FORBIDDEN PASSION

"I've never met a woman like you, Morning Star," Joe murmured. "I want to be with you all the time. I know I shouldn't, but I want to hold you in my arms."

Sun Cloud's daughter raised her hand and stroked his cheek. "It is the same with me, Joe. What shall we do?"

The desire in her voice was more than he could resist. With a ragged sigh, he captured her sweet lips in a fierce kiss.

"I want you so much, Morning Star. I can't help myself," he whispered.

Before she could tell him she felt the same way, his lips met hers once more. How could such powerful feelings be wrong? A savage and bittersweet longing swept through her. She could not summon the will to refuse what she wanted and needed with all her soul . . .

JANELLE TAYLOR

Forever Ecstasy

ZEBRA BOOKS
KENSINGTON PUBLISHING CORP.

ZEBRA BOOKS

are published by

Kensington Publishing Corp.
475 Park Avenue South
New York, NY 10016

First printing: June, 1991

Printed in the United States of America

For:

the family of Hiram Owen, in loving memory of my
dear Dakota friend, translator, and adviser
who passed away 8/31/88.
Wakantanka nici un.

Eileen Wilson, who loves Gray Eagle
and his heirs as much as I do.

Debbie Keffer, for her kindnesses.
and,
my many friends and readers at Sinte Geleska College
and St. Francis Indian Mission.

Acknowledgments and Special Thanks to:

Marvene Riis, Archivist, Cultural Heritage
Center in Pierre,
Lawrence Blazek, Mayor of Marcus,
Gary LeFebre of Lodgepole,
The Pierre Chamber of Commerce,
Ken Wetz, Mayor of Newell,
The staff of Bear Butte State Park,
Spearfish and Sturgis Chambers of Commerce,
and
many historical societies and staffs of historical sites
in the friendly and generous state of South Dakota.

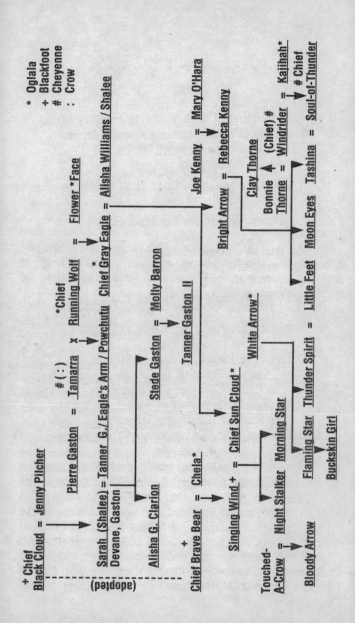

* Oglala
+ Blackfoot
# Cheyenne
: Crow

Chief Black Cloud + = Jenny Pilcher

Pierre Gaston = Tamarra x #(:) = Tanner G./Eagle's Arm/Powchutu Chief Gray Eagle * = Flower Face * Running Wolf *Chief

Sarah (Shalee) Devane, Gaston = Tanner G./Eagle's Arm/Powchutu

Alisha G. Clarion

Stede Gaston = Molly Barron

Tanner Gaston II

Alisha Williams/Shalee = Bright Arrow

Joe Kenny = Mary O'Hara

Rebecca Kenny

Clay Thorne

Bonnie Thorne = (Chief) # Windrider = Kajihah *

Chief Brave Bear = Chela *

Singing Wind + = Chief Sun Cloud *

White Arrow *

Touched-A-Crow = Night Stalker *

Bloody Arrow

Morning Star

Flaming Star   Thunder Spirit = Little Feet

Buckskin Girl

Moon Eyes   Tashina = Soul-of-Thunder # Chief

(adopted)

Prologue

Dakota Territory, 1831

"As the sun last slept, Grandfather gave me a vision," Standing Tree told the men gathered in the meeting lodge at their winter camp in the Black Hills. "Before I speak it, let us prepare ourselves."

The Oglala shaman lifted the sacred catlinite pipe and fingered the smooth red bowl on a four-foot stem that had ceremonial beads and feathers attached at the joining point. His wrinkled fingers packed tobacco inside it, then took a burning stick from the fire and lit the fragrant contents. Standing Tree raised the pipe upward to honor Wakantanka—the Great Spirit—and downward to honor Makakin—Mother Earth. Next, he saluted each of the four directions: the east to summon enlightenment and peace, the south where warmth was born, the west which brought rain, and the north which offered fortitude. "As I share your breath, Grandfather, open my heart and mind to receive and accept your sacred message," he invoked. He drew the smoke deep into his lungs, held it there for a moment, then exhaled curls of smoke that went heavenward. He passed the pipe to the man at his right, the Oglala chief, Sun Cloud.

Strong hands accepted the sacred item. The supplication to the Great Spirit was repeated. Then the pipe was passed to the next man, to continue around the group until all participants had done the ritual four times. During this reverent

7

ceremony, no one talked and all meditated.

Sun Cloud gazed at the buffalo skull, weathered and bleached by *Wi*—the sun—and *Makajou*—the rain, that was lying on the mat before the shaman in a place of honor. It was painted with the colors and symbols of nature, and was stuffed with a mixture of sweet grasses. The buffalo was viewed by Plains Indians as the most powerful animal of the Great Spirit's creation—a generous and clever gift to His children to provide them with food, shelter, clothing, tools, and medicine.

Sun Cloud shifted his gaze to the Medicine Wheel that was mounted on a tall cottonwood post, the same tree chosen for the Sun Dance ritual. The wheel's surface was divided by four bars which represented the four directions: west for danger, north for life, east for knowledge, and south for quiet: the influences and forces of life. Made of brain-tanned hide stretched taut over a willow hoop, its roundness told of their belief in the Circle of Life: *Canhdeska Wakan*. Hair, heart-beads, fur, and feathers decorated it. Another buffalo skull was attached to its center to signify *Lakol wicho'an*, the traditional way of life, and *Pte Oyate*, the spiritual life. All spokes radiated toward the center—the heart and meaning of life, which was total harmony with one's self and with nature. That skull was painted white to express purity. A Hoop of Life hung beneath the Medicine Wheel.

The Hoop of Life symbolized all stages of man's existence: the never-ending circle of life from birth, to maturity, to old age, to death, then rebirth in the Spirit World. Four bars and four feathers were displayed on its surface for the four virtues of wisdom, courage, constancy, and generosity. The four directions to which it pointed were the same as those of the Medicine Wheel. Here, too, the four points radiated toward the center for total harmony. The chief repeated the pipe ritual a fourth time.

A fire glowed in the center of the large tepee. Its undulating flames created shadows against the buffalo-hide wall which seemed to breathe with a spiritual life of their own. A flap was opened at the top to allow smoke to escape, but it

8

did not release the fire's heat. It was cold outside the meeting lodge on the moonless night. The floor was the earth upon which the Indians lived. The men sat on buffalo mats, huddled in several circles around the blaze, their bodies also giving warmth to each other.

The only sounds heard were the soft breathing of the men, the invocation words, and the crackling of burning wood. No wind howled around the tepee. No dog barked. No child cried. No horse neighed. It was as if all creatures and forces of nature sensed and honored the gravity of this moment.

Many smells filled the air: the sweetness of cherrywood sticks and special grasses in the fire, the animal-skin mats upon which they sat and the hide walls which surrounded them, the fragrant tobacco in the pipe, the dirt beneath them, and the grease—human and animal—upon their bodies for protection against winter's chill. No man seemed to feel the stinging of smoke in his eyes or mind the familiar odors. All were too ensnared by suspense and a feeling of oneness.

The Oglala chief, council members, and high-ranking warriors were eager for their shaman to reveal his vision. Standing Tree commanded their respect, awe, and loyalty. He was a man of wisdom, mystical insight, healing skills, and "powerful magic." All remained still and silent as the spiritual leader of their tribe rose to enlighten them.

"Grandfather spoke to me in a sacred vision while I slept," he began. "We have been at peace with the white-eyes for many winters, a peace that came from the loss of our great leader, Gray Eagle, father of Chief Sun Cloud. But Grandfather warned that a season of bitter conflicts and greed will destroy that peace. The Great Mystery showed me two men. One's face was hidden from my eyes, but Grandfather said he carries Oglala blood. A chief's bonnet lay at his feet, torn from his head by evil. In the winters to come, Grandfather will make his heart grow restless. He will call the lost warrior back to the land of his people to share our destiny." The shaman was quiet.

Chief Sun Cloud pondered the holy man's words. Bright

9

Arrow—his brother—had been driven away by evil, but had returned. Powchutu—his father's brother—had been driven away by evil, too, but had returned. Both were dead now. "Your words confuse me, Wise One," he said. "If he is of our blood and tribe, why do we not know of him? What evil drove him from our people? When was the past moon that witnessed such a black deed?"

"I do not know," the sixty-year-old man answered. "His face and markings were not clear. We will know his words are true when he speaks them to us. When white trappers and traders came to our land, we met them as friends. We let them trap our streams and hunt in our forests. We made truce and trade with them. What they have seen and done here calls other white-eyes to our lands; many of them will be evil and dangerous. A dark moon in the winters to come will flood our land with white-eyes, and war will thunder as a violent storm across it."

"Why would the soldiers attack?" the chief reasoned. "Since my Grandfather's time, we let the whites roam our lands and draw maps of our hills and valleys, our forests, plains, and rivers. We let trappers and traders build posts to sell goods to whites and to Indians. We let soldiers cut trees and build forts so we could observe them and learn their ways. When battles came between our two peoples, it was the whites' doings. They asked for treaties, and we gave them. Eleven winters past we made a new truce with them. The one called Derek Sturgis took the paper I signed to their Great White Chief Monroe. The fort was abandoned, and the soldiers left our territory. As promised, they have not returned to threaten us. When Colonel Leavenworth came with troops eight winters past to seek our help to defeat the Arikaras, we gave it; they thanked us, presented us with gifts, and rode away." Sun Cloud kept his probing gaze on the older man.

"Such good things will not halt what is to come, my chief. Trouble will be reborn, but its life will be cut short by the warrior Grandfather sends to us. A long peace will follow—"

Smiles, nods, and murmurs of relief took place before

10

Standing Tree could finish his sentence. They ceased when he continued. "But more white-eyes will journey here in great numbers. Their hungers will bring even darker and bloodier suns. They will crave all Grandfather has given to us: our lands, our animals, our rocks and trees, our grasses, our lives, our honors, and our freedom. They can have none of those sacred gifts unless they destroy us. Many seasons after I begin my walk at Grandfather's side, they will try to do so, and my people will resist. The white-eyes will come to fear and do battle with the Dakota Nation as they do with no other. The Tetons will lead all tribes of the Seven Council Fires and our allies in the last battle for survival. Grandfather did not reveal the final victor to me."

Sun Cloud was angered by this news. "We trusted the White Chief, and we kept our word. Why can he not honor his? Must we drive all whites from our land and stop others from coming? Will not their number and strength grow faster and stronger than the grasses upon our plains?"

"We cannot keep them away until time is no more. Feed upon the seasons of peace ahead, for many of starving will come. The first trouble will bring the two men that Grandfather revealed to me in my sacred vision."

"How can this be?" Sun Cloud asked. "My brother was slain in battle with the Crow this summer past. Bright Arrow has no sons to challenge me. He has no grandsons who match your words. My memory knows of no man who lost the chief's bonnet and was driven away. If it was long ago, how can a distant evil hold such power? Who seeks my rank?"

"My vision did not say he wants to take the chief's bonnet from Sun Cloud. It said he was denied his rank, land, and people and that Grandfather will draw him to us for help in a time of great danger."

Sun Cloud's heart pounded inside the bronzed flesh of his broad chest, scarred by the Sun Dance ritual. "My son is ten winters old. Do you speak of him? Will he be taken from us, but returned one moon?"

"I do not know. His face was kept hidden from me. When the moon comes, Grandfather will reveal all to me. I will

11

speak His words to you."

"What of the other man, Wise One?" a council member asked.

"He is a white-eye who will come to help us defeat our enemies. He is unlike other white-eyes. He will prove himself worthy to become our blood brother. His words and ways will be hard to accept and obey, but we must do so to survive. The white-eyes will not honor the treaty we signed. After many snows have covered Mother Earth with their white blankets, our land will be darkened by dangers. The blood of many, Indian and white, will soak into Mother Earth. Peace lies within the grasp of the white-eye whose hair blazes as the sun and in whose eyes the blue of sky lives. His heart will side with us. Many foes, Indian and white, will try to defeat him. An Oglala maiden will be chosen to ride with him, and she will become a skilled warrior at his side. She will guard his life and help defeat foes."

"Why does Grandfather use a white man?" another elder asked.

"I do not know. But I do know his eyes are as blue and calm at the sky when he will appear. His voice will blow as a strong wind one moon and as a gentle breeze on another. His attacks will beat as heavy rain upon our foes. His glory will shine as brightly as the glowing ball in the heaven where the spirits live. His anger at those who threaten us and betray us will rumble as loud thunder. As with snow in our sacred hills, his heart and mind are pure. He will come when Grandfather says the time is here. The maiden who is chosen to battle with him will know a great destiny; her legend will speak of She-Who-Rode-With-The-Sky-Warrior."

"Who is this maiden, Wise One? Why must a female ride with a white warrior to defeat our enemies?" A third man asked the question in all their hearts.

"I do not know."

During the ensuing silence, Sun Cloud glanced at the pictorial history of his Red Heart Band that was painted upon a tanned buffalo hide that hung on the lodge's wall. It recorded the events that had taken place since the birth of his grandfather, Chief Running Wolf. It told of past conflicts

12

with whites and with enemy tribes. Sun Cloud dreaded the scenes that would be added to it one day. His dark eyes scanned the faces of his warriors and tribal leaders. He wondered who would live to see those ominous times. The thirty-four-year-old chief wondered if he would still be their leader then. "When will this black sun come?" he asked in a grave tone, believing the shaman's medicine powerful and his counsel wise.

"I do not know," Standing Tree said once more. "But not for many, many winters." He took a seat cross-legged on a buffalo hide.

Sun Cloud did not understand the meaning of this strange and distant vision. Yet he trusted and believed the mystical shaman and the Great Spirit. His father, the legendary Gray Eagle, was with Wakantanka; as was his mother, Alisha Williams, a white captive whom his father had loved and married. Bright Arrow and his wife had joined their parents last summer. Sun Cloud felt it was good and merciful when the Great Spirit called mates to His side on the same sun, as it had been with his parents and his brother. He knew it must be hard and lonely to live without the love of your heart.

Sun Cloud heard the others leaving the meeting lodge while he was deep in thought. Except for the Crow, Shoshone, and Pawnee, peace had ruled their land since the treaty with Sturgis in 1820. That truce had followed the ambush of his father and a painful struggle with his brother over the chief's bonnet. He had won that honor and duty and won the hand of Singing Wind. Years of joy, success, and love had ensued.

Now it was nearing time to begin his son's warrior training, and he prayed the man in Standing Tree's vision was not his only child. Singing Wind, his beloved wife, would bear another child when summer came. Perhaps it would be another son. No matter, a second child at last would bring much pride and happiness to his heart. He would make certain there was no confusion or conflict over which child would follow him as chief, as there had been with his brother eleven summers ago.

The Red Heart chief of the Oglala/Teton branch of the Dakota Nation got to his feet. He flexed his muscular body and told himself that if dark moons were ahead, he must enjoy all the bright ones until then. A man's destiny could not be changed; his Life-Circle was drawn by the Great Spirit before his birth. There was no need to worry over distant threats. Grandfather would always be there to guide, protect, and love His people.

A hungry smile softened his handsome features. Sun Cloud headed for his tepee and his wife, who would chase away the night's chill with fiery passion. Until Grandfather sent Sky Warrior to them, he would forget the perilous times ahead. For the present, all the chief wanted to think about were his wife, his young son, and the child Singing Wind carried.

Chapter One

"Hello in camp! Can I join you for coffee and rest?" Joe called out before approaching the camp. It was a precaution he had quickly learned to take in this wild Dakota territory to avoid getting shot by accident.

"Come on in," a voice replied, "but take it slow and easy."

Joe dismounted and secured his reins to a bush. He didn't unsaddle the animal, since he always liked to be prepared for a quick escape. It was chilly tonight. He removed his leather riding gloves and stuffed them into his saddlebag, but kept on the thin wool jacket he had donned a mile back.

Joe headed through the wooded location toward a fire near the riverbank. As he passed two wagons, he saw a beautiful Indian girl secured to one of the wheels. Her arms were extended, her wrists tied to the spokes, and her legs were bound at the ankles. He was intrigued by her presence, but ignored her for now. He had other matters on his troubled mind.

Not far away, he noticed, eight horses for pulling the two wagons were tethered and grazing. An abundance of trees, with the river eastward, had forced the men to leave those wagons thirty feet from their waterside camp. Yet the spacings of oaks and cottonwoods and a three-fourths waxing moon made the female prisoner visible to her captors.

Joe's azure gaze studied each of the three men as he approached them, just as they were eyeing him with interest. The condition of the camp—the large amount of coals, the trampled ground, more than a few hours' smell of manure, and the many items scattered about—told him it was several days' old. When he'd found their trail, he had known the wagons were a few days beyond him. He hoped he wasn't wasting valuable time and energy on what could be an impulsive chase. "Thanks," he answered the man. "I was getting tired, sore, and hungry. This area is mighty deserted. I'm glad I happened up on you men. Mind if I share your coffee and beans? My last meal was a long way back."

"Help yourself, but ain't you out late tonight, stranger?" a barrel-chested man remarked. He gestured for the new arrival to sit on the ground.

As Joe poured himself some steaming coffee and set the tin cup on the grass beside him, he explained, "I was about to make camp earlier when several Indians chose the same clearing I had. I thought it best to let them have first choice," Joe jested with a wry grin. "It doesn't take long in this wild territory to learn you don't want to meet up with them when you're alone."

"What tribe was they?" the youngest man asked.

Joe glanced at the towhead with dark-blue eyes as he guilefully remarked, "Indians are Indians, aren't they?" He took in details: the man was just under twenty and had a long knife scar on his left cheek.

"Nope" came the reply. "Some are friendlies; others, real mean."

"Friendlies, hell. They're all blood-thirsty savages. Ain't worth the salt it'd take to cure 'em fur dog meat. Only good ones are on your payroll or dead," the third man refuted with a cold chuckle, then sipped his whiskey.

Joe didn't like these crude men. The third one was tall and slender, with a pockmarked face and dirty hands wrapped around the bottle he was nursing. He appeared to be about thirty. His brown hair was as filthy as his clothes, and his hazel eyes had an emotionless expression that put Joseph Lawrence, Jr., on guard. His father's friend Stede Gaston had told him to never trust a man whose eyes stay frozen

16

when he smiles. He had found that warning to be accurate.

Joe stopped dishing up beans to feign surprise. "Indians work for whites?" he asked. "I thought they were independent free-roaming men who lived only to hunt and raid, and that they made their women do all the work."

"If ya give enough trinkets, they'll do most any chore fur ya."

The burly man scowled and spat on the ground. "What you work too much is your jaws, Clem. Put up that fire water; you've had enough. What are you doing in these parts?" he asked the stranger.

To be convincing, Joe used half-truths. "My father's in the shipping business, and I got tired of making voyages for him," he said. "I hated being a sailor. Sea trips aren't any fun when you spend most of your time heaving your meals over the rails. I heard it was exciting and challenging out here, so I decided to leave dull Virginia and seek a few adventures."

Joe smiled to relax the wary man with his scraggly beard and muddy brown hair that flowed over his broad shoulders. It looked as if that tangled mane hadn't seen a comb or brush in ages, and it didn't take a keen observer to realize that their clothes hadn't seen a washpot in weeks. It was apparent these rough characters cared nothing about their appearances. "A man who lacks pride in himself usually lacks morals and a conscience," his father had told him, "so sail clear of him, son. Even poor folk, if they're decent and honest, keep themselves clean and neat." That wise remembrance told him to be vigilant. "My name's Joe Lawrence," he introduced himself. "As I said, I'm glad I came upon you tonight. I'll admit I was getting a little nervous out here alone. Who are you?"

"I'm Zeke," the leader replied, watchful of the newcomer. "That's Clem." He nodded to the disobedient man who had the bottle to his lips once more. "And that's Farley." He named the youngest of the group.

No last names were supplied, and Joe wondered if there was a special reason. He also noted that Zeke had silenced Clem to prevent him from revealing any facts the leery man wanted kept secret. The wariness aroused Joe's interest as much as the contents of those wagons. Between bites he made small talk to calm them while he tried to entice slips of the tongue. "Where's the best place to look for work in this area?"

"What kind of job you got in mind?" Zeke asked, lazing against a tree.

"Haven't thought much about that, but I'm not joining the cavalry. I don't want to trade one boss for another one. If I didn't like soldiering, I wouldn't want the Army hunting me down as a deserter. Since I don't know this territory, scouting is out. Besides, I don't care to go tangling with hostiles every other day or two. When I get ready to return home, I want to take my hair with me," he said with a chuckle. "From what I've read and heard, Indians like to take scalps as trophies, especially blond ones."

"You kin bet your boots an' pants they do," Farley concurred. He stroked the lengthy knife scar on his boyish face and frowned.

Joe caught the hint. "I'm not much of a gambler, so I'll take your word, friend. Where are you men heading? Maybe I can tag along for safety, if you don't mind." Joe took a few more bites of beans, then washed them down with strong coffee. Neither tasted good; his appetite was lagging, but he pretended to enjoy the scanty meal and company.

"Sorry, Lawrence, but we're heading for a private camp."

Joe focused his attention on the leader. "No jobs available there?"

"The boss don't like to hire strangers or greenhorns."

"I learn fast and follow orders good," Joe told him, then set aside the tin plate and empty cup. "Most people say I'm easy to get along with, even on my bad days. I'd be grateful for help. I'll give you a cut of my salary for a while to get me hired on and to teach me my way around these parts."

Zeke tossed the two dishes and spoon into a pile with other dirty ones. "That's a tempting offer, Lawrence, but no. Strangers are too nosy, and greenhorns are too dangerous. Both cause too much trouble."

"Iffen he's good with fightin' and shootin', Zeke, the boss might want him. We kin always use a skilled—"

18

"Nope. You know the boss's orders, Farley. If I was you, Lawrence, I'd ride to Fort Tabor where the Missouri joins the White River or to Pratte's Trading Post at Pierre. Men looking for work do best there." Zeke's distrustful gaze roved Joe as he talked. "You don't appear a man to take to trapping or trading. If you don't want to join the Army or do scouting, best I can think of is guarding places or hauling goods."

Joe glanced at the two wagons thirty feet away. He knew they were loaded because of the deep ruts the wheels had made, the ones he had located and followed. He tried not to look at the female prisoner who was watching all four men with her dark eyes. The blond-haired man presumed she must be cold so far from the fire and without a blanket or long sleeves. But for now he had to ignore her plight. Later he would decide what to do about her. He looked back at Zeke and casually inquired, "That what you do, transport supplies?"

Zeke kept his gaze locked onto Joe's face. "Not exactly."

Joe sensed the man's caution and let the touchy subject drop. He noticed how Zeke's eyes stayed on him as tight as a rope on a capstan. The leader looked tense, and his dirty fingers kept drumming on one thigh.

"If you came from Virginny," Zeke asked. "Why didn't you stop at Fort Tabor or at Lookout? Or head upriver to Pierre? What kind of work you expect to find in a wilderness? This area's a long way from civilization."

To calm the still edgy leader, Joe decided to start speaking more like these men and drop the correct English that he'd been taught during his years of schooling. "I was ridin' for Benton near the headwaters of the Missouri," he fabricated. "I got a friend there who's been beggin' me to join him. He hired on with the American Fur Company in '47. Been with them ever since. I figured I'd see more of this wild territory if I rode across country, rather than take a boat the long route by water. I heard the Missouri gets mighty treacherous in places, and I ain't one to challenge crazy water much. I had my fill of that workin' for my father back East."

"Maybe I know your friend. I've traded with lots of trappers."

19

"Ever met Ben Murphy? About forty—short, husky, black hair."

"Nope. I thought I knew all those American Fur boys."

"Ben's quiet. He usually keeps to himself. We trapped together back South. He taught me most of what I know. When we'd take off huntin' or trappin', my father always sent somebody to fetch me home if we didn't return in a month or two. He was determined I was going to learn his shippin' business and take it over one day. I figured if I joined Ben out here, I'd be too far away for Old Joe to find me and drag me home again. I guess I got too used to being on my own at school, and I didn't take to Old Joe's runnin' my life from dawn to dusk like he did his company."

"So why you looking for a job in these parts if it's to Benton you're heading?" Zeke asked. When an owl hooted, he glanced in that direction, his nerves obviously on edge.

"I been ridin' for weeks and my tail's tryin' to grow to the saddle." Joe answered. "I need a rest. It's a long way to Benton. Frankly, I ain't lookin' forward to crossin' Crow Territory. It drained me to come this far through Sioux land."

"Don't let them hear you call 'em Sioux," Zeke warned, "or they'll lift your hair for sure. That's a chopped-off French word meaning 'treacherous snake.' They call themselves *Dakotas,* 'friends.' Best remember that."

"Are they?"

"Are they what?" Zeke asked, confused.

"Friends, friendly," Joe hinted as a reminder.

"Sioux are about the lowest and meanest savages alive." Zeke spat again, as if clearing his mouth of a foul taste.

"*You're* working this area and you still have your scalp. You got a truce with them?"

"Sioux don't make no truces with whites, but they'll leave you be if they think you're smarter and stronger than them. I've beaten some of their best warriors, so the others avoid tangling with me."

"Sounds like you're the right man to join up with in this area."

"I don't need nobody else to tend or to slow me down. Clem and Farley do more than enough of both. You'll do

20

better to head for Crow Territory than hang around in Sioux."

"Why is that, Zeke? Don't they hate whites, too?"

"Not like the Sioux. Don't show no fear of them when you're alone, and Crow'll let you pass. One of their prophets told them his vision said not to war with whites. All Injuns are big believers in them peyote dreams they call visions, but braves will still ambush and rob you if you act scared."

"Hell, Zeke! Most of 'em are cowards and beggars. They'd rather have a trinket 'an fight a real man for his scalp," Clem said between chuckles.

Zeke glared at his companion before giving his advice to Joe. "If you ain't heading on to Benton at first light, you best ride east to one of the trading posts on the river. For a few dollars you can catch a boat to join your friend. Trappers who don't work for companies mostly come to sell their winter catches before long. They spend a month or so jawing, drinking, whoring, and gambling. Then they resupply and go back to their trapping grounds. River's the safest way to get there from here. It's eastward. We're heading southwest. You don't need to ride in that direction."

Joe knew the man was lying. The trail he'd followed for days was heading northwestward and Crow Territory and Benton were both in that direction! Zeke's careless mistake and odd behavior told Joe he'd been smart to follow his gut instinct. But it was clear that the ruffian was adamant about them parting ways at sunrise. When the others remained silent, Joe yawned and flexed his shoulders. "I wish I could change your mind, Zeke, but I understand." "I'll get my gun and help keep guard tonight," he offered. "I don't want any Indians sneaking into camp while we're asleep."

"No need," Zeke said. "We take two-hour shifts each, even when it seems safe. We've done scouted the area. The Sioux are still holed up in their winter camps south of here, and it's a good ways to Crow Territory. You can rest easy tonight, then be on your way at dawn."

Joe smiled, then asked Clem, "You got another bottle of that good whiskey I can buy? It's been a dusty and tiring ride today."

Before Clem or Zeke could reply, Farley said, "Plenty, if-fen you got—"

"No!" the hefty leader interrupted and came to his feet. "The way Clem's been slopping down our supply like a bottomless pig, it's about gone, except for that bottle I got in my gear. You're welcome to a swig or two of it, Lawrence. I'll fetch it. You stay here with the boys."

Joe saw how the large man got to his feet with ease and agility, then left the smoky fire to head for the front wagon. With Zeke gone, maybe he could get answers to the beautiful mystery nearby, he thought. "One of you having trouble with your squaw?" Joe inquired in a genial tone as he nodded to the captive some thirty feet away at the second wagon. The moon's angle and tall trees now placed the confining wagon and young female in almost obscuring shadows, but Joseph Lawrence had a mental picture of her that would never vanish.

The half-inebriated Clem glanced in the beauty's direction, chuckled, and revealed, "We're taking her to the boss. Caught her whilst we wuz scouting. He likes 'em young, full of spirit and fight. She oughta last a few weeks, maybe months if he's more careful this time. He uses 'em up fast. Just 'twixt us, Joe, I'd like a bite of her flesh meself. Maybe we can talk—"

"Shut up, you drunken fool," Zeke warned, his eyes narrowing as he passed Joe the half-empty bottle. "Don't pay Clem no mind," he said. "His brain's sour mash by now. He's teasing you. But if he don't stop drinking and lying so much, I'm gonna get rid of him. He knows I traded for her in a Crow camp yesterday. You can see she didn't care much for being sold by her pappy. She'll settle down soon and make me a good squaw."

Joe noticed the bite mark on Zeke's hand that he rubbed as he lied. The woman presented Joe with a difficult decision: rescue her and lose this contact, or ignore her imminent fate so he could try to stay with these offensive men. With Zeke so mad at Clem, maybe he could persuade the leader to let him join them. If he pulled off that feat and they reached their destination, he'd never be able to free her. Yet if these men were connected to the murderous villain he was after . . . "She's beautiful, Zeke. I'm sure a strong man like you will have her tamed fast. I've always heard that a woman with fire is more fun than one who's quiet and cowardly. I'd say you got a good deal, a real challenge." He sipped whiskey and deliberated which course to sail tonight.

The Oglala maiden was awake and alert, and she tried to ignore the chill on her flesh. Morning Star hated the men who had taken her prisoner and the dark fate they had in mind for her. And now there were four to fight against. Although she pretended not to understand their words, her parents had taught her English. Years ago she had practiced that skill with any light-skinned visitor who had come to their camp. Those days were gone because of the recent trouble between the two cultures. Her father had signed a treaty with the palefaces in 1820, and peace had ensued for years. But during the past two summers, sporadic fights and false charges had marred that truce.

A new breed of encroachers seemed determined to war with them now, a breed that was to provoke even more hatred and trouble between the Crow and the Oglalas. Soon her people expected more conflicts, violence, and false accusations. Yet she could not forget that her family and tribe had befriended some lightskins. Nor could she forget that her grandmother and aunt were of white blood, or that she carried a trace of it. She had concluded long ago that not all palefaces were bad. It was unfair and wrong to judge an entire race by the evil doings of some of its members, as most whites did with Indians.

This past winter had been tranquil. In fact, she had known mostly peace since her birth and had not witnessed the new troubles, so a fierce hatred for all whites did not exist in her heart. She wanted to study them and discover why there were such hostilities and differences between them. Only by learning from a problem could it be resolved, and bloodshed be prevented. Yet her captors seemed to be proving that her brother's ominous words about most palefaces were true.

Morning Star prayed that the Indians the last man had

23

mentioned earlier were from her travel party and not Crow warriors arriving early. The Crow were fierce enemies of her people, the Dakotas, and had been for generations. If she were recognized as the daughter of Oglala Chief Sun Cloud, the Bird People would demand to buy her as a slave. She could imagine the horrors — or even death — she would endure at their hands. Yet she must not lose hope and courage. She must not lose her wits. She had to remain ready to seize any opening. When that glorious moment came, she wanted to flee with as much information as she could. She forced herself to concentrate on the men's conversation.

The last man's words revealed he was new to her land. He seemed different from her cold and mean captors. She sensed that the big foe did not trust the handsome stranger. Morning Star decided that the sunny-haired man would be lucky to get away from the others alive.

Sun Cloud's daughter tried to ignore Joe, as she needed to concentrate on the others and their plans. She wished she knew who was the "Boss" they had mentioned several times within her hearing and wished they would reveal more. She knew there were weapons inside the wagons for the Bird People to use against her tribe. She needed to discover why these men wanted to create an inter-tribal war.

Morning Star watched them drink and talk. She knew the stranger had noticed her but was pretending she did not exist. Even if he were a good man, she could not cry out for his help. He was as outnumbered as she; he was also white, and that probably made him a foe.

She closed her eyes and leaned her weary head against a spoke of the wagon. She was thirsty and hungry; the men were punishing her with the denial of food and water for battling them, especially the big one. Several times he had shaken her, slapped her, and shouted of horrible things he would do to her if she weren't a gift for his boss. Then he had laughed — an evil sound — and said she would soon wish he were her owner instead of the other man! Despite her fear, she had pretended not to understand his threats.

The wind's coolness and strength increased and blew over her flesh, causing her to tremble. She wished she had been given a blanket to ward off the night's chill, but told herself that her comfort wasn't the most important thing at this time, even if she *were* miserable. Her outstretched arms ached, and her tightly bound wrists caused her fingers to tingle and lose feeling. The hub of the wagon pressed into her back and made it beg for relief. Her buttocks were sore and numb from being confined to the same awkward position for hours. It was a struggle to accept such torments in silence, to resist fatigue, and to quell her fears. She prayed her party had not been misled by the false trail her captors had set for them. If so, her world could be lost forever. Once she was enslaved and used, even if she escaped, how could she return to her tribe without her honor?

"You can toss down your bedroll and sleep here," the Oglala maiden heard the big man say to Joe. "Best get an early start tomorrow; you got a ways to ride." She heard Joe excuse himself and saw him vanish into the denser trees and bushes to the right of the campfire. The other men huddled and whispered. A bad sign, she decided. No doubt they were—

Morning Star perceived someone's stealthy approach behind her under the wagon. The scent was unfamiliar. Her heart rate increased and she quivered in suspense.

Joseph Lawrence, Jr., could not allow an innocent girl to suffer the terrible fate that Clem had mentioned before Zeke had silenced him. If he could free her without getting caught, he would continue his deceitful attempt to join up with the suspicious men. If not . . .

Joe had removed his jacket to keep from putting telltale stains on it. He used his elbows and feet to wriggle to the female. He hoped the shadows and her pinioned body would conceal him. He lifted himself to his knees and leaned close to her head. "I hope you understand me, woman, because I don't have much time," he whispered. "I'm a friend, but those men over there are real bad. I'm going to cut you free, but keep still and quiet until I get back to the fire and distract them. I'll leave my knife beside you. When I have their attention, free your legs, then sneak away. If you understand what I'm saying, nod your head."

25

Morning Star did not know all of the words he used, but she grasped his meaning. Though she worried that the man's strange behavior was a trick to make her expose herself, something within her said to trust him. She gathered her courage and nodded.

"That's a relief," Joe murmured. With caution, he sliced through the rope at one wrist, then the other. As ordered, the female didn't move from her strained position. He slid his knife to her right side. "Make sure they aren't looking when you free your legs. Hide until they stop searching for you. I'll get back to the campfire to spy on them. Good luck."

Joe worked his way from beneath the wagon and retrieved his jacket. After brushing the debris from his shirt and trousers, he slipped on the jacket and sneaked into the concealing trees. So far his plan was a success, but he remained guarded. He began to whistle as he walked along the riverbank to camp. He entered the clearing with his shirttail hanging out, as if he had relieved himself and hadn't straightened his clothing. The other men were bedding down, their weapons nearby. Joe wondered why no guard was being posted, as Zeke had talked about earlier. He wondered if it had been a ruse to keep him rifleless. He came to full alert and decided that perhaps he should get away while he could, as soon as the girl was safe. To stall for time and conceal his wariness, he remarked, "That coffee and whiskey ran through me fast. I'd sure love a bath if that water wasn't so cold. I'll fetch my bedroll and join you. I'll be—"

Clem looked toward the lovely reason why he was in trouble tonight. His shout cut off Joe's sentence. "That Injun gal's escaping, Zeke!"

All eyes riveted to the wagon and the female, who was leaning forward and cutting the bonds on her ankles. She glanced up, then hurried back to work on the rope. Zeke and Farley tossed aside their covers and leapt to their feet to halt her. The drunken Clem moved slower. The three men hesitated only long enough to glance about for warriors, as somebody had obviously aided her escape attempt. They saw and heard none.

Morning Star almost panicked when the alarm was given,

26

as she was so close to freedom. Her heart beat as a kettle drum. With haste and shaky fingers, she severed her ankle bonds. Keeping the knife, she jumped to her feet and dashed toward the thick treeline.

Zeke aimed his rifle in her direction. Instinctively Joe lunged at the big man and thwarted his intention, causing the weapon to discharge upward in a loud roar. "You can't shoot a woman!" he shouted. "Let her go!"

As soon as she was concealed by trees and darkness, Morning Star halted to observe the perilous scene left behind. She saw Joe arguing with Zeke and blocking another shot at her. The big man was clearly furious. As Zeke tried to fling Joe aside to fire again, Farley halted his pursuit of her and attacked Joe. With a speed and skill that impressed her, Joe struck him a stunning blow across the jaw that sent him backward.

"You'll die for that, Injun lover!" Zeke shouted. "You helped her!"

The sunny-haired man whirled to meet Zeke's assault. Zeke's blow to Joe's stomach doubled him over for a moment. Morning Star knew her rescuer was in trouble, but how could she help without a weapon? What could a knife do against powerful guns? How she wished she had a bow and arrows or a lance. Her head screamed for her to flee, but her heart and feet refused to obey that cowardly and selfish command. She lingered and watched with wide eyes.

Joe yanked his head aside before the burly man could bring down his clenched hands on his neck, then Joe rammed Zeke's stomach, sending him to the ground in a noisy fall.

Farley recovered enough to rejoin the fight. Joe knew he had to disable the youngest man fast, as Zeke, cursing, was getting to his feet and Clem was fetching his gun. Joe lifted his knee and sent it with force into Farley's groin. The towhead screamed in pain, dropped to his knees, then rolled on the grass as he cupped the injured area and groaned.

Morning Star knew she must go back and help Joe. The stranger had risked his life to free her, so she couldn't leave him to battle three wicked men. Her gentle heart and conscience spurred her into motion.

From the corner of his eye, Joe saw the Indian maiden using a sturdy limb to club Clem unconscious. He was astonished that she had returned to help him but happy she was repaying his kindness to her. Knowing he had only Zeke to conquer, Joe confronted the large man with renewed energy and resolve. He soon learned that Zeke was hard at best.

The two men struggled for the upper hand. The girl used her club to land a hard blow on Zeke's back. The big man then turned and shoved her to the earth.

"Run!" Joe yelled to her as he slammed his lowered shoulder into Zeke's stomach. He was glad to see she obeyed, but, distracted for that instant, Zeke sent him tumbling to the ground with a fisted jab to his chest that claimed his breath for a short time. When he saw the leader stalking toward him with a kill-gleam in his eyes, Joe knew he had to recover and move fast.

Morning Star raced to the first wagon and retrieved her bundle from where she had seen the large man toss it. She hurried to the men's horses and freed them. She loosened the reins to her mount, then went for Joe's.

The sunny-haired man scrambled to his feet just in time to avoid Zeke's next attack. The two men circled each other, then Zeke landed a blow to the side of Joe's head, almost stunning him. Joe fell to the earth, entangled his legs with his opponent's, and twisted his body. The movement caused Zeke to trip and fall hard.

"*U wo!*" The girl on horseback shouted for Joe to come to her.

While Zeke was down, Joe obeyed without a second thought. He leapt upon his horse and took the reins from her extended hand. Their knees urged the horses to flee, and the animals obeyed. The furious Zeke grabbed for Clem's rifle, aimed, and fired a shot before they vanished into the darkness. The ball passed through Joe's upper right arm but missed the bone. Though he grunted from the pain, it didn't stop or slow his retreat.

"When I find you, I'll kill you, you bastard!" they heard Zeke threaten as they rode out of rifle and hearing range.

28

They galloped for over an hour before they halted to rest the horses.

Joe twisted in his saddle and looked behind them but heard and saw nothing of a pursuit. They had escaped, but what now? he mused.

"They not coming. I free horses," she told him. "They be slow to catch and follow. We rest, ride, find secret place till gone."

"You speak good English. I'm glad, because . . ." He couldn't say he didn't want to give away the fact he knew a little Lakota from Stede Gaston. He thought it was best to keep that skill a secret for now. "Thanks for what you did back there. I couldn't have escaped without your help."

Morning Star was surprised that the man wasn't the least embarrassed or angered by a woman's assistance; most warriors would be both. She liked his warm and grateful smile. She wished she could see him better, but the moon's early ride across the heavens did not allow a clearer study. "You good white man," she told him. When rushed or flustered, she often skipped words in sentences, and she didn't get much practice in using her English these days anyhow.

"That sounds as if you haven't met many good ones," he hinted.

Her smile faded. "White men *sica,* bad," she replied in a grave tone. "They hate, fear Dakotas. They kill, steal from Dakotas."

"For no reason?" Joe prodded to learn her feelings. He needed to discover all he could from this maiden about the Indians and quickly, too, before his throbbing wound dulled his wits. He felt warm, sticky moisture easing down his arm and wetting his shirt and jacket.

Unaware of his wound, as she was positioned to his left, Morning Star mistook the meaning of his question. "They have reason; we Indian."

"That's no reason to kill anyone." Joe's voice was serious as he refuted, "I'm white and you're Indian, but we helped each other. Surely there must be more to any trouble between the two peoples."

"You not been here long. If yes, you know I speak truth."

29

"I wasn't calling you a liar, miss. I was stating a fact."

"A fact is truth?" she questioned for clarity.

"Yes. Who are you? Why were those men holding you captive?"

"Talk later. Story long. Must find good place to hide. They after us soon." She needed to hurry in case her group was still nearby and searching for her. She must warn them about the Crow band and, if possible, stop their enemy from receiving the powerful weapons.

"Wait a minute. I need to tie a strip around my arm to halt this bleeding. Soon I'll be leaving a trail even a child could follow."

"*O-o?* You wounded, shot?" she asked. Morning Star edged closer to him and peered around his body. She saw his darkened sleeve.

Joe also eyed the wet area. "I took a ball in my arm back there as we were leaving. I'll be fine. Just help me tie a bandage around it."

As Joe pulled a cloth from his saddlebag, Morning Star guided her mount to his other side. *"Si. Makipazo we,"* she said in a firm tone. When he looked at her, she translated. "Be still. Show to me." She eased the jacket off his right shoulder and hand, then pushed up his sleeve.

Joe handed her the cloth. "Will you just bind it for me?" he asked. "We have to hurry. I don't want them to catch up with us. We'll tend it later."

Morning Star leaned toward him and bound the wound with gentleness and care, then she pulled down his sleeve and helped him put his jacket back on. "I tend with medicine when camp. Must find place to hide. They search for us soon. Crow party meeting them on new sun."

That was a clue Joe had been searching for, but it wouldn't do him any good now. Rescuing her had severed any chance of using that contact. He was back to the first step in his difficult journey to the truth. Unless this woman knew more . . . "Why meet a Crow party? What's in those wagons? Who are those men? What were you doing with them?" he questioned in a rush.

Morning Star was intrigued by his reaction. "Must go fast.

30

Speak later." She readjusted the bundle on her lap.

"Lead the way," he said. "I don't know this territory."

"Come. You safe if be good white man. Oglalas honor words to others."

"Oglala? That's your tribe?" he asked.

Morning Star sensed curious pleasure in the man. *"Han."*

"That means yes?" he knowingly inquired with a grin.

"Yes. Your eyes say you heard of Oglala tribe of Teton Dakotas."

"Does anybody come to this territory and not hear of them?"

"No. This be Teton land. This always remain Teton land."

"What Oglala band are you from?" Joe pressed with undisguised eagerness. Maybe his luck hadn't run out tonight; maybe it had improved.

Morning Star became wary. She wondered why he was so pleased to learn her tribe, but lacked time to question him. She decided not to ride for her last campsite, as that would give their trackers a point to begin a search. With a Crow band helping the white men, her small party could be overtaken and slain. "Must go. Not be captured again. Come."

Joe realized she was nervous about the impending arrival of the Crow, and he knew why: they were fierce enemies of the Dakotas. "I'm ready to ride," he proclaimed.

The white man and the Indian maiden galloped for another hour until they entered the Black Hills. He followed her over grassy terrain and into a treeline. They journeyed up a hill and into a rocky section that demanded vigilant riding. By the angle of the moon, it was getting darker by the half hour. When they came to a wide stream, they guided their horses into it, and followed its course. When they reached an area where the bank was trampled into mire by numerous hooves, they left the water.

"Soon, many buffalo come to drink. They cover tracks. I know place to hide. Men and Crow search hard for me. Come, Joe."

"Why do they want you so badly?" he questioned during their slow pace, but she didn't explain or even speak again. The area was steep, and had been named accurately for the black boulders and towering pinnacles. Roots and rocks jutting from the earth forced the horses to move slowly as they picked their way over the rough terrain. It was a jarring and sluggish pace. Joe was exhausted and weakened by his wound. He had ridden since yesterday morning, and knew it must be Wednesday by now. His tension had not lessened since catching up to those men of whom the Indian woman was so afraid. He wanted to know her identity and why she was such a valuable captive.

Morning Star led him to a sheltered area that was surrounded by dew-covered spruce, pine, and ash. Joe inhaled the fresh smells that were enhanced by mountain air. He heard animals moving in the darkness, no doubt spooked by their arrival. He was relieved when she halted.

"We hide in cave. Must rest. Must tend arm." She slid off her horse and tied her reins to a bush. "Come. You need help?"

"I can make it fine," Joe said, dismounting and securing his reins. He ignored his discomfort to give his loyal steed relief by removing the saddle, then tossed it over a small boulder. He was glad to find a seep there from which the animals could drink and lush grass where they could graze. This female was smart, and familiar with the area. He saw her waiting for him clutching a small bundle against her breasts, and he joined her with his saddlebags.

"You ride with skill, woman, and fight like a warrior," he complimented her, and then he remarked on the mottled Appaloosa that she had ridden bareback with ease and agility.

She sent him a smile for his kind words. Love was in her tone as she responded, "His name Hanmani; it mean 'to walk in the night.' He clever in darkness, not step wrong. Your horse good; he strong, much wind."

Joe glanced at the roan with the white splotch on his forehead. "His name's Star. I've had him a long time, and he's been a fine mount." When he saw her grin, he asked, "Why are you smiling like that?"

"My name *Anpaowicanhpi*." She laughed as he tried to repeat it before she could explain her amusement and the meaning of the word. She then told him how to pronounce it. "Ahn'pao'we'con'hpee'. It mean 'the dawning of the morning star;' that why I laugh at horse's name."

"Morning Star," he murmured as he studied her in the remaining moonlight. "It's beautiful." He halted himself from adding, *just as you are.* Her long ebony hair was shiny and soft, her eyes a warm brown. No one could call this golden-fleshed, smooth-complected beauty a "redskin." He guessed her height at around five feet seven-inches. Her nose was small and dainty, and her lips were full. She was the most exquisite woman he had ever seen. His stare brought a curious gaze to her eyes, so he halted it.

"Come, we go. It dark. Hold hand." She held one out to him and she noticed how he grasped it with eagerness and speed, a grip that exposed strength and trust. His hand was warm and pliant, and its inner surface revealed marks of hard work, while the back was smooth. She liked the contact with him, didn't consider Joe an enemy. And she sensed he felt the same. She entered the cave and walked into the shadows that engulfed them. Morning Star knew the center of this path was clear of obstacles, as she had played and camped there many times since birth. When she reached the area she wanted, having counted off the steps, she halted and said, "Be still. I light torch."

Joe waited in the blackness after she left him. He heard movements, then saw a spark. Soon, a glow revealed the interior and Morning Star to him. He watched her build a small fire with bush left there from another time. "How do you know your way around in the dark?" he asked.

"Come here many suns and moons since Life-Circle begin. Many times tie cloth over eyes to play games. Other times, cover eyes to test skills and make them grow larger. There not always light to guide feet when danger come. It good to be friends with darkness."

"You're right. I'd never thought of that before," Joe said. His eyes had adjusted to the amount of light from the fire, and as he looked around, he decided it was a safe hideout. There was a spot where a stream trickled down the rocky surface and formed a pool to supply them with water. There was enough brush to keep the fire going for another day or two. The floor was smooth in most places, and several areas had lengthy ledges like bunks. He didn't detect any musky or foul smell in the cave. It was a fresh, clean, and unusual chamber. With a fire and a beautiful woman, it was cozy—too cozy.

"Take off shirt. I tend wound," Morning Star said.

Even with her gentle assistance, Joe winced as he removed his jacket and shirt, but he was pleased that the snug binding had stopped most of the bleeding. He watched Morning Star open her parfleche and remove several things. He kept his gaze on hers as she examined the injury.

"White man's ball go in and out. That good." She asked if he had a bowl, but he didn't. She took the tin cup he handed to her. Morning Star knew Joe watched her as she crushed the pond lilies that would halt his bleeding completely. She pulled a small pouch suspended from a thong around her neck from beneath her top, loosened the string, and poured dried herbs into her palm, then finger-brushed them into the cup. She added enough water to blend them and prepare a mixture to prevent infection. She took care not to hurt him while smearing it onto the entrance and exit wounds. Afterward, she bound his upper arm with a clean cloth.

"What was that?" Joe inquired, pointing to her medicine pouch.

"*Pezuta wopahte,* medicine bundle," she explained.

"I meant those herbs you used."

"I not know. They halt wound from growing red with fever and stop bad yellow water from coming. Payaba gave to me. He shaman many seasons past. I seek herbs, plants, barks for him when captured. Hawk Eyes is shaman these suns. Payaba was Standing Tree in seasons past. His name Payaba these suns, 'Pushed Aside.' Hawk Eyes say his magic and skills larger, but Morning Star not believe. Payaba eighty winters. His legs and mind walk slow these suns, and many times not go where he wishes them. When he sick on mat for many suns, Hawk Eyes tell council Standing Tree soon go to join Grandfather; he say our people must vote for new medicine chief with many seasons until his Life-Circle end."

Joe realized the young woman spoke better English when

she talked slower and chose her words with care. It was also apparent she did not like Hawk Eyes or the retirement of her friend Standing Tree, now Payaba. "Why do you gather medicines for him if he's no longer your shaman?"

"Many visit Payaba's tepee; his powers strong. He cannot seek herbs, plants, and barks he needs; Morning Star gathers for him."

"That means your camp can't be too far from here."

"You not know how long I captive."

"Not long enough for those plants in your pouch to die and rot."

She grinned. "You see and know much, Joe Lawrence."

"Tell me how and why you were taken prisoner," he urged, feeling more at ease with her by the minute. It was a strange but good, sensation.

"Must sleep. Morning Star tired. Joe tired, hurt. We talk later."

"You sure you won't sneak off during the night?" he asked.

"Night flees. *Wi* awakens soon to climb into sky."

"You'll be here when I wake up?" Joe asked again.

"Morning Star be at your side." She moved to a place where she could rest her head on her folded arms on a rock, then closed her eyes.

After Joe put on his shirt, he went to the woman to slip his jacket around her shoulders. When she opened her dark eyes and looked at him, he couldn't seem to break their gazes or move back to his place.

Firelight flickered on the man's face. Morning Star saw that he had sky blue eyes to go with his handsome face and sunny hair. He was tall, about half a foot taller than herself, and strong; he possessed a good spirit and could be trusted. She enjoyed his smile and voice, and felt strangely warmed when he used them on her. When he had removed his shirt, she saw that his chest was as hairless as an Indian's. She liked this stranger who made her feel safe and happy. There were not many whites like him, and that was why lasting peace was impossible. She had no urge to sneak off from him while he slept, but she didn't know what she would do with him when the time came for parting. She hated to send him back into danger, as he didn't know this territory.

"You be in our land many suns?" she inquired.

"Yes, Morning Star, for many, many suns. I'll explain everything after we sleep. You're right; I'm exhausted." He knew he had to return to his place in the cave, as this woman was more tempting than any he'd ever met.

The daughter of Chief Sun Cloud observed Joe's retreat and sensed a reluctance in him to leave her side. She asked herself if he failed to grasp the differences in them, in their cultures, in their skins. He looked at her as a man of her kind would. She found that odd but pleasing. Soon they would learn more about each other. She closed her eyes.

Joe reclined on his side to prevent staring at her. He tried to believe it was her connection to the Oglalas that held his interest, but he knew it was not; it was Morning Star herself. He warned himself to stop thinking such crazy thoughts about her; he was here on a vital mission, not to woo a woman, especially one so different from him.

In a short time, the two fatigued people were asleep, only to dream of each other.

When he awoke, Joe yawned and stretched. He noticed that his wound was not as sore as he had expected. Perhaps it was because of the herbs Morning Star had placed on it. He glanced at the spot she had taken last night; no, early this morning. It was empty! Morning Star was gone!

Chapter Two

Joe jerked to a sitting position and looked around the cave. A small fire was burning. He listened, then caught her voice far away. He got to his feet and headed for the entrance. He saw Morning Star outside with her horse, stroking and speaking to him. His blue gaze moved over her shapely figure in the buckskin dress. He assumed the hidden part of her body was as firm and supple as her arms and legs. As if sensing his approach — or maybe she'd heard it — she turned and smiled.

"You close eyes long time, Joe Lawrence. *Wi* climb high. Morning Star see, hear no danger. We rest. Joe heal until *Wi* come again and enemies gone. Morning Star return home, and Joe ride away."

"Where is your home, Morning Star?" he asked, joining her.

"Must go in cave. If danger come, Hanmani warn. Hole in cave for escape. Hanmani, Star have water and grass. They fine."

Joe followed the Indian maiden back inside the rock shelter. "You never answer my questions, Morning Star. Why? Do you distrust me?"

"*Hiya,*" she replied with haste. "No. Story long, hard. Morning Star *yuonihansni,* shamed by evil whites' capture. Eager to scout and not hear Hanmani warning. Morning Star foolish, pride too big."

"Don't scold yourself. If it hadn't been for you, I would be dead now. You helped me better than any warrior could

37

have. I can understand why you'd want to spy on those men. You said they were taking guns and whiskey to your enemies, the Crow."

She stared at Joe in dismay and sudden mistrust. "Morning Star not speak such words! Say they meet Crow band on this sun. Not say why they meet or what in wagons. How you know such things?"

Joe noticed that she had strapped a beaded belt with a knife sheath around her waist and that her hand had shifted to the weapon. He had let her beauty steal his wits, and he'd made a slip. He didn't know who she was, where she was from, or if the Oglalas were involved in the trouble as charged or merely being framed. "Somebody is trading guns and whiskey to the Crow, and it's going to cause big trouble. Their tracks told me those wagons were loaded heavily; that's why I trailed them. When they acted strange and didn't want me around, I added up the clues."

"Why you care if they trade with Bird People? Crow friends with whites. Crow and whites want Dakota land and lives! Do you trick Morning Star to take you to her camp, to return to destroy it?"

"I swear that isn't true. We helped each other back there because we're good people and we want peace."

To see his reaction, she told Joe, "Dakotas cannot have peace with whites. Palefaces lie, cheat, steal, kill. They forget words of truce on paper. They want all we possess."

Her eyes and tone did not agree with the evocative words she spoke. If she believed them, she would not have helped him or remained here with him, he reasoned. "Some whites do, Morning Star, but not all of us, not me. I want peace. You can trust me."

The dark-haired beauty stared at Joseph Lawrence. His blue gaze was filled with honesty, hope, and gentleness. "Tell why you here. Why track men? Why rescue Morning Star?"

Joe sat down on a rock as he decided what to tell her. "I was traveling with a friend of mine. We got separated at Pratte's Post east of here. Tanner was knifed badly. Before he died, he mentioned guns and whiskey, a boss called 'Snake-Man', and something about picking up a big load. When I came across those wagon ruts, my instinct told me to follow them. I've heard about the trouble between the Crow and Dakotas and that the Army thinks the Dakotas are going on the warpath again this year. I was going to join those men until I could find Tanner's killer. While I was getting justice and revenge, if I could stop a war between Indians and whites by getting at the truth, I'd be glad."

"People lie to you. We not want war," Morning Star said adamantly. "We not start war. We defend our lives and lands from attack. Whites are ones who not honor words. Oglalas make treaty many winters past. Have peace long time. Five winters past, white men make trails on Lakota lands. Many wagons use. Some whites stay in Lakota lands. They start new troubles. More soldiers and forts come to help them. Crow help them; they help Crow. When *Wi* hot and long last season, more trouble come. I not see, but hear of bad deeds. When cold and snow come, whites and soldiers quiet. They afraid to attack in winter camp; we too strong. Soldiers send message that we stop attacks we not make. We tell truth; they no believe. We say Crow do; Crow say no. They take Bird People's words. Bands find tracks of white man's horses at wicked sights. Not know who. Father say more trouble come when we hunt buffalo soon, when warriors gone from camp and defense low. How have peace?"

"By helping me prove your people are innocent and want peace."

"Tokel he?" She asked him how.

"Take me to your people. Let me talk with them. I have to discover who this Snake-Man is and why he's trying to start a war here."

Her eyes widened and her voice lowered. "We hear of Snake-Man. He have powerful magic. He evil. We not know his name and face. You must go, or die." Her tone and expression were filled with worry.

"Your people would kill me? But I'm trying to help them."

"Not my people. Bad whites and Crow allies."

"Not if your people help me. I need a guide and translator. If I can get proof as to who is to blame, the Army will stop the evil whites and the sly Crow."

"Toke he?" She asked why. This situation was befuddling her.

"They killed my best friend, and they want to stir up a war. I don't think you want a bloody war to start, either, so help me prevent one."

"Make no promises to Joe, but take to Father to talk."

"Who is your father? How far away is your camp?"

"Ride fast, two suns. Father called Mahpiya-Wi, Oancan: Sun Cloud, Chief. Great Spirit create Dakota Nation in three parts: Lakota, Nakota, and Dakota." She explained the major divisions of what the whites called the Sioux Nation. "It like three branches with many limbs on big tree called *Dakota Oceti Sakawin:* 'Seven Council Fires of the Dakota.' Tribes like limbs. Dakota/Santee branch have four limbs: Mdewakanton, Wahpekute, Wahpeton, and Sisseton. Nakota branch have two limbs: Yankton and Yanktonais. Lakota branch have one big limb: Teton. It have many small limbs: Oglala, Brule, Hunkpapa, Blackfeet, Two Kettle, Sans Arc, and Minneconjou. Small limbs have many bands like pinecones. Morning Star belong to Red Heart Band of Oglala tribe, Teton limb, Lakota branch of tree. Dakota/Santee branch not same as big Dakota tree. When Santee sign Pike's Treaty, they give whites part of their territory far away. Whites think Dakota/Santee sign for Dakota tree. That not true, not same, not one."

Joe knew about the 1805 treaty where the Santee ceded some of their territory in Minnesota to the United States for forts. That treaty confused whites who didn't know the Santee chief could not speak for the entire Dakota Nation, as the President ruled and represented America. Most whites believed there was a treaty with all Dakota Indians and they could come and go as they pleased in any Dakota area. But, in truth, the woodland tribes had no claim or control over their Plains brothers' regions. It would be like the governor of Virginia selling someone land in Georgia without Georgia's permission or knowledge. Suddenly, Joe realized who Morning Star really was. Stunned, he asked, "You're Sun Cloud's daughter? Sun Cloud, son of Gray Eagle?" And also Tanner's cousin, he added to himself.

She was pleased by the awe in his expression. *"Han,* yes, it so. You hear of Father and Grandfather."

"Many times. They're both great legends, men as tall as the sky. Thank God I didn't let those bastards harm you. It would have been a bloodbath for certain. How did Zeke and his men get you? I'm sure your father has a search party out looking for you."

"Word not reached his ears. Take friends five moons to reach camp from place Morning Star captured on past sun. Joe rest, heal. We ride on new sun. Catch friends on trail. Friends ride this sun, travel slow; have women, children, old ones. Evil whites hide capture trail; mark false one to Crow Territory. Friends not know Morning Star near; cannot ride into Bird People lands to attack, rescue. Need more warriors for big fight. They ride home, tell Father. Take many moons."

"Are you sure we shouldn't leave right now? They might travel fast with such bad news. We could catch up to them before they tell your father."

"No. Will ride fast; be close behind in two . . . days. If not stay hidden, evil whites and Crow find. Must not guide to friends; they be slain."

"You're right. We'll wait until tomorrow. Tell me about yourself and your people," Joe coaxed. "I didn't know Sun Cloud had a daughter. The more I learn before I reach your camp, the better we can all work together. First, I want to hear about your capture, and what you heard those men say."

"You strange white man. Morning Star speak, but Joe must . . ." She halted and looked toward the entrance. She touched a finger to her lips for silence, then cupped an ear with her hand: sign language for *listen.*

Joe remained quiet and alert. He heard what had captured her attention. Slowly and carefully he reached for his Sharp's '48 rifle. He must not allow anything to happen to this valuable woman, even if it cost him his life.

With caution, Joseph Lawrence and Morning Star crept toward the entrance of the cave. They heard the roan's shoes and the Appaloosa's hooves striking against rocks as the two horses shifted about in rising anxiety. Their ears caught a whinny several times as someone or something frightened their mounts. Joe motioned for his companion to stay back, but she continued to follow him. His rifle was ready for use, as was the knife in her grasp.

Joe peered outside to the right of the opening. He gave a sigh of relief and relaxed his taut body. "Look," he said, pointing to the seep where a porcupine was drinking.

The horses knew it was wise to give the prickly creature all the space it wanted. When the animal had drunk its fill, it waddled through the bushes and vanished. The horses settled down the moment the porcupine was gone and returned to their grazing.

Morning Star laughed and dismissed her own tension. "It wise not to challenge *pahin* when he thirsty."

Joe chuckled. "Or any other time. Those spines give a nasty bite."

"Hawk Eyes say quills have poison; Payaba say it not so. It hard to work with them. Pricks sting; they . . . become sore; they not kill. Hawk Eyes say they no kill Red Heart women because we bathe hands in *ska utahu can* when we done; medicine bark heal pricks."

He noticed the tone of her voice and the look on her face. He knew they held unintentional clues he might need later in camp. "You don't like or trust Hawk Eyes, do you?"

Morning Star glanced at Joe and frowned, but at herself, not him. "It wrong to think, speak bad of shaman. Hawk Eyes not always this way. His son, Knife-Slayer, desires great rank and power for his father and for Knife-Slayer. He places . . . mischief in Hawk Eyes' head. Many times wish they not Oglalas. Morning Star fear their hunger for war against bluecoats and whites will bring much suffering to our people. Think others not see bad in them."

Morning Star's dark-brown eyes scanned their green-and-black enclosure before she continued. "Hawk Eyes want Buckskin Girl as mate. He have two; one die. She say no; Morning Star tell her say no. Buckskin Girl Morning Star's friend. She granddaughter of White Arrow; before he join Great Spirit, he great warrior and friend to Gray Eagle,

42

Morning Star's grandfather. They live, hunt, raid as brothers from birth until leave Mother Earth. Morning Star not know Gray Eagle; he killed long before she born. Bad bluecoats slay in trap. Father become chief when Grandfather ride Ghost Trail. Bad bluecoats punished. Father make treaty with white leader to have peace. For past two summers, whites forget truce. More trouble coming."

The Indian maiden realized she was rambling to take her mind off the white man. She did not understand his potent effect on her. She wanted to caress the bruises on his face from the battle to rescue her. She longed to tease her fingers over the dark stubble that was growing along his strong jawline, cleft chin, and above his lips. She liked the way his sunny hair, slightly mussed from sleep, journeyed like low, rolling hills from his head to his collar. She could stare into his azure eyes forever. She liked the size and shape—not too large or too thin—of his nose, and the appealing fullness of his mouth. His shoulders were broad, his muscles well defined and toned to sleek hardness. She enjoyed his calming smile, his soothing voice, and his nearness. She felt at ease with him, yet tense in his presence. When his gaze met hers, her body warmed and trembled without warning. It was confusing, alarming . . . and forbidden under her tribal laws.

Joe saw how she looked at him. It was as if strong currents were pulling them into the same whirlpool and spinning them around together, drawing them closer and deeper by the hour. She was beautiful and tempting—irresistible. The sides of her lustrous black hair were braided near a flawless face; the rest flowed down her back like a silky and shiny river. He was surprised it wasn't tangled or mussed this morning. Perhaps she had a brush in the parfleche from which she had taken her knife and sheath, after she had returned his blade he had lent her during her rescue.

Entranced, he studied her from head to toe. Morning Star's eyes were wide in the center, then tapered to fetching points at the outer edges. Her lashes were thick, and her brows were thin. They traveled above her eyes in perfect harmony. A straight nose that attempted to tilt upward was above full lips that evoked a desire to kiss them many times.

43

Her oval face had bone structure any female would delight in having, and it was the same with her figure. Without a doubt, many warriors craved this beauty.

The tawny dress she wore was a different shade than her golden-brown flesh, and it was stained in several places, probably from struggling with her captors. The sleeves and tail displayed short fringes that swayed with her movements. She wore low-cut moccasins with lovely beadwork, which he surmised she had made.

As they gazed at each other, both forgot their peril and her last words. A hawk's shrill cry overhead startled them back to reality.

Morning Star was bewildered by her lapse of attention and wayward thoughts. She could not comprehend how their spirits could touch so soon and so powerfully after meeting less than a sun ago. "We go in, be near escape hole if danger come," she suggested, suddenly feeling apprehensive.

"I'll join you in a minute. I need to . . . have privacy," he hinted.

Morning Star grasped his meaning and left him alone. After Joe relieved himself nearby, he joined her in the cave.

Morning Star had listened intently to Joe's use of English and she called to mind her past lessons. She spoke slowly in an attempt to be correct. "We must put out fire. We must not let smoke or smell show hiding place. We will hunt and eat when dark come and danger gone. Yes?"

"Yes." Joe set aside his rifle, retrieved his saddlebag, and withdrew a pouch of dried venison strips he had purchased at Fort Laramie. "We can chew on these and have water until later. You must be hungry. I didn't see Zeke give you anything to eat, and there were only three dirty dishes in the pile."

Morning Star was impressed by how little escaped his senses. She *was* hungry. She hadn't eaten since leaving her people's camp yesterday morning, and, accepting the meat, she said, *"Pilamaya."*

"You're welcome," he responded to her thanks, but neither noticed that and other slips. He used his cup to fetch

44

water from the nature-formed basin, then shared it with her. Joe chewed off a bite of the jerky. "Not too good, but not too bad," he jested.

The sun's angle cast a bright glow into the cave's entrance and prevented them from being in total darkness, though its power diminished the farther it drifted into the interior. It was a pleasant spring afternoon that Joe decided must be the fourteenth of May. The night's chill was gone; the odor of a fire lingered in the air. Water trickled down rocks and flowed into the small pool that must have an opening beneath, because it did not pour over the sides into the cave. A hawk signaled to its mate and warned an intruder away from his domain. Crickets chirped in the darkness behind them. Birds sang in the bushes and trees and beyond the cave. The dirt floor gave off its own unique odor of earth. The strong but not offensive smell of jerky filled their noses as it was consumed. It was harder to eat than fresh game, but it removed any hunger pangs. The cool and refreshing water they shared was the best part of their meager meal.

Morning Star toyed with one braid as she reflected on their past conversations and the one she had overheard in the white men's camp. She looked at her companion and remarked, "You spoke lies to white men. Why you come to Oglala land with friend? Who is Murphy and Old Joe? To trust and help, must know more, must know truth."

Joe swallowed the water in his mouth, then coughed to clear his throat. Her first statement had caught him off guard. She had keen wits, so he needed to be as honest as possible. He didn't want her to mistrust or fear him. "I was trying to trick them with words so I could join them, but they were too nervous around a stranger and they were hiding something. I was hoping they'd lead me to Snake-Man. That seemed like the only way to track down Tanner's killer. It wasn't all lies, Morning Star. I did come here for excitement and challenges with Tanner and his father; a man needs those kinds of things sometime in his life."

Joe slid off his rock seat and moved to the ground where he could stretch out his long legs. He propped his back against the rock, then continued. "What I told them about

45

Ben Murphy was true, except the part about him coming out here to trap for a fur company. Ben still lives back South. It seemed a good way to explain my presence in this secluded area. The other man is my father, Joseph Benjamin Lawrence, Sr. I was named after him: When you have the same name, the father is called senior and the son is called junior. He's a good man, Morning Star, but I wasn't ready to get deeper into the shipping business yet."

"What is . . . the shipping business?" she inquired.

Joe contemplated a way to clarify it for her. "Large boats are called ships. When you use them to carry supplies to other places, it's called shipping. Business is the work you do. We own many ships and we get paid money to deliver goods for other men. Some of those places can only be reached by water. To other places, it's faster, easier, and cheaper by ship."

"What is 'cheaper'?" she queried another word she did not know.

"It's like when a man asks for two horses to take your supplies to another camp to sell or trade, but a second man only asks for one horse to take them. You hire the man who asks for one because he's cheaper. A ship is very big; it can carry a lot of supplies, not a few as in a wagon. A ship can hold more supplies than six trading posts; it could hold an entire Indian village. Ships can move faster and easier over water than wagons can over land. One day, I'll go home and work with my father. But . . ."

When he halted, she pressed. "But?"

"My father forgets I'm no longer a boy. He wants me to follow orders like a hired man. I need to prove my worth to him and to myself. I want to experience more than water and ships. I want to face challenges. I want to see this wild land. So much is happening out here; the country's growing. I want to be a part of it before I settle down. My father didn't understand these hungers in me. He was disappointed when I left home."

"Morning Star understand. Father and people see only a woman. Morning Star can battle, hunt, and track as warrior. Can shoot bow with skill. Morning Star arrows, lance, and

46

knife not miss targets. Morning Star hunger to see and do many things before . . . settle down. Others say no. Say woman must cook, fetch water and wood, wash, make garments, join, and bear children: do only woman's chores. Such work must be done, but it give no . . . excitement. We much alike."

"Yes, we are." He noticed how she worked to improve her English, and he was impressed by her quick intelligence. He moved to a topic of great interest to him. "Those men who held you prisoner, what did they say? Why do your people let them roam your lands freely?"

"Father sign truce many winters before daughter born not to kill whites or make war with bluecoats. Whites not honor their part of treaty. If they attack, we must defend lives and lands. If they not attack, we let travel on and beyond our land. They must not come and steal Oglala land. They must not slay buffalo and many creatures for hides. Buffalo give life to Oglalas and our brothers. Bad whites raid sleeping places; steal warriors' weapons, garments, all their possessions. They kill hunters; they take scalps to sell and trade. White law say no give guns and whiskey to Indians, but greedy whites trade to Crow to kill Oglalas. Whites steal horses, burn mark on hide, put shoes on feet, and claim. Warriors know all ponies in herds. Tell soldiers to make return. Soldiers say brand make Oglala ponies white man's horses. They not to build more forts if Father and tribe say no. They not to steal trees from face of Mother Earth and makes cuts in her body for . . . farms. They not to graze spotted buffaloes on grasslands."

Joe knew the Indians called cattle by that peculiar name. He listened with interest to her list of grievances against his people.

"White men not know Morning Star speak English. They not know much Oglala. They not talk much where Morning Star can hear many words. Big man say they . . . de-liv-er supplies to Crow. They go back to man called Boss. They speak no name and no call him Snake-Man, so not know if Boss is same man. He say Crow be mad soon and attack Oglalas. Not know why. He say, when Sioux gone, all be fine, Boss can do his plans. They hope Crow slay us, so we can no return to battle another su— another day," she corrected herself. "You must ride far. They search for you to slay for saving Morning Star. If you ride here to look for friend's killer, you be killed. Morning Star not want Joe Lawrence killed. You good man."

Joe was moved by her concern. "I have to stay and avenge Tanner. I promised myself and his father. Tanner was like a brother to me."

"Task of *watokicon* dangerous," she warned.

"What is that?" he asked.

"Avenger. Snake-Man is *wakansica,* a Bad Spirit. Cannot slay spirits."

"He's not a spirit, Morning Star, Just an evil white man using tricks to scare and fool the Indians. Why do you think he's a spirit?"

"Knife-Slayer and raid band see him with Crow. They hide to watch; they not have enough men to attack enemies. *Wakansica* have snakes on arms. They crawl up arms, with heads here," she said, gesturing toward her breasts, showing him how the "snakes" curled around the man's arms, over his shoulder, and downward to his breasts. "Spirit Snakes big and many colors. They have bad eyes, sharp fangs, long tongues. They no see Spirit Snakes move or strike; they sleep on *Wakansica*'s body. Hawk Eyes say they powerful and evil medicine. Band see *Wakansica* do magic. He throw little balls into fire; make much noise and smoke. Make little suns glow and dance in wind. When suns and smoke gone, Snake-Man gone. His men ride away in wagons. Band no attack Crow in evil place where Bad Spirit hiding. Might return and slay Red Hearts."

Joe realized this clever Snake-Man was using Indian superstition and their lack of knowledge to frighten and delude them. "Those were only cunning tricks, Morning Star. I've seen such things before during my travels far away. The snakes are painted into his skin, they're called tattoos. They're much like the pictures painted on tepees and shields. Across the big waters, there's a place called the Orient. Wise men live there. They make the balls that shine and give off

48

smoke. That's where Snake-Man gets his magic tricks from. I've seen how men can sneak away when the air is filled with heavy smoke; it blinds the eyes for a short time. He probably slipped to the wagon and hid there while the Indians couldn't see. He wants the Crow to believe he's a powerful shaman so they'll work for him to destroy your people. If I traveled in my ship to that land, I could buy balls like those and do the same tricks. It's not real magic. It has no power, except to fool people who don't know about them. When we reach your camp, I'll ask Knife-Slayer how Snake-Man looked. That will help find him."

"No good. His face behind ceremony mask, head of big snake."

Joe was disappointed. "Because he didn't want anyone to recognize him," he murmured. "He chose a good disguise and scheme. He's clever."

"What is disguise and scheme?"

"Disguise is when you use things like masks to hide who you are. A scheme is a wicked plan to fool people. I wonder if Zeke, the man who captured you, is smart enough to be Snake-Man."

"He no have snakes on arms. I claw and bite when captured."

It didn't surprise Joe that Zeke wasn't his man. "How did he capture you, Morning Star?"

"Small party go to Mato Paha, Bear Mountain. It sacred place where go to pray and give gifts to Great Spirit. Men go to seek visions and to think much. Holy mountain where we given Sun Dance and our beliefs by Great Spirit after he create Dakotas. We hang prayer cloths and tokens on trees that grow on sleeping bear hill. Sometimes white men steal; that bad medicine. Not even Crow steal sacred gifts from trees. Grandfather punish."

She sat down near him and crossed her legs. "Morning Star go there with brother, Night Stalker. He take wife and son. He go to pray for safety of our people when we ride for summer camp and for good hunt when we seek buffalo. Others go with us. Hawk Eyes go to seek vision, take his wife. Flaming Star and Thunder Spirit go to give thanks and

49

to pray. They sons of White Arrow. They have many winters on their bodies; may never go to sacred mountain again. Mates go to tend chores. Buckskin Girl travel with parents, Flaming Star and Morning Light. Little Feet is wife of Thunder Spirit; she daughter of Bright Arrow, brother to Father. Bright Arrow walks Mother Earth no more. Crow war party kill before Morning Star born. Summer Rain and son go with Lone Horn; he war chief. He give thanks and seek vision to lead warriors if attack come soon."

Morning Star sighed heavily at that distressing thought. "We stay at Mato Paha five suns, days. We ride for village. Stop at Elk Creek for men to hunt game for journey in Paha Sapa, means Black Hills. This sacred place, where we make winter camps, where old ones rest on *wicagnakapi wiconte,* death scaffolds. Spirits and Thunderbirds live in black mountains. Much game here. This Oglala land and must defend to death," she said with deep feeling, then returned to her story. "Women stay in camp and make ready to ride when hunters return after *Wi* passes overhead. Morning Star finish chores and go seek medicine plants for Payaba. Touched-A-Crow, she brother's wife, go with Morning Star. She gather roots and plants. She take son. He two winters; he bad boy many moons. He bad on trail; she must return to camp. Morning Star ride on to do Payaba chore. Stay near edge of forest. Morning Star think, walk too far, hear noise and hide."

Her dark eyes grew wide and she spoke faster with excitement. "See two white men scout. Get bad feeling. Follow them on Hanmani. They go to Mato Paha. They take prayer tokens! Morning Star angry, but have only knife as weapon. Cannot attack. While thinking, man—big one—sneak up and capture. Morning Star fight. He strong, mean. He take to others. They put on horse with big man. They take Hanmani to make false trail to Crow land. They drop Crow arrows and cloth to fool Red Heart band. They know small band cannot ride into camp of many Crow. They know others must return home, cannot challenge Bird People. We ride to river. We travel water far to wagon camp. Morning Star bound and given no food, no water, no blanket. Wait all

50

sun. Moon and Joe come. Joe help escape."

"We *are* a lot alike," Joe said, grinning. "We were both trailing them to gather clues. That was smart and brave."

"Not smart; got captured," she refuted, then frowned.

"That happens sometimes even to the best warriors," Joe reassured her. "I came along to help you, and you returned to help me. We're both good fighters and we make a good pair. After I see your father, if he'll work with me, we'll put a stop to this trouble before it leads to war."

"Joe's voice and eyes say much. You seek men who kill friend. More to Joe's ride and task. Is not so? What more you seek?"

Joe decided if he told her the truth he might win her help and trust. If so, it would be easier to obtain her father's. "Ever hear of a white man named Thomas Fitzpatrick? The Indians call him Broken-Hand." She eyed him strangely, but nodded. "He trapped in this territory for twenty years, and later worked as a wilderness guide. He became the Indian agent five years ago at Fort Laramie. Know where that is?"

Again, Morning Star nodded.

"Tom's honest and fair and smart. He knows this territory and the people here, white and Indian. He's working on a big treaty between all tribes, and between Indians and whites. Tom suspects that somebody doesn't want the Indians to make peace among themselves and keeps stirring tribes up one against the other. He knows that if intertribal warfare breaks out, whites will be caught in the middle. Besides, it's against the law to sell weapons and whiskey to Indians. There are many clues that point to the Red Hearts and other Lakota tribes as the troublemakers. Tom thinks this Snake-Man may be behind the problems. He's talked to Crow, but they won't tell him anything. He's talked to Lakotas, too, but they claim they don't know anything. Tom wants me to find out who Snake-Man is, what he's trying to do here, if he's the guilty one, and how he can be stopped. The United States government and our chief don't want a war with your people or any other Indian tribe."

"Why bluecoats attack hunters if this be so?" she argued.

"To keep them from killing white settlers who come here

and from killing white immigrants passing through your territory heading west. Many wagon trains are attacked. Boats on rivers and soldiers on patrol have been attacked. Settlers and farmers have been burned out. Trading posts have been robbed. Almost every time, Lakota arrows have been found."

"It not Oglalas, not Red Hearts. Inkpaduta and Little Thunder raid wagons on trails; they not Oglalas; they Santee and Brule. They part of Seven Council Fires, but not same tribe. Whites have land and game where *Wi* awakens. Must not come and steal Lakota land and creatures. They stay in their land, they be safe; we be safe. No trouble, no battle."

"That sounds simple, Morning Star, but it isn't."

"What is . . . simple?"

"Easy, not hard . . . what's right. The smart and good thing to do."

"It be simple, if whites honor truce and not come to our land."

"More settlers, trappers, traders, and others will come. This area is beautiful and exciting," he said, then thought, *like you are.* "Many whites want new or better lives, Morning Star. Things are bad for them back East, where the sun awakens. Some don't have money to buy land, and they want to make a good place for their families. They can do that here. This land is big. There's plenty of room for everyone. Sometimes I've ridden all day without seeing one Indian. If we can stop the troublemakers and become friends, everybody can live in peace in the same territory. Some of the people on the wagon trains have to stop here because they can't make it all the way to Oregon or California. They get sick, or tired, or discouraged; or they run out of money. Some just fall in love with this territory."

"They try to take land, claim it, not use it, not share it," Morning Star argued. "Grandfather owns the land. They kill His creatures for furs and hides; they waste meat. When game killed, all of creature must be used. They bring strange sickness. They scare game. They build across animal trails and confuse creatures. They want best hunting grounds. They want trees in sacred hills. They not travel as we do.

52

They camp in one place; they destroy it. They bring whiskey to dull warriors' wits. Traders and trappers speak false; they cheat Indians. They bring trouble; they blame Indians. They use false words to get more forts and bluecoats. When whites come and we let stay, it tell more whites to come. Soon, no land and game for Indians. Crow are fools; they no see whites trick and how much hate Crow. If agent Tom want peace, he keep whites away. Simple." She used her new word.

Joe changed his position and faced her fully. "Lordy, I wish it were. I don't want to see your people or other tribes destroyed. If war comes, Morning Star, that could happen. The whites have many more people than the Indians; they have more and better weapons. To challenge them is a mistake. I hope your father will work for peace."

She did not like that scary information, but said with confidence and courage, "If peace means lose land, honor, and lives—he no make peace."

"I hope I can help him obtain peace with honor and without losses," Joe said. "That's hard when each side wants the same thing, and each side thinks they're right. The man I came here with feels and thinks the same way I do: Tanner's father. He's an observer and adviser on the situation for President Fillmore," he said, then explained the situation, after deciding how much and what to tell her about Stede Gaston.

"Tanner's father is like a scout and speaker for the Great White Chief Fillmore. He learns what's happening, then tells our chief what he thinks must be done to prevent problems and war. Our chief trusts him and will listen to him. Many of the white man's problems have been halted, so more white-eyes are on these lands. We had many enemies, like you have the Crow, Pawnee, and the Shoshone. We made peace with them. War ended with the Mexicans, people who live south. Our border conflict with the British was settled. We traded money for a large track of land that includes this territory. Indians say land can't be owned, but the French claimed this territory and sold it to us years ago. Whites do believe land can be owned and claimed. The United States now claims this territory. The path wagon trains use is called

53

the Oregon Trail; the one near it is called the Mormon Trail. Many whites use the trails to travel west.

"There's another problem about a yellow rock called gold that white men desire. A lot of it was discovered west of here in a place called California. Many of the men passing through this territory went there and are still going there to search for gold. Trying to stop passage through your lands can't be done."

Joe stretched out his legs again. "With more whites coming here and through here, Morning Star, they demand more forts, trading posts, and roads. Roads are cleared trails for easy and fast travel." He knew she would not understand what the Topographical Bureau was and he didn't know how to explain it, so he skipped over the survey they had done near Laramie in '49. "You can't stop settlers any more than you can stop the rain. But rain and soil work together to give life and beauty to the land and people. Whites and Indians can do the same. First, peace is needed, but that can't come until evil men are caught and punished. Those working in your territory don't attack where they can be seen and caught. They trick the Crow into fighting for them. They don't do their own dirty work because they don't want the Army involved. Tanner and I were to travel around and be his father's eyes and ears. Tanner saw or heard something dangerous; he was killed so he couldn't tell others. If I'd been with him, he'd be alive. I was getting a new shoe for Star. He'd thrown one on the way to Pratte's Post."

When Joe became silent, Morning Star grasped his grief and guilt. "If you be with him, you be dead like Tanner dead."

"Maybe," he half agreed. "I'm going to find who killed him, then get justice. After I buried him, I went to Fort Laramie to tell his father. Lordy, that was hard. He would have come back with me to find the killer, but his leg is broken and he can't ride. I was returning to Pratte's Post to search for clues when I found Zeke's wagon trail. A gut instinct told me to follow it. I'm glad I did. Meeting you was fate, Morning Star."

"What is fate?" she asked, intrigued by his tone.

"Destiny, something meant to happen, part of my Life-Circle that must cross another person's at a certain time and place."

She liked his explanation. "It so. You want peace much as you want Tanner's killer. This be good. Morning Star help you find both."

He felt there wasn't anything she could do other than help him with her father and people, but he didn't refute her words or refuse her offer. "If anything happens to me, tell your father to send word to Captain James Thomas at Fort Tabor. Make certain the soldiers know you want peace so they won't be tricked by Snake-Man and the Crow into attacking your camp."

"Captain James Thomas," she repeated. "Morning Star remember."

Joe was feeling stiff and restless. She was too close to ignore. "Are you sure your band would head for home without you? If not, we should warn them of the Crow coming today. If they stayed, they're in danger."

"They gone. When Morning Star not return to camp, Night Stalker search. He good hunter and tracker. When he see trail to Crow land, he not follow. He leave to protect others. It our way. It wrong to risk many lives to save one. If Night Stalker foolish and stay, must not lead Crow and evil whites to their camp. Most are old ones, women, and little ones."

He noticed something in her tone that told him she wasn't convinced her party was gone. "You think your brother might stay here and search for you?"

"Morning Star pray he do not trail to try rescue. Not sure," she added, being honest with him. "Night Stalker have much to learn from Father before he be chief. He hunger to drive whites from land and slay all Crow. He hunger to earn many coups and much honor. He not want to think and talk. He want to use wits and skills to defend hunting grounds, sacred lands, and people. When winter quiet, he grow restless. He not trust whites. He thirty winters, years, old. Father fifty-four years. More trouble comes. It not Night Stalker's time to be chief. Father must teach more. Morning Star pray brother listens. Knife-Slayer whispers words into ear Morning Star not think good. Morning Star pray Great Spirit opens all Oglala hearts and ears to Joe's words for peace."

"So do I, Morning Star. If a strong truce isn't made soon and your people attack the whites, the Army will retaliate." Joe fretted over the interference and resistance he suspected he would get from Knife-Slayer, Hawk Eyes, and Night Stalker. He would have to do some fast and clever talking to convince Sun Cloud, Red Hearts, and other Oglalas to cooperate with him and his cohorts, Stede Gaston and Tom Fitzpatrick. "If I only had some evidence against Snake-Man to show your people to prove I'm . . . That's it! In the morning, you ride home and I'll track Zeke to spy on his meeting with the Crow. Maybe I can get some proof. I'll come to your camp as soon as—"

"*Hiya!* Go with you. It too dangerous alone and wounded. Men bad."

Joe gazed into her defiant face. He knew it was bravery speaking, not impulsiveness. "No, Morning Star. They could capture you again. Then the Oglalas would attack the Crow, and war would surely follow."

She was touched by his concern for her safety and his desire to help Lakotas. Yet it was more her problem than Joe's, so she must assist him. "We be careful. Morning Star know land and tracks. Go with you, help."

Joe saw how determined and confident she was. He knew arguing was a waste of time and energy, and she was right. "You can come, but we won't get too close. We're not taking any risks."

"Good. Simple," she added and grinned, her eyes sparkling. Morning Star was glad he yielded. Riding together against foes sounded exciting. Her body quivered with anticipation. The chief, tribal council, and warrior societies controlled everything in Indian camps. It was thrilling to be half in charge for a change. Until they reached her village, she could use her skills and wits on something besides female chores. It was delightful not be refused and scolded because she was "only a woman." She could not help but be impressed by Joe's generosity where her help was involved.

56

They had talked in their hideout for hours. Dusk approached and dimmed the cave's interior. Both decided their foes must be gone by now.

Morning Star got to her feet. She was hungry, and needed privacy. "Joe stay. Morning Star hunt, track and kill with knife. It silent. Gun loud. You make fire to cook. Morning Star return soon."

Joe reasoned that any threat to them had ended, but still he protested her plan. "What if they're still looking for us? I can't let you go alone."

"Morning Star know hills, and one hunter best. Morning Star be alert, not be foolish. Be safe."

Once more, Joseph Lawrence realized he couldn't change her mind. After seeing her in action he believed she could take care of herself. She was on guard now; it was dusk; and she was familiar with the area. "Don't stay long. I'll worry until I see your face again."

After the Indian maiden left, Joe used a safety match to light a fire. As he worried over her safety, he drifted into serious thought. He knew this mission was going to be difficult. He would have foes, resisters, and dangers on both sides. Yet his tasks seemed challenging and stimulating ones. He tried to keep the loss of Tanner Gaston off his mind, as it could distract him. At a time when he was surrounded by perils, distractions could cost him his life and success. If everything worked out, he would avenge the death of his best friend, help establish peace for Stede's people and for innocent whites, and spend time with Morning Star. Once his tasks here were done, he would return to Virginia and never see her again. That thought evoked a curious ache within him.

Tanner's cousin was enchanting and unique. She stirred feelings in him that he had experienced before, but never this strong and deep. He warned himself that he could not act on those desires. She was Sun Cloud's daughter; and they were a world apart in upbringings and beliefs. If only she and her people weren't in such peril . . .

What he had told her about needing a strong treaty and no attacks or else the Army would retaliate was true. There were eight forts within a week's ride of the Dakotas' enormous territory: Atkinson and Kearny II to the south; Dodge, Ripley, and Snelling to the east; Benton to the northwest; Laramie fringed it to the southwest and within it was Fort Tabor on the Missouri River. From what Tom Fitzpatrick had told him, it wouldn't be long before Bridger, Union, Lookout, and Pratte's posts would have forts. The Oglala's lands were almost surrounded by military sites, most of which were well armed with men and weapons.

The forts had been constructed to battle outlaws, hostile tribes, and renegades, to act as supply depots for wagon trains and other forts, to guard the immigrant trails west, and to encourage white settlement. Fort Laramie was the largest and strongest nearby, and that was where Stede Gaston, Tom Fitzpatrick, and Colonel David Twiggs were posted. Twiggs, commander of the western division of the Army, controlled the 2nd United States Dragoons, two companies of Mounted Riflemen, one company of 6th United States Infantry, and various other soldiers. The Oregon, Mormon, and California trails passed near Laramie, a major stop for wagon trains and gold seekers and an area that had become like an enormous kettle of assorted types of people.

Into a large pot were tossed disdainful soldiers, scared recruits, passing immigrants, determined settlers, prospectors, countless traders, and reckless hunters. Added to it were a batch of rival fur companies and trappers, then mistrustful Indians, warring tribes, and defiant renegades were included. Tossed in were a pinch of surveyors, scouts and explorers. That mixture had stewed for years—especially since '46—and was beginning to simmer after being spiced with greed, guile, fear, and misconceptions. To have those people and emotions provoked to the boiling point by a blackheart like Snake-Man made for a lethal meal. Worse, hotheads on both sides added new fuel weekly to the cookfire.

If the evildoers were halted and both sides made an honest attempt at getting to understand and respect each other, real peace was possible. If a southern shipper like himself could come here and grasp so much in less than a year, Joe reasoned, so could others. He had learned a great deal about the Indian. A warrior's world was his tepee, his family, his tribe, his ancestors, his hunting grounds, his enemies, his coups, and his culture. A woman's was tending to the needs of her family.

The Dakotas were a strong, proud, independent nation, born to a way of life that had existed for centuries with few changes. Their lives were simple, nomadic, and in harmony with their god and the land. They valued their allies, and they battled their foes. Intertribal feuds were passed from father to son, then kept alive with continual aggression and retaliation. They saw wars and raids as the path to glory, high rank, and livelihood. They battled to retain their ancestral, sacred, and hunting grounds. Yet most coups were earned for touching a foe or stealing his goods, not by slaying him. Scalping—taking a small lock of hair, not the whole head— was a symbol of courage, prowess, and cunning. Joe concluded that the Indians were not as he had imagined, even though Stede Gaston had told Joe many things before his arrival here.

After Stede's father—Powchutu—had been slain during the same ambush that had taken the life of Gray Eagle and made Sun Cloud the Red Heart chief, peace had ruled this area until '46, except for a few conflicts. Many events since that time had compelled more whites and soldiers into this area, which they had promised to leave in peace and privacy. The Canadian border dispute had been settled in '46. Oregon had opened up and beckoned pioneers. The Mexican War had ended in '48, giving the Union more territory to explore and settle. The gold rush to California had come in '48. More forts and posts had been constructed in '49 and '50, and more troops had come to Laramie. Some territories had become states, California just last year, making thirty-one in the Union. The whites and their states had advanced steadily: Missouri, Illinois, Iowa, and Texas. Word was Minnesota would follow suit within a year or so.

Plans for more encroachment and progress were ongoing back East. Asa Whitney had spoken to Congress in '49 about extending roads and railroads from the Great Lakes through this territory to Oregon and the Pacific. The Department of Interior, headed by Secretary Stuart, had been established in '49 to handle settlement. President Fillmore was having a difficult time over the slavery issue — which he hated but endured until he could abolish it safely — so he wanted eyes and ears on another matter. Expansion in the West offered him that solution, that reprieve. For these reasons Fillmore had sent Stede Gaston to this area to prevent any bloody confrontations borne of fear of settlement.

Joe was apprehensive over rapid advancement. He doubted the Indians realized the strength and number of whites or how impossible it would be to keep this territory to themselves. Did they, Joe mused, know how many other Indian nations and tribes — mainly eastern — had been destroyed, conquered, or moved aside for white habitation? True, he had come to be with Tanner and to share adventures with his best friend, but he had witnessed and learned enough to get him as deeply involved in this cause as was Tanner's father.

Tanner Gaston . . . Stede Gaston . . . Joe wondered if Sun Cloud and his people recalled those names from the distant past. He had not spoken them to Morning Star, for a good reason. What would happen when he mentioned Gaston to her people? By Oglala blood and tradition, Stede had more of a right to the Red Heart chief's bonnet than Sun Cloud did . . .

Morning Star's father and grandfather were legends in the worlds of the Indian and White men who had signed treaties in the past. But after each treaty, new trouble had arisen, and promises were forgotten or disregarded by the whites. Perhaps Sun Cloud and the Oglala had lost all faith in the whites. Joe couldn't blame them and he could not help but worry about what would happen if he failed in this awesome task. What if fierce war broke out between the Oglala and Crow, between the Oglala and whites? What if Sun Cloud was slain in an ambush as his father had been in 1820? From what Fitzpatrick, Stede, and others had told him — as with Gray Eagle — Sun Cloud could control and lead; he could cool hot heads or inflame restless hearts. He was loved by his people and allies but feared and hated by his enemies. He was the epitome of the perfect warrior and leader. Joe was eager to meet this great legend — son of a past legend, father of the woman with him now — to learn the truth for himself.

Joe worried what he would do if what he'd been told wasn't true or accurate and if the Oglala were at fault or partially guilty. What if they didn't want peace anymore or desire a new treaty? What if they murdered and scalped him the minute he entered their camp?

Joe had watched southern belles work their wiles on men. He knew how cunning and daring some could be, all the while looking and sounding as pure as angels. Could Morning Star have him duped by her many charms? Could she knowingly be leading him into a lethal trap? Was she fetching the white-hating warriors she had told him were gone? Was it logical for an Indian maiden to trust and help a paleface?

Chapter Three

Morning Star chased the careless rabbit into an area enclosed on three sides by fallen rocks that were jammed close and tight and offered no hiding place or route to freedom. She dragged broken tree limbs into the opening to entangle her catch and prevent its escape. She eased toward the captive who was huddled in a snug ball against the rocks. She grabbed his ears, then struggled to get him under swift control as his squeals could summon a predator. She trapped the creature between her knees and cut its throat with speed, mercy, and skill. Slaying the rabbit did not evoke guilt because it was food provided by the Great Spirit, and hunting was their way of life.

Morning Star removed the head and skinned away the furry hide. She gutted it and left the entrails to feed another of the Great Spirit's creations. She took apart the barrier and went to a nearby stream to wash the meat and her hands before heading for the cave. She halted long enough to cut a sturdy limb for a skewer and two strong ones for pronged holders.

During her walk back, Morning Star thought about the white man awaiting her. Her father, uncle, grandfather, and tribe had made friends with a few whites in the past. Joseph Lawrence seemed to be the kind of man they would like and trust, as she did. His plan for peace was daring and clever. She prayed it would succeed. She knew many in her camp would speak against it and him, but hopefully the vote would go in his favor. As her rescuer, he should be safe. But his kindness would not earn him their help. If the council refused his request and he was sent away, she might never see him again. That thought displeased her.

It was strange how she wanted to watch him, to learn from him, to share more exciting and dangerous adventures with him, and to become closer. She liked the way the sun played in his golden hair and reflected its radiant glory. She lost herself in his eyes that mirrored the blue heaven and in his voice that flowed as warm honey over her. He was a good man. If she could become his guide and translator, she could help her people survive. But would Joe allow a woman to join him? If so, would her council agree? Her father?

Morning Star entered the cave as darkness settled as a cozy blanket over a chilled land. She went to the fire and sat down. *"Mastincala* to cook and eat." Her skilled hands positioned the two holders with forked ends into the ground. She skewered the rabbit with the last one and suspended it over the fire, resting the limb on the two Y-shaped ends.

"How did you get him without a trap or a bow or gun?" Joe asked.

"Buckskin Girl teach how. She," Morning Star revealed as she gestured thirty-six with her fingers, "Winters. Morning Star," she said and motioned eighteen. "We . . . best friends. How many win— years is Joe?"

"Twenty-eight," he answered, signing the number of his age as she had.

"Tell more. Where you from? When come here?"

"I'm from a place called Virginia, far away. I traveled to Fort Laramie last fall with Tanner and his father. That's the season between summer and winter. We wintered there, as your people do in these hills. When spring came, Tanner and I started riding from post to post scouting for his father." Joe didn't want to think about Tanner's death again today, so he chatted lightly. "I have one sister, Sarah Beth; she's older than I am. She's married to Andrew Reardon, who works with my father in the shipping business. They have one son, Lucas, four years old. I miss my family, especially my mother. Her name is Annabelle; you'd like her—she's a fine lady, the best."

Morning Star watched the array of expressions that came and went on Joe's face. She was glad he felt this way about his people. Families, friends, and ancestors should be important to one.

Looking at Morning Star, Joe suddenly realized that his brief doubt of her had come as a defense against his potent attraction to her and a fear that he could not resist her. Somehow he knew she could be trusted. "When we talked before, I didn't mean to sound as if my father and I aren't good friends; we are. We love each other. I guess I'm as much like him as any son could be. I just had this hunger inside that I had to feed before I settled down. I wouldn't want you to think those words I told Zeke and his men were true."

"What people see outside not always how we are inside," Morning Star commented. "Many think Morning Star too bold and act before thinking. Morning Star not try to be a warrior, but women must know skills to hunt and to defend camp when men gone. If not learn how to strike target with arrow and lance, not be able to protect and feed loved ones. A man enemy most times stronger than woman's claws and teeth. Must learn tricks to use when power is smaller than foe's. How can others say such things wrong for woman?"

"It isn't bad or wrong, Morning Star," Joe assured her. "And it doesn't make you less of a woman or a lady."

"What is lady? You say mother is lady."

Joe mused for a minute, then said, "A special woman from a good family and high birth rank, one who knows how to do the right things at the right time and place. You're from a line of great chiefs, so you have a high birth rank and a good family. You're a very special woman, so you're a lady."

The Indian maiden beamed with pleasure, and the fascinated male returned her smile. Neither realized the strength of the bond and mutual attraction between them, nor how rapidly they both were increasing. Many things had inspired their easy rapport and trust. They were sharing a heady adventure. They had depended upon and helped each other. They possessed similar dreams and goals. They were in a secluded and intimate setting where it seemed for now that only they existed.

The fire crackled and danced flames as wispy smoke rose, then vanished into the blackness. They sat on the cool earth with the fire separating them and highlighting their features. They had touched when she had tended his wound and when she had led him into the dark cave. He had shown his trust in her when he had followed her lead on the trail and into the hideout and when she had left to hunt. She had shown her trust by remaining with him. Instinct told Morning Star that Joe would not harm her, and it told Joe that she knew she was safe with him. They felt at ease, as if they had known each other for a long time.

"Are you married?" he asked.

She understood the word and replied, "No. And you? Do you have a mate?"

"No. What about a sweetheart, a special man?" he clarified.

"No. Is same for you?" she asked, and prayed it was.

"I have no special woman at home, but I'm surprised you're still free."

"I not shared a blanket with any brave or warrior." Morning Star explained the custom of romance. Privacy for courting was often hard to find. When a brave came to woo his choice of a mate, they would stand before her family's tepee and she would cover their head and shoulders with a blanket. This allowed for closeness, stolen kisses, whispers, and plans. It was the custom that everyone pretended not to notice the half-hidden couple. If a female was in great demand, she could share a blanket with many braves until she decided which one she wanted to join, marry.

"That sounds most enjoyable. I bet a brave gets jealous and scared when his choice shares a blanket with others. I would."

They laughed, then gazed at each other until Joe felt warm and tingly. "Smells good," he said, nodding at the rabbit.

Morning Star understood why he was changing the subject. Their talk had been personal. She had listened to his words carefully, and she tried to speak correctly as she said, "It is cooked. Do you have . . . dishes?"

"We'll have to share," he said, fetching a tin plate and handing it to her. He went to the pool and filled his cup, then sat beside her to feast off the shared plate and to drink from the same cup.

The rabbit was crisp, moist, and delicious. They licked their fingers after finishing each piece she carved before fetching another. The meat was nourishing and satisfying. When it was consumed, Morning Star washed the dishes and set them aside to dry. The fire had burned low. She added more wood to chase away the blend of night and cave chills.

"We must sleep. We ride when *Wi* awakens."

"We scout tomorrow," Joe reminded. "Nothing more."

"Morning Star obey. We must live to find peace for my people."

"There's something else you must understand and accept: my tasks are important. I'll do and say anything necessary to carry them out. I'm a stranger here, so I need help from your father and people. I don't want to lie to them or trick them even a little. But if I must, I will. If I don't make truce and find victory, your people and lands can be destroyed. If they're guilty of the charges against them," he added, "I'll have to report that to Fitzpatrick. No matter who's to blame, the main thing is to prevent a bloody war out here. I owe that to Tanner, and I promised his father."

She observed his expression for a moment as she mused on his words. "Morning Star understand." She claimed the same location she had used last night. She had refused Joe's polite offer of his sleeping roll, that even he had forgotten about last night. She rested her head on her parfleche and snuggled into Joe's warm jacket that held his masculine scent.

Joe felt guilty using the bedroll even though Morning Star had pointed out accurately that he was more accustomed to sleeping on one than she was. He wished she were lying beside him and curled in his arms. He scolded himself for such carnal desires about the "lady" nearby.

Joe was glad she had accepted his last words without anger or resistance; it told him that peace and survival for her people was her goal. He was cognizant of the many differences between himself and the lovely Indian maiden. Nothing serious was possible between them, yet his body ached for hers and his very soul seemed to reach out to her. He warned himself to stop thinking of her and craving her, but his heart and body refused to obey his mind's urgings.

Morning Star experienced the same longings and hesitations. She asked herself why no Oglala or ally had touched her as this sunny-haired, sky-eyed white man did. If so, she would be joined by now! She told herself she must not be drawn to him, as nothing could come of such feelings. She told herself it was wrong to want to be near him, to want to . . . She changed her position and ordered such wicked thoughts to leave her in peace. She couldn't help but wonder if the Great Spirit—Wankantanka—had guided him to her on the past moon and was using him to save her people. Wakantanka often worked in mysterious ways.

Joseph Lawrence could be one of those ways. Just as many warriors were talking of war with the encroaching whites, a special white man arrived to try to prevent new conflicts and bloodshed. Despite his skin color, she trusted Joe with all except her heart. That she must never yield to a man her people viewed as one of the enemy.

Each heard the other's restless movements. Both hoped theirs were not as noticeable. Both knew the suffering and shame any weakness would bring to themselves and their families. To allow their bond to tighten and strengthen would be like willingly leaping into a roaring fire. To even think of each other as only a man and a woman would be perilous, shameful, and destructive. Each prayed such forbidden emotions would vanish. Each knew they would not. They closed their eyes and begged for sleep to imprison them, free them. They didn't know who or what awaited them tomorrow . . .

Joseph Lawrence and Morning Star left the cozy cave and sneaked to Zeke's campsite. They found it was deserted. The age of the coals, wagon ruts, and horse droppings revealed that the three white men had left early the previous morning. Two whiskey bottles, a coffee tin, broken knife, a flattened metal cup, and an old St. Louis newspaper had been left behind.

The Indian maiden looked at the mess. "They make face of Mother Earth ugly with their leavings. Fire die after they ride away. It dangerous not to kill with water. Plenty nearby. If fire jump rocks, it run far; bad."

Joe understood her dismay. It was the same along the trails that the wagon trains took through Indian territory: various

67

items—wagon wheels and parts, pianos, heavy furniture, broken bottles, fancy clothing, trunks—and garbage from spent supplies were strewn about from beginning to end. Skeletons of mules and horses overburdened by overloaded wagons could be seen, as well as farm animals that had died along the way. Graves and crosses caught the eye at places where fatal illness or accident had occurred. Sometimes such eyesores couldn't be helped, but used tins and such should be buried, not cast out to steal the land's beauty, Joe and Morning Star concurred.

"Let's track the wagons," Joe said. "But we have to be careful. They're probably watching for us to follow," he reminded her. As they studied the ground, Joe remarked, "Looks as if they all left together. I'm surprised they didn't come looking for us. Let's ride, but keep your eyes and ears alert. If trouble strikes, you ride for home."

"If trouble come, Joe follow Morning Star fast."

He shook his head. "No," he told her. "I'll lead them in the other direction. I want you to get away safely. Don't worry about me."

She looked into his adamant gaze. "No good to be apart. Joe must follow men. Morning Star. Safe with Joe, not safe alone."

He thought over her argument and nodded. "You're right. You're more valuable to them than I am. If we're ambushed, we make a run for it."

They followed the deep ruts and numerous hoofprints northwestward. After a few miles, they saw buzzards circling beyond them.

The hairs on Joe's body seemed to bristle in warning. "Maybe they shot an animal or one of their horses died," he remarked. "Let's move slow and easy. I'll keep a lookout for an ambush, and you keep us on their tracks."

Morning Star shared his feeling that something was wrong ahead. She watched the trail, while Joe kept his concentration on their surroundings. She didn't want either of them trapped by their enemies and tensed with apprehension and alert, summoning forth all of her skills and instincts to aid them.

When they neared the place the vultures had found their

next meal, they noticed a man's body with arrows protruding from it.

Morning Star recognized the garments. "It man called Clem," she said.

Joe's gaze scanned each direction, but he didn't see or sense anyone's presence. "Stay back. He may be alive. It could be a trap."

"Death birds no come unless smell death."

"Wonder who attacked them," Joe murmured as they approached the grim site. He warned himself to stay on guard for trickery.

Anger filled Morning Star as she eyed the arrows, as each tribe had their own colors and markings. Clem was lying as if he'd been shot and had fallen from a horse, then left behind while others fled for survival. "It trick. My band gone."

"What do you mean?"

"Those Red Heart arrows. White men steal and use to make others think we attack and kill. It not true."

"You sure your band left this area? What if they did attack?"

She shook her head. "They no do. See, no pony tracks. He die or big man kill. Leave here so others blame Red Hearts."

Joe dismounted and examined the ground and Clem's body. Perhaps Clem had died from a blow to the head during the battle for their escape, Joe thought. He had taken a hard fall after Morning Star's attack with the limb, and he had been drunk, in addition. Or, from the forceful bash on Clem's skull, she could be right about Zeke getting rid of a problem. The group's leader was clearly taking advantage of the situation; he was framing Red Heart by using their arrows to mislead whoever found Clem's body. Joe couldn't allow that lie to be reported. He broke the shafts and put the feathered ends into his saddlebag. With no way or desire to bury Clem, he mounted. "Let's go," he said.

They rode to the spot where Zeke and his men had met with a large Crow party. They didn't dismount until they visually scouted the area.

"They didn't stay long. They joined up and left together. Their trail heads into Crow territory, doesn't it?"

"Han. We follow while, maybe catch up, spy."

"No, it's too dangerous, too many of them. I wanted to see which direction Zeke and his boys took after their trade, but that's not possible. We can't ride into a Crow camp or risk an ambush."

"You speak wise."

"We'll head for your camp so I can meet with your father. Then I have to ride to Fort Tabor to meet with Captain Thomas before I start looking around for clues. Thomas might know something helpful. I also want to give him the names of those men and their descriptions. If they come around the fort, Thomas can keep an eye on them. When I finish there, I'll return to your camp to get that guide and translator I need."

"You think white soldier help Oglalas?" she asked in a doubtful tone.

"Some of them will; this one will."

"We see. Come, camp in trees. Long ride."

They skirted the eastern side of the Black Hills. At times they had to journey slow for rest and because of hilly terrain. That change in pace allowed them to take in the beauty of the rugged peaks and towering spires in midnight black. The dark hills were a striking contrast to a deep-blue background and verdant foreground. The area was alive with green and fresh-smelling spring growth: spruce, pine, asp, cottonwood, oak, and sometimes dense underbrush. Almost every hill and meadow displayed a multitude of flowers in vivid shades. Streams were encountered frequently with sparkling water that seemed to dance and swirl around rocks with new moss. It was some of the most peaceful and inspiring scenery Joe had ever seen; he understood why Morning Star's people loved their territory so much.

They heard birds singing and calling to others as if they were the freest and happiest of God's creatures. They spooked shy deer, large elk, graceful antelope, and one coyote who looked sad to be alone. He loped away at a leisurely pace, but glanced back several times with eyes that seemed to say he wished he could join them.

They saw an enormous herd of buffalo grazing in a valley of sweet and short grasses. The beasts were massive and strong, yet they deceptively appeared to be gentle and slow. About one-third of them were lying down, but all were on alert. They hadn't shed the lighter-colored winter coats that looked like tangled curls against their dark bodies and heads. Numerous babies played near their mothers. Heavy bulls walked around as if guarding females they had selected as members of their harems. The herd evoked an impression of power, mystery, unity, and wildness. It was a stirring sight.

Wildflowers gave the valley splashes of blue, yellow, red, and white atop the green covering. Bees worked amidst countless pollen-filled offerings to gather sweet nectar. Jackrabbits, abundant in the area, darted from one hiding place to another as the couple's passing alarmed the furry creatures.

They rode until dusk, having stopped at intervals only to rest and water their mounts. They hadn't seen or heard any other travelers, but Joe had spotted and shot two quail, and the fowl were secured to his saddle. After eating cold rabbit this morning and chewing on jerky at midday, they were eager to camp and cook the birds.

When Morning Star pointed out a sheltered glen with lush grass and water for the horses and protection for them, Joe smiled and thanked her. "This is perfect. The hills and trees will hide our cooking smoke from enemy eyes. I doubt anyone could sneak up on us here, Morning Star."

"Oglala warriors can jump on the enemy before he sees or hears danger. No time to grab bow or knife. You be safe. You with me."

Joe noticed how she spoke her first sentence slowly and correctly but how the next few came swiftly and with words missing amidst her laughter and smiles. He realized how much English she knew, and how much she was either learning or remembering while riding with him. He was glad.

"You smile like cunning fox, Joe Lawrence. Why?"

"I was just thinking how smart you are. I'd better watch out or you'll show me up on the trail. Show me up—prove you're better than I am."

71

"Is bad for woman to show . . . better skills?"

"If you know what's best in something, you should do it and teach me. Mistakes are what's bad; they can get you killed. It's worse to hide skills."

Morning Star reasoned for a time, then smiled once more. "You teach Morning Star more English and white ways?"

"Yes, if you won't be insulted when I correct you. And I won't get mad or be insulted when you teach me something about your people and land."

"Is good trade."

He sent her a smile and a gentle correction. *"It* is a good trade."

"It is a good trade," she repeated. "Morning Star gather wood."

"I will gather wood. When you speak of yourself, it's I or me." Joe gave her many examples of when to use either word.

"You . . . will teach . . . me when right. No, when it is right to use."

"You're sharp, quick, and smart. I hope I will be, too."

"We make good partners."

"Good partners. *Han. Pilamaya.* You'll teach me more than *yes* and *thank you* before we reach your camp, won't you?"

"I teach Lakota; you teach English. It is a good trade."

Joe yearned to trade more than words and ways with the exquisite woman, but knew he could not. Too much was at stake to think of himself, particularly when a match between them was impossible and could hurt many people. If only—

"You look sad. What wr— What *is* wrong?"

"When my task is over, I'll have to leave your land. I'll miss you. We made friends fast and easy. With Tanner gone . . ."

"You miss him. It is bad not to have peace in death."

"He'll have peace when I find his killers and punish them."

"Revenge will not steal pain in heart. It must leave when ready."

"You're right, but at least they won't go free after taking his life."

"It is our way to punish enemies. Morn— I will help you."

Joe smiled and thanked her, but didn't comment on her

72

offer. "Let's get wood collected so we can eat. I'm starving."

Together they gathered wood, built a fire, cleaned the quail, and put them on a spit to roast. While the fowl cooked, they tended their horses and freshened up in the stream. A full moon journeyed across the eastern sky, and shadows crept over the landscape. Except for nocturnal insects and creatures, it was quiet.

Morning Star listened to the crickets, frogs, and night birds. Their songs always relaxed her. She watched a mild breeze ruffle leaves. She saw grass and blossoms sway as if lulling themselves to sleep. She heard the distant howl of a coyote, and was glad to hear a mate's answer to the lonely wail. Water rippled around rocks and twigs in the stream. An owl hooted nearby, then again from farther away. Once in a while, the horses neighed or shifted their stances. Her world was good, safe, and happy. How she hated the thought it could be destroyed or stolen, how she and her people could be pushed out or slain.

The blond-haired male observed the Indian maiden who sat so serenely graceful as she meditated. He noticed how the moonlight shone on her midnight hair. He longed to stroke it to see if it was as soft and silky as it appeared. He wanted to caress her skin to see if it had the same feel. He had the crazy urge to nibble at her proud chin, her dainty ears, her full lips. She looked more exotic and tempting than any island or Oriental beauty he had seen during his many travels. But something had stolen the glow in her dark eyes and brought a serious expression to her face. "Now, you're the one who looks sad," Joe said, intruding on her thoughts.

Morning Star's deep-brown gaze fused with Joe's blue one. Simply hearing his voice and looking at him caused her heart to race and her body to warm. She wondered what strange and powerful magic he possessed to enchant her this way. To conceal her interest in him, she told him what she had been thinking earlier. "Oglalas must remain here forever to tend and save this land for Grandfather. If harmony is broken, the land dies; the creatures die; the people die; all is gone. The white man is not one with the land and nature; he changes and destroys. He would slay all of one creature. When one is gone, nature's Life-Cycle is broken. It changes those of all other living creatures.

It is wrong, dangerous. The white man does not care; he feeds on greed and deceit. If the grass is trampled by wagons and farms, what will feed the buffalo? If the buffalo starves or is slain, what will feed the Oglalas? If trees are stolen, what will give shade and wood? If streams are changed or claimed, what will Oglalas drink? If more land is settled, where will Oglalas live and hunt? Where will Oglala dead rest?"

Joe understood what she meant. He had learned how the Indians lived, how they used all the parts of a slain animal for food, clothing, utensils, pouches, and sewing materials. Wood was gathered for tepee poles, then used in the fire, or enough trees died or shed limbs for burning. Nothing in nature was ever totally destroyed. Each creation had its purpose in nature's life-circle.

"What you say is true, Morning Star," he commented, "but some people don't understand the harmony of land and nature. Some take what they want or need without thinking about the destruction they're causing. My family has a plantation back home. It's like a big farm. We grow things, gather them to eat or to sell, then plant seeds to grow more. As long as we keep seeds, we'll have those plants. It's foolish for a man to eat all he has and not save seeds for growing more food and plants for clothing. We don't kill all of our creatures for meat and hides. We breed them, so the line will continue. We make roads for travel, so grasses won't be trampled. Many white men are this way. Many are growers, not destroyers."

Morning Star spoke slowly and carefully as she tried to explain matters to her companion while she practiced her English. She hoped she would have even more use for it soon as she wanted to become Joe's guide and translator. "We have seen and heard of such men. Those who come to our land are destroyers, not growers. They steal from our forests, streams, and prairies. They cheat and deceive when they make trade. They bring guns and disease to kill. They bring whiskey to weaken minds and bodies. They say they will be friends, but they work as enemies. They say they wish to share, but they take. They wish us to become as they are. We do not want or need white man's laws and ways."

Joe held silent as she checked the roasting quail; he didn't

74

want to disturb her line of thought.

"Some come to say we must accept their . . . religion; but the white man has many religions. We have one, Wakantanka the Great Spirit. Those called missionaries say it wrong to kill and steal, but whites do not follow the words in their Bible and religion. Father say white men cannot be trusted. They call us savages, hostiles, wild animals. They do not try to understand Oglalas. They put words on papers to sell to others to turn all whites against us. Papers say only good about whites and evil about Indians; big lies. Father say much evil done to other tribes where the whites live. He say many tribes destroyed or driven from their homelands. Many treaties signed by other tribes with white man; they not honored. Many use treaties to say they traded goods for Indian lands. The land cannot be owned or sold. When white man say he bought land, soldiers and white leaders use paper words Indians do not understand to take away their land. My people hear and learn much about whites in past winters. They do not want more here. Your task will be hard, Joe Lawrence."

"Not all white men are bad, Morning Star."

"It is . . . different with you. Joe comes in peace, to learn, to help. You do not come to steal and kill, to stay. It is not so with others."

"There are other whites like me. They only want a good and safe place to settle and live. They want peace, too, Morning Star."

"How can peace come when they take Oglala land and insult us?"

"Both sides must change and share; they must learn about each other."

"We do not go to white lands to take them."

"There's more land here, and too many whites back East. It's the way things are, Morning Star. To refuse to change is dangerous and unwise."

"To defend our land and lives shows courage and honor."

"If the Oglalas and other tribes agree to stay in their own territories and let whites settle in lands between them, all can live nearby in peace; that's what Fitzpatrick wants for everyone. Oglala territory is big, Morning Star; there's room for others to live in areas they don't use."

"What would Joe do if Crow rode to your . . . plantation and took it? Would Joe make truce and share parts he does not use?" she asked.

Joe started to say that was different, but he stopped himself. She had a good point. "My family's land is small, Morning Star," he tried to explain. "All of it is used for growing food, plants to make clothing, and for raising animals. Many others live on our land and tend it for us."

"They are friends, not enemies. What if enemies settled there?"

"That's not the white way. White laws protect our lands from others."

"If we accept the whites and their laws, it would be the same here. They would claim land and keep Oglalas away from grass, water, and game."

She was right, but Joe hated to agree with her. White advancement and progress were heading to this area. If a compromise wasn't reached, it would mean bloodshed. It was a scary and costly predicament.

"Your eyes say you know my words are true, and that troubles you."

"Yes, it does. We can't stop the rain of whites from coming, Morning Star, but we can prevent a destructive flood from washing away your people. If I can get your father's help and stop these present conflicts, it will hold back the rains for a while. That's all I can promise you or them."

"I will help you in all ways," she promised in return.

The daughter of Sun Cloud liked the way Joe did not try to trick or deceive her with clever words or cunning lies. Even when the truth was bad, he spoke it. Her father had made treaty to earn a few years of peace for his people; it had stretched into thirty. Without Joe's help and victory, that truce would end and war would begin. With them, perhaps another stretch of peaceful years lay ahead. She had heard her father say many times that the white man could not be stopped forever but that he would resist their intrusion for as long as possible, even with his life. Chief Sun Cloud had said that Wakantanka always sent an answer to a problem, and Joseph

76

Lawrence must be the answer this time. She had found him, saved his life, tended his wound, taught him things, and befriended him; it was her right to ride at his side to save her people from his. For now, she would not suggest that idea to him, though, for she surmised he would resist it.

After they had eaten, they doused the campfire and bedded down for the night with only a few feet separating them. Both lay there thinking for a time, then drifted off to sleep.

Their schedule was the same the next day. Neither talked much as they made camp. Both privately reflected on their meeting, their time together, and what confronted them soon. Each knew that once they reached Morning Star's village, things would change between them. Each knew that if something went wrong, tomorrow would be their last day together, and that caused them to share a strange apprehension.

They ate rabbit stew, this time simmered to tenderness with wild vegetable roots that Morning Star had found. After their meal was consumed and their horses tended, Joe spread his sleeping roll and a heavy blanket on the grass. He stretched out on the bedroll while Morning Star lay down on the thick blanket.

"We reach my village before next moon. Be strong and brave," she encouraged. "I will speak for you and peace to my father and people."

"Pilamaya," he said. Joe noticed how uneasy Morning Star was tonight. Though she faced away from him, he could see the tension in her body. Was she afraid her people would harm him, or even kill him? Or, did she dread their parting, as he did? Even if he were given the chance to see her again, he knew it would be reckless and cruel to court the temptation. He couldn't stay here longer than six months; he had promised his family he'd be home by Christmas, and traveling by horseback required four or five weeks. She couldn't leave with him, *wouldn't* leave with him. Anything between them was hopeless. So, he asked himself, why did that thought hurt so much? It wasn't just physical desire gnawing at him. Morning Star was fun, witty, dependable, brave, intelligent, strong, and gen-

tle. It was so easy to be with her. He wanted more than friendship!

Morning Star sensed Joe's eyes on her, and his thoughts seemed to reach out to her. She knew it was wrong to weaken toward an enemy, but her heart kept telling her he wasn't a foe. He had not come here to settle and live, and he would leave before the winter snows returned. She didn't want him to go. But, even if he remained in her land, she could not turn to him. She knew what people — Indians *and* whites — called Indian women who mated with or married white men: squaw. Worse, a *witkowin:* whore. Their lives and ways were so different, too different. A relationship between them was the same as one between a deer and a buffalo. It could not come to pass, and she must do nothing to encourage either of them to seek the impossible. Yet . . .

Joe dared not question the woman's restlessness, just as she dared not query his. Both knew that to talk at this moment was perilous and could cost them victories in the battles that were raging inside them. At last, the two weary people fell asleep.

When Morning Star told him they were nearing her camp, Joe halted their journey to remind her, "Remember I'll do and say whatever I must to win your people's trust and help. If nothing more, I need their promise they won't raid or attack while I'm working on peace."

Her gaze roamed his clean-shaven face, and she read urgency in his eyes. "Come. Scouts will see us. We must speak with Father first."

It was almost dusk. They had ridden fast to reach her village today. From the trail they had found of the group returning from Bear Butte, they knew they would arrive only a few hours after it. They had not encountered a rescue party yet, and concurred that one must be planning to leave the village at sunrise on Monday morning. They had spoken little today, and both were apprehensive about seeing Sun Cloud.

As they entered the edge of the large camp, people halted their tasks to stare at the strange sight. Warriors reached for weapons, then followed the riders toward their chief's tepee.

Word of Morning Star's return and the white man spread rapidly. A curious crowd gathered.

Morning Star dismounted and called to her parents, *"Ata! Ina!"*

Singing Wind rushed outside when she heard her daughter's voice and the loud commotion. *"Anpaowicanhpi! Tokel oniglakin kta he?"* She asked what had happened as they embraced with deep love and relief.

"Ina, he mi ye," the girl replied, saying she was home safely.

Singing Wind asked how she had escaped her Crow captors.

Sun Cloud joined them, his dark gaze going back and forth between his daughter and the white man. He listened, waited, and watched.

Morning Star told her mother she'd been tricked and had much to tell her. *"Taku ota eci ciyapi kta bluha yele."* Morning Star embraced her father, then related details of her misadventures.

While she talked, Joe stood still and silent. He had been told that Sun Cloud was the reflection of his father, Gray Eagle. He was tall, lithe, and muscular for a man of fifty-four. There were few strands of gray in a midnight mane that flowed past broad bronze shoulders and down a strong back. Sun Cloud's eyes were almost as black as his hair and thick brows. His bones were as finely chiseled as any aristocrat's. The one eagle feather secured behind his head and traveling downward was said to be worn always in honor of his slain father. He was not wearing his chief's bonnet, but had a necklace around his throat that depicted his name. He was clad in a breechcloth, leggings, and moccasins. Sun Cloud was indeed the epitome of a great leader, an awesome warrior, and a dignified man.

Joe let his observant gaze slip to the woman with the chief and his daughter, Singing Wind. At fifty-four, as well, she was still beautiful and slim. He sensed a spirited nature in her that her daughter had inherited, as well as her awesome beauty. Her eyes were as brown as rich chocolate, but her hair was not as dark and long as Morning Star's. The few wrinkles on her face did not detract from its loveliness. She carried herself as a lady, a woman of high rank and birth, a woman of importance. Joe detected no vanity or arrogance in either female, nor in Sun Cloud. That pleased him.

Joe assumed the warrior nearby was her brother, Night Stalker, who had been the leader of the pilgrimage to Bear Butte and who had returned home without her. He looked surprised at his sister's arrival and angered by Joe's presence and part in the rescue. He wasn't as tall as his father, but he was more muscular. Nor did he have Sun Cloud's handsome face and dignified carriage. A lance scar ran down his left side, and Sun Dance scars marred his broad chest. His dark hair was worn loose, but a headband held it in place. Joe knew this man would be one of his obstacles.

Joe's eyes were pulled to a warrior next to Night Stalker. The man's dark gaze was narrowed and chilled by the story he was hearing. Joe guessed his age in the early twenties and his height at five feet eleven inches. His hair hung in two thick braids, with coup feathers suspended near the bottoms of both plaits. A small knife was suspended from a thong about his neck. He, too, was wearing only a breechcloth, leggings, and moccasins. Joe perceived a coldness and arrogance in this bronze-skinned warrior whose chest displayed Sun Dance scars that proved his prowess. The only time the Oglala's gaze altered was when it touched on Morning Star; then, open desire was apparent. Joe felt his temper rising against the warrior who craved Morning Star. He didn't have to be told this was Knife-Slayer, and an enemy.

Many others, men and women and children, gathered around the group, but Joe returned his attention to the talk in progress and tried to catch a word here and there to learn how it was going.

"Why did you bring a white foe to our camp?" Knife-Slayer demanded in Lakota. "He will learn our strength and tell others, if he is not slain."

"Hiya! Ito kawe kin papsunpi sni ye!" Morning Star shouted, saying not to spill Joe's blood. "He is a friend," she continued in her tongue. "He helped me. He is here to help us. Father, you must spare his life and heed his words."

"How can an enemy help us?" Night Stalker asked.

Morning Star focused on her father. "He is our friend, Father. He *can* help us. He has a plan to draw our real enemies

80

from hiding. If he does so, the soldiers will punish them." To Joe, she said in English, "Speak the words to my father you say to me on trail."

Joe's blue gaze locked with Sun Cloud's dark one. "I know only a few of your words, though Morning Star is teaching me more, so you must forgive me for addressing you in my language. I am not your enemy, Sun Cloud. The Great White Chief and most Americans want to live in peace with your people and all other Indian Nations. I am here with a man who is seeking answers to the troubles between whites and Indians. We're here to help Agent Tom Fitzpatrick at Fort Laramie obtain a new treaty that all peoples can accept and honor. The real enemy in your territory is called Snake-Man. He sells guns, whiskey, and supplies to the Crow and encourages them to destroy the Lakotas. We don't know why he wants war, but we must stop him before he begins a bloodbath in this area. If the Crow and Oglala go on the warpath, the Shoshone and Pawnee will side with the Crow; and the Cheyenne and Blackfoot will aid their allies, the Dakotas. Whites will be trapped between the warring tribes. More soldiers will come. Fitzpatrick has sent word to you about the new treaty, but you have not responded. Many things have happened, and your tribe has been blamed. I don't think you're guilty, but I need help proving it. I have to discover who Snake-Man is and capture him. If not, this area and all people here can have no peace."

"If he is white, why do you side against him?" Sun Cloud asked.

"He's evil. His actions cause the deaths of innocent Indians and whites. He enflames the hatred between the Oglala and Crow. It must stop."

"We have always warred with Bird People!" Night Stalker shouted.

"That time must end, Night Stalker. If both tribes honor the new treaty and remain in their territories, peace is possible. I need a guide and interpreter, someone to teach me your people's ways."

"You seek to learn our ways to use them to destroy us," Knife-Slayer accused in English. "You must die!" He reached for the blade at his waist.

81

Morning Star covered his hand. *"Hiya! Wicake! I'ye waste!"*

Sun Cloud noticed how the girl shouted in the white man's defense, claiming he spoke the truth and was a good man. He didn't have time at that moment to worry over the tone of her voice or the expression in her eyes.

"If we harm him, we harm ourselves!" Morning Star added in Lakota.

Knife-Slayer noticed her tone and gaze, and retorted in his tongue, "You are a woman, and his cunning rescue has blinded you. He must die."

"I want peace and survival for my people. I am no coward. I will ride, track, and fight with him. I will be his tongue, ears, and teacher," she avowed.

"No!" Knife-Slayer shouted. "He will trick you again, and slay you."

The girl glared at the warrior for his subtle insult. "If such a threat was true, why do I stand here now, alive and unharmed?"

"You are his path to our camp, sister," Night Stalker replied. "My band was riding at first light to rescue you. I could not come after you in Crow Territory. I saw many tracks. It was my duty to get others home safely."

"It was your duty, brother, and I do not blame you for leaving me behind. The false clues were cunning. I knew you would be tricked by them. You must listen to this white man; his words are wise and true."

Sun Cloud raised his hand and asked for silence. "Hold your tongues, my people. We will hear his words before his fate is decided. First, I must speak with him. We do not strike a death blow before we learn the truth."

Though Joe could not grasp the rapid flow of Lakota between Morning Star, Night Stalker, and Knife-Slayer, he surmised that the two men were speaking against him and that Morning Star was pleading his good cause. Joe knew it was unusual for a woman to argue with men, especially in public. He was glad when Sun Cloud halted the heated words and turned to address him.

"For many winters, the Red Heart Band had a treaty with

82

your leader and people. Why has it been broken? Why does White Chief Monroe let more whites and soldiers enter our lands? Why have more forts been placed on the face of Mother Earth? Soon they will encircle us and tighten as a rope on a wild stallion's neck to choke the life from us. Why do they make more trails through our lands? Why do they settle on our sacred and hunting grounds? Why do they give and sell supplies and weapons to our foes? Why have they set their eyes upon the buffalo, our life's blood? Why do they bring their diseases to sneak upon us in the night and slay us?"

Joe held silent and let the chief continue.

"We were foolish to allow the first white footprints on our land. Now their tracks are everywhere. They refuse to leave, and they battle us to stay. We are forced to fight them to save our land and people. The leader called Broken-Hand at Laramie asks us to sign a new treaty with the whites and our foes. It is no good. The whites and Crow would not honor it."

Joe had listened closely and respectfully and hoped he wouldn't forget any of Sun Cloud's questions, even though most had been spoken as statements of fact and feeling. "Tom Fitzpatrick, Broken-Hand, is a good man. He is fair and honest. You knew him when he trapped in this area. He respects your people, and he knows the Indian ways. He wants peace between all tribes and whites. As long as tribes war against each other, white travelers are in danger and more soldiers and forts will come to give them protection. You don't want that, so it's wise and good to make treaty so all sides can survive and be happy. Most battles are fights over hunting grounds and revenge for raids. If every tribe stays in its own territory and doesn't attack another, peace will come, Sun Cloud."

"We have warred with our enemies since long before the birth of my grandfather and his father," Night Stalker shouted. "How will marks on a paper stop a war passed from father to son for more winters than are marked on the buffalo record of our people?"

"By everyone wanting and needing peace and survival more than scalps and war prizes," Joe responded in a calm and careful tone.

"Words come easy from your mouth, White man. Honor

83

does not come easy from the Crow or your people. Another treaty matters not."

"The first treaty never reached the hands of the White Chief Monroe," Joe revealed. "Derek Sturgis, friend to Gray Eagle and Sun Cloud, was injured in a fire that destroyed his dwelling and the paper. He did not live to return to make another one. Our new White Chief is President Fillmore. He desires a treaty. I am here as his helper to make truce."

"You speak for the new White Chief?" Sun Cloud asked.

"Yes. I speak for him through the man who brought me here."

"He lies to save his life," Knife-Slayer charged. "He will betray us."

"It is true many forts have been built in this vast territory," Joe revealed, "but they are to protect our Indian allies as well as white settlers. They defend everyone against bad whites, called outlaws, and against bad Indians, called renegades. Such men attack good Indians and good whites. Fort Tabor's soldiers do not attack the Lakotas. Neither does Fort Laramie where Broken-Hand lives and works for peace. When the soldiers battle, it's to punish and halt attacks on innocent people. It's true a trail crosses to the south of your lands. Most whites are riding far to the west to begin new lives. Some halt and settle here; they're tired and have no money to continue to their destination. They want to live in peace. They—"

"Peace!" Knife-Slayer interrupted in anger. "They—"

Sun Cloud halted the furious warrior and said, "Let him speak, Knife-Slayer. He did not break into my words. You can speak later."

"The white man who sells weapons to your enemies is bad," Joe continued. "He must be caught and punished. Your father, Gray Eagle, was a great chief. He wished for peace and survival. Long ago, you did the same. It must be that way again, Sun Cloud. Give me the help I need," he urged.

"How do we know this warrior would be safe at your side?"

Joe anticipated resistance to the suggestion he was about to make, but his plan was clever enough to work. "What I need and request is a brave and smart woman to lead me to the Crow camps and white settlements. The evil whites would not suspect a white trader or trapper with an Indian wife of being a spy. We could go anyplace together and search for clues."

"You speak of my sister, Morning Star?" Night Stalker asked.

"Another trick!" Knife-Slayer charged. "He will hold her prisoner. Think of Morning Star's value to the bluecoats."

"If I wished to take her captive, there was plenty of time on the trail," Joe pointed out.

"You did not so she would lead you to our village!"

"That isn't true. Besides, I don't want Morning Star as my helper. It's too dangerous. I don't want Sun Cloud's daughter harmed. That would cause more distrust between us. Select the woman best trained to help me."

"I best," Sun Cloud's daughter stated. "I know Oglala land. I speak English and understand Crow signs. I have warrior skills."

"No, Morning Star. I can't risk your life again. It's too perilous. Sun Cloud has lost too many of his family. It must be another female."

As Knife-Slayer, Night Stalker, and Morning Star argued amongst themselves, warriors whispered and watched. Those who knew English explained the situation to others nearby who didn't. Then they passed along the shocking news to Red Hearts distant from the center of activity.

A man with narrow, piercing eyes stepped forward. *"Wicakewala sni. Wowocake sni. Kastaka."*

"Who is he? What did he say?" Joe murmured to the stunned girl at his right. He had a dark suspicion of his words, and dread washed over him.

Morning Star felt her heart race and her mouth go dry. A chill passed over her as if she were standing barefoot and naked in the snow. She had feared this man's resistance and hatred, and, more so, his power. It was up to Joe to change her people's mind. "Hawk Eyes, our shaman, father of Knife-Slayer," she replied. "He says you lie and must be slain."

Joe knew it was a bad sign for such a powerful man to talk against him. He saw the looks on most faces that said they agreed or would follow any advice given by their medicine chief and holy man. He read mistrust and hostility in some faces. He read confusion in others. In a few stoic expressions, he could glean no clue to their thoughts and feelings. "I do not lie, Hawk Eyes. All I have said is true. I come as a friend, an ally."

"I say his mouth must be silenced by death this moon!" was the shaman's reply, this time in English and spoken as a command.

Two strong warriors seized Joe's arms. Morning Star panicked. Even if they refused to give Joe help, she could not let him be slain. But what could she say or do to save his life? Nothing came to her terrified mind.

Alarmed and desperate, a bold and cunning idea entered Joe's head. He prayed Morning Star would understand his motive and keep his secret. If he didn't attempt it, he was a dead man, and war was a certainty. If he did and she exposed him, he was a dead man. He glanced at her frightened expression and decided his ruse was worth the risk he would take.

Chapter Four

Joe shouted over affirmative "yips" of the Kit-Fox cult and murmurings for and against killing him, "Sun Cloud! I'm Tanner Gaston! The son of Stede Gaston! Son of Powchutu, son of Running Wolf, your grandfather! I only use the name Joe Lawrence to trick evil whites! I'm Tanner Gaston!"

As the warriors, who did not understand English, yanked at Joe, Sun Cloud raised his hand and ordered them to halt and release him. The chief stared at the white man as those shocking words struck home like flaming arrows. The braves unhanded Joe and looked at their leader for an explanation.

"He speaks words I must hear," Sun Cloud related in Lakota.

"Do not listen to more lies!" Knife-Slayer shouted.

Sun Cloud sent the Sacred Bow Carrier a warning glance to be silent, then returned his probing gaze to the stranger.

Joe took that as a sign to finish his startling revelation. "Stede Gaston, my father, is the man who brought me here. He's waiting for me at Fort Laramie. He works with Broken-Hand and President Fillmore for peace. My father is old and injured. I'm here as his legs, arms, eyes, ears, mouth, and heart. The Great Spirit called him to his father's lands to make peace."

While Sun Cloud and others who knew English gaped at the white stranger and Morning Star did not interrupt him, Joe hurried on to save his life and his mission. "My grandfather, Powchutu, was the firstborn son of Running Wolf. If the chief's bonnet hadn't been stolen from his head by evil when his mother married a French trapper and denied Running Wolf his son, Powchutu would have been chief in Gray Eagle's place. When my grandfather was forced from these lands he loved and his rightful rank was stolen from him, my father was born and raised as white, as was I. When danger came to these lands, the Great Spirit troubled his heart and called him here to help save his people, the Oglalas. We are of the same bloodline, Sun Cloud. Would you slay your cousin? Your friend? Your ally?"

Night Stalker found his voice and shouted a translation to his people. He dared not accuse the stranger of lying until his father decided it was or wasn't the truth. He didn't want the white man's arrival and words to intrude on his life and desires. The Oglala had been given many challenges from the whites and Crow during the last few years, but his father had continued to urge for peace. Night Stalker didn't believe peace was possible. He believed his warriors should confront their enemies in glorious battles—battles that would drive the whites and Bird People from their lands forever; battles that would bring him many coups, wealth, and prestige as in the olden days. He wanted to prove his wits and prowess, especially after failing to rescue his sister. He wanted to defend his lands and people, and to earn the chief's bonnet soon. He did not want to lie around and grow lazy and fat. He did not trust the whites, and he was restless from the long, quiet winter in camp.

Payaba made his way through the whispering crowd. Once known as Standing Tree and shaman, he declared in the Lakota tongue in a strong voice that belied his eighty years, "I say he speaks the truth. Has Sun Cloud and the council forgotten my vision of twenty winters past?" For those who didn't recall it and those who hadn't heard it, the old man repeated it. "Look at his eyes and hair. Think of his bloodline and words. As my vision warned, a season of bitter conflicts and greed have destroyed truce with the whites. Two men have come to our land to help us defeat this first trouble. He speaks the truth. He is Sky Warrior, the white helper we have awaited for twenty winters. I say we must listen and accept his words. We must help him. To do so obeys Grandfather's commands in my sacred vision."

The elderly man had spoken too fast for Joe to catch more than a few words that didn't make sense to him. All dark eyes had shifted from the past shaman to him. Joe sensed that something important about him had been revealed. An array of emotions filled the Oglalas' faces: awe, confusion, trust, anger, and apprehension. When Morning Star translated for him, astonishment, tension, and befuddlement filled Joe. He knew the Indians were believers of what they called visions, but he was amazed by the exactitude of one that had taken place twenty years ago. He wondered how the old man could have foreseen this episode. Yet Payaba had! The past shaman's insight and prophecy baffled Joe. "What does it mean?" he asked Morning Star.

Morning Star studied him closely. This was the first time she had heard of the *wowanyake,* a vision coming true before her senses. She was stirred by the news of the woman in Payaba's vision long ago, as Joe had asked for a female helper now! Her actions were justified, foretold! The vision matched Joe and the current situation perfectly! She had done nothing more than be used and guided by the Great Spirit! She was blessed and honored and proud. What did it matter who defeated their foes and won peace? She must prove her mettle to become that vision woman. Yet she replied, *"Slolwaye sni;* I do not know." She needed to learn more before she could explain things to Joe.

"Morning Star told him such things on the trail," Night Stalker charged. "He is not Sky Warrior. He does not carry Oglala blood."

"I did not tell him such things!" Morning Star retorted. "I did not know of them until this moment! I believe the vision and his words. Grandfather crossed our path so I could bring him to our camp to fulfill his destiny and ours. A vision must be obeyed, my brother."

"How do we know Payaba did not have a dream?" Knife-Slayer asked.

"If it was a sacred vision, why was I not shown it?" Hawk Eyes added.

"How can only a dream match what has come to be?" Morning Star reasoned, then reminded them, "All know Payaba was a great shaman who was taught by Mind-Who-Roams, the powerful medicine chief who led our tribe under Gray Eagle. His powers and insight have not vanished. Grandfather let Payaba live to speak to our people on this sun about the forgotten vision. Only Grandfather knows why He did not share the truth with Hawk Eyes."

Sun Cloud was shocked by the man's claims. Joe had no Indian coloring or bone structure; he bore no resemblance to Powchutu. He remembered his father's half brother. They had become close friends before Powchutu's death at the side of Gray Eagle during the white man's ambush in 1820. Afterward, he had signed a treaty with Derek Sturgis because he wanted to save his people, his family, his ways, and his lands. But troubles over the past few years had stolen his trust in the white man and their great leader. Now he must confront that same decision again: war or peace. "How do we know you are Tanner Gaston, son of Stede, grandson of Powchutu? Why did you not tell Morning Star? Or speak it sooner to me?"

"There are many charges against your band," Joe replied carefully. "I didn't want to reveal my identity until I was sure I could trust you. I thought you would speak and act differently to Joe than to Tanner. When the first whites came, you met them in peace. You did not resist settlers until they began to intrude in large numbers and to claim parts of your land. When gold — the yellow rock white man craves — was discovered in California, many prospectors and traders swarmed over your territory as countless bees. When land was purchased or claimed in Oregon Territory, white pioneers had to pass through your lands to reach it. Many stopped and remained. Troops were sent to patrol the area, to protect the whites, and to obtain peace with the Indians." He saw Sun Cloud nod.

"When the numbers of the settlers, traders, trappers, and soldiers became too large, your people and other tribes, as well, worried that they would steal all lands from you. There are many differences between the two peoples, Sun Cloud. The whites do not understand how bad it is to kill the buffalo that sustains your way of life. They cut timber to build homes, fences, forts, and barns. They don't realize that their guns scare off game. They don't understand why they can't let their stock graze on the same grasslands with buffalo, deer, and elk. They don't know that you believe they scar the face of Mother

90

Earth when they clear land to grow food, to raise stock, and to build homes, forts, posts, churches, and schools. They clear land for roads because they're easier for wagons to travel than trails. They don't know Indian ways. The same is true of the Oglalas and other tribes; they don't understand the white man's ways. Many events in history are beyond the control of a leader and his people. What happens here is not, Sun Cloud. What you decide and do will become history — good or bad — and it will affect the lives of these people and all generations to follow."

Sun Cloud was impressed and silently concurred, but he responded, "Those are wise and good words, but they do not make you Tanner."

Joe did not comprehend how Payaba had prophesied his coming, but he could not ignore the strange truth. The mystical holy man had described him — not Tanner Gaston — accurately! Some power greater than all of them was at work and had led him — not Powchutu's grandson — to this place and problem. Yet he needed that blood connection and his lie to make the remainder of the "vision" come true.

Confident he was doing the right thing for all concerned, Joe reasoned, "There's no way I could have known about Payaba's vision to use it to deceive you. I'm as shocked as you are to see me here today fulfilling it. I don't understand such magic and mysteries in life, but I know I'm here to help. I'll tell you what Powchutu told Stede and he told me. Powchutu lived and worked as a half-breed scout at the fort; that's where he met your mother, when she lived as Alisha Williams after she was stolen from your father by soldiers. When she was returned to your grandfather, she was proven to be Shalee, long-lost daughter of Chief Black Cloud. She didn't understand or believe such claims, and she fled Gray Eagle with Powchutu. Gray Eagle tracked her to St. Louis, told her the truth, and brought her home. Powchutu was said to be slain by the white enemy holding your mother captive, but he was only injured and had been sold into white slavery. For many years, he didn't remember his name. When the Great Spirit returned his mind, he left your grandparents in peace and married a half-white woman. But you know the truth about her," Joe hinted.

Yes, Sun Cloud knew the truth about Sarah Devane Gaston. She was the real Shalee, abducted daughter of Black Cloud, the woman whose identity his mother had used until her death the same day as Gray Eagle's. Yet only a few people knew and had known that secret because it would have been damaging to many. He also knew that Powchutu's mother was a Crow, not a Cheyenne as recorded on the family history hide. Love between enemies was torment for all involved. That was the main reason Running Wolf had been denied his firstborn son from a forbidden love for a Bird Woman and the impossible union between lovers of enemy tribes.

"When my grandfather returned to his people thirty-one years ago, he became Eagle's Arm," Joe continued. "Running Wolf had confessed the truth of his first son to Shalee, and she revealed it to Gray Eagle. All was forgiven and they became brothers. Powchutu rode to the fort with your brother Bright Arrow to spy on the soldiers; that's how he earned his way into your tribe. He became the friend of Sun Cloud, and you shared many talks. When he rode to the fort with Bright Arrow, he sent a letter to my father and told him such things. He rode at Gray Eagle's side the day both were slain. You became chief. You sent Derek Sturgis away with a treaty. Sturgis came to see my father and told him of *his* father's death. He gave my father a letter written by Powchutu before his death; it told us the truth of his birth and all that happened after his return to his homeland. It told the truth of my grandmother," he reminded the observant chief.

Joe withdrew the necklace he had taken from Tanner's pocket after his death, the one Stede had told him to keep for assistance. "You gave this *wanapin* to Sturgis that last day. It's a replica of Gray Eagle's that you used when you rode as his ghost to frighten the soldiers. Sturgis thought my father should have it. My father, Stede, gave it to me to use as a sign to you that I'm telling the truth. Oglala blood runs swift and thick in Stede Gaston's blood. As with his father when he grew old, he felt called home to his people and ancestral lands. We came to prevent war."

Sun Cloud caressed the *wanapin* of a white eagle and recalled the day he had placed it in Sturgis's hand. He remembered the days he had worn it, along with the chief's bonnet and garments, to "haunt" the soldiers who had murdered his father. "Seasons past, the whites and soldiers were afraid of the Oglalas because of my father's prowess and power, even of his ghost," he said. "That time is no more. Whites and soldiers grow too bold and greedy."

"They fear you just as much as they feared Gray Eagle. That's why Snake-Man is so eager to destroy your people. He knows he can't take over this territory as long as Oglalas remain here. He's tricking the Crow into attacking, and he supplies them with weapons and goods. He's tricking the whites and soldiers into believing your people want war and that you're raiding and killing. They see the image of Gray Eagle in you, Sun Cloud. You have his wits, courage, prowess, and power. They know you can band the Dakota tribes and your allies together, as Gray Eagle once did. The last time there was trouble, you met and worked with good white men. Together you battled evil white men. But there were and are evil Indians, too. Have you forgotten about Silver Hawk, Red Band, and renegades?"

Sun Cloud wished he hadn't mentioned the treacherous and traitorous Silver Hawk, who had been his wife's brother. "They are not Oglalas."

"Just as all Indians aren't the same, Sun Cloud, all whites aren't the same. Most whites want peace; they're looking for new lives here. Most soldiers are only obeying orders, so we have to make certain those orders are kind ones. Broken-Hand Fitzpatrick is a good white man. So is Captain Thomas at Fort Tabor. These men want to help your people."

"Soldiers provoke and attack us! If we retaliate, they say we challenge for war!" Night Stalker charged, dreading how Joe might effect his life.

"Even if you refuse to give me help with a guide and translator, at least don't attack for a while—only defend yourselves. Give me time to unmask Snake-Man and his tricks. Let me go to the Crow camps and gather clues. Let me prove your people are blameless and want peace. You don't want bloodshed; the whites don't want bloodshed. Allow me time to find this villain and then stop him. I'll ride to Fort Tabor and speak with

Captain Thomas. Broken-Hand says I can trust him. I'll see if he has any clues. Then I'll return here and make plans with you."

"No!" Knife-Slayer shouted. "He will lead bluecoats to our camp."

"You have my word of honor, Sun Cloud; I will not betray my grandfather's people. When he's healed, I'll bring Stede to see you."

"A chief leads his tribe, but all warriors can speak, and the Council must vote. We must think on your words and claims, then call the Council to meeting. Morning Star, take him to my tepee to await our answer."

"Put him at the captive's post!" Knife-Slayer demanded. He did not want Joe around Morning Star any longer. He was suspicious and envious of the way the woman whom he desired, trusted and defended the stranger. He was determined to win the chief's daughter as his wife. He was furious about the days and nights she and the white man had spent together on the trail, alone.

Sun Cloud eyed the hostile warrior, and again worried over his effect on Night Stalker and others. "He will be our friend and ally until we prove he is our foe. Your chief can say and do this much without a vote."

"Thank you, Father," Morning Star said. "Come, Tanner. I give you food and tend your wound while the Council meets."

"For the sake of both sides, Sun Cloud, you must trust me and help me." Joe headed for the chief's colorful tepee with the Indian beauty. He glanced back to see Night Stalker, Knife-Slayer, and Hawk Eyes huddled together and talking. Dread washed over his weary body, because he knew the awesome power those warriors possessed. If they even suspected he'd lied, he was a dead man. If they sent for Tanner's father and Stede exposed him, he was in deep peril. Right now he wanted to learn why Morning Star had taken his side and kept his secret . . .

Morning Star guided Joe inside her home, then turned to him. "You lie," she remarked. "You not of Running Wolf bloodline."

"Why didn't you challenge me?" Joe inquired.

94

"I trust other words. I believe you here to help."

"I swear it. I hated to trick your father and people, but I had to save my life and get their help. You know what will happen if I fail. Tanner was my best friend. He wouldn't mind if I used his name and bloodline to save his father's people. Everything else is the truth, Morning Star."

"You seek to avenge Tanner's death," she said in slow speech.

"It's true that Stede is hurt and he's at Fort Laramie. It's true he's working for the President. Stede heard and read stories about what was happening out here. He wanted to come to learn where and how his father had lived. He wanted to meet his relatives and help them. He wanted to learn more about his ancestors. If Powchutu, his father, hadn't been denied his birthright, Powchutu would have been chief of the Oglalas, not Gray Eagle. If that were true, Stede could be chief now, not your father. But I think fate worked in the best way. No leaders could be better than Gray Eagle or your father. Fate sent Powchutu away, so his son could return at this time to offer a path to peace. It's Life-Circles touching again. When I came here with Stede and Tanner, it was to share adventures. Now that I've learned the truth and Tanner is dead, their task is mine."

"Great Spirit capture my tongue when you lie. I understand. You Sky Warrior, man in Payaba's vision long ago. Other man Stede Gaston, Grandfather's brother. I must ride with Joe. We friends; we must help each other. I wish to become warrior maiden in sacred vision."

"No, it's too dangerous. I don't want you hurt."

"I speak not with false pride, but I be best trained female. You say I ride with skill and fight as warrior. You say I save Joe's life. You say we make good pair. Great Spirit let Morning Star be captured for us to meet and work together. In Joe's mind, he know and want this. Why does Joe's heart battle what should be?"

Fatigued, hungry, and concerned with the council meeting, Joe's wits were not as sharp as usual. He didn't deny the truth that troubled his heart. "You know why, Morning Star. When peace is won and the treaty is signed, I must go far away. My family, home, and destiny are there; my Life-Circle is there."

"My family, home, and destiny here, so I must help save them."

"It's too dangerous for us to ride and work together. From the first moment I saw you in Zeke's camp, you gave me a funny feeling inside. It's best if I keep that feeling buried. With you at my side, my head wouldn't be clear. I have a hunger for you that I can't feed."

"You speak bold words to woman you know for short time," she replied as her heart raced.

Joe knew he must be honest. "I speak the truth as a warning to both of us. When I said I didn't want you hurt, I meant more than your body and more than by others. Our lives and cultures are different, Morning Star. With you as my helper, I'd be too tempted to forget that. If we did, it would be hard and painful for both of us when all this is over."

"If you not take best woman, you may fail and die. We both strong and brave. We let nothing weaken our wills and defeat our duties."

"That's also why you kept quiet; you didn't want me killed by your people. Don't you see how we've been pulled toward each other?"

"I silent because of sacred vision."

"You held silent before it was revealed. When I look into your eyes, Morning Star, I see the same things I'm feeling inside. You would never leave here with me, and I can stay only until winter. We mustn't trap ourselves in a hopeless situation. I don't want to hurt you, and I don't want to be hurt. Please forget your desire to become this vision woman. If I lost control with you, Sun Cloud would slay me — not to mention that the mission would fail."

Before Morning Star could respond, her mother returned to the tepee with fresh water. She turned to do her chores to hide her expression.

"Loyacin he?" Singing Wind asked.

"English, Mother," the girl reminded in a gentle tone.

"Are you hungry?" the older woman inquired once more to Joe.

"Yes, ma'am. We rode hard and fast to get here before the rescue party was sent out."

Singing Wind dished up meat stew and served it with buffalo berry wine and bread pones that were speckled with dried
fruits and nuts. She handed them to the white man, then observed him as he ate. It was the Indian custom for men to eat
first, then women and children; but Joe was not Indian, so
Morning Star joined him. As the couple devoured the best
meal they had eaten in days, Singing Wind watched with interest. She couldn't help but wonder if her daughter was to be the
woman in Payaba's vision . Despite her fears and worries, she
couldn't help but hope that was true. In her younger days, her
Blackfoot people had called Singing Wind — headstrong,
bold, and impulsive. She had been one with deep and strong
emotions, with a wish to do more than a woman's work. She
had wanted adventure and excitement. She had learned the
same skills that warriors possess, the same ones her daughter
now possessed. How could she fault Morning Star's behavior
and traits when they had been hers so long ago?

Each of them was from a long line and respected tepees of
chiefs. Morning Star's maternal grandfather had been the
Blackfoot chief Brave Bear, adopted son of Chief Black
Cloud. Following Brave Bear's death, she herself had been
raised by Chief Medicine Bear and trained by his sons.

What worried Singing Wind were the powerful currents she
was perceiving between her youngest child and the stranger. If
Morning Star turned to one of the enemy, she and her family
would know great loss of face. A marriage between them was
not possible or right. For either to seek one would cause bitterness, antagonism, and suffering.

Yet the older woman knew how willful and strong love
could be, and how fast it could work. She had pursued and
yielded to Sun Cloud while promised to his brother! Even
knowing what anguish and shame her actions and desires
could cause she had been unable to control herself; it had been
the same for her husband. They had risked humiliation and
banishment, perhaps death, to win each other. Everything had
worked out, and they had been happy for thirty-one years.

There had been other mixed unions in her husband's bloodline. Gray Eagle had joined a white woman; Bright Arrow had
joined a white woman; Alisha/Shalee's alleged father, Chief

97

Black Cloud, had joined a white woman. Singing Wind knew that Sun Cloud and his people would fiercely resist more enemy blood weakening his Indian line. If Morning Star leaned toward a paleface, it would appear that his bloodline preferred white—enemy—mates over their own kind. It would bring great *yuonihansni*—shame, loss of face, dishonor—to their tepee. Added to that sting, mixed marriages were hard on a couple. Whose ways would they choose? Which side would they take during warfare?

Singing Wind knew how like herself Morning Star was. She prayed her daughter would not forget her traditions, family, duties, and people. She prayed her child would not yearn for what could not be. She prayed that her instincts and intuition were mistaken.

"Takucahe, Ina?" Morning Star asked her mother what was wrong.

Singing Wind remembered that Joe had said he knew a little Lakota, so she responded in English, "We talk later, Daughter. Eat. Rest."

As he ate and waited, Joe wondered what was taking place in the council meeting, as it affected more than his own fate.

Morning Star asked her mother if she could go see Buckskin Girl while the council was in progress. Singing Wind gave her permission. After telling Joe to relax and that she would return soon, Morning Star left. But she did not go to the tepee of Flaming Star to visit his daughter, her friend. She sneaked toward the meeting lodge to eavesdrop. She was glad the large and colorfully marked tepee was erected in an area near concealing trees that would aid in her bold action.

The Oglalas' camp was situated between black rock formations and a large lake, amidst fragrant pines and spruces. It offered more privacy than their nomadic summer camps on the Plains when tepees formed ever-widening circles around the chief's tepee and meeting lodge. Here, they spread out amongst trees, along the lakeside, and before hills and rocks.

Night had settled on the land, and a full moon's light was dulled by curious clouds that gave her an eerie sensation. Women were inside their conical dwellings, occupied with children and chores. Council members and other warriors

98

were at the meeting. Any other people were in their tepees or at waterside campfires discussing the strange event that had occurred earlier. She passed rope and branch corrals at many places, as there was no need in this safe and secluded location for warriors to picket their horses beside their tepees. She was relieved they knew her scent and stayed calm.

Morning Star slipped from tree to tree, halting to look and listen at each one to make certain her forbidden behavior was not discovered. She had to hear what was being said and by whom . . .

Inside the crowded lodge, the ritual pipe smoking and prayers had taken a long time with so many participating. The meeting in 1831 where Payaba had revealed his vision had been attended by the Council. Tonight, all warriors of high-standing were present to voice opinions.

Members of the O-Zu-Ye Wicasta stood in circles around the councilmen who were seated on buffalo skins in the center of the group. There were several warrior societies represented whose jobs were to preserve order in camp and during moves and hunts. Some punished offenders of their laws. Some guarded the camp, led battles, and oversaw feasts and dances. Some were the keepers of the tribe's heritage and traditions. All were highly trained warriors with numerous coups and great prowess. Most were members of the Tall Ones or Kit-Fox cults, military societies that demanded courage and honor. A few were members of the Sacred Bow cult, to which Sun Cloud had belonged in years past. Presently, Night Stalker and Knife-Slayer were Sacred Bow carriers: two of four men who took places at the fronts of battles. It was a perilous rank and had to be earned. The Sacred Bow test was as difficult and dangerous as the Sun Dance. After proving himself, a Sacred Bow carrier could resign with honor, as Sun Cloud had done when he became chief.

Sun Cloud, other chiefs, shamen — past and present — and mature, renowned warriors were members of the Big Belly society. They were responsible for the tribe's leadership. Since they were advanced in years and their skills were not as sharp as in earlier days, ten younger warriors — "shirt wearers" — were appointed by them to carry out their orders. Night

Stalker and Knife-Slayer were also "shirt wearers."

Payaba, a Big Belly was one of the few Oglalas who was also a member of the Elk Dreamer cult. It was considered powerful and special and he took his rank seriously. He knew that if a man disobeyed a vision, he would be punished, usually by death. He prayed his people would heed his vision of long ago. He waited with patience.

Wolf Eyes, the ceremonial chief, said before taking a seat, "In the east where *Wi* rises, the whites are as many as the drops of rain that have fallen on our land since Grandfather created it for us. They do not come here to nourish it as rain does; they come to flood, destroy, and change it. But their weapons have as great power as the lightning. If they grow many and strong and we challenge them, they will roll over us as the mighty thunder when it roars with anger."

The man once called Standing Tree stood tall and proud after he rose to speak. Long white hair traveled his shoulders. His eyes were clouded by age, but he saw things these days with a sharp mental vision. Numerous wrinkles lined his face, but did not take away from his pleasant expression. Gnarled fingers made tasks difficult for him, but he never complained. There was a gentleness about him that men like Hawk Eyes and his son mistook for weakness. Yet his resonant voice and dignity evoked love and respect in nearly all of his people. "We cannot fight our allied foes and the white-eyes. If we go from battle to battle, how can we make enough weapons? Or hunt buffalo for food and other needs? How can we laugh and sing, with many to place upon scaffolds? How can our women have children without fathers to plant their seeds? If we ride into battle, who will protect our camps and people? If we do not make peace, there will be no time for hunts, joys, smiles, births, or ceremonies. There will be only battles, sadness, tears, deaths, and war dances. I say we fight only in defense. I say we make truce with the whites-eyes and Crow."

"Both are evil," Night Stalker said. "The Crow have slain many of our tribe. They attacked and killed my uncle, Bright Arrow and his mate. They have become friends with the whites. They are unworthy of our truce."

"Their truce with the white-eyes lets them survive and grow

stronger. Have you forgotten how many Bird People we have slain for their bad deeds? How many prizes we have brought home after raiding their camps? We do not have to make them allies and blood brothers as with the Cheyenne and Blackfoot; but we can make truce with the Crow, Pawnee, and Shoshone. The white-eyes made truce with their enemies, the Mexicans and the British. If Indian nations remain separate and foes, the united white one will be strongest. One by one, they will defeat nation by nation, and take all Indian lands. The badger is fierce and cunning, but we respect his skills and territory. Can it not be the same with our white and Indian foes? If the white-eyes and Crow band together, the Oglala will be destroyed, and Crow will get our lands. The Great Spirit has sent us a path to truce and survival. We must help Sky Warrior ride it for us."

"We fight our own battles and make our own truces. We need no white man to do them for us. I say, kill him, then ride against our foes."

"That is why the Crow and white-eyes will listen to him, Knife-Slayer, because his skin is white. The Great White Chief honors Tanner's words, and all white-eyes must obey the White Chief's words and their laws."

"The White Chief's words, laws, and ways are for *his* people. They are not for Oglalas and our brothers. They have made what they call reservations in many places and confined whole tribes as captives. Have you forgotten what the trapper told us the winter after your . . . vision? He said the White Chief had made a law called the 'Indian Removal Act' so they can drive the Cherokees and other tribes toward the setting sun. If we do not resist, they will come to drive us far from our lands. We must live free or die fighting."

"The treaty will protect our lives and territory, Knife-Slayer. To give a challenge with no hope of victory is foolish and deadly."

"A new treaty will protect us only until the whites crave more land. Such a warning was in your past vision," Catch the Bear reminded.

"It is so, but that is a battle for another season. While there is peace, we can grow strong with children, weapons, and skills. If we battle every moon, we will grow small and weak; Oglalas will perish. All living things need rest, as the trees in winter. When spring comes, they are strong enough to grow taller and larger. If foes cut into their bodies and chop off their arms, they die. It is the same with the Dakota Nation."

"Payaba is wise and his words reach deep," Sun Cloud said. "We must not speak or act too quickly and rashly. What do others say?"

Flaming Star, son of White Arrow who was best friend to Gray Eagle, said, "My heart says the words of our chief and our past shaman are wise. My hatred of the Crow is great for slaying my friend Bright Arrow. I took many Crow scalps and ponies in revenge. But it is time for my sons and grandchildren to know peace. I will bury my hatred to seek it for them."

"When the Cheyenne and Blackfoot unite with the Seven Council Fires," Night Stalker said, "we will be stronger than the whites or the Crow. It is wrong to crawl as a frightened or wounded dog to our foes. We must fight."

"Do you forget Payaba's vision?" Talking Rock asked. It commands truce. Speak it again, Wise One, for all to hear and understand. Tell all the white man said, for those who missed his words."

So for those who might not have caught everything during the excitement and loud noise, Payaba repeated his past vision. Then, Sun Cloud related what Joe had said earlier.

"We do not know whose hands claimed the messages Powchutu sent long ago," Knife-Slayer debated. "Any eyes that touched upon them would learn the secrets inside. We do not know if Stede Gaston told others what his father told him? We do not know if this white man is his son. A hunter and warrior must live by instincts. Mine say he is not Sky Warrior."

"How would he know of the vision he fulfills?" Plenty Coups asked.

"It was told to the Council and others long ago," Knife-Slayer replied. "Warriors and hunters sometimes fall prey to white captors. Perhaps the vision was forced from one's lips."

"No Red Heart would reveal our sacred secrets," Tracks Good refuted, "not even if he is tortured and slain."

"Not all Red Hearts are as strong and wise as members of our great council," Knife-Slayer retorted. "The white man has whiskey to dull wits and strange sicknesses to burn heads with fever. Some men will speak secrets when their minds are stolen by such evils. At Night Stalker's side, we ride against our foes and shoot them from their horses with our Sacred-Bows. They have never failed us. We must do so again."

"You cannot make and fire enough arrows to win such a battle," Sun Cloud replied, "even with a powerful weapon of the Sacred Bow Cult. It would be hard for the same white man to steal the letters written long ago and sent far away to Stede," he pointed out, "to learn of the past vision here, and to have his face match it. I do not believe such a thing is possible. What do you say, Hawk Eyes?" he questioned the medicine chief.

"My heart and mind war over all I have seen and heard. I must seek counsel from the Great Spirit before I know what is right for our people. When I traveled to our Holy Mountain for guidance, I did not see this white man in my vision. If Payaba's vision was real, not a dream, perhaps this man is not the Sky Warrior who rode in it. Evil can work in powerful and mysterious ways. The words of my son could hold strange truth."

"The words of Grandfather that I revealed long ago are the same as the story he told to us. I say, let him live and ride to the fort. If he lies, we will slay him when he returns." Payaba said, glancing at Sun Cloud to see if he agreed.

Hawk Eyes spoke again. "After I seek my vision, if it says he is Sky Warrior, we will help him. If it says he is not, we will remove his evil tongue and heart and feed them to the death-eating birds. We have known much evil from the whites. They will not change their bad hearts."

"What of the other Dakota tribes?" Jumping Elk asked.

Long Horn, the war chief, replied, "When Sun Cloud and Lone Horn visited the camps of our brothers, some spoke for peace and some for war. Brave Bear of the Brule wars against the whites and attacks travelers on the white man's trail west. Little Thunder of another Brule tribe speaks for war. Wamdesapa's son leads his Santee as renegades; Inkpaduta's band is for war. Tashunkopipape sees the power of the soldiers and restrains his Oglala band until we choose a path, at which time he will ride the same one. Red Cloud has joined the Bad Faces

103

Band to his mother's Old Smoke Band. He resists the white man's encroachment, and he carries much power among the Tetons; but he desires peace with honor. Sitting Bull and Gall of the Hunkpapas will join us in battle; they do not trust the whites. Jumping Buffalo will vote for peace. He has many white friends, as the white trapper who gave him his medicine symbol from the raccoon and calls him Spotted Tail. Even at ten winters, his nephew Crazy Horse rides with him. Many say he will be a great warrior and he urges his uncle to fight. Wacouta, who took Walking Buffalo's chief bonnet of the Red Wings, wants peace and will sign a new treaty. Walking Buffalo signed treaties in what the white man calls '1815' and '1825,' but he refused to sign again fourteen winters past. Most of the Santee Council Fires warred at the sides of the British against the whites when they fought their two great wars seventy-five and thirty-nine winters past. The British promised not to enter Dakota lands if the Dakotas helped them defeat their white colonists."

"The colonists were stronger and defeated the British even with the help of the Santee tribes," Payaba reminded. "The whites are more numerous and stronger now. How can Lakotas alone defeat such a force? We cannot."

"Once," Flaming Star said, "the Dakota Nation ruled more land than the whites and other tribes claim as theirs. But the woodland bands of the Santee Council Fires to the east let the Chippawas and whites push them closer to us. They were foolish to make trade with Pike for part of their territory; Mother Earth cannot and must not be sold."

Catch the Bear repeated the story he had been told, "They know this. They tricked the whites to get money to buy guns to battle their foes. Pike's Treaty is worthless. The same is true of the Prairie de Chien Council and Treaty twenty-six winters past. The whites think their words and papers made truces and boundaries. They think they gave the Dakotas a large territory. The land belongs to Grandfather and is for the Dakotas' use. The white man says we took these lands from our foes, and they will take them from us. But Tetons have been here since before the fathers of our father's fathers. We have always been Dwellers of the Plains, as our name says, and we will always remain here."

"Our Indian brothers to the east—the Sauk, Fox, Shawneee, Ottawan, and Chippewa—where are they now?" Hawk Eyes asked. "Indians to the south—Cherokee, Seminole, and others—where are they now? What of the Nez Perce and Yakima to the west? What of the Kiowas, Apaches, and Comanches who fiercely battle the whites for three winters now? What of the Cheyenne and Arapaho whose lands the whites look upon with greed these suns? The whites want us to live and think as they do. They want us to worship their god. They say we must accept their laws. They write words in what they call newspapers to arouse all whites against us. Some chiefs did not understand the meanings of their treaties; they believed the whites gave them supplies to use their lands, not to buy them. The whites used the papers the chiefs signed to get the white government to take Indian lands when the chiefs argued and resisted leaving. Some whites are good, but they are few. The bad whites are strongest and rule all whites."

"Hocoka is the center of all things," Walks Tall said. "All power comes from the Sacred Hoop. As long as it is unbroken, our people will live and flourish. If we let the whites break our Circle of Life, we will die."

"We did not invade their lands to the east; they must not invade ours. Most come as settlers, not warriors," Thunder Spirit, brother of Flaming Star, stated. "Their armies are great. We do not want our sons and daughters, our parents and their children slain. We must not challenge until we are certain of victory. The whites do not understand our ways. They believe they purchased Dakota lands. One man cannot sell another's horses. The Santee cannot sell the Plains. The French cannot sell the Plains. Thunder Spirit can say Walks Tall's horses are his, but it would not be so. If Thunder Spirit steals Pawnee horses, they are his to claim and sell. The French did not conquer our territory, so they cannot sell it to the whites."

"We accepted many whites among us," Night Stalker said. "When my uncle Bright Arrow traveled with the men called Lewis and Clark, he saw and learned many things. He told my people much when he returned. That was long ago, before I was born. Since that season, many whites have followed their trail to the big waters, into the territory called Oregon. They make homesteads there and push out villages. When Indians resist, whites say they are provoked to war, so they can kill and take all. Other tribes accepted them as friends, but whites did not honor that friendship. It will be the same in our territory. We must stand against them this season."

Charging Dog, one of the oldest men in the Big Belly Society, asked, "Many have forgotten or do not know of the visit from Tecumseh, the Shawnee chief, before the last white war with the British. Tecumseh called Dakota tribes together to warn us of white danger. Many Teton bands went to the council. Many Oglalas went: Gray Eagle, White Arrow, Plenty Coups, Charging Dog, Payaba when he was Standing Tree, and others. The Shawnee chief told of eastern tribes who were massacred by white settlers. He spoke of camps and villages burned by blue-coats. Each winter, the whites journey closer to our lands, claiming all they pass. Tecumseh came to urge all Indian nations to band together against the whites. He told how they greeted the first whites in peace; whites were given food, blankets, and help. Whites grew strong; they wanted more land, from the rising to the setting suns; they killed all Indians who resisted their desires. He told of how whites hated, cheated, insulted, and abused Indians. We did not join him, and his warnings have come true. The Great Spirit gave the whites lands across the big waters and gave us these lands. The greed of the whites brought them across the big waters and into our lands. I say for Hawk Eyes to read the words spoken by Tecumseh, written on the Tribal Buffalo Record. Those words are as powerful as Payaba's old vision."

"A vision must be obeyed, Charging Dog," the elderly man urged.

"It was long ago, Payaba," Knife-Slayer said. "You should seek another vision. Perhaps Grandfather no longer wants us to obey the old one."

Payaba did not display the anger he felt toward the trouble-maker. "If such is true, Knife-Slayer, why did he send Sky Warrior to us?"

"Evil is strong these suns, Old One. Perhaps Evil sent the white man to trick us. I have not heard the warnings of Tecumseh. Read them, Father. All must hear them before we vote

106

which medicine is strongest."

All of the council members and warriors were silent as the shaman retrieved the tribal record from its place in the meeting lodge.

Hawk Eyes stood to read it, so all could hear the words clearly, as he wanted the vote to go the same way his son did. "Tecumseh told us; 'Brothers, if you do not unite with us, they will first destroy us, and then you will fall an easy prey to them. They have destroyed many nations of red men because they were not united. The white people send runners amongst us; they wish to make us enemies, that they may sweep like devastating winds. Where today is many other once powerful tribes? They have vanished before the avarice and oppression of the white man, as snow before a summer sun. Think not you can remain indifferent to the common danger. Your people, too, will soon be as fallen leaves driven before the wintry storms. Every year our white intruders become more greedy, oppressive, and overbearing. Let us defend to the last warrior our country, our homes, our liberty, and the graves of our fathers.' His words have come to be."

Everyone was silent and thoughtful for a time.

Sun Cloud reflected on words his mother had told him long ago: "You must be strong, Sun Cloud," she said, "for many dark days are ahead. Being a chief is difficult and painful, but your father has trained you well. Lasting peace is gone forever. You must defend your people; you must guide them wisely. You must seek truce if the whites will allow it; only through peace can the Oglalas survive. You must learn to share our lands, or the whites will take them by force. You must learn to accept them, or they will destroy all you know and love. They are powerful, my son. Know and accept this fact, or you will battle for a victory which can never be won. Seek peace with honor, even if you must taste it as a bitter defeat . . . Some white leaders and peoples are not evil; it is those you must seek out and work with. . . . I lived with the whites, and I know them. Truce, however bitter, is better than Mother Earth with no Oglalas. One day, the white man will realize his evil and he will halt it. Until that day, you must make certain the Oglalas survive." Sun Cloud remembered the last words she had spoken to him: "Life

107

is often brief and hard, and you must feast on its rewards each day. . . . Do not allow the white man's hostilities to harden your heart." His mother had been a wise and kind woman, a white woman. Yet her words were as hard to accept today as they had been shortly before her death. But he was chief, and he must think of his people before himself.

Sun Cloud rose from his buffalo mat. His fingers clutched the *wanapin* Tanner Gaston had returned to him. His other fingers touched the eagle feather behind his head as if drawing strength and wisdom from the man it represented. He gazed around the circles of men of many ages and ranks. He had fought battles at the sides of most of them. He had watched some grow to manhood. Some reminded him of fathers or brothers lost during raids or wars with whites and with Indian foes.

Sun Cloud glanced at his thirty-year-old son. He knew Night Stalker was not ready to become chief, and he wondered where and how he had failed to make him the man *his* father had made *him*. If only Gray Eagle and Shalee had lived long enough to influence and guide Night Stalker along the right trail, as they had done with him. At his son's age, he had been chief for seven years. If he believed his son was ready to accept the chief's bonnet, he would yield it to the skilled warrior. At fifty-four, Sun Cloud felt soul-tired from years of bearing burdens for so many people; he wanted to enjoy the rest of his life. He was willing to complete his Life Circle as a Big Belly. But Night Stalker was too hotheaded, too impulsive, too consumed by hatred for the whites and a hunger for war, too swayed by Knife-Slayer, for him to turn leadership over to his only son. But for now there was the decision to make about Tanner Gaston and his mission. "We must vote," he said.

Morning Star's heart drummed with trepidation. After listening to everyone's words, she could not guess how the decision would go. It was getting late, and she couldn't remain hidden there much longer. Her mother might become worried and search for her. If her mischief was discovered, everyone would blame Joe for her bad conduct. With reluctance, she started to leave, then more words halted her in mid-step . . .

Chapter Five

"Is there more to say before our sticks are tossed?" Sun Cloud asked?

"There is a glowing ring around the full moon tonight," Payaba said. "It is an omen to say this time is important. We must vote for peace."

Knife-Slayer had seen the hazy look that seemed to encircle the moon. "I say it is black magic, evil magic, to warn us to vote for war."

Hawk Eyes wanted to agree, but held silent.

"Our vote this moon must be only about the white man's life," Flaming Star suggested. "I say, let him live. We must give him time to prove his words and learn if he can win us peace with honor."

Thunder Spirit added to his brother's words. "What harm can giving him his life for saving Morning Star's do? What harm can it do to let him seek and destroy the one who sells weapons to our foes? What harm can it do to let him work for an honorable peace? If he fails, we can war later."

"His task will distract our foes while we hunt buffalo and make more weapons," Walks Tall said.

"Payaba's words carry much strong medicine," Catch the Bear said. "We must test his vision and this white man. Free him to prove himself to us."

When it was silent for a while, Wolf Eyes assumed everyone had given their feelings and opinions. He explained the voting procedure. "If you wish to free the white man and to allow him to attempt his mission, toss your white stick into the basket. If you do not, vote with your black stick."

Hawk Eyes spoke again. "If the vote is no, he must die. If he is slain, we will call another council to talk war. It is true he rescued Morning Star, but if we vote we do not trust him, he must die to protect the secrets he has learned in our camp."

"I say that the white man's story matches Payaba's vision," Sun Cloud told his people, "so we must accept both as truth, as Grandfather's message. We must let Tanner prove he is unlike other whites and will side with us. If peace lies within his grasp, we must not slay him. It is true his words are hard to accept and obey. Look at our tribal record," he said, pointing to the pictorial history of the Oglala depicted on a tanned buffalo hide. "Until these past few summers few conflicts were painted on its surface after our treaty. The 'time of great danger' Payaba spoke of has arrived, so have two men who match the vision. I speak for peace. The day for a great war will come, but this is not that season. If we do not allow Sky Warrior to defeat Snake-Man and the Crow, our lands will run fast and dark with Oglala blood. That will be Grandfather's punishment for not obeying the sacred vision he gave to our shaman long ago."

The men who were wavering in their decisions made them after the chief's final words. Sun Cloud was loved, awed, and respected. Many older eyes still saw the image of the legendary Gray Eagle in him. Others knew what a wise and brave leader he had been for years. All eyes closed and the basket was passed from man to man. Sticks were dropped inside.

When the basket was dumped before Wolf Eyes, the ceremonial chief, for him to count the votes, all sticks were white — yes — except for three.

Sun Cloud guessed that two "no's" were from Night Stalker and Knife-Slayer; he presumed the third was from Hawk Eyes. It disappointed and worried him that his son — the future chief — and the tribe's shaman were so against peace, if won with honor. The other "no" did not surprise him.

"He is to go free," Wolf Eyes announced.

Knife-Slayer told the group, *"Puzani ni kte lo. I'ye sica yelo,"* and left.

Morning Star watched the furious man stalk away, having behaved as no honorable warrior should have. Before others left and she was exposed, she hurried to Flaming Star's tepee and called to her friend.

Buckskin Girl came out and embraced her, then started to ask rapid-fire questions.

Morning Star smiled and silenced her. "I must hurry back to

110

my tepee. I am fine and will tell you all things tomorrow." She rushed home.

In the meeting lodge, Sun Cloud did not heed Knife-Slayer's warning: "You will see you are wrong. He is bad." He was eager to reach his tepee and speak with Tanner, the grandson of his long-dead friend. He quickly thanked his close friends for their votes, then departed.

When the chief ducked into his tepee, he glanced first at his wife, who was sewing on a new shirt for him, then looked at his daughter, who was beading a new pair of moccasins. Morning Star smiled at him, but her eyes were filled with concern over the fate of her white rescuer. Well trained in their ways and a respectful girl, she did not question him about the council meeting. Sun Cloud thought how like her mother she was in looks and personality. If only she were a son, an older son, she would be worthy of their chief's bonnet. It was sad that Night Stalker didn't have more of her good traits. Sun Cloud went to sit beside the dying fire near the man who had entered their lives to change them forever.

Joe met the chief's probing gaze. It told him nothing of their decision. He was impressed by this great man, and lying to him gnawed at his conscience. One day he would confess the truth. If his mission succeeded, hopefully Sun Cloud would understand and accept the necessity of his deceit. Although anxious, he waited for the older man to speak.

"Many whites have visited our lands and camps," he began. "The first ones mentioned on our tribal record came in my grandfather's day, Verendrye brothers who were accepted as friends. Many trappers and traders followed. One called Manuel Lisa created the Missouri Fur Company and had many posts and men. He died the year my father was slain. Pierre Chouteau claimed his territory and called his post American Fur Company. First they came for beaver, muskrat, and otter; later, for any and all hides and pelts. More posts were built: Pratte at Pierre, Columbia at Lookout, McMichael to where the Sahiyela and Mnisose rivers join. Each season, more follow."

Joe knew he was referring to the confluence of the Cheyenne and Missouri rivers where Orin McMichael owned and ran a trading post. He and Tanner hadn't made it that far north before his friend's death, but they had been told the Scotsman was friendly with all Indians.

"Now, they seek deer, elk, and buffalo. They kill without feeling and with much waste. If the game are all taken or frightened away, the Oglalas will die. When Indians try to trade furs to them, they pay little, and they ask high for their goods. They are filled with greed and deceit."

Singing Wind handed both men buffalo berry wine to wet their throats and to calm them during the tense situation. She returned to her sitting mat and backrest to work and listen.

"We have helped the bluecoats. In what you call '1823,' we rode with Colonel Leavenworth and U.S. troops to defeat the Arikaras. We let the man called George Catlin come to our villages and paint pictures of us on strange paper. We let the one called Francis Parkman visit camps and write words about our tribes and Nation. He stayed long with Chiefs Old Smoke and Whirlwind. Lewis and Clark journeyed our lands. They drew pictures of trees, animals, and plants. They made maps of forests, streams, hills, and trails. They were not harmed. Joe Kenny, father of my brother's wife, was our friend. Soldiers like Sturgis and Ames were our friends. In the old days, few wars came between whites and Indians. Those days are gone."

Joe held silent, alert, and respectful while Sun Cloud sipped his drink. He didn't know which direction this talk was taking.

"Once the Dakotas ruled from Canada to the Platte River, from Minnesota to the Yellowstone. Many of those hunting grounds and streams have been stolen by whites. Tribes have left them or been pushed out by soldiers. When your people signed a treaty with the French called the Louisiana Purchase, it was wrong. They did not own these lands. Now your people will not confess their mistake and leave us in peace. Our ancestors live in the winds that blow over us, in the rains that refresh Mother Earth, in the trees and grasses and flowers that make her beautiful. They live in the glows of the sun and moon, and in all forces of nature that claimed their bodies from death scaffolds. Their spirits live in the hearts and memories of those left behind. They live in the legends they created, in the images of their bloodlines, in the scenes on the tribal record hide, in our songs and stories, and in all they taught us. Now your people want us to forget our dead, our ways, our world. How can a man forget all he is? Does that not make peace cost too much? If you steal all a man has, what good is survival without his spirit and dignity?"

"A good man can't forget what he is, Sun Cloud," Joe concurred. "That's why Stede Gaston came here. We don't want your lands, and we want to make certain others don't steal them. A man can't live without his dignity and honor. The Americans know Dakotas sided with the British during their war for independence and during the War of 1812; what they don't know is that it wasn't the Oglalas. The Dakota Nation is viewed as a whole, and the Americans know it's a strong and large nation. They don't want to fight you."

"They ask for treaties. When we sign, they use them to make soldiers force us from our lands. If we do not mark our names on papers, they cannot lie about us; they cannot say we sold them our lands."

"If you'll sign the new treaty with Fitzpatrick, I'll read every word to you. I'll make certain no tricks or lies are included. You can record every word in your language, then have them sign your paper. If trouble comes again, you can read the treaty to the authorities to prove you're right."

"Their words on paper are worthless."

"No, Sun Cloud," Joe answered him. "Treaties are legal. They're like laws; they can't be broken unless your side declares war on us. If one side wants changes made, a meeting must be called so differences can be discussed. A treaty isn't and can't be destroyed without a good reason. We signed treaties with the British. They're our friends now. We haven't battled in thirty-six years. We visit their countries and trade with them, and they do the same with us. Can you say that about the Crow? President Fillmore will honor the treaty."

"What if another white chief takes his place?"

"We do change leaders more than your people, but new leaders honor treaties and laws other Presidents made. It's our way, Sun Cloud. If you made a treaty with us, wouldn't Night Stalker honor it when he became chief? Wouldn't he need a good reason to break it?"

Sun Cloud watched the white man as he said, "Night Stalker

does not trust whites; he voted against you. If I am slain or hand the bonnet over to him, he will speak against you and for war. Most follow the chief."

Joe was stunned by that revelation, as Morning Star had told him the voting was cast in secret, even though most men voiced their opinions aloud. Unless everyone voted against him and all sticks were black, how could Sun Cloud know which way his son voted? His concern showed.

Morning Star came to sit beside her father. She could stand the suspense no longer, as she knew how worried Joe must be. She gazed into her father's eyes with a pleading she hoped would coax exposure of his good news.

Sun Cloud grasped her unspoken request and the warring emotions within her. He was concerned over how the vote would affect his family. He prayed that she was not the female in Payaba's vision, but feared she was. He speculated that was why the two had been thrown together. He was acquainted with her skills, so he knew she could handle the task. But he didn't want her traveling with Tanner alone for so long.

"What did you vote, Sun Cloud?" Joe asked to break the silence.

"I voted to free you," the older man revealed, then explained the meeting to the other man. "If you lie, I will slay you with my own hands," he warned. "You will leave when the sun rises. Go to the fort and speak with the man you trust there. Return and meet with us. A female will be chosen to travel with you. We will give you until the end of buffalo season to seek and destroy our enemy, or until the bluecoats attack. We will not raid against whites or Crow. If you fail, you must leave our lands."

"It is agreed, Sun Cloud." Joe smiled in relief.

"It is good, Father," Morning Star concurred in excitement. Now that her father had related the events of the meeting, she wouldn't have to fear unmasking herself with careless slips.

"We shall see, Daughter."

"I will gather supplies to be ready to ride when . . . Tanner returns."

"No, Morning Star."

"I am best trained," she argued as dismay filled her.

"Your father's right, Morning Star," Joe concurred

114

prematurely.

"There will be a contest while he is gone. All women who wish to enter may do so. The winner will ride with Tanner Gaston. It will be the female with the most skills and courage who wins. All must have the chance to become She-Who-Rode-With-The-Sky-Warrior. Grandfather did not reveal her face and name to Payaba, but he will choose her in the test."

Joe didn't like that idea, as he somehow knew Morning Star had spoken the truth when she told him she was the best trained. Still, it was a fair way to make a choice. If Sun Cloud's daughter won, it wouldn't be the same as him selecting her above the others, so it shouldn't cause jealousy and trouble. He was elated and alarmed by the prospect of being alone with her.

Morning Star beamed with joy and anticipation. She was eager for the contest to begin, as she felt confident about winning it. What other girl in their tribe could shoot, ride, hunt, and fight as she could? None.

"We must sleep. Have you tended his wound?" Sun Cloud asked.

"Han, Ata," she replied.

"You sleep there," he told Joe, pointing to a mat away from the other three which were positioned close tonight on the other side.

"Pilamaya, Mahpiya Wi," Joe thanked him.

"It is good you learn our tongue and ways. Knowing them, you will not offend with mistakes that can bring shame and death." Sun Cloud glanced at his radiant daughter, then returned his meaningful gaze to the newcomer.

Joe captured the hint in the chief's words and nodded understanding and acceptance, though he knew how hard it would be to keep his word.

They took their places to pass an unusual night. The small, rock-enclosed fire had died. For a time, an unoffensive odor of smoke lingered in the conical dwelling. The top flap was adjusted for the flow of fresh air, but the entry flap was closed for privacy. Except for distant sounds of nocturnal birds, insects, and frogs, it was quiet in this secluded area.

The clean, neat tepee told Joseph Lawrence that Singing Wind was an organized woman. He knew that she and Morning

115

Star had tanned these hides, gathered these poles, and constructed this cozy surrounding. Even though it was too dim to see much, his keen eyes and alert senses had taken in many details during the evening. Six large poles—tall, straight, and debarked—made a sturdy framework, then many slender ones leaned against them to provide strength, support, and shaping. The fifteen-foot pointed cluster was covered by buffalo skins that were laced together by deft hands to stay in place, especially during brisk winds and storms.

A colorfully painted dew-cloth, an added layer of brain-tanned hides stitched together to form a lengthy roll, was suspended from a height of five feet to the ground; this strip discouraged drafts at the base and provided added warmth and beauty for the simple home. It also diverted the rain that could run down the poles to the outside, and created an air flow that forced smoke upward and out the top flap. The numerous lining ties were secured to a rope that went from post to post and was attached to each. Possessions hung from the strong rope: medicine bag, parfleches—the equal of white man's drawers and chests for clothing and such—sewing pouch, weapons—which women never handled—backrests, larger pouches for holding dishes and cookware. When not in use, sitting and sleeping mats were rolled and kept near the tepee base. Joe was amazed that all their worldly possessions could be contained in such a small abode.

Yet Joe knew that Lakotas were nomadic, and that they lived a simple and routine existence. Other than horses, acquired by trade or theft, they cared little for collecting "worldly" riches. He mused on the number and variety of items in his home and in his father's office in Virginia, when this family could hold almost all of their goods inside one Lawrence closet. He thought of the amount of clothing and jewels most women of his acquaintance owned, when Morning Star had only a few garments and modest beadwork. He reflected on the foods and treats that whites loved and demanded during a meal, particularly when dining out, when these people had a simple diet that they themselves gathered or killed.

As Joe's mind drifted before slumber claimed him, he realized again how many differences there were between himself and the daughter of the Red Heart chief. Whites worshipped in churches and learned in schools, while Indians used nature's surroundings or their tepees. Whites executed or jailed criminals, whereas Indians slew or banished theirs. Lakotas met other tribes for exchange fairs or, on a rare occasion, dealt with a post or traveling trader; there were no stores, specialty shops, and busy towns in this territory. There were no trains, ships, or coaches here—only horses and *travois* for travel and transport. There were no theaters for plays and orchestras to offer enjoyment, or casinos for gambling, or businessmen to obtain wanted items, or workers to hire for laborious tasks, or seamstresses to make clothing, or large homes for parties and dances, or servants for doing daily chores.

He had been reared by a wealthy and educated family. But he had Stede, Molly, and Tanner Gaston to thank for teaching him about down-to-earth living. He had learned much from them over the years since meeting Tanner at school. He had spent many holidays in their home and shared many trips with the family. Not that his parents had allowed him to become spoiled, self-indulgent, or lazy—but the Gastons had honed his best traits and had inspired others. To him, Stede and Molly had been like a special uncle and aunt; Tanner had been like his brother.

Tanner—his loss was terrible. Joe couldn't imagine never seeing his best friend again or sharing good times with him. It was painful to think of never hearing Tanner's voice and laughter, of never viewing his lopsided smile, of never hunting and riding side by side, of all the things they would never get to do together, of him missing this soul-stirring adventure. Anger and bitterness gnawed at Joe, and he knew he must find Tanner's murderer.

Tanner would have liked Morning Star and his other Indian relatives. He was liked by nearly everyone he met. He had possessed an instinct about people and he'd known how to deal with all types. Many times Tanner's wits and skills had gotten Joe out of a bad situation or prevented one. Tanner had been easygoing and unique.

Unique, as was his beautiful Indian cousin. Joe was aware of Morning Star's close proximity. Her essence was in the still air

117

and it seemed to engulf him, as if her spirit was touching his flesh from head to toe. He admired and respected her and her parents. He was pleased and proud of his success today. When he left in the morning, he would miss the young woman nearby. He would hurry to return from his trip to Fort Tabor to see Captain James "Jim" Thomas. At least he was grateful that Zeke and his boys were heading in the opposite direction, unless they had used another false trail to mislead him!

Joe was fatigued from riding and worrying, but he was relaxed over the council vote and his acceptance by Sun Cloud. His heavy lids drooped and closed. Soon, he was asleep.

Morning Star was not a captive of slumber but an emotional prisoner of the white man in her home. His pattern of breathing told her his restive spirit had found release. It was wrong, but she wished she were lying on the mat with him. She had felt safe but stimulated at his side. Any distance between them now seemed to evoke a feeling of denial. Yet she must conceal those emotions, must halt and prevent such forbidden desires. Her father believed in avoiding temptations to prevent yielding to them.

Morning Star was tired, but elated. She was eager for Joe to return, and hated for him to leave even for a short period. Soon, they would share so many adventures and confront so many challenges on the trail. She glanced at the shaft of light coming through the ventilation opening at the tepee point. The full moon could not pierce the heavy hides, so the enclosed area was nearly dark. If only they were alone in this cozy . . . Morning Star warned herself again to cease such hopeless yearnings and dreams. She forced her eyes shut and told herself to go to sleep.

Neither was Singing Wind asleep. She hoped that Sun Cloud hadn't noticed the strong pull between their daughter and the grandson of her husband's uncle. She knew that her love, her chief, had enough to worry over without including their youngest child. When Sun Cloud gathered her closer to his body, Singing Wind relaxed and eased into slumber.

Sun Cloud wished he could do the same. He perceived the restlessness in everyone in his tepee. He sensed the attraction between his daughter and new-found cousin. He trusted Morning Star, but love was powerful, often irresistible, as it had been between himself and his wife long ago. He remembered the risks and chances they had taken to be together. He didn't want his child to be hurt by craving a food she must never taste. If only he could keep them apart, their temptation would be easier to control. Maybe she would not win the contest to become Tanner's helper. He would do all he could to make certain she lost. If she won, it would mean it was the will of the Great Spirit. He had made many sacrifices in the past for his people. Surely Wakantanka would not make his daughter another one . . .

As Joe saddled Star, Sun Cloud gave him directions to the fort. The chief tied a beaded band around his forearm with markings that revealed Joe as a friend of the Red Hearts. "If other Dakotas approach, point to the *isto wikan* and say, *Mahpiya Wi, mitakola, mita tahansi*. It means, Sun Cloud, my friend, my cousin. They will let you go in peace. If Crow or Whites approach, remove from your arm and hide."

"*Pilamaya.*" He thanked the chief, then secured his bedroll and rain slicker behind the cantle, and positioned his saddlebags. He suspended a canteen and supply sack over the horn and slid his Sharp's rifle into an oblong leather holster. He was wearing a Colt pistol at his waist, and a knife sheath above his ankle. Tanner had trained him to be a near expert with guns and knives. Joe turned to Sun Cloud. "I'll tell the Army your people aren't responsible for those raids on boats, wagons, homes, and soldiers," he said.

"We raided Crow camps to look for Red Heart arrows to learn if they seek to make us look guilty," Sun Cloud said. "We found none. Many times we find tracks of shod horses, white man's shoes, but we do not know who rides them. They travel too far to follow. We will wait to learn if you can stop the war breeding this season. If you cannot, leave our land and do not get trapped between us."

Joe asked a troubling question. "One thing I don't understand, Sun Cloud; why did you allow a small party to journey to Bear Mountain when there are Crow and bad whites in the area?"

"No Crow or other enemy band will attack a sacred party at a holy place. We did not think the evil whites would be in that area

119

this soon. We believed they would wait for us to move our camps to the plains to hunt buffalo before they cause trouble. Whites do not honor sacred lands and times. Others went because they felt the Great Spirit's call; it is our way."

Singing Wind joined them and handed supplies to Joe: *papa,* dried strips of meat similar to the white man's jerky, *aguyapi,* pones of bread of which half were plain and half were speckled with dried nuts and fruit, and *wakapanpi,* prepared meat and berries — what the white man called pemmican. Still unadjusted to speaking English at this time, she told Joe, *"Ake ecana wancinyankin kte. Wakantanka nici un."*

Morning Star smiled and said, "Mother says, Good-bye, I see you again soon. May Great Spirit go with you and guide you."

Joe smiled and responded, "I'll return as soon as possible. Good-bye, Sun Cloud, Morning Star, Singing Wind. Thanks for everything. I'll do my best to win peace for your people."

Joe mounted his roan, glanced at the three upturned faces, smiled again, and left the camp. As he rode away, he recalled what the chief had told him was the council's orders: the vote was to spare his life, to let him seek an honorable treaty, to allow him to defeat Snake-Man, and to distract their foes during the buffalo hunt. If Joe failed, there would be another council meeting and vote for war. This morning he had noticed Knife-Slayer, Hawk Eyes, and Night Stalker watching his every move and listening to his every word. He prayed that Sun Cloud could control them while he was gone. He kneed Star into a gallop.

Morning Star stood with her father for a time, but she was careful not to stare after Joe as he departed or to expose her warring emotions. It was the first time they had been alone since her return with the white man.

Sun Cloud said in his language, "I am happy you returned home safely, Daughter. It was rash to stray so far from the others."

Morning Star accepted the gentle reprimand with love and respect. "I was distracted while gathering herbs for Payaba, Father. When I saw the two white men, I had to follow them and spy to decide if a warning to our people was needed. They could have been scouts for an attack. My father did not raise a coward, and my mother did not birth a reckless fool. I knew the risks, but chose to take them. A chief's people and his duty come first to him; I am a chief's daughter, so I feel the same. Would you have me do less than I am able because I am a female? I believe my capture was the Great Spirit's plan to allow a meeting with . . . Tanner."

"I believe it is so," he concurred. "You were wise and brave to trust him and to bring him to us, Daughter. Pride lives in my heart for your deed. You have much of your mother's wits, skills, and daring. At your age, she was this same way. But her emotions often ran too deep, like a stream hidden beneath the face of Mother Earth. When heavy rains come, the stream can burst forth from its secret place and do much damage. Too often her love of adventure made her impulsive and willful. The first time I realized how strong my feelings were for Singing Wind, she was trailing white men to spy on them. Many times she rode alone and ignored dangers."

Morning Star laughed and replied, "Those things made her a strong and brave woman, Father, a special one who captured your eye and heart. Only such a woman can be the best wife for a chief."

Sun Cloud grinned and agreed. Then he warned, "If you are to ride with Sky Warrior, Morning Star, always remember you are Oglala, daughter of the chief. Do not let his white ways enter your head and heart."

"I will remember your words and obey them, Father," she responded, then prayed she could keep that promise.

After they parted and she headed to begin her daily chores, Night Stalker approached her. "It is a good day, Brother," she greeted him.

"A good day," he scoffed, "when a white man rides from our camp to expose our strength to the soldiers so they can return and attack?"

Morning Star was dismayed by his distrust and bitterness, by his dangerous need to battle the whites at any cost. "He goes to help us, Brother," she argued, "not to betray us. He and his task were revealed to us in a sacred vision. How can you not believe, accept, and obey that?"

"I am not convinced the vision is real. If it is true, how do we know he is Sky Warrior? Even so, he is but one wolf attacking a herd of strong buffalo. He cannot slay or halt its stampede. He will cease to try and will join them. We have vowed to battle the whites to victory or our deaths. There is no white man's peace without defeat and dishonor. Every treaty has been broken or used against Indians. The whites invade our lands and seek to steal them. They challenge us, spit upon us, curse us. They desire all we have and will slay us to get it. If this is not so, why do more soldiers come and why do they build more forts? They do so to prepare to attack and take. The white man cannot be trusted. He is evil and greedy. He must be pushed back to his lands or destroyed. We wait for Tanner to seek truce while our foes get stronger. It is foolish and deadly."

"No, Brother. If we challenge the whites, we will die. If we do not seek truce with the Bird People, the wars with them will continue forever and will endanger all children to follow us. I will help Tanner seek peace."

Night Stalker's long black mane moved about as he shook his head. "It is not our way for a woman to be a warrior!"

"Our way will die if our foes are not defeated. Tanner is the one to lead us to victory. And I am best trained to become his helper."

"Prove it, Sister," he challenged. "What will you say when you lose the contest Father plans? Will you shame your family with a pride too big? The warrior who boasts loudest is usually the weakest. When the time comes for him to prove his words, his skills fail and dishonor him."

"What will Night Stalker say when his sister wins the contest, and when, at Tanner's side," she retorted, "she obtains peace for our people? You will be chief one day, Brother. The time must come when you think and seek more for survival of our people than for personal coups and honors."

As she stalked away, he murmured to himself, "The granddaughter of Chief Gray Eagle, the child of Chief Sun Cloud, and the sister of future Chief Night Stalker must not shame us or help the whites destroy us. I will make certain you do not, my sister."

Morning Star and Buckskin Girl knelt at the lake's edge and

talked as they washed clothing. The chief's daughter told her best friend of her capture, treatment by the white men, and her time with Joe. Yet she withheld the secret of Joe's true identity and her mixed feelings about him.

The lovely and gentle Buckskin Girl remarked, "I was so worried when you vanished. When scouts found clues to your capture, fear shot into my heart as a flaming arrow. Night Stalker wished to track them and rescue you. If the others had not reasoned with him and changed his mind, he would have done so."

"My brother is blind to the wrongs in his heart, Buckskin Girl. I pray the Great Spirit will clear his eyes and uncloud his mind. When Tanner wins peace for us, Night Stalker will be forced to accept the truth. It will be so exciting. She-Who-Rode-With-The-Sky-Warrior is my destiny."

"What if it is not?" the daughter of Flaming Star asked as she kept her gaze on her chore. "What if it is another's destiny? What if he is not Sky Warrior?" Buckskin Girl hinted at but did not reveal her suspicions or her hopes. The hopeful woman did not want Tanner harmed, but she prayed the real Sky Warrior would arrive soon. No, she corrected, would *return* soon. It was obvious that everyone—except her—had forgotten about his existence. He had been gone for sixteen years from this territory, driven away by shame and anguish, after the war chief's bonnet was stripped from his head by evil. He had gone to the white world to seek himself. Everyone seemed to have forgotten about *Notaxe tse-amo-estse,* the Cheyenne name for Sky Warrior. His father was Cheyenne and his mother was white, but his grandmother was Oglala. Perhaps Stede Gaston was the first man in Payaba's vision, but *Notaxe tse-amo-estse* was the second! His looks and Life Circle matched the vision words perfectly! Soon, the Great Spirit would call him home to her side and to his great destiny!

She missed the blue-eyed, sunny-haired warrior, and she loved him with all her heart. The day Sky Warrior had said, *"Na-ese,"* she had understood the Cheyenne words: "I'm leaving." It had broken her heart, but she had believed he would return one day, especially after she learned of the sacred vision years ago. She had refused to join with another and had lived for the sun when he came back to take his place of honor as foretold in the sacred vision. She knew that Morning Star did not think of Sky Warrior because her friend had been only three winters old when he left. But Tanner's coming was strange. If the vision *was* about Tanner and Morning Star, Buckskin Girl worried, her dreams were over.

Morning Star shook her friend's arm with a wet hand. "You do not hear my voice and words, Buckskin Girl. Where has your mind traveled? Why do you say such things? How can you doubt Payaba's vision?"

Buckskin Girl's dark gaze met her friend's worried one. "I do not doubt it, Morning Star. But you must not dream rashly. I do not wish you to be unhappy if you lose the contest and if Tanner is not the vision helper."

"How can such be true, my friend? I do not understand."

The older maiden chose her words carefully. "It is possible the first man is Stede Gaston, but the second is not his son. Tanner is not the only man with sky eyes and sun hair and white blood. You hunger for him to be the man and you to be the woman, but that will not make it so."

Morning Star looked toward camp as the ceremonial drum, the *can cega,* alerted men to a coming announcement. A verbal message rang out in the air: *"Omniciye ekta u wo"*—Come to the meeting. She knew the contest would be discussed and she was anxious to enter and win it. "You sound as doubtful of Tanner and the vision as my brother and Knife-Slayer. I wish this was not so, my friend."

Buckskin Girl knew how Morning Star would feel tomorrow when she became her challenger, but it was something she must do. She knew that the daughter of Sun Cloud was skilled in many areas, but so was she. She must win the contest, so she would be at her love's side when he replaced Tanner Gaston! But, until everyone was shown the truth of this mistake, it was best to withhold her secrets. If the Great Spirit had a purpose for this episode, she must not intrude. "I am sorry, my friend, but I cannot help what Grandfather places in my heart."

"That is true," Morning Star conceded with reluctance and understanding. She glanced at her friend from lowered eyes. She sensed that something was troubling Buckskin Girl, but a friend did not pry. A good friend stood close and patient until the right time arrived.

As the two females worked in silence, Morning Star wondered how Hawk Eye's vision-quest had gone this morning. She knew the shaman had purified his body in the sweat lodge, then gone into the hills to "find his way to a spiritual path to Grandfather" with the aid of a peyote button. She wondered if the medicine chief would see the truth and, if so, would he speak it? Again, she chided herself for having such wicked thoughts about him.

As Morning Star hurried from the woods with her burden at dusk, Knife-Slayer halted her and said, *"Wociciyaka wacin velo. Unkomani kte lo."*

She did not want to speak with him or to take a walk with him today or any day, and wished he would halt his pursuit of her. "I am busy, Knife-Slayer," she refused in a polite tone.

Morning Star continued on her way, with the man trailing her and urging her to spend time with him. They came to Sun Cloud, Singing Wind, and Hawk Eyes.

Singing Wind smiled and said to her daughter, "You work late. We have eaten. Your food is by the fire. Do not let it get cold."

"I was gathering wood for Payaba and Winter Woman," she responded as she adjusted the loaded carrying sling on her back. The much loved and elderly couple had no children left to help with their chores so many Red Hearts assisted them. Morning Star had deep affection and respect for the past shaman and his wife, and she often did their tasks. "I must fetch water for them from the lake before I eat. Thank you, Mother."

As Morning Star left the small group, she heard Hawk Eyes tell her father that the Great Spirit had told him in his vision today to wait, that He would reveal all soon. She didn't know if that pleased or dismayed her. She heard Knife-Slayer quickly excuse himself from the group, and she prayed he would not follow and join her. She was glad when he did not.

Later, when Morning Star entered her tepee, she sat down by the dying fire, removed the cloth from a bowl, and ate her evening meal.

Sun Cloud and Singing Wind returned an hour later. The

chief explained the contest, revealed the judges, and related the rules. He said it would begin tomorrow and would require all day to complete.

Morning Star was thrilled but apprehensive. By tomorrow night she would know if she was to ride with Joe. She scolded herself for allowing her brother and best friend to shake her self-confidence. Yet what if they were right? What if she did lose? But surely it was not vain or wrong to believe in herself and her skills. Surely Grandfather had thrown her and Joe together to meet and to work as partners.

Morning Star curled into a tight ball and clutched her stomach with her arms. She was nauseous, feverish, and shaky. Beads of moisture dampened her flesh and caused her hair and garments to cling to her body. She heard her stomach rumble in protest as something evil attacked and slashed at it with an unknown knife. Pain seared through her, and she trembled. Her perspiration increased. Her head ached. Her throat warned of a violent eruption in the making. Without pulling on her moccasins, she crept from her sleeping mat and entered the woods near their tepee, thankful for its close location during winter camp.

For over twenty minutes, her body emptied itself. Her weakness increased, and the agony mounted. She shook from illness and fear. Her mouth tasted terrible. She felt awful. Dizziness swept over her, and she clutched a tree to steady herself. When she felt relief for a time, she cleaned the area as best she could.

Morning Star went to the lake to wash out her mouth and to cool her face. She knew she wasn't finished with the strange illness, but she had to lie down or risk fainting. She sought her mat once more.

It wasn't long before she was compelled to dash for the woods again. This time, Singing Wind followed her daughter and asked, *"Nikuja he?"*

When she felt a little better, Morning Star replied, "Yes, Mother, I am sick." She explained the curious illness. "What medicine do you have? I must get well before morning for the contest."

When Singing Wind asked where it hurt, Morning Star

pointed to her stomach as she replied, *"Lel mayazan."*

"I will take you to your mat, then seek Payaba's help."

Morning Star's torment was too great to refuse, despite the late hour. Holding her mother's arm, she return to her mat.

"What is wrong?" Sun Cloud asked from the shadows.

"Anpaowicanhpi li'la kujape." She replied that their child was very ill.

"Do you wish me to call Hawk Eyes to her side?" he inquired.

"Hiya," Morning Star refused in a weak voice.

"Do you wish me to call Payaba?" he offered.

Morning Star nodded and said, *"Han."*

Sun Cloud went to the past shaman's tepee and called out softly to avoid awakening others.

"Tuwa kuja hwo?" The old man asked if he knew the problem.

"It is Morning Star, Wise One." The chief related the symptoms.

Payaba gathered his medicines and followed Sun Cloud to his tepee. Singing Wind had started a fire to give light and to heat any water needed. The white-haired, slump-shouldered man went to the girl's mat and knelt. Her parents hovered nearby, waiting and watching, praying and worrying.

Morning Star and Payaba talked for a time. Then he went to work to prepare a medicinal tea from white oak, water avens, and several herbs to halt the diarrhea and vomiting.

Before it was ready to consume, Morning Star knew she was about to be sick again. "I must go, Mother."

Singing Wind assisted her child into the forest. Morning Star was hunched over with pain, and she could not suppress her groans. When she was finished, they returned to the tepee. The younger woman sank to her damp sleeping mat, exhausted and frightened.

When the tea cooled enough, Payaba handed it to the quivering girl.

When he saw how she was shaking from weakness and fever, Payaba held the cup for her. "Drink, precious one. It will make the leavings of the body firm, not as the running of water. It will stop the food from retreating on the same trail it took inside."

Morning Star drank the bitter liquid, fearing it would return

127

before her aching stomach kept it long enough to do its task. *"T'mapuze."*

"No, you must not drink water until the medicine heals you inside."

For several hours, Morning Star continued her treks into the forest, then returned to drink more tea. She fretted that the liquid was not working and she would grow weaker. Surely she had nothing left inside her body to expel!

At last the bouts ceased and the herbs worked their magic. When she drifted off to sleep, Sun Cloud thanked Payaba and walked him to his tepee. The old shaman had warned Singing Wind not to give her daughter anything to eat or drink until he checked her, in two hours, in the morning.

Sun Cloud cuddled his weary and relieved wife in his arms. He whispered into her ear, "I do not think she can enter the contest today. She is too weak. Perhaps it is the Great Spirit's way of letting another win."

Singing Wind did not believe that was true, but held silent.

The sounds of dogs barking, horses neighing, and people talking and laughing awoke Morning Star. She ached from head to foot. Her mouth was as dry as grass burned by a scorching sun after months without rain. Her stomach was sore from emptiness. Her throat scratched its discomfort. Her chest protested breathing after its exertions last night. She felt as limp as a wet cloth. She was in trouble . . .

Tears misted her dark brown eyes and she fought to control them. She felt awful; but worse, she felt weak as a newborn. How could she participate in the events in the contest today: race, ride, battle a warrior, track, shoot? In her condition, even a strong child could beat her!

"Help me, Great Spirit," she prayed with all her soul and might.

A day's ride from the Red Heart encampment, Joe reined in his horse and stared at the scene before his wide eyes. He was in trouble . . . "God, help me," he prayed with all his soul and might.

Chapter Six

A mounted Indian party had left the trees ahead and had taken a position in Joe's path, watching him with brandished weapons.

The blond-haired man knew it was too late to remove the armband — Sun Cloud's safety token and a connection to the dreaded Sioux — and conceal it. His keen mind, which hadn't detected their presence earlier, took in fifteen warriors who were ready to pursue him if he fled. Yet they appeared content to let him make the first move; be it one of peace, aggression, or cowardice. He was glad they were not wearing warpaint and hadn't ambushed him before giving him time to speak. If he was lucky and clever, and if he made the right choice, maybe he could save his life. He ordered himself to appear unworried, as he'd heard that most Indians respected courage in a foe. He kneed Star's sides and walked his roan toward the waiting men, hoping they were only curious about him.

When he was close enough to view their clothing, Joe recognized the geometric beading design of the Lakotas. Realizing they were not Crow, relief washed over him like a calming wave. Then he remembered Morning Star telling him some bands hated whites and rode as renegades against them. If this was such a band and their hostility was deep, they might not honor Sun Cloud's message. Yet all he could do was approach them.

Joe reined in his horse and used the little sign language he knew. He greeted them by making a combination of three signals: *sunrise, day,* and *good.* He raised his right hand to neck level — palm out and with index and middle fingers touching and extended — then lifted his hand until his fingertips were even with his face: the sign for *friend.* Next he moved his left hand, palm up, to his waist and grasped it with his right, allowing his thumb to rest on the back of it: the sign for *peace.* So far no brave moved, spoke, or threatened him.

The only emotion the chief exposed was interest. His black hair, parted in the center, was straight, breast length, and shiny. His most prominent facial feature was a long nose with a large base. His wide mouth was full lipped; and it was relaxed, neither smiling nor frowning. Joe decided the leader's expression and mood were calm and controlled, as was expected of a man of his rank. An air of dignity exuded from the chief, who appeared to be a sailor's knot under thirty. Then Joe noticed a clue to his identity, or hoped he had.

"Lakota kitnla ia," telling them he spoke very little Lakota. As he waited a response before continuing, his mind drifted for a moment. The elder Tanner Gaston — Powchutu — had taught his son Stede sign language and the Lakota tongue before returning here and dying, almost as if he'd known the man would need them one day. Stede had taught his son and had tried to teach Joe during the journey here and the winter at Fort Laramie. Joe found the Indian language difficult to learn. Their words were not positioned in the same sentence order as English: time was always mentioned first; adjectives and prepositions followed nouns; direct objects went before verbs; plurality was shown with verbs, not nouns; and certain endings identified the sex of the speaker or listener. In many cases, *is* and *was* were left out of sentences, which explained why Morning Star often skipped those English verbs. Too, the Dakota, Nakota, and Lakota dialects differed in some spellings and pronunciations; all reasons why he needed a translator for his coming task.

When the Indians held silent, Joe pointed to his armband, which he was sure had been noticed, and told them he was Sun Cloud's friend and cousin as the Oglala chiefs instructed. *"Nituwe hwo?"* he asked.

"Sinte Galeska," the chief replied. "Spotted Tail of the Brules. I speak white tongue. How is man with white face family of Sun Cloud of Oglalas?"

With brevity, Joe explained his assumed identity and mission to the dark-skinned man wearing a raccoon tail as his medicine and name symbol. His guess was correct; the leader was Spotted Tail, a Brule, a tribe of the Teton branch, as was the Oglala. Tom Fitzpatrick had told him the names and tribes of the most important chiefs in the territory. Spotted Tail was said to be a clever man who was cautious and cunning in his dealings with the whites, a man who preferred truce to war.

Spotted Tail had heard stories of Powchutu and the 1820 ambush, which had occurred three years before his birth. "Evil white men like mist, hard to capture. Wet hand give clue he been there, but bad spirit gone. I trade and speak with whites many times. Since trouble come, whites no trust any Dakota. It bad to see good and bad Indians as one people to attack. It good to seek peace; it hard to find between wolf, buffalo, and bird."

"Han," Joe agreed. Indian Agent Tom Fitzpatrick had told him to use the Indian way of speaking to relax them, to reveal respect, and, of course, to be understood clearly. His comparison was, "Game does not come to a warrior's tepee; he must hunt it or starve. It is the same with truce; peace must be sought and taken into the body or it will die from war wounds."

A suppressed smile caused the chief's eyes to shine. "You speak wise and good for white man," Spotted Tail remarked. "Need more like you."

"Pilamaya." Joe expressed his gratitude.

Spotted Tail translated for his band before telling Joe, "We ride to Sun Cloud camp to speak of new trouble. War rides the wind this season. If you find victory, war not dismount to attack both sides. Go in peace, Tanner Gaston. You be safe in Dakota lands and camps."

Joe signed *good-bye,* then continued his journey. Thoughts of the two great chiefs he had met entered his mind. If all Dakotas were like Sun Cloud and Spotted Tail, he concluded, his search for truce would succeed. But he needed to work rapidly and victoriously before trouble changed their minds. If he didn't fail and it went fast, he would be gone by fall.

Morning Star wandered into his head at that possibility. He could envision her without closing his eyes. She was like stimulating rain that followed a drought; she refreshed his thirsty landscape, gave him new life, and brought beauty to his surroundings. Her aura was like the fragrances of certain flowers whose scents lingered in the air. Being with her was like riding waves in his ship: some were calm and quiet, others tempestuous and rough. He would love to take her on a voyage around

131

the world on one of their ships, show her wonderful sights, and teach her many things. She was too brave and adventurous to be frightened by exotic lands and busy ports. She would be enthralled by all the world offered. There was so much that she didn't know existed, and her hungry spirit would feast on all of it. She was eager to confront the unknown, to overcome obstacles, to endure hardships, to battle dangers. But her challenges were here in her land, for her people, in her culture.

How could an Indian maiden with a simple rearing fit into an aristocratic setting — balls, dinners, theater, and such? He could easily sail anywhere with Morning Star, but he couldn't take her into his society. His fear wasn't that she would embarrass him, as the smart female could learn all the correct things. She would be beautiful in a walking dress with a parasol clutched in her dainty hand or in a riding habit racing over their plantation or in an expensive ball gown with her black hair piled atop her head. Yet she would be like a lost child in his world; she could be hurt, humiliated, and scorned. Too many whites feared and despised all Indians, viewing them as savages. What *she* lacked was the background and education to help her become an accepted part of the southern scene she would enter if . . .

Joe shook his head to clear it of those crazy dreams. He hadn't ridden far when he realized he might have to make camp soon and possibly lose a day's travel. He hated for this trip to take even an hour longer than necessary, but it looked as if it couldn't be helped . . .

Payaba entered Sun Cloud's tepee and went to Morning Star's side. He forced his achy body to kneel beside her mat and his gnarled-fingered hand touched her cheek with gentleness and affection. "Do not fear, precious one," he coaxed. "All goes as Grandfather plans. Does your body heal?"

The weakened maiden related her sorry condition to the wise old shaman who had been like a grandfather to her, as her natural one had died long before her birth. "I will lose, Payaba. I have not the strength to win."

Payaba sent her an encouraging smile. "Drink this soup; it will give you the strength you need. Many special herbs are inside."

Singing Wind returned with water she had fetched. *"Toniktuka he?"*

"I am fine, Mother," Morning Star replied, but knew she was not.

"She must drink the medicine soup. Take her to the water to bathe. It will bring new life to her weary body," he instructed the older woman.

"She must stay on her mat today, Payaba. She is weak and ill."

"No, Singing Wind, she must enter the contest. She will win."

"Was this in your vision, Wise One?" the mother inquired.

The past shaman felt it was not the time to reveal the whole truth. "It is in my heart and head," he replied. "They say she is the one to be chosen."

"How can she enter the contest when she cannot walk from her mat?"

"Before the kettle drum summons her challengers, she will be ready."

The two women watched the elderly man get to his feet with great difficulty and leave their abode.

"Help me to do this, Mother. We must let Grandfather choose."

Singing Wind assisted her ailing daughter to a private area at the serene lake and helped her bathe. Morning Star donned cleaned garments and her moccasins. Singing Wind brushed her hair and braided it, to prevent it from getting into her eyes during the events. When they returned to their tepee, Night Stalker was awaiting them.

"Father says you are not well, Sister. Do not enter the contest. Do not shame us with your loss. Does this illness not tell you the truth?"

Morning Star could not bear the thought of another woman riding with Joe. "It tells me there are evil forces against me, Brother, but I will win."

Before they could argue the issue the *can cega* and *wagmula*—the ceremonial drum and rattle—sent forth the message for the contestants to gather for the beginning of the ritual.

Morning Star summoned all of her strength, will, and courage to face what was before her today. The outcome was in the

133

Great Spirit's hands. She walked to the crowded area with her mother and brother. Her father joined them, and in a quiet voice questioned her health. She told him she was fine, but both realized she was not at her best.

Ceremonial chief Wolf Eyes stepped to the center of the gathering. There was no purification rite in the sweat lodge as the men participated in before their special rituals, and for that, the weakened Morning Star was grateful.

Wolf Eyes lifted the sacred buffalo skull in his hands. It was used in all important ceremonies. Its horns were wrapped with long grass, on which the life and life-sustaining buffalo grazed. Its interior was stuffed with sweetgrass, herbs, sacred tokens, and spring flowers. The painted images upon its prairie-weathered surface depicted sun, rain, lightning, and hail: all forces of nature that his special vision had said to paint there.

Wolf Eyes raised the skull heavenward and used it to salute the north for life, the east for knowledge, the south for quiet meditation, and the west for danger. "Hear us, Grandfather. Your people call you to witness this great event. Judge the women who enter this contest and choose one to carry out the vision you sent to Payaba long ago."

The ceremonial chief placed the skull on a short pole. "*Whope,* sacred White Buffalo Calf Woman, who honors girls as they enter womanhood," he called out. "She who has the power to heal with her touch, whose eyes can pierce the shadows that hide the future, who helped Wakantanka with the creation of His people, watch over and guide your blessed ones this sun."

Morning Star was anxious for the contest to get underway before the little energy she had regained deserted her, but she did not view the ritual as a waste of time. She felt as if her legs were filled with water. She hoped her tremors weren't noticeable to others. Beads of moisture made her feel as if she needed a bath rather than she had just taken one. Her fever was gone, as were her other disturbing symptoms, but the illness had left her feeling powerless in body and spirit.

"Who will step forward to attempt this great task?" Wolf Eyes asked.

Flying Feather, granddaughter of Catch the Bear, was first. Gray Squirrel, granddaughter of Tracks Good, was second.

Comes Running, granddaughter of Wolf Eyes, was third. The fourth competitor shocked Morning Star: Buckskin Girl, her best friend and child of Flaming Star. The daughter of Sun Cloud made the fifth and last contestant.

As this was the result of Payaba's vision and he was one of the few members of the Elk Dreamer Society, he stepped forward to do the ritual dance while the spirits gathered to observe and bless the event. A hair hoop wrapped in flattened and colored porcupine quills with a white downy eagle feather suspended from its center was in a head of white hair, coarse and dulled by age and dryness, above Payaba's left ear. A circle was painted around his body of sagging muscles to symbolize the Hoop of Life. He carried an Elk Dreamer hoop, called a rainbow, in his left hand. The hoop was made from a flexible willow limb, wrapped in furry elk hide and adorned with clusters of herbs, animal claws, and other special tokens revealed to him in his vision. The power of elk medicine was considered very strong and rare.

As the elderly man chanted and danced about the cleared circle, Morning Star's renewed strength faded like a sinking sun. She feared she would faint before he finished and the first event began. Her fingers clutched her thighs to control their quiverings. She locked her knees to halt their wobbling. Nervous perspiration broke out all over her body and heat rosed her cheeks.

Payaba ignored his body's pains to perform the beloved task. His movements were steady, measured, and self-assured. His shoulders and back were bent, and his flowing white hair concealed his lined face as his feet followed a pattern and drumbeat he knew well. When the right moment came, he lifted his head skyward and invoked, "Hear me, Grandfather; Sun Cloud and his people need your help and guidance. Speak to us. Send us a sign."

Those words echoed through the Red Heart chief's head from a distant time when he had spoken the same ones during his Sun Dance ordeal. Many images and memories of that tormenting season raced through his mind, but he tried to push them aside.

Before Payaba completed his prayful chant and sacred dance, the reason Joseph Lawrence feared the delay of his journey neared the camp.

"Icamna lecetkiya," Singing Wind whispered.

Morning Star glanced eastward to see the dark clouds moving toward them fast; it was going to storm, as her mother warned. Suspense and joy filled her heart. Surely that was the answer to her desperate prayers, as a violent storm would postpone the contest and give her time to heal.

The others were so attentive to the ritual that they failed to notice the changing weather. But they couldn't ignore it when the wind suddenly gusted through the trees and clearing. Within minutes, it yanked at hair and garments, stirring up dust. Its power increased rapidly and caused trees to sway and grasses to wave. The sky darkened with speed and vivid flashes of lightning shot across the heaven, followed by a thundering boom. The storm closed in on the encampment, sending forth more streaks of light and loud roars. The sound seemed to echo off the rocks, cliffs, and earth. Large drops of rain began to fall. First the water came down slow, then fast and heavy.

In a short time, everyone was soaked. Drenched garments clung to bodies. Dripping hair stuck to skin. Many women with babies and children raced for their tepees. A dazzling bolt of lightning struck a tree near the edge of camp; it crashed to the ground, and all forces rumbled together. Falling water became as loud as the thunder and the wind.

"It rains too hard!" Wolf Eyes shouted over the combined noises of stormy nature. "The contest must wait until the new sun when it is gone!"

"No! It is bad medicine!" Knife-Slayer shouted. "Payaba used his power and magic to call the storm here to protect Morning Star! She is ill and he fears she will lose! Will it not storm when the winner must do her task at Tanner's side? This is a good test of her skills!"

The ceremonial chief, whose granddaughter was involved, reasoned, "How can they track when rain washes away trails? It must wait."

"If Grandfather has halted the test, Wolf Eyes, there is a reason," the young warrior persisted. "He tells us the test, our help, and a truce are wrong. He shows his anger and prevents it."

Payaba stepped closer to be heard. "Your words are not true.

136

I did not call down the storm. My Elk Dreamer hoop does no evil magic. Grandfather has a reason for us to change the test until another day. It is not my doing."

Three girls shivered and huddled as the chilling rain beat down upon them. Buckskin Girl stood with her father, and Morning Star with hers. The five females, as others still present, could hardly see from the water streaming into their eyes. Mud splattered on everyone's moccasins and legs. The entrants glanced at each other, but none gave her opinion.

Nor did Sun Cloud want to give his, since his daughter was involved. He waited for council members, who would be judges, to cancel the competition. Within minutes, a verbal vote brought the decision nearly all had hoped for: postponement until the next day, if the weather improved.

"Why can we not continue when the rain stops?" Knife-Slayer reasoned. "The ceremonies are done; the spirits have been called."

"And they have spoken for another sun," Payaba responded.

The participants were excused for the day and all raced for their tepees. Sun Cloud grasped his daughter's arm and assisted her back to her home. He turned his back while Singing Wind helped Morning Star get out of her soaked clothes. She dried off the trembling girl and covered her with a warm buffalo hide after she lay down. Before she let her daughter fall into exhausted sleep, Singing Wind urged more herbal tea down her throat.

Morning Star closed her eyes and relaxed; she was rescued for now. She tried not to worry over Buckskin Girl's challenge in the contest. Yet she wondered why her best friend would go against her in this matter. Knowing Flaming Star's daughter, there must be a good reason.

She wondered where Joe was along the trail and how he was doing. She had spent only a short time with him, but she missed him, and longed for his quick and safe return. He inspired such excitement and happiness within her. He made her feel as if she could do anything she attempted. It was as if she were more than only a woman with him. He made her feel braver, smarter, more alive than anyone ever had. With him, she could be her best. She wanted to use and enjoy every moment she could have with him.

137

If only he were truly Tanner Gaston and had Oglala blood and if only he could remain here forever, she daydreamed. No, her drifting mind told her, that would make them grandchildren of half brothers. Was that kinship too close for joining? Before she could reason on the matter, the herbs, warmth, and her fatigue carried her to slumberland.

As Morning Star napped and Singing Wind sewed, Sun Cloud sat on his mat and reflected. He heard the storm unleashing its fury outside and it brought a similar one to mind. Shortly after his father's lethal ambush, which had provoked a rivalry with Bright Arrow for the chiefs bonnet, he had submitted to the Sun Dance. A man's body was all he truly owned and was the most important thing he could offer willingly to the Great spirit as a sacrifice. He had chosen the hanging position which Gray Eagle had endured many seasons earlier. Most warriors used the standing one that allowed their feet to push against the earth to help obtain freedom. The shaman had worried over him participating after just finishing the Sacred Bow ritual and race — which he had won — and subjecting himself to two purification rites in the sweat lodge. He had been tired and weakened, but determined.

The Sun Dance could cost a man his life if his stamina was weak. His chest was pierced with an eagle's claw and thongs were secured around the freed muscles. Then he was suspended by them in the air from a cottonwood post. Never had he known such physical agony. He had hung there for hours as his flesh refused to tear free and release him. It meant either a victory or death ordeal. His face had been painted with the markings of his name and medicine symbols. Just when he feared failure, as Morning Star had today, a violent storm had arisen. The sacred pole had swayed and his body had twirled, shooting more torment through it.

The shaman had jumped to his feet to dance and chant, and no one had left the scene. A vision for victory over their white foes had been given to him, along with personal messages. Lightning had struck the pole, as it had the spruce today, and freed him, as today's storm had rescued his daughter from certain defeat. Rain had smeared his facial paint to make it reflect that of his father's markings. The storm had ceased and the sun had peeked from behind a large white cloud: nature had created his name and symbol in the sky. Many had thought it was the Great Spirit's way of displaying His selection of Sun Cloud over his brother for chief.

"What do you think of, Husband?" Singing Wind inquired.

Sun Cloud related his thoughts. "The Great Spirit and forces of nature helped our daughter this day as they helped me long ago. All within me cries out that she not be the one, for I fear it will take her from us."

"If it is the will of Grandfather, we cannot battle it, Husband."

"That is true. But I will pray she is not His choice."

"As will I, my husband and love."

Wednesday was a glorious day. Payaba came early to check on Morning Star. He asked if she was well and if she could do the contest.

"I am better, Wise One, but my strength is less than usual. I will try to win. Is all prepared?"

"Yes. Our people gather. Come."

Morning Star accompanied Payaba to the chosen area. The ground was soft and wet, but was drying out from sun and breeze. She joined the others. Buckskin Girl did not look her way, and that saddened her. She listened as Wolf Eyes listed the thirteen events. He told how a stone would be given for each victory, and the one with the most stones would be the winner. There would be a drawing in case of a tie, he said.

Wanji, the first event, was in self-defense. Her judge was war chief Lone Horn. The warrior who would test her was Hoka Inyanke, Running Badger, grandson of Plenty Coups and a skilled fighter. It almost seemed as if this first test was meant to eliminate her quickly, as if they doubted her skills and wits following her capture by the white men! At least she would battle the twenty-three-year-old man while she was at her freshest and strongest. She saw the ceremonial chief hand each of the five warriors a strip for binding the wrists of a captured girl — the show of defeat. The females were told they could run anywhere or try anything to elude their captors. The winner was the one who remained free the longest.

139

A signal was given. The girls fled in different directions. Running Badger raced after his target. He was fast and surefooted on the softened terrain, but so was Morning Star. When he closed the distance between them, his arms banded her chest. Quickly she lifted her arms and slipped from his grasp like a slimy eel, causing him to hesitate in surprise. She whirled, rammed her head into his abdomen, and sent him stumbling backward — a tactic she had seen Joe use in the enemy camp. Off she ran once more.

Gaining on her, Running Badger reached the large rock behind which she took refuge to recover her wind. They circled it a few times as the warrior laughed and grinned, but Morning Star never took her eyes from his. Her father had taught her that was where a man exposed his next move if you learned how to read the signs. She didn't drop her attention or laugh when he told her she was as slippery as a wet fish in a greasy hand.

She saw Running Badger step one way, turn rapidly, then flip himself over the obstacle. She got her breathing back under control, dodging his body and eluding his grasping fingers. She ran toward a tepee, but his hand snaked out and seized one of hers. Morning Star yanked it to her lowered head and bit him! When his other hand sought to loosen the one under attack, she clawed at it and jerked free. Once again, she fled.

Running Badger caught up and lunged at the maiden, throwing her off balance. As she landed on the ground, she grabbed a handful of wet dirt and flung it into his face, but it did not have the same effect as when dry and dusty. Thinking fast, she entangled his ankles with hers and tripped him, another trick she had seen Joe use while fighting Zeke. She was up and behind a horse before the warrior could react.

Over the animal's back, the man teased, "You battle dirty."

"Only to win," she retorted. "Today you play my bad enemy, not my good friend. I must do all to defeat you." As those last words left her lips, she stooped and sent her foot upward into his groin beneath the animal's belly. It was a naughty action she hated to use, but felt it necessary.

Running Badger, who had been standing with his legs spread, dropped to his knees and moaned. He saw the sneaky girl race away and knew he must recover and pursue quickly, as his male pride was stung.

A quick glance toward the ceremonial chief told Morning Star the others were captured and bound. Still free, she ran to the war chief's side and asked, "Do I continue, Lone Horn?" To conserve energy, she hoped he would say no.

Wolf Eyes responded for the judge. "The others are bound," he said. "You run free. You fought well. You are winner. Give her a stone, Hawk Eyes."

Morning Star clutched the hard-won prize, then handed it to her father to hold. They exchanged smiles, his eyes full of pride.

The others were cut free for *nunpa,* the second test: English. Thunder Spirit, son of White Arrow, was to quiz and judge her, as he spoke the white man's tongue.

When the event was over, there was a tie between Morning Star and Buckskin Girl, whose father was as skilled in English as his brother, her judge, and he had taught his daughter well.

Hawk Eyes held out his closed fists to the woman he had been wooing for a long time for her to choose first. When he opened the one Buckskin Girl tapped, the second stone was awarded to her.

Morning Star was upset that her best friend had denied her a second victory. Now each possessed one stone. She wondered if the medicine man had intentionally stared at the hand which held the coveted prize.

Yamni, test number three, was to play the part of a squaw, the role which would be used at Joe's side. Each girl acted out a part before the council, who voted on their performances. Each was told why she lost. Morning Star heard that she talked too much and kept her eyes up: squaw should be quiet and humble and almost grovel in fear of her owner! The stone was handed to Flying Feather, who held it up and giggled.

Topa, test number four, was with the bow and arrow. Tracks Good was Morning Star's judge. She tried not to dwell on the two losses and three-way tie, but had trouble keeping them off her mind.

Flaming Star whispered to her to take her time, as he knew she had been ill and weak. He, too, wondered why his child was competing.

When all five of her arrows struck the center of the target,

141

Morning Star won her second stone. She took a deep breath that did not lessen her tension. She knew she was tiring again from her recent sickness. She also knew what loomed before her.

Zaptan was a knife-throwing test. Buckskin Girl won the fifth stone easily, tying her friend once more with two stones each.

Sakpe was a lance-throwing test. Morning Star ordered her arms to stop trembling. She grasped the lengthy weapon and flung it with all her might, but it did not hit the center of the circle drawn on the ground. She watched with apprehension as the other girls hurled theirs. She mopped away glistening perspiration before she handed her third stone to Sun Cloud.

Wolf Eyes announced a break for the girls to rest and to take refreshments. They were given thirty minutes until the next event.

Morning Star went to her tepee and lay down. She had to relax. She had to gain strength. She had to win. She kept recalling what her brother had said about the shame of losing after being so cocky about winning. She admitted that her pride had been too large. The contest was not the "simple" victory she had envisioned it to be.

"Toniktuka he?" Singing Wind asked how she was.

"Weak as a rabbit the moon of its birth," the maiden responded.

"Must you do this, Morning Star? There is no shame in stopping because you are weak from sickness. It is worse to continue and lose."

"As Morning Star, would you quit a task so important?" she asked.

"No, my daughter, I would continue."

'Thank you, Mother," she replied, grateful for the honesty.

Payaba arrived and gave Morning Star soup and tea laced with herbs. "They will give you strength, precious one. Do not be discouraged."

Morning Star consumed the liquids and rested until it was time to rejoin the others. She noticed Hawk Eyes speaking with Buckskin Girl, praising her and wooing her. A surge of anger, frustration, and disappointment engulfed the daughter of Sun

Cloud, and she hurriedly quelled those feelings.

Sakowin was a test for reading tracks and trail signs. Catch the Bear was her judge. It included fourteen parts. She guessed the three smoke signals correctly: one puff for *danger,* two puffs for *all is safe,* and three puffs for *send help.* As each Indian nation had different moccasin prints, it was vital for a tracker to be able to recognize those he found and trailed. She guessed correctly for the Crow, Dakota, Cheyenne, and Pawnee prints. Trail signs were tested, as they gave crucial information: directions, warnings, water locations, and so forth. Most were made of grass bunches tied differently, or rocks stacked in certain patterns and numbers, or cuts made on trees. Morning Star read all seven accurately.

Pleased with herself, she waited for the others to finish. It was another tie between her and — this time — Gray Squirrel for the seventh stone. Tracks Good, her grandfather, had taught her competitor well.

The drawing did not go in her favor, and she lost another stone. It was terrible to lose an event she had done successfully! At least, she reasoned, she was still ahead by one victory. She had to try harder!

Saglogan was another tracking test, a skill vital to survival and success: locating or avoiding enemies and finding game. Each girl was shown to a different starting point and told to return with a certain object. Morning Star's was her father's *wanapin,* his name and medicine symbol. The clues and tracks had been made and the objects hidden during the break. Whoever returned with her object first was the winner.

Morning Star followed the clues into the woods and located her father's medallion. She hurried back to camp, but Gray Squirrel was there holding the eighth stone. She almost wanted to scold Tracks Good for teaching the girl such expert skills. Again, she had succeeded, but still had lost. Perhaps her renewed fatigue was slowing her down and dulling her wits. Now Flying Feather possessed one stone, Buckskin Girl and Gray Squirrel had two each, and Morning Star owned three. Ahead, she fretted, but in danger of being caught up to and passed. At least three of the remaining five events were in her strongest areas, if her lagging body didn't fail her.

The test of *napciunka* should be easy for her: sign language, vital for communicating with friends and foes of other tongues. Hawk Eyes was her judge for the fifty-six chosen signals. She cautioned herself to make no mistakes. When the shaman spoke a word, Morning Star made the motions for it. Some included: counting, tribes, greetings, responses, foods, supplies, colors, trade, gratitude, names, and farewell. Her last two were for indicating tribes. For Crow, she signaled *bird* and *Indian;* for Dakota, she signed "throat cutter," used by others over the correct meaning, *friends*.

Hawk Eyes went to meet with the other judges. Then Wolf Eyes announced a tie between Morning Star and Gray Squirrel. The two females approached the shaman, and Gray Squirrel won her third, the ninth, stone to tie Morning Star in the running for victory.

The chief's daughter was visibly dismayed and fatigued. Buckskin Girl touched her arm and smiled in empathy. At that moment, Morning Star did not feel kindly toward the woman who possessed the two stones she would have herself if Buckskin Girl weren't a challenger. She sensed something was terribly wrong, as if dark forces were trying to defeat her. If only she could draw first one time; if there was another tie, maybe her luck would change! She chided herself for thinking the shaman was to blame for her losses.

"Kiinyanka iyehantu." Wolf Eyes called out it was time to race.

Event number ten — *wikcemna* — was to prove escape skills. The course was marked, and the council as a whole would observe and judge. The five females lined up, readied themselves, then took off at the signal.

Morning Star gave it her all, but she was too weak by now to keep up. After a stumble and near fall, she came in fourth. She watched with envy and discouragement as Comes Running accepted the tenth stone.

"Kuwa iyehantu." Wolf Eyes announced the hunt for food.

Morning Star was aware of her friend's skill with the knife, as Buckskin Girl had taught her how to trap and slay small animals with one! This event was in two parts — *Ake wanji* and *ake numpa:* number eleven was with knife, and number twelve was with a bow. In each, the first girl to return to camp with a kill by the specified weapon was the winner.

After Buckskin Girl accepted her third stone for skill with a knife hunting, there was a three-way tie between her, Morning Star, and Gray Squirrel. Hawk Eyes praised the oldest woman highly.

At the signal, Morning Star raced into the woods, determined not to lose another event and stone. Her pride was taking a beating, as were her body and spirit. She urged herself to win this hunt and the last test. She saw a fawn tangled in underbrush. She knew she must hurry. With reluctance, she lifted her bow, placed her arrow, and drew back the string. From the corner of her eye, Morning Star caught a glimpse of a beautiful doe. The mother deer moved about nervously, sensing danger and refusing to leave her baby imperiled.

Morning Star knew she could not slay the panicked fawn, and knew what her tender-hearted generosity could cost her. She put the bow aside and freed the small creature, who hurried to its mother. She watched the two race off into hiding. She retrieved her weapon, then heard noisy chatter overhead. She looked up and saw a fussing squirrel. Carefully she took aim and brought down the furry rodent. Size didn't matter, only that she used an arrow and returned to camp before the other girls.

Morning Star succeeded, and claimed her fourth—the twelfth—stone. Again, she was one victory ahead of her two closest competitors.

"*Akanyanka iyehantu.*" Wolf Eyes said it was time to test riding skills.

The last event — *ake yamni* — would reveal who could mount, ride, retrieve objects astride the horse, dodge thrown objects as substitutes for arrows and lances, and dismount the fastest.

Morning Star was an expert rider, but so were two of the other girls. To win, she must ignore her lack of strength and energy, as she didn't want another tie or loss. Flaming Star was her judge to see how many or *if* any objects struck her, and to see if she retrieved others fairly. As she lined up with the four girls behind their mounts, she was stunned to see that Buckskin Girl would be riding Knife-Slayer's pinto, a well-trained animal. That told Morning Star that her friend's romantic pursuer wanted her to lose! All she could do was hope that Hanmani did not fail her today.

The signal was given and all ran to their horses having no trouble mounting swiftly and agilely. After three runs of a marked course, each girl raced to her assigned testing area. As each rode her course, warriors jumped from behind rocks, trees, and tepees to try to hit the contestant with soft leather balls. The judge was to count how many struck the female target. Afterward, she was to ride past posts and grab various-size hoops from them, then return to her judge.

Morning Star wondered why her beloved animal faltered several times and seemed agitated. She was third to reach her assigned area. As she galloped that course, only one warrior succeeded in hitting her, and only one hoop was left behind— both results of unusual mistakes by her horse. She urged Hanmani to hurry back to Flaming Star, then dismounted and handed him the hoops. She spoke soothingly to the Appaloosa and noticed how wild-eyed he was. She must ask Payaba to check him.

Wolf Eyes met with the five judges, then announced a tie between Morning Star and Buckskin Girl.

Sun Cloud's daughter knew that if she got the stone, she would win with five of them. If she did not, it would be a four-stone tie, and a final drawing. As feared, Buckskin Girl won her fourth—the thirteenth—stone.

As the council complimented all of the girls on their skills, courage, and victories, Morning Star fretted over another drawing, as she hadn't won a tie yet. She was suspicious of several things—Hanmani's strange behavior, the three drawings to settle ties with a challenger always choosing first and right, and her curious illness the day before. If the Great Spirit rescued her yesterday and helped her save the fawn today, why was He deserting her now? It was disappointing enough to lose fairly, but infuriating to lose unfairly.

"The others also have skills, Morning Star, but that makes yours no less great," Flaming Star murmured. "You did not lose the ties because your skills were less, but from bad luck. If you had not missed one sign, you would be winner without another draw. It is my fault you missed it, as I am the one who taught you

146

and practiced with you."

Morning Star gaped at her elder. "What do you mean? I missed none."

The sixty-eight-year-old Big Belly looked surprised. "Hawk Eyes said you missed one. That is why you tied, then lost."

At that moment, the shaman called the two women to settle the tie and the championship. "Victory is in the hands of the Great Spirit," he said, then extended both closed fists to Buckskin Girl to select one first.

"No," Morning Star refuted, pushing her friend's hand away before it touched Hawk Eyes' left fist. She worried over a loss of face by her challenge of their medicine chief. Yet she despised cheating and defeat.

Sun Cloud stepped forward and asked, "What is wrong, Daughter? It does not matter who chooses first. Grandfather is in control of victory."

Morning Star's determined gaze met her father's confused one. "Flaming Star said a strange thing," she explained. "Hawk Eyes told the others I missed a signal in the sign language test. That is why Gray Squirrel tied with me and she drew the winning stone. I say, I missed none!"

The crowd was silent and alert. Sun Cloud looked dismayed by his daughter's challenge of the shaman's honesty. Hawk Eyes looked angered by the bold insult on his honor. Morning Star locked her gaze to the shaman's.

"I missed none, Hawk Eyes," she stressed with confidence.

"She did not give the correct sign for *treaty*," he alleged. "She —"

"No!" The girl shouted at him to halt, shocking everyone. "Speak only the word, then Wolf Eyes will watch me give it to see if I was wrong."

"You say I did not speak the truth?" Hawk Eyes asked indignantly.

"I say you made the mistake, not Morning Star," she replied.

Sun Cloud was distressed by his daughter's behavior. A woman did not speak this way to a man, especially to a holy man, a council member! Even though she had chosen her words and reply carefully, she had called him a liar, a cheater. If she was wrong, she and all in her tepee would be dishonored. Yet he had

147

never known his daughter to be rude and unkind. It was obvious she believed she was right and that this victory was important to her. Too, she was still suffering from her recent illness and was not herself.

Wolf Eyes eased a difficult situation by saying, "I will ask her."

"If you give our chief's daughter a chance to correct a mistake, to be fair, you must do the same with the others," Hawk Eyes argued.

"I made no mistake," the maiden emphasized.

Wolf Eye asked the other females if they would be troubled by his testing Morning Star's challenge.

Flying Feather, who had entered the contest for the fun of it, replied, "I lost the other stones fairly. I do not wish to repeat any test. It is her right to lose only because she was wrong. Ask the word again."

"It is the same with me, Grandfather," Comes Running added.

Gray Squirrel, who was serious in her vie for the championship, said, "Morning Star is skilled in sign language. It is strange she was wrong. If she missed before, she will miss again. Ask her, Wolf Eyes."

Buckskin Girl had no choice but to say, "I wish to win, so my feelings are confused. I will accept the ceremonial chief's decision."

Morning Star, who was well liked by the other girls, was grateful for their understanding and help and relieved that none of them protested. She sent each girl a smile of thanks. Even though she did not comprehend Buckskin Girl's motive for competing, she appreciated her honesty.

"It is agreed to test the word again," Wolf Eyes said. "Morning Star, what is the sign for *treaty* between two tribes?"

The maiden moved her hands to give the signals for *much, smoke,* and *handshake.* "Is that not right?" she inquired with confidence.

Hawk Eyes debated. "She is right this time, but in the test, she gave the signs for *handshake* and *white;* that is the sign for treaty with a white man, not with another tribe."

"She is right," Flaming Star announced to the whispering

crowd. "She must be proclaimed winner."

"She was ill and shaky; she was wrong," Hawk Eyes protested.

"No," she argued on her own behalf, "I was not. Perhaps in the excitement, you were confused. Flaming Star taught me well. I did not confuse the two different signs. I swear on my life and honor."

Wolf Eyes, ceremonial chief, suggested, "Why do we not repeat one of the events to settle this disputed tie? This will make the victor win on her skills, not on luck or mistakes."

The council members quickly nodded agreement to the solution.

"The sun will sleep soon," Hawk Eyes said. "Tracking is too long. They are skilled at all others. Use the foot race. It is quick and fair."

Morning Star guessed why the medicine chief selected that event; he realized she had little or no strength left to run a race against Buckskin Girl. Yet, she could not demand one of the other tests, in which all knew she was strong; she could not refuse a deciding test she had risked dishonor to obtain. She nodded.

Buckskin Girl knew she had an advantage in strength over Morning Star so she held silent. She wanted to win. She truly believed the white man was not Sky Warrior in the sacred vision. When her lost love returned and claimed that rank from Tanner Gaston, all would understand her motive, especially her friend. To ride at her love's side, she must become the vision woman. Perhaps the Great Spirit had weakened Morning Star so she herself could become victor. With her friend at her best, the contest would have been won easily by the chief's daughter.

Darkness settled on the land as the talk took place. "Night blankets us," Wolf Eyes said. "They will race when the sun returns. They can rest and grow strong while *Wi* sleeps. The race will be fair to both."

Hawk Eyes disagreed, as did his son, but they were out-voted. The shaman wanted the race run immediately and for Buckskin Girl to triumph so everyone would be convinced he had not cheated to prevent Morning Star's victory. He was annoyed that Flaming Star had exposed the error, and furious that she had

149

challenged him. He had promised his son to help defeat the chief's daughter, whom Knife-Slayer was determined to take as wife because of her beauty and rank. His son would do anything to keep Morning Star from riding away and spending time alone with a white man. If the contest had taken place yesterday while she was sick, she would have lost quickly and easily. After everyone left the clearing and there would be no tie-breaking draw, he tossed away a stone from each hand . . .

Upon rising, Morning Star pulled on her soft buckskin garment, braided her hair, and left to be excused in the nearby forest.

Knife-Slayer entered the chief's tepee when the maiden was out of sight. He greeted Singing Wind and handed her berry-and-nut speckled pones. He smiled and said, "Mother says they will help Morning Star regain her strength. She does not want Singing Wind and her daughter to believe Father thinks badly of Morning Star for her challenge."

As he talked, Knife-Slayer noticed the empty bowl that indicated Sun Cloud had eaten his early meal and left. He saw two others prepared for the women. Upon his entrance, Singing Wind had set one down from which she was about to eat. That told him the other bowl was Morning Star's. When the woman turned to put aside the gift he had brought, he dropped herbs into the bowl.

Singing Wind faced him and said, "Thank Waterlily for her kindness. Tell Hawk Eyes we have no bad feelings for the mistake on the past sun."

Knife-Slayer did not debate her choice of words. He smiled, nodded, and left. He went to prepare himself to witness Morning Star's defeat and to give her comfort in his arms.

Morning Star returned to her tepee, lifted a bowl, and ate . . .

Chapter Seven

Morning Star glanced up as her mother returned to their te-pee. "Where did you go?" she asked. "Your food grows cold."

Singing Wind related the visit by Knife-Slayer, then said, "We have plenty, so I took the fruit pones to Winter Woman and Pay-aba."

"Knife-Slayer and Hawk Eyes waste words on apologies that do not come from their hearts," Morning Star contended. "Both desired me to lose." She revealed her suspicions to the shocked woman.

"You should not say or think such wicked things, Daughter."

"Should I hold silent to my mother about what is in my heart?"

"No, Morning Star. I am happy you share all things with me. I worry that the contest is too important to you and blinds you."

"Have you known me to do my skills so badly?"

"You have been ill, Daughter," Singing Wing reminded.

"What of Hanmani's strange behavior? What of losing all ties? What of letting others always choose first in the draws? What of Hawk Eyes' mistake? What of his protests and the bad feelings he showed?"

"Payaba said your horse is fine. Perhaps Hawk Eyes did not realize he made you choose last each time or did not want to show favor for his chief's daughter. You challenged him, Morn-ing Star, and he feared trouble and dishonor. He only wished the contest to be fair for all who entered it."

"That is why he insisted upon a foot race when he knew I was too weak to win it?" she asserted skeptically.

"All agreed it was the best choice to settle the dispute."

"All did not demand it be run in darkness."

"Do you have ways to prove your claims against him?"

151

"No, Mother, and I will say nothing to him or to others."

"That is best. In this time of trouble and danger, we do not need more. You are well this sun. The race will be fair."

"I would be winner without trouble if Buckskin Girl had not entered the test. She is my friend. I do not understand why she challenges me."

Singing Wind saw how hurt and confused her daughter was. "It is a great honor to become the vision woman," she pointed out. "Buckskin Girl has many skills. Must friendship make her deny them and not chase after her desires?"

"But she knows how much I want this task."

"And you must see how much *she* wants it. What did she tell you?"

"She asked, 'What if it is another's destiny? What if he is not Sky Warrior?' How can she doubt the truth? He matches the vision."

"Are there clues in her words?" the mother inquired.

The younger female mused a minute, then suggested, "Perhaps she thinks it is her destiny. She told me she could not help what Grandfather places in her heart. She did not warn me she believed His message was for her to enter the contest! There is a strangeness in her gaze and spirit she will not explain. I do not know why she makes me wait for the truth. We have not kept secrets from each other before this time."

A brief moment of guilt chewed on Morning Star as she remembered she did withhold a large secret from her best friend. Her tone altered from dismay to anger as she revealed, "She does not trust Hawk Eyes, but she did not speak for fairness or defend me on the past sun. I do not wish this to come between us, but she hungers too greatly to win."

"And Morning Star does not hunger just as greatly to win?"

"I have good reasons," the girl avowed.

"How do you know she does not, if she holds silent?"

Morning Star wondered if Buckskin Girl wanted to win to keep her and Joe apart. Did Buckskin Girl sense her feelings and dangerous weakness for "Tanner" and was trying to protect her from herself and shame? Or protect her from the journey's perils? If such was true, why not reveal it? No, the maiden deduced, that was not her friend's motive.

"Accept what happens as Grandfather's will," Singing Wind urged.

The troubled girl nodded a promise, then changed that subject. "Eat, for we must do our chores before it is time for the race."

Singing Wind reached for her bowl. It was gone. "Did you take the food from here?" she asked, pointing to a sitting mat.

"Yes. Was it not for me?"

The older woman smiled and answered, "It was mine, but it does not matter. I will take the bowl I prepared for you and left by the fire."

"I go to see if Hanmani is fine this sun. I will return soon for chores."

Spotted Tail and his party arrived in Sun Cloud's camp. The Red Heart chief greeted them and talked for a while. He invited the Brule chief to his tepee for refreshment, as was their way. The other warriors made camp at the edge of the village, then spread out to visit with friends.

Morning Star saw the visitors arrive and enter her home. She went to the lake to tell her mother of their guests. Singing Wind's water bags were there, but she was not. The maiden looked around, but did not sight her. She filled the bags and joined her father and Spotted Tail. After welcoming the young chief to their camp, she served the men water and fruit pones. "While you speak, I will fetch Mother. She does chores now."

Morning Star searched for her mother, to learn Fast Hands saw her enter the trees earlier. The maiden followed the woman's directions. She called out, *"Ina!"* and her ears captured a faint response. When she located Singing Wind, the older woman was doubled over and violently ill. *"Ina?"*

She looked up at her daughter and said, "Help me to my mat."

Morning Star realized that her mother was attacked by the same strange illness she had had. Recalling how many times she had dashed to the woods for her body to empty itself, she knew her mother would not want to display such private and uncontrollable behavior before a visitor. "We have a guest. Chief Spotted Tail visits with a small band. I served pones and water, then

153

came to seek you. I will take you to Payaba. He will make you well, as he did Morning Star. Do not worry; I will tend our guest."

As the ailing woman lay in misery on a mat in the old shaman's tepee, Winter Woman and Payaba tended her. She drank the healing tea that the old man prepared from special herbs.

"Did you eat any of the pones Knife-Slayer brought to you?" Morning Star asked in a near whisper.

"No," the woman replied, but she grasped her daughter's meaning.

"Were our bowls waiting while he was there?" Morning Star asked.

"Yes, but he was not alone with them. I looked away but a moment."

"Evil can work swiftly, Mother. Did he know which was mine?"

Singing Wind thought a moment, then admitted, "Yes. I was holding mine when he entered. He saw me place it on the mat. You ate it."

"And you ate mine, after he left. Have you forgotten I ate from another waiting bowl before I became ill? Knife-Slayer heard you tell me it was ready. He heard me say I had a task to finish before I returned."

"Do you say he put something in both to make you ill?"

"He wants for me to lose, Mother. He was with the horses before the race to fetch his for Buckskin Girl. Perhaps he gave something to Hanmani."

"That is wicked, Daughter, your thoughts and words," she chided.

"No, Mother, what he has done is wicked."

"There can be truth in her claims, Singing Wind," Payaba related. "There are plants which bring on such sickness. Hawk Eyes knows them. In my vision long ago, Grandfather warned that some would try to stop it. I have not forgotten how Hawk Eyes convinced all I was dying and took my place. He is the reason I am called Pushed Aside, not Standing Tree."

Morning Star saw how this conversation was distressing her mother. "We will speak of this later when you are well," she said.

"Until he is caught doing evil, do not accuse him, Daughter.

154

Your father has many worries on his mind. Without proof, do not add another. After your challenge of Hawk Eyes, it will make bad trouble."

Morning Star stroked the woman's moist brow. "We will say nothing, Mother, but we will be alert to more mischief."

Payaba nodded agreement to the necessary silence. He, too, had been suspicious, but hadn't mentioned it to anyone. He was glad Morning Star had the intelligence to notice the same clues he himself had. "I will heal her. She will remain here with us. Go, tend your guest. Win the race."

"It is to be, Wise One; I feel it in my heart."

The white-haired man smiled and nodded agreement once more.

"Mother is ill, Father. Payaba tends her in his tepee. Do not worry. He says she will be fine by the new sun. When the race is over, I will prepare food for Spotted Tail, our honored guest."

"Your father told me of the vision and contest, Morning Star. If the storm had not forced us to camp all day, we would have witnessed it. I wish victory this day for the daughter of a great chief. On the trail I met the white man called Tanner Gaston, family of Sun Cloud. His task is large."

"Obtaining peace is never an easy one, our friend. Will you vote for treaty when the time comes?" she couldn't help but ask.

"Peace with honor is a greater task. If the whites offer it, I will accept. When you ride with Sky Warrior, seek rest and safety in my camp."

Morning Star smiled and thanked him. News of Joe warmed her heart and sent surges of energy through her body. She felt wonderful today, her old self again. She could tell that Joe had impressed the Brule chief, and that pleased her. She wondered if he had been delayed by the storm, too.

The ceremonial drum began its summons for the race. Morning Star left the tepee and headed for the clearing ahead of her father and guest. Her brother halted her before she reached the appointed spot.

"I have seen Mother in Payaba's tepee. She is very ill. You brought the white man's disease to our father's tepee and our camp. It attacked you and Hanmani, then our mother. Pray

155

your evil does not slay her and others."

Morning Star resented his remarks. She was not to blame. "That is cruel, Brother. And how did you know Hanmani was sick?" she asked, wondering if she had judged the wrong man guilty of wickedness.

As he stroked the lance scar on the side of his face, inflicted by a Crow weapon, he answered, "I heard you tell Payaba to check him. Why do you do this evil thing, Sister? Your words shamed you and your family on the past sun."

She stared at him and wondered how he could be so different from their father. "If a man is wrong, does Night Stalker not challenge him?"

"I am a man. As a woman, you gave great insult to our shaman."

"Should I yield and lose so great a victory when he was mistaken?"

"Was he, Sister?" her brother scoffed.

"Yes, Night Stalker," she responded. She was tempted to reveal her suspicions, but kept her promise to keep silent about them. Besides, her brother was close friends with Knife-Slayer, and he was in favor of war. When the truth was placed in her hands, she would pass it to his!

Morning Star left Night Stalker standing there, staring at her retreating back. She encountered Buckskin Girl on her way to the clearing to compete with her. "Why do you challenge me, my friend?" she asked her friend.

"When the time comes, you will learn all things," the daughter of Flaming Star replied. "I must do this, Morning Star. I do not challenge to hurt you. When the truth is revealed, you will understand and accept why I seek to win. I cannot speak such words today, but I am happy we race when you are stronger. It is fair. Know you are my friend and I love you."

As the female walked away, Morning Star prayed, Wakantanka, *omakiyi:* Great Spirit, help me. This was it, her final chance for victory.

The two competitors lined up at the starting point. After her earlier words, Morning Star glanced at Buckskin Girl and smiled. No matter if she was wrong, Buckskin Girl was her friend and felt she must do this deed. Surely Grandfather had a

156

good reason for it, one He would reveal soon.

Wolf Eyes gave the signal, and the two females raced toward a marked point. They remained even at the turning spot and down the return stretch. At the last minute, Morning Star thought of Joe and surged forward to be the first to cross the line drawn on Mother Earth. The ceremonial chief handed her the thirteenth stone and announced her as the winner.

Morning Star grinned at her father as she recovered her breath. Buckskin Girl congratulated her with a sad smile and walked away in an aura of depression, to be halted by Hawk Eyes wanting to console and woo her. Morning Star wondered why her friend was so upset, but knew she would learn the reason one day. She read pride and concern in her father's gaze. When she joined him, he spoke to her.

"This sacred event must be painted upon the tribal and our family's buffalo records. I am proud, my daughter," he said before the others, but his heart drummed in trepidation of what the victory could cost him.

Spotted Tail smiled and remarked, "It is good to know Morning Star will become the legend She-Who-Rode-With-The-Sky-Warrior."

"Pilamaya, Sinte Geleska."

As Morning Star envisioned her coup upon the pictorial records, her heart raced with excitement and pride. She had known Joseph Lawrence for the passings of only seven moons, and already he had changed her life. She could not imagine exactly how traveling and working with him for many full moons would alter her and her existence. Yet she knew and accepted that he was a vital part of her destiny.

At dusk, Joseph Lawrence reached Fort Tabor. Sunday's storm had passed his location quickly, then settled over the Black Hills without delaying him. After concealing his Lakota armband, he entered the military site, a small one built in '49. He located Captain James Thomas and introduced himself. As he sat across the desk from the officer in charge, he looked into the brown eyes of the sandy-haired man with tall and lanky body and pleasant expression who immediately said to call him Jim.

Joe revealed that Tom Fitzpatrick had said James was the man to see in this area. "He has great faith in you, Jim."

"That's good to hear, but why did Tom send you to me?"

"You know about the big treaty he's working on . . ." Joe began and the officer nodded. "He thinks somebody is trying to prevent it, to stir up trouble between the Dakotas and Crow. If those two nations go on the warpath, whites will be trapped in the middle of a bloody and violent confrontation. Every wagon train passing through this area will be in danger, and so will every soldier and settler in these parts. The trappers and traders won't be any safer, either, despite how long they've been here."

Joe explained who Stede Gaston was and why he had come to this territory. The captain recognized the names Sun Cloud and Gray Eagle, and he displayed instant interest. Joe disclosed his mission with Tanner, and Tanner's subsequent murder. He told Jim about his run-in with Zeke and his boys and about his rescue of Sun Cloud's daughter and the visit to the Oglala camp, and described his meeting on the trail with the Brule chief. "From what I've seen and heard, Jim, I think somebody is trying to frame the Dakotas, make whites terrified of them so the Army will wipe them out for him. I believe the villain is Snake-Man." Joe passed along the scanty description that Morning Star had given him from Knife-Slayer's spying.

Captain James Thomas propped his arms on his desk and leaned forward. "I've heard rumors about such a man, but I haven't talked to anyone who's willing to say he's met him. The Crow say he's a good spirit, not a real man. They claim he doesn't give or sell them weapons and whiskey. They claim the Dakotas lie to provoke soldiers into attacking Crow camps to recover arms and firewater that do not exist."

"They're wrong, or lying to cover their guilt and connection. He's real, and he's fooling them with Oriental magic," Joe insisted, then explained his suspicions. "I know Zeke and his boys were hauling guns and whiskey, probably to the Crow; that's where their trail headed."

"I've seen Zeke, Clem, and Farley around here and at trading posts. From what I know, Zeke works for himself. He hires out to any trader to haul goods. But I didn't realize he was carrying illegal supplies to the Indians. I'll question him later."

"Zeke might claim he works for himself, but he doesn't. He's hired by somebody he calls 'Boss.' I heard his boys slip up and so did Morning Star."

"I'll keep that in mind, and I won't drop any clues to him. If he knows you're on to him, he'll be more careful."

"After what happened between us on the trail, I can't get near him. What I'm certain of is that the Dakotas, most of them, want peace, and they're not making those attacks I've heard about. They're still in winter camps. Spotted Tail was traveling only to speak to Sun Cloud about the new trouble and accusations. I was impressed by both chiefs."

Jim sipped his cool coffee. "I've been here almost a year and I haven't met either one. I'm surprised you got in and out of that Oglala camp alive with your light hair. You're lucky they befriended you."

"They had good reason; I claimed to be Tanner Gaston so they'd accept me and help me. Once the treaty is signed, I'll tell Sun Cloud the truth. For now, as long as he thinks I'm his kin, I'm safe. You'll need to keep my work for Fitzpatrick and that lie to Sun Cloud secret."

Jim leaned back in his wooden chair and relaxed. "You have my word. I want peace, too, so I hope you succeed. I'll give any help I can."

"Tell me, what would Snake-Man have to gain with new trouble?"

Jim leaned forward again, his expression serious. "If he gets the Dakotas pushed out by Crow or whites, and he has enough men and money to take control of large tracks of land, he'll be rich and powerful. There are valuable furs and hides for the taking or buying. Most of the timber, certainly the best, is along the rivers and in those Black Hills. Endless miles of grasslands make for good ranching. The soil is fertile for farms, and not much clearing is necessary. There are plenty of rivers for water and for easy travel. In he gets into trading posts, supplies for settlers and wagon trains could bring in a fortune. Not to mention if he brings in women and whiskey for soldiers. Some old-timers speak of gold, but even the Crow won't tell where it is or use it for trade. That's one secret all Indians realize is dangerous. All he has to do is stop the treaty and keep gaining strongholds. To do that, he has to stir up big trouble. I hope you're wrong, but I'm afraid you aren't. How you planning to work this mission?"

Tom Fitzpatrick had told him to confide in and to work with this man, so Joe trusted Jim. "When I leave, I'm going back to Sun Cloud's camp. They're letting me borrow their smartest female to act as my guide and translator. I'll pretend to be a traveling trader and she'll be my squaw. We should be able to get into and out of most Indian camps and settled areas. If all goes well, I should pick up clues."

"Sounds clever but dangerous. Don't tangle with Zeke again. He'll be looking for you with blood in his eye. He's big and mean and strong."

"Does he work one post and area more than the others?"

"Not that I know of. Most of my time is spent on the post or close by."

"Tanner and I met some of the men at Lookout. Those Columbia Fur boys seemed all right; nothing that sparked suspicion. Simon Adams at Pratte's was busy and only talked to us a little, but we overheard some things he said to others. He didn't make any secret of how much he hates the Indians, but a lot of white men feel the same."

"If you'd been here as long as some of them and experienced what they have," Jim explained, "you'd understand their feelings, even though most are mistaken. Trouble is, all Indians get blamed for the raids and brutalities of a few bands of renegades. Overeager or confused officers order retaliations on the wrong bands. Or whites join together and attack hunters. Then the Indians blame all whites and soldiers for the actions of a few. It's a crazy circle, Joe. Biggest problem is that neither side takes the time to get to know the other. We're all too wary. I doubt that will ever change. All a new treaty will do is hold off the inevitable a while longer."

Joe feared the captain was accurate in his assessment. He returned to Simon Adams. "Men who have something to hide and protect usually aren't as verbal as Adams was about their feelings," he said to Jim. "I could be wrong; it could be an act. He was a big man and he wore long sleeves. He could be this Snake-Man. He warned me and Tanner about the Lakotas, just before my friend was killed. I'm sure Tanner saw or heard something more than he was able to tell me before he died. At least, they thought he witnessed something damaging. The owner, Bernard Pratte, wasn't around, so I don't have an impression of him. We didn't make it north to McMichael's post."

"Bernard Pratte's a last choice for Snake-Man," Jim asserted. "He's been there since '31; that's a long time to wait to cause trouble. Most Indians like him and deal with him over the other traders. Orin McMichael seems a pretty good fellow, too, a jolly Scotsman. Hasn't given us any trouble. He stays close to his post and runs it himself. I do know Zeke hauls for Pratte. Why didn't you and Tanner come to see me before roaming around?"

"I wish we had; he might still be alive. Tanner suggested we look around and get a feel of the area before seeing you. I was riding with him, so I let him do the planning and deciding."

"You don't have any idea who killed Tanner Gaston or why?"

Joe revealed what his friend had told him. "Not much to go on, but that's why I followed those ruts left by Zeke's wagons."

"Too bad you didn't find anything out. Make sure you visit me often now and keep me informed of what you learn. I won't make out a report on this. I wouldn't want someone finding that file about you. A man doesn't always know whom he can trust. Who will you be traveling as?"

"Joseph Lawrence. I don't want anyone connecting me to Stede Gaston at Fort Laramie. Besides, Simon Adams and Zeke know me by that name, and know about Tanner's murder, so it might stir up suspicions if I use his name. I'm sure Snake-Man has spies everywhere."

"Was Zeke around Pratte's that day? You said he knew about Tanner."

"I didn't see him. But if he's working for Snake-Man, he knows."

They talked a while longer. Then Jim stood, shook hands with Joe, and said, "Good luck. Be careful out there. And don't forget your reports."

"Thanks, Jim. I can use your help. I'll keep you informed."

Before Joe left Fort Tabor the next morning, he wrote and mailed two letters: one to his parents and one to his married sister. He told them all of his challenging work here with Stede for peace, of meeting Stede's Indian kin, and of how beautiful this area was. He didn't mention Tanner's death, as he didn't want to worry them. He closed by saying he would be home in six months. He asked his sister to keep an eye on their parents until he returned, as his father had been upset by Joe's decision to come here. In time, he hoped his father would understand why it was so important to him.

As he rode away, Joe's mind was on the loss of his best friend. He wished Tanner was with him, sharing this ultimately fulfilling task. He wished Tanner could have met his Indian relatives. He missed their talks and friendship. It was hard to accept they were gone forever. He vowed anew that he would not rest or quit until his friend's murderer was punished.

Joe pushed his grief into the back corner of his mind by thinking of Morning Star. He could hardly wait to see her again. Soon . . .

The daughter of Sun Cloud completed her chores and visited with Hanmani, whose curious behavior had been exhibited only during the riding event. It had been four moons since the winning race against her friend. Spotted Tail and his band had left the following day to visit with Oglala chief Red Cloud, another powerful leader. Singing Wind had healed within two days, as Morning Star herself had. Her brother was still urging her not to ride with Joe. Though her father had painted her coup upon the pictorial records of the tribe and their family, she had noticed how quiet he was; she knew he did not want her to leave but felt he must say and do nothing to stop her.

Buckskin Girl had not explained her curious challenge, but still vowed to reveal the motive soon. Her friend seemed disappointed over her loss of the contest. They continued to share chores, but something was different between them. Buckskin Girl seemed unsure of herself and a little distant. Morning Star wished she knew why.

Morning Star recalled an exciting episode that had taken place two days ago. Wind Bird's vision quest had shown him an elk and he had been taken into the Elk Dreamer Society. Payaba was teaching and training him to be a shaman. Naturally that did not please Hawk Eyes, as a tribe had only one medicine chief. She hoped something, a message or sign from the Great Spirit, would return Payaba to that rank; or He would let it pass to Wind Bird. She had been polite to Hawk Eyes, but his resentment toward her remained obvious.

Knife-Slayer, his son, was pursuing her with frequency and boldness since her victory. As if thinking of him summoned him, the Indian brave approached.

"*Wociciyaka wacin yelo.*" He said he wished to speak with her.

"*Takuwe he?*" she asked, dreading another annoying conversation.

"*Ye sni yo. Hecetu sni ye. Hanke-wasicun, sunka-ska* Tanner!*"

She was vexed when he told her not to go with Joe. She was angered by him calling "Tanner" a half-breed and a white dog. "*Wacin nis econ akinica he?*" She asked him if he wished to argue.

"*Hiya,*" he quickly refuted. "*Waste cedake. Nis wacin.*" He vowed his love and desire for her.

Morning Star knew that desire was to marry her, and though she had rejected him many times, he kept asking? "*Okihisni Anpaowicanhpi.*" She told him she could not accept.

"*Micante petani niye,*" he vowed.

The maiden did not believe she was the fire in his heart. She replied, "*Micante wookiye wacin,*" telling him that the fire in *her* heart was a flaming desire for peace. She accused him of wanting to go on the warpath, which they both knew was true. "*Zuya iyaka nis wacin!*"

"*Oyate makoce unkita kici kiza ecinsni toktuka hwo?*" he contended.

His words—"How is it wrong to fight for our people and land?"—drummed through her head. He was a quick and clever debater. Yet she countered with haste, "*Wiconi wowahwa.*"

He wanted to shout her foolish words—"Peace is life"—back into her beautiful face. How could someone so smart, brave, and skilled work for costly peace against such fierce enemies? he fumed. "*Wimacasa yelo! Wicasa iyecel mat'in kte yelo!*" he vowed: I am a man! I will die like a man!

Morning Star shook her head in vexation, turned, and left

163

him.

Knife-Slayer glared at her retreat and vowed to himself, *Mitawa Anpaowicanhpe! Wicasta wanzi tohni icu kte sni!*

If Sun Cloud's daughter had overheard the ominous words of his vow — "Morning Star is mine! I will let no man take her from me!" — her troubled heart would have pounded in trepidation.

The following day, as Morning Star and Singing Wind left the forest with loaded wood slings, both sighted Joe's horse tethered near their tepee at the same time. Apprehension washed over the mother as she realized what the white man's return meant, the departure and perilous task of her daughter. But suspense and joy raced through the maiden as she comprehended that the moment to seek her true fate had arrived.

"Tanner has come," Singing Wind murmured. "Soon, you must go."

"Do not be sad, Mother. This task will bring peace for our people."

"I pray it is so, Daughter, but great fear lives in my heart."

"We will take no risks. Grandfather will guide us and protect us. Have you forgotten the sacred vision told of our victory to come?"

Singing Wind did not doubt that success would be won; she only worried over what their journey together could cost her family. Observing the expression in her child's eyes and the happiness in her spirit over the man's return warned Singing Wind of how strong her daughter's feelings were for the grandson of Powchutu/Eagle's Arm. She sent a mental prayer to the Great Spirit to keep Morning Star's mind clear. The two females entered the tepee to find "Sky Warrior" and Sun Cloud talking.

Joe glanced at the beautiful maiden who had filled his thoughts for days. Learning she had won the contest hadn't shocked him, and his worries had become overshadowed by excitement. He had never doubted her skills and wits, as he had witnessed them during their trek together. After greeting the mother, he focused his attention on his impending partner. "Hello, Morning Star. I'm proud of your victory. Your father showed me your coup painted there," he remarked, motioning to the pictorial family record suspended from the tepee-lining

164

rope to dry. "I told Sun Cloud about my meetings with Jim at the fort and with Spotted Tail on the way there. I'll tell you everything after we're on the trail tomorrow. We're riding out at first light. I want to start before more trouble arises. Can you be ready to leave early in the morning?"

"*Han.* Yes," she switched to English for practice.

"Good. I almost made it here yesterday, but the sun gave out on me. I camped about ten miles away because I thought it might be dangerous to ride in after dark. I didn't want to risk getting shot as an intruder." He smiled.

"We break camp in five moons to ride for the grasslands to hunt buffalo," Sun Cloud reminded his daughter. After the customary signal of tepee dismantling by the chief's wife, the others would begin their tasks to journey to their first summer camp. He told her where he would make trail signs to let her know which direction they took, which was determined by where the most buffalo grazed. As the great herds moved, so did the Indians and their nomadic camps. They would begin in the lush plateaus and canyons that composed or surrounded the area known as Maka Sica, what the white men also called the Badlands.

Joe was delighted that Morning Star could read trail signs and could locate Sun Cloud's new location after they left this one on the first of June. He noticed how she kept her gaze controlled and off him unless he spoke to her, and he suspected — and hoped — it was to conceal her joy at seeing him. He also tried to keep his frequently straying mind on the business at hand. He was eager to begin their journey and to participate in the ceremony tonight that would make him a *Tanhan-We,* blood brother.

"Rest, Tanner," the chief said. "We talk more before the moon rises."

Morning Star and Singing Wind began the final preparations for their departure. They packed supplies, but Joe didn't offer help because that was "woman's work." Sun Cloud loaned them one of his horses to carry their supplies; it would be loaded in the morning.

Joseph Lawrence gave the women privacy as he strolled around the Indian encampment. Dogs raced about and barked or lay in the warming sun. Horses were held in rope and brush corrals or staked beside tepees that were positioned between black hills and a serene lake. The pointed dwellings with many poles reaching heavenward were colored from the use of different colored buffalo hides, varying from light tan to almost black. Spring grass was lush and green, the sky clear and blue. Reeds and water plants grew along the lake's edge, and assorted wildflowers offered beauty here and there. It was a lovely and peaceful setting.

Joe encountered older women and youthful maidens doing chores. Most halted to stare at him, with the youngest cupping their mouths to whisper and giggle. He was relieved and delighted not to sense hatred in them; their behavior told him that he and his task had been accepted. His keen mind took in details of camp life.

At the lake, women washed clothes or fetched water. Others went to or returned from gathering wood or edible plants. Some were hanging strips of meat on racks to dry and preserve. A few were beading, sewing, or flattening quills with their teeth. Cradleboards, travois bindings, securing thongs, and saddle pads were being made or repaired in preparation for the moving of the camp soon. Small children entertained themselves nearby, girls with toys made to teach them their roles in life: miniature tepees, wooden horses, travois, and grass-stuffed dolls. Babies slept or played on buffalo mats near their mother or tender's sides, and older children — especially boys — were off enjoying themselves.

As Joe roamed the active area, teenage boys also delayed their games to eye him as he passed them. He witnessed mock hunts to hone instincts, races to acquire speed and agility, balls of tightly rolled buffalo hair tossed into distant baskets to learn accuracy for when the ball changed to a lance, and the rolling of a willow hoop with a stick for dexterity and control. Soon, many of them would go into serious training to one day ride with their fathers on hunts — or perhaps raids if the truce parley failed.

Most fathers and older brothers were occupied with important tasks. Some warriors and braves were away hunting or scouting for enemy tracks. Others sat near their conical abodes or in the forest shade to work. Joe lingered for a while at a few groups to watch them sharpen old weapons whose blades were dulled from use or repair edges that were chipped. He observed the preparation of feathers for one end of the arrow shafts, as they controlled the flight of the most frequently used weapon. He saw how they smoothed slender and sturdy limbs chosen for shafts, as any rough spot could change its speed and direction. He watched them chiseling away at certain stones to make arrowheads with sharp and jagged points, and how they attached the tips and feathers to the shafts. Joe was intrigued by the men's deftness, and how they balanced the weights of each piece to construct a lethal and accurate weapon. He observed men restringing bows, their strength and skill displayed in rippling muscles and agility. Some of the elders sat with them smoking pipes, telling stories, or gambling. Joe was impressed by their comradeship and hard work.

He liked the way they smiled or nodded at him and allowed him to spend time with them. Those who could speak English explained the details of their chores to him. Some were more genial and open than others. Most of them had ridden with Sun Cloud over the years, and a few with the legendary Gray Eagle. He wished he had gifts of gratitude and friendship for each of them, but he had made purchases for only one man: Payaba, the old shaman who had foretold his coming and aided it.

Joe went to his horse and retrieved the knife and small ax, more like a hatchet. He headed for the past medicine chief's tepee, as he'd seen the elderly man return home earlier. From the custom he had learned, he called out, asking for permission to come inside and visit.

"U wo." Payaba granted it.

Joe held out the knife and hatchet. "I bring you gifts of friendship and thanks, Payaba. I don't understand visions, but yours was filled with knowledge and truth. Morning Star speaks only good and loving words of you. I'm honored to know you. If there's a chore I can do for you today, my hands and mind are willing."

"Your heart is kind and pure, Tanner Gaston. Payaba thanks you. Many others see me as a grandfather, brother, and uncle; they do chores for Payaba and Winter Woman. They fetch wood and water, and bring food. Morning Star gathers herbs and plants for my medicines. I need nothing more. My heart is warmed by your generosity and friendship."

Payaba retrieved something from a medicine pouch and wrapped it in a small piece of hide. "It is medicine to tend the cut you place on your hand in the ceremony this moon," he explained. "It will halt redness, bad water, and fever. No evil spirit must be allowed to sicken a man who has a great task before him."

Joe thanked him for the gift. "Payaba's medicine is strong. Morning Star used it to tend a bullet wound I got after I helped her escape those white men. It's almost healed now."

"Cover the cut. Let no dirt or insect enter. The evil white-eyes put many bad things into Mother Earth."

As the snowy-haired man watched Joe's departure, he reflected on the dream he had experienced following the contest. He decided it would be damaging to reveal it to his chief. Besides, if it was more than a dream — as he suspected — destinies of those involved could not be changed. There was no need to worry his leader until the time came . . .

As Morning Star went through her possessions one last time to make certain she had packed everything she would need on the trail, she lifted her flesher and gazed at it with pride and joy. At a girl's ritual introduction to womanhood, she was given a special elkhorn upon which her good deeds were recorded by whomever was in charge of an event. The color, shape, and number of dots revealed the reasons for those marks. Some were for tanning hides and making robes, for winning beading or quilling contests, for helping others construct their first tepee before a joining ceremony, and for performing a charitable or brave deed. Possible suitors often asked to view a woman's flesher before he shared a blanket with her or asked her to become his wife. For a female, counting her dots was comparable to a warrior counting his coups of prowess and generosity.

Many women had earned a new dot for helping Morning Star prepare for the great task before her. The Lakota beading was removed from all her possessions and replaced with the colors and symbols of the Arapaho, a tribe that was neither ally nor foe of either the Dakotas or the Crow. It would be a safe identity to assume as Joe's squaw. Even her new necklace and wristlets were Arapaho.

Morning Star wondered where Joe was and how he was doing in her camp. As soon as the last task was completed, she would look for him.

Knife-Slayer returned from hunting with a buck across his horse. He sighted the white man near a corral and headed to speak with the paleface before skinning his kill. As he approached, the hated rival heard him.

Joe noticed the cold glare in the warrior's narrowed eyes and the hostility in his expression. He perceived hatred and resentment in the Indian's aura. Hoping to avoid an unpleasant confrontation, he complimented the man. "Your hunt was successful; that's a fine buck. How many arrows did it take to bring him down?" he attempted to converse in a genial way.

"A skilled hunter slays his game with one shot, White man. Knife-Slayer is a skilled hunter and a skilled warrior. Can you do the same?"

Joe tried to make peace by grinning and replying, "Most of the time, but I wouldn't want to compete in hunting and shooting with a man of your prowess. I'm glad we're on the same side. You'd make a tough enemy."

The Indian avowed, "We are enemies, White-Dog. You do not trick me with your words as you blind others with them. Before many suns and moons pass across the heaven, you will prove to my people you are false, that your skills are few, and your task futile. When the whites and Crow attack us on the plains, war will come. Until my people see the truth, protect Morning Star from danger. And do not touch her," he added with a coldness that startled Joe.

"I'm not your enemy, Knife-Slayer," the blond argued. "I'm here to help your people. How can you doubt and reject a sacred vision?"

Ebony braids with coup feathers attached near their ends grazed strong shoulders as the warrior shook his head. "You cannot stop a war we have battled with the Crow since Grandfather created us. You cannot stop the whites from attacking.

169

Yes, Half-Breed, we are enemies. Your white blood and ways are strongest. When war comes, you will side with them. On that sun, I will slay you with great joy. If you try to steal Morning Star from me and her people, I will slay you sooner."

Knife-Slayer's insults and warnings angered Joe, but he controlled his temper. Joe knew the warrior was arrogant, as no other one wore his coup feathers in camp. He glanced at two Sun Dance scars on the bronzed chest of the man who craved the same woman he did; they told him the warrior could endure as much pain as he could inflict on foes. He couldn't imagine Morning Star marrying and yielding to this fierce male. She was too gentle, kind, and smart. Yet, if Knife-Slayer stopped others from wooing Morning Star and made himself her only suitor, and if he offered many possessions to her father for her hand in marriage, would Morning Star feel compelled to accept her only proposal to avoid embarrassing her family by having no mate? The idea of her being entrapped by the wicked warrior vexed Joe. With boldness, he chided, "Your heart is filled with hatred and bitterness. Men like you are the only ones who can prevent peace with the whites and the Crow. It's wrong, Knife-Slayer, to endanger and destroy your people."

"A man fights his own battles, White-Dog."

"Your intrusion can create a battle you can't win, Knife-Slayer."

"There is no battle I cannot win! There is no foe I cannot defeat!"

"Then why didn't you attack and slay Snake-Man when you located him and spied on him?" Joe challenged, his own blue eyes narrowed now.

Although only two inches separated their heights, Knife-Slayer drew himself up tall and stiff to level their gazes. "He is an evil spirit," he responded. "They cannot be slain, except with powerful magic. I am no shaman."

"He isn't a spirit. He's only a man, a white man, a clever man."

"You have not seen him! How do you know such things?"

"In a land far away, I have seen the kind of magic he does. They're only tricks to fool Indians who haven't seen them. I'm going to defeat him. Like you, he craves war, but I'll find him

170

and stop him."

"If he does not find and stop you first."

"At least I'm not afraid to go after him," Joe snapped unwisely.

"Knife-Slayer fears no man and no task, Piss of the Coyote!" Provoked, Joe spoke his mind. "You fear I have the prowess to steal the woman you desire. You fear I have the prowess to gain a treaty to halt another war. You fear my victory will earn me a bigger coup than you've won. You fear that victory will put an end to the bloody raids you love. Fear is a strong and wicked power, Knife-Slayer, one you'd better defeat or learn to control for the good of your people and lands. If you change your mind about me and peace, I'll offer you my hand in friendship," Joe finished, but only to avoid more hostility. He walked away.

Morning Star was concealed behind a tree. After she saw Joe depart, she joined the warrior and warned, "Remove such fears and doubts from your mind and heart, Knife-Slayer, or they will bring much trouble and suffering to many. It is wrong to insult a man with Oglala blood, the same blood that lives within your chief and in my body. When the great task is done and peace rules our lands, I will return to my people and he will return to his. He is not what stands between us. We are too different."

"If he tries to steal you, I will challenge him to the death."

"He cannot steal from you what you do not own," she retorted. "If you intrude on the sacred vision, you will be banished or slain. We have known each other since children. I do not want such shame and torment to enter your mother's tepee. Visit the sweat lodge to purify yourself of such wickedness. Pray to Grandfather to change your heart. Endure a vision-quest to receive His warnings of wisdom. Seek another female to share your love and tepee. Only this way can you survive and be happy."

"I do not wish to survive without my love, my lands, and my honor."

"You do not love me, Knife-Slayer," Morning Star corrected, "you desire me and you crave the daughter of your chief as first wife. If you are patient, a true love will come to you. If you are patient, Joe will win truce, and your honor and our lands will not be endangered."

"Why do you call him Joe?" He pounced on her slip.

Thinking fast, she explained, "That is the name he uses to fool the whites. I practice to avoid mistakes when we travel together. No one must know he is the grandson of Powchutu who was first called Tanner Gaston."

"You are wrong, Morning Star. My love and need for you are as strong as my doubts of him. Do not shame our chief and people by not returning."

"Have you forgotten we are of the same bloodline and cannot mate? Have you forgotten we are different? Morning Star cannot go to the white lands and accept the white ways; I am Oglala; I will always be Oglala. I swear to you, he will return to his home far away when his task is done."

"Swear it to Grandfather, for you will not break your word to Him."

"Nothing I say or do will change your mind, Knife-Slayer. I am troubled by the feelings I see in you. I pray they are gone when I return."

Morning Star encountered her brother before she reached her tepee. She knew that meant another quarrel, and she dreaded it. She smiled and greeted Night Stalker, hoping he would be kind today.

"I pray you can return safely after the truth is revealed, Sister. Know, if you do not, your brother and Knife-Slayer will avenge any harm to you."

"I will be safe with Tanner, my brother."

"He was raised white. He is a half-blood. Do not trust him."

"His bloodline is as strong and true as ours. Tanner said Powchutu joined a half-white woman. Both bloodlines have Indians and whites."

Coldness entered the proud warrior's dark eyes. "No, our blood is almost pure. His has been weakened and stained many times. Enemy blood came to Tanner from his paleface mother, his half-white grandmother, and a paleface parent before her."

Seeing how upset Night Stalker was, she debated in a soft tone, "What of Shalee's mother? What of Jenny's parents? All were white, my brother. Much as you despise the truth, you cannot remove it or forget it. If Running Wolf had claimed his first-born son, Powchutu would have become Red Heart chief, not

172

Gray Eagle, the second born. If Powchutu had been chief, his son — Stede — would now be chief, not our father. If so, Tanner/Sky Warrior would be next in line, not Night Stalker."

He glared at her and alleged, "If Powchutu had become chief, he would not have met his half-breed woman in the white world he joined by choice. Do not forget, Powchutu loved our grandmother; if he had become chief, he would have taken Shalee as wife. All would be the same for us. I would still be chief next."

"It would not be so, Brother. Different mates bear different children. We would not exist if Gray Eagle had not won and mated with Alisha/Shalee."

"You are wrong, Morning Star. The Great Spirit and *Whope* give a maiden her seeds when she comes to season. No matter which man brings one to life, the child is the same."

"If that is true, how does a white captive bear an Indian child, as Alisha did our father and uncle?"

"Because the Great Spirit makes a warrior's water of life overpower the white woman's seed."

"If that is true," she reasoned again, "Powchutu's flow overpowered his mate's seed to make Stede an Indian, and Stede's flow overpowered his mate's to make Tanner an Indian. As Oglala, you have no fight with him. To you, Tanner must be as Indian as you are, my wise brother."

Night Stalker realized she was turning his argument against him, but he vowed to open her mind! "The Great Spirit does not live and work in the white world where Powchutu fled and mated. Stede was raised as a paleface and he joined to one. The Great Spirit did not intrude on their mating, and their son was born of her white seed. Tanner's face marks him as white, and he carries little Oglala blood."

Morning Star asked herself if her brother's explanation was right, or even partly right. She did not know how either Stede or the real Tanner looked, and she told herself to ask Joe when they had privacy. Yet every child of a mixed union that she knew looked Indian or revealed only a tiny mark of their white heritage. Except Alisha/Shalee, she reminded herself. "Does that mean the Great Spirit did not intrude on the mating of Black Cloud and Jenny Pilcher?" she questioned. "All say Shalee had hair of fire and eyes like grass when Mother Earth renews her face. Why would the Great Spirit let a white captive's seed be stronger than a Blackfoot chief's?"

"Perhaps the Great Spirit was angered when Black Cloud took his white captive as wife."

"If so, was the Great Spirit not more angered when Gray Eagle — the greatest warrior to ever live — took his white captive as wife?"

"It is not the same, Sister! Our grandmother was half Indian. That is why the Great Spirit did not mark our father and uncle as half-breeds or whites; He made them Indian to show He was not displeased."

"Perhaps the Great Spirit gave grandmother a white face to show all that some whites are good. How can you hate the son and grandson of Powchutu when our grandmother and her mother also carried white blood? The Great Spirit chose Tanner as our helper; He does not hate or reject all white blood. If you battle him, you will be punished," she warned.

To silence her, he accused, "You speak too strong for him, Sister."

"I trust him and believe he can help us. A sacred vision does not lie."

"I fear I see more than trust in your eyes."

"Do not be foolish, Brother. We are of the same bloodline: Running Wolf's. We cannot mate. Is that what troubles you about my leaving?"

"I have not seen this strange glow in your eyes before. He touches your heart, Sister, but be certain he does not touch your body."

"Your warning is not needed, for I know and accept such things."

"Do you, my sister? Remember, if you turn to him and we are betrayed, you and your family will be shamed. You will be banished."

Morning Star fretted as she watched her brother leave. He and Knife-Slayer suspected her feelings for Joe; her mother had hinted at them, and her father was too quiet and watchful. That could only mean she was not doing a good task of concealing her forbidden emotions! She cautioned herself to be more careful. She did not want anything, especially her weakness for Joe,

174

to hinder the sacred mission before them. The fact that Joseph Lawrence was a man of pure white blood made him as taboo as if he were her blood cousin. She was vexed by the contradiction that an Indian male could take a white female but that it was a disgrace for an Indian woman to take a white man!

Morning Star scolded herself for worrying about such an impossible situation. Joe was not like Knife-Slayer, a man who would take a female he desired even if he couldn't join her! Joe had pride, honor, and goodness. Joe knew they were unmatched, and would not pursue her. Yet a curious sensation washed over her. She prayed it was too late for anything or anyone to prevent her from leaving with him in the morning.

Chapter Eight

After the evening meal in Sun Cloud's tepee, Joe, the chief, his wife, and Morning Star joined the Red Hearts who gathered in a clearing near the water for the unusual ritual to make a white man a blood brother.

Green spruces and pines, obsidian hills, and a blue lake surrounded the people with colorful beauty. A half moon floated across an indigo sky with countless silvery stars which reminded all of an artistic piece of Indian beadwork. The water's surface was as tranquil as a lazy southern evening; it reflected the partial moon rising above it as if the moon held a narcisisstic spirit who wanted to view its image in nature's mirror. Frogs, crickets, and noctural birds sang loudly and merrily as if joining in on the special event, their tunes competing at one time and blending at another. Tepees were outlined against the firmament, their protruding poles like skinny fingers pointing to the heaven. The wind was calm, so no limb or grass blade moved. It was a pleasant night.

In the center of the large gathering was a bonfire with leaping flames of red, orange, and yellow. Soon it would die down to an almost intimate glow. The fire was a signal to draw close to share something special with the tribe; it was a unifying spirit. Near it, there was a post with the sacred Medicine Wheel and Wolf Eyes' Ceremonial Skull: vital symbols of the culture and beliefs of the Lakotas. The four eagle feathers suspended from the wheel's bottom and representing the Lakota virtues — wisdom, bravery, constancy, and generosity — did not flutter in the still air. Morning Star had told Joe they were the first coup feathers earned by the last four Red Heart chiefs. When Night Stalker, or another, became chief, his first coup feather would replace Red Hawk's, as only four could dangle there. The four intersecting bars of shiny metal glittered in the firelight. The center of life was represented at the place where they met in the middle: harmony with the Great Spirit, with oneself, and with nature. It depicted a neverending circle, the continuity of Indian life.

In the forefront of the circle of bodies, the Big Bellies sat on furry mats in the location of importance and control. Next came the cult members of proven warriors, hunters who had not been taken into a society yet, and male elders who were not members of the ruling society. The circle of Indians was completed with the women and children.

The first step of the occasion was to give thanks for past blessings and to summon the Great Spirit to witness this solemnity. Wolf Eyes then continued. "We take *Mahpiya Wicasta*, Your helper, into our hearts and band, Grandfather. You called him home from where *Wi* rises to bring peace and enlightenment to Your children. Tanner seeks harmony with himself, with his grandfather's people, and with Mother Nature. We ask You to give him these things. Tanner has shown the four virtures we honor, as with the eagle feathers on our sacred Medicine Wheel. You have joined his Life-Circle to ours once more. As we share Your breath, prepare our hearts and minds to become as one in purpose and feeling."

The second step in the ritual was pipe smoking, to share the breath of the Great Spirit and to inspire solidarity between the men. Normally the ceremonial chief was first, followed by the tribal chief, the war chief, the shaman, and other Big Bellies. Afterward, all warriors of high rank took their turns. Tonight, their honored guest was third to smoke.

Joe sat on one side of Sun Cloud, Morning Star on the other. Though she was a part of the sacred vision and mission ahead, she did not share the smoking rite. Women were never allowed to touch men's sacred objects or weapons, for it was believed they would steal their magic and strength.

Wolf Eyes packed the red stone bowl, lit the tobacco, drew deeply and reverently from its long stem, and handed it to their leader. Sun Cloud inhaled smoke, then released it. He passed the pipe to Joe, who repeated their actions while Morning Star observed.

When the pipe was passed four times, Wolf Eyes stood to pray for the safety, survival, and success of Tanner

177

Gaston and Morning Star.

As the maiden listened to the words being sent to her god, she knew He would not punish her and Joe for their necessary deception. If the Great Spirit was angered by it, He would have exposed them or even slain them by now. She believed that Stede and Joe — not Tanner — were the vision helpers. It could not be bad or wrong to do the will of her god, even if she had to lie to her loved ones for a while. Once peace was won and the villains defeated, surely her family and tribe would understand and forgive her trickery.

The ceremonial and medicine chiefs performed a special dance and chant to the timing of stone-filled gord rattles, eaglebone whistles, and a kettle drum that was beat upon by eight men using sturdy sticks with ends wrapped in buffalo hide. As the almost hypnotic music played and the two men moved around the fire with matching steps and words, Sun Cloud withdrew his knife and made a slice across the palm of his right hand.

Joe did as the chief had instructed earlier, and took the firesterilized blade and sliced across his hand. Sun Cloud had told him of his mother's warnings about cuts made with dirty weapons and left untended. Morning Star had told Joe how refusing to inflict "mourning cuts" upon his body after his parents' deaths had angered many tribe members and almost cost her father their votes for him as chief over Bright Arrow. Joe held up his bleeding hand and, when Sun Cloud lifted his, he grasped it and mingled their blood. As the red liquid eased down his arm, Joe knew he had done the right thing by claiming to be his murdered friend. Their gazess met, each exposing friendship and belief in this ceremony. "I will always be your friend and blood brother, Sun Cloud."

"Your eyes and voice say your words are true, friend and brother."

Morning Star was touched by the scene of uplifted clasped hands and stirring words between her father and the man who was stealing her heart. She couldn't help but think of the physical differences in the two men, and between Joe and KnifeSlayer whose glare exposed his ill feelings. From their positions with Sun Cloud between them, she could barely see Joe, and she dared not lean aside to peer around her father's body. As she waited, she envisioned how he must look in the sienna breech-cloth, fringed leggings, and beaded moccasins that her father had loaned to him. She could almost see the adoring flames dancing on his handsome face.

With his face shaved and his chest hairless, Joe almost stole her breath! For a few wild moments, she imagined him riding across the Plains as a band leader or a hunter, dancing around a campfire in only a breechcloth with sweat glistening on his taut body, and battling their foes in warpaint. Of course he would mark his face with blue, white, and yellow to represent his new name: Mahpiya Wicasta, Sky Warrior.

The daydreaming maiden pictured how the blue paint would enhance Joe's azure eyes, and how all three colors would look against his sunbronzed flesh with a golden mane flowing past his strong neck. That sunny hair grazed the top of powerful shoulders that tapered into a sleek middle. In Indian clothing, with his sparse body hair, strong bone structure, and darkly tanned skin, if it were not for his blond hair and sky eyes, he wouldn't look so different from her people. Yet it would always be those eyes and hair which reminded her of the impassable canyon between them.

Morning Star felt proud and honored to be a special part of this period in her people's history. She was ready to challenge dangers, confront the unknown, and to learn more about Joseph Lawrence and herself. She was the only one who knew the truth about him, and that trust warmed her. He could have fooled her too, but he hadn't. He had confided in her from the start, proving her faith in him was justified. As soon as his cut was tended and night passed, they would leave. But before her departure, there was something important she had to do: make peace with Buckskin Girl. She would do so when the ceremony ended.

After the ritual, the men's cuts were tended and they chatted with others and enjoyed refreshments. When things quieted down, Sun Cloud asked "Tanner" to join him for a walk to speak privately.

The chief did not want his daughter to return home and overhear the matter that troubled him tonight. He guided his blood brother beyond the last tepee and settled himself on a large rock near even larger boulders. Sun Cloud motioned for the man to sit. "We must talk before you ride, Tanner. There is a promise you must make to me."

Joe sat down near the Indian. "What is it?" he asked warily.

"After you left nine suns ago, I remembered what you said when you first entered our camp. You know the truth of my mother and your grandmother," he ventured, more as a statement than a question.

"Yes, Sun Cloud, I know Sarah Gaston was the real Shalee, not your mother. I know Alisha Williams was a white woman, not the abducted daughter of Chief Black Cloud. Powchutu told Stede the truth about his mother, and he told me before we came here."

The Red Heart Chief exhaled audibly. "For many years I have believed all who knew that dangerous secret were dead, except for me and Singing Wind. My parents, White Arrow, Powchutu, my brother, and the old woman who placed the *akito* of Black Cloud on my mother's body when she lay near death are gone. I did not think of Powchutu telling his son. Matu meant no harm when she placed the mark of her chief on my mother; she wished to return home to die with her people. When Black Cloud came to claim my father's captive as his long-lost daughter, my parents did not know of Matu's trick. If Father had revealed his suspicion, Alisha and Matu would have been slain. Father believed it was the Great Spirit's way of giving him the woman he loved and needed, so he held silent and took her as wife. When Matu died, only Father, White Arrow — his best friend since birth — Mother, and Powchutu knew she was not the real Shalee. All held silent to save Mother's life, to protect my father's honor, and to prevent disharmony. In a time of war — unity, friendship, and trust are important. To reveal such a trick then or now would destroy them."

"You're telling me that only you, Singing Wind, Stede, and myself know the truth? Night Stalker and Morning Star don't know this secret?"

"They do not, and the secret must never leave the mouths of the four of us. Swear as my blood brother and friend you will not betray my trust. If we must war with the whites, my people must be as one in spirit and action. They cannot follow a leader whose honor and face are stained by lies. Night Stalker hates whites, and his spirit is troubled. If my son learns the truth, he will become bitter and dangerous. He will do terrible things to prove he is more Oglala than white. It must not be. If Morning Star learns the truth of her grandmother, I fear she will be pulled toward the white world; and that will destroy her. My daughter was raised Oglala and looks Oglala. You know how Indian women are treated in the white lands. It must not be."

"You have my word of honor I won't tell anyone this secret. Stede Gaston will hold silent, too. I understand why everyone who knew the truth kept quiet, and I agree with what they did. So does Stede. Powchutu only wanted his son to know who his mother was, which makes him who *he* is. Stede knows his father loved Alisha Williams, and he wouldn't do anything to stain her memory. Neither would I. We've heard the glorious legends about Gray Eagle and Shalee. They were remarkable people who let love overcome the differences between them and their cultures. That rarely happens. When it does, it's too beautiful and special and powerful to destroy. I won't ever do that, Sun Cloud. I promise."

"Does your father wish to return to our tribe?"

Joe grasped the unspoken meaning behind his question. "Only to visit. When peace is won, we'll return to our homes far away. Stede believes the Red Hearts have their rightful and best chief: you. His father believed the same thing about Gray Eagle."

"When the time comes, I'll meet with the son of my uncle. Long ago, Powchutu was a close friend when he lived and rode as Eagle's Arm with my father. He lives in my memory and in our legends."

"Your family gave him the peace of mind he needed before he died. It was good he returned to his father's land to seek it. His heart was troubled by all the problems he made for your parents. It's good they all made peace before they died."

"As it is good his son and grandson return to help us."

Joe realized he had been saying "Stede" and "Powchutu" rather than my "father" and "grandfather." If Sun Cloud had

181

noticed that curious slip, he didn't seem suspicious. Joe surmised that the chief must assume he was using their names for clarity. "I'll do my best for peace, Sun Cloud. So will my father," he added as a safety measure, and prayed the foul taste of that lie in his mouth didn't show in his expression.

"That is all any man can do, Tanner—his best."

After the men left the secluded area, Morning Star relaxed her strained body. She had stayed motionless behind the large boulder so their keen senses would not detect her presence. She had not intended to eavesdrop, but they had arrived just as she finished excusing herself and she hadn't wanted to be caught at such a private moment. She had assumed they would talk of the impending task, then leave. The conversation had frozen her in place.

Its implication shot through her keen mind. Her grandmother was not half Indian, or any Indian! She herself, her father, her uncle, and her brother were more white than she had been told! She knew of the Blackfoot custom of a father using a sharp bone to scratch his symbol—*akito*—into the buttock flesh of his children. Ash was rubbed into it to make the mark permanent. It was used to identify children stolen during raids by enemies, especially if it was many years before their rescue and their faces had changed. Perhaps Snake-Man had used such a practice to make the symbols on his body—those Joe had called tattoos—but had rubbed colors into his scratches instead of black ash. But Snake-Man left her thoughts quickly.

This news was astonishing, but not distressing. Why should she be upset to discover she had a little more white blood than she had known, particularly when it came from an exceptional female? Alisha Williams, who had lived as Shalee, had been a strong, proud, and brave woman who had gone from white captive to wife of Gray Eagle, a chief whose legendary exploits had never been matched. Alisha had saved Gray Eagle's life when he was captured and tortured by whites. She had led her husband to a past villainous enemy so Jeffrey Gordon could be defeated. She had made Black Cloud's last days happy ones. She had saved Running Wolf's life. She had saved their tribe from a cavalry attack. She had given Gray Eagle and the Red Hearts two

182

great leaders in Sun Cloud and Bright Arrow, and had raised them to be superior men. She had taught her sons English and white ways to help them with peace and understanding.

Alisha/Shalee had become Indian in heart and spirit. She had been a lesson in courage and strength to everyone. She had earned the love, respect, and acceptance of Gray Eagle, the Red Hearts, and other tribes; something she could not have done as a white captive. Becoming Shalee, even by deception, had given her that chance and all had learned from it. She had lived a full and rewarding life. The love she had shared with Gray Eagle was so powerful that they had even died the same day. The Great Spirit had blessed and honored the loving couple. They would never be forgotten by her band or the Dakota Nation. It would be wrong and cruel to stain their golden memories.

Morning Star understood why her father and the others had kept the truth concealed, and why it must remain buried in the past. She knew Joe would keep his word to Sun Cloud. Without their knowledge, she would help protect the truth. Yet the Great Spirit had led her to this spot tonight to discover it, so He must have a good reason for enlightening her.

Just as Buckskin Girl must have a good reason for her curious actions, which she had not revealed during their short visit. Buckskin Girl had promised to tell her everything soon. Whatever distressed the other female, it could not — must not — destroy their friendship.

Morning Star pushed what she had learned tonight into a special corner of her memory, then headed for her tepee for much needed rest. She would deal with both matters another time.

The exciting moment arrived, and many gathered around Sun Cloud's tepee. Morning Star embraced her mother, father, Payaba, and Buckskin Girl. She comprehended how anxious her parents were, how excited the old medicine man was, and how depressed her friend was not to be going. She spoke to other friends and tribe members, all of whom wished them well.

Morning Star noticed how her brother stayed in the background. His wife, Touched-A-Crow, did not approach the genial group either. The woman's action did not surprise her, as the Brule female kept mostly to herself. Touched-A-Crow was uncommonly quiet and not very smart. She had shown no interest in the stirring contest and had not visited Morning Star and Singing Wind when they were ill. Sun Cloud's daughter wondered why Night Stalker did not take a second wife, unless he didn't want a crowded tepee or to assume responsibility for another person.

As Joe conversed with others, Morning Star's gaze settled on her nephew in Touched-a-Crow's arms. Blood Arrow's lips protruded in an angry pout, as usual, and the defiant gleam in his eyes was visible at that short distance. The two-year-old squirmed to get down, but Touched-a-Crow refused to release him. When the moody boy began to whine and to slap at his mother, Night Stalker apparently ordered his wife to take their son home, no doubt to spare the warrior embarrassment at Bloody Arrow's misbehavior. Morning Star hated to imagine what kind of man her nephew would become if not disciplined soon.

Morning Star looked at her older cousin, Little Feet, who was near the age of her father. The eldest daughter of her slain uncle had well behaved and happy children, and a loving husband in Thunder Spirit. The maiden decided that was how she wanted her own family to be someday.

Joe clasped wrists with the chief and said, "I'll guard her life with my own, Sun Cloud. After we gather enough information, we'll report to you in the new camp. You won't be disappointed by your decision to make peace."

"I will trust you to do what is best for all, Tanner, nothing more."

Whether or not the chief intended to make a dual point with his words, Joe took it that way. He smiled and nodded.

The white man and maiden mounted, and Sun Cloud handed Joe the reins to the pack horse. Farewells and waves followed them from the scene. Neither Joe nor Morning Star failed to notice the icy stares of Knife-Slayer, Hawk Eyes, and Night Stalker.

As both Morning Star and Joe wondered what would happen during their trek together, they rode for a long time without

184

talking or glancing at each other. Though their trust had not vanished, nor any uneasiness settled in, each realized the most difficult part of their task was controling their emotions. Neither wanted to tempt or be tempted beyond their strength to refuse what both knew existed between them.

When they halted to rest themselves and the horses, Morning Star told Joe, "I worked on English while you gone. I practiced with Father, Mother, and others who speak white tongue. You teach me more."

Joe asked, "Can you read any English?"

Morning Star surprised him by replying, "Little," as she held up her hand with her index finger and thumb about an inch apart. "Grandfather, Gray Eagle, have learning book from white captive who schoolmarm. Grandmother teach him more; she teach sons, Bright Arrow and Sun Cloud. Father teach Mother more after they joined. Father teach Night Stalker and Morning Star. Many white words hard. Indians not have as many for same thing. Even same color have many white names. Words put together and confuse; whites say 'it's' and 'you'll' for it is and you will."

"Those are called contractions. Whites use them in speaking, but they aren't — are not — in formal English, best English." Joe had noticed how she glowed when she spoke of Alisha/Shalee. "Your grandmother was a special woman. I've heard many wonderful stories about her. It's a shame you never knew her. From what I've seen, you have many of her good traits." His mind wandered back in history. Sarah/Shalee had taken after her white mother, so she had been "rescued" by soldiers, then sent to New Orleans as a small child, where she was adopted by Dr. Devane. As fate would have it, Powchutu had met and married her as Tanner Gaston, then discovered Black Cloud's *akito* that revealed her true identity.

Morning Star saw Joe's attention escape for a moment, and she knew where it had fled. She felt it was best to relate the story she had been told of her heritage. "I not know what Powchutu tell Stede and Stede tell Tanner and Joe. I tell you about Grandmother. She part white. Her father Blackfoot chief Black Cloud. He take Brave Bear, Singing Wind's father, as son after his father killed. Shalee stolen when two winters. Many summers later, Gray Eagle capture white girl. He come to love, but cannot join; she enemy blood. Soldiers steal Grandmother from camp; he attack fort and take back. She ill, and he tend. He find mark of Black Cloud on her body. He happy. It fine to join chief's daughter with white blood. She great woman; all loved her. Morning Star have little white blood," she finished, making the same motion with her fingers as before.

"It not trouble me, but Brother would make many cuts on his body if they let white blood flow out. He not know Grandmother; he born next winter. If so, he not hate all whites so much. She legend. She . . . lady," the maiden finished with a bright smile. "He not remember *Wahea* — it mean Red Flower, 'cause she have red hair. He nine winters old when she killed. She uncle's wife, white woman. She do many good deeds. Whole tribe love and accept. She lady, too. When captured by Bright Arrow, she have bad time; he have bad time. He banished many years. They do good deeds; tribe forgive and take back, but no can become chief. It good for all."

Joe couldn't blame Gray Eagle for allowing the misconception about his love to stand so he could have her. He couldn't blame Sun Cloud for letting it continue to protect his parents' lives or for both chiefs to prevent disrupting the unity of the tribe. The Red Hearts had accepted a white woman into the life of their beloved chief only because they hadn't known the truth about Alisha. His lie about being Tanner Gaston, was an example of how sometimes deception was necessary for the good of all. What if, Joe mused, he never exposed the truth about his identity? As part Indian, could he claim Morning Star as — No, his mind shouted; staying Tanner made them kin! He could pursue her only by exposing his identity. By doing so, he made a match between them just as impossible. Besides, why was he thinking this way?

"What trouble you, Joe?" she asked the quiet man.

"I was planning our strategy," he said, hating to deceive her.

Morning Star sensed he was taking a different trail to mislead her, but didn't contradict or challenge him. "What is stra — te — gy?"

"A cunning plan to surprise and trick the enemy," he

explained.

"What stra-te-gy we use?"

"After your rescue, I can't join up with Zeke and his men. Maybe we can find them, trail 'em, and spy on them. First, we need to locate clues to see where to begin. We'll ride and look for tracks to follow."

"Ride to place where Zeke met Crow to see if they do so again. See if pick up trail or signs to follow," she suggested.

"That's a good idea; it could be a regular rendezvous point. Meeting place," he clarified. "That'll give us time to get to know each other before we enter any white or Crow areas. If you're my squaw, we don't want to seem like strangers to each other. That'll create suspicions."

"You right. We ride and become friends before see whites and Crow."

"We *are* friends, aren't we?"

Morning Star gazed into his hopeful eyes. She smiled and said, "Yes, we friends. Morning Star and Joe friends not same as white man and squaw friends. Is not so?"

He grinned and nodded. "That's true. We'll have to pretend . . ."

"What is pretend?" she inquired when he halted and looked uneasy.

"Like playing a game, a trick, behaving in a way that isn't true to fool others. Pretend we're . . . married, man and wife."

"Like disguise." She used one of her new words. When he grinned and nodded again, she added, "Not all squaws join to men who buy. Some join in Indian way, but not in white eyes and laws."

"Which do you want? Joined or not?" he asked.

She considered her two choices for a moment. "We pretend joined; that more fun, bigger challenge. Good disguise. Others we meet respect squaw more who claimed by white man. Not so with squaw not joined."

He grasped her meaning; she didn't want anyone — friend or foe — to view her as an unchaste mistress, or captive property. "You're right; wife it is. To make it seem real to us, we'll have a pretend joining ceremony."

"*Taku?*" she asked, astonished by his suggestion.

187

What? his mind echoed. Feeling mischievous, Joe asked, "Why not? If we pretend to join, it'll make it seem more real when we claim we are."

"We not have ceremonial chief to say words. Joe have no gifts for Father. We not shared the blanket. How can seem real?"

Joe untied a blanket from his saddle, grinned, and tossed it over their heads. "One rule covered," he jested in the dimness. "Your Great Spirit and my God are watching over us. Aren't They the highest chiefs of all before whom to say words?"

"It . . . is so," she faltered in confusion and suspense.

"My gifts to your father are my blood, friendship, and peace. Surely they're as valuable as horses. The whites say, Before God, I, Joseph Lawrence, Jr., take you, Morning Star, as my wedded wife." Her expression of pleased astonishment yanked Joe back to reality. He asked himself what in blazes he was thinking and doing! She was so close, so entrancing. To halt or to say it was a joke could offend her, so he needed to carry out the pretense he had begun. Yet he didn't think it wise to use the remaining words that leapt into his head. "Your turn."

Little space separated their bodies, something she was too aware of beneath the cozy cover. She trembled and warmed. Curious emotions surged through her. Recalling his words, she spoke slowly, "Before Great Spirit, I, Morning Star, take you, Joseph Lawrence, Jr., as my wedded . . . husband. Is that all? Are we pretend joined?"

Gazing into her dark eyes and having her so near, Joe lost his wits again. "All white weddings end with a kiss. It makes a bond between husband and wife and their vows to each other. If you'd rather not do that part —"

"It fine to do ceremony right," she interrupted before her courage deserted her. "It hot, hard to breathe; must hurry," she prompted him.

Joe's hands lifted and cupped her face. He looked deep into her dark-brown eyes. "You're my wife now, Morning Star," he murmured, then covered her lips with his.

Morning Star experienced new sensations of pleasure and heat. Running Badger and Knife-Slayer had stolen kisses before; she had been unwilling, and they hadn't felt like this one. Joe's mouth had a nice taste and a gentle pressure that was pleasing and enticing. His lips guided hers toward the correct response. When his arms banded her body, she did the same with his. The kiss became as powerful and hot as a wildfire racing across dried grasslands. It was wonderful to touch him this way.

Joe's arms tightened, and he felt his body reacting to her contact and response. He didn't want to pull away, but knew he should. His breathing altered, as did hers, and he knew she was as affected as he was. He tossed aside the stuffy blanket. The kiss continued.

Hanmani stomped one foot and whickered from a fly bite, causing the two almost to jerk apart. When the pesky insect tried to steal blood from another foreleg, the animal repeated his discouraging action, which gave the couple time to recover their wits.

"We are pretend joined?" she asked once more.

"Yes, you're my woman," he responded, and it was how he felt. "Let's ride." Joe scooped up the blanket and rolled it.

They mounted and rode on.

It was almost dusk when they halted to make their first camp near a tree-lined stream that offered shade and cover. Joe tended the horses while Morning Star unpacked their supplies and prepared their meal. The ride, skirting the Black Hills, had been an easy one with a pace that hadn't allowed much chance for talking. The maiden had led the way; Joe had followed close behind and kept his wits on alert for trouble.

Joe sat on the ground and stretched out his long legs. He watched her work with skilled hands. "Tell me about the contest," he coaxed, as the silence and serenity were sending his mind in a hazardous direction.

Morning Star continued her chores as she related the events. "It was not . . . simple as Morning Star thought. I win, but it hard. It . . . fate. It hard because I sick and weak." She explained her strange illness, her brother's cruel words, and her suspicions of Knife-Slayer and Hawk Eyes.

Joe was troubled. He ignored his romantic rival for the time being and said, "I can't blame Night Stalker for being scared of white men's diseases. We have some bad ones, but they harm Indians more than whites, because we know how to avoid them and tend them. They're strangers to Indians and they can wipe out an entire tribe."

"Long ago, white man's disease almost destroy Cheyenne camp of our allies. It Windrider's camp and tribe when he was chief and best friend to Bright Arrow. White wife of Bright Arrow and white captive of Windrider, who powerful medicine woman, save tribe. Disease steal children from both. Windrider take white shaman as wife. Windrider son, Soul of Thunder, now chief. He joined to Tashina, daughter of Bright Arrow."

"How did Bright Arrow and his wife die?"

"Crow attack camp when warriors and hunters gone. Bright Arrow return and battle. He killed. Wife killed saving children from Crow who capture for slaves. Others return and slay all Crow."

Morning Star passed Joe his wooden dish. As he devoured the meat that was softened in heated water and flavored with unfamiliar seasonings, he ate the wild vegetable roots she had cooked with it. He washed them down with flesh water from the stream, as did she.

"Agent Fitzpatrick told me how your grandfather was killed in an ambush by wicked soldiers, but when did you lose your grandmother?"

"She die same day, just go to sleep when Great Spirit call her name to come join Grandfather. Both die before I born. I know from stories and songs about them. I not know Mother's parents. Brave Bear die in battle. Chela die when Mother enter life. She made daughter of new Blackfoot chief. Father say it best for mates to leave Mother Earth on same sun."

Joe liked her poignant statement. "I agree. I'm sure it's hard on the one left behind to face life alone. How did your parents meet?" he inquired to keep up the casual conversation. Still, it was hard to keep his mind off the fetching female. He kept remembering how she had felt in his arms and how her lips had tasted upon his. He kept recalling how she seemed attracted to him, too. The playful ceremony had exposed to him how he wanted her as a wife. But how, even if he could persuade her, could she fit into his world? How could he take her away from all she knew?

When she finished chewing and swallowing the food in her

mouth, she sipped water before answering. "Blackfoot and Oglala been allies many winters. Old chief was my grandmother's father. He was good friends with Running Wolf, Gray Eagle's father. When Black Cloud hear daughter returned, he come to camp and take Shalee home. Gray Eagle wish to join. She refuse, been captive and angry. Black Cloud want to join her to Brave Bear. Gray Eagle come and fight challenge for her. He win. He give promised one — Chela — to Brave Bear to join. Make good choice and truce."

Morning Star saw how intrigued Joe was by her family history, so she continued it. "Bright Arrow was good friend to Singing Wind brother, Silver Hawk. He bad; he side with evil soldiers; he slain after Gray Eagle die, and before parents join. Rebecca, she Bright Arrow mate, missing long time, stolen by white men. Father and uncle both want Singing Wind and chief's bonnet. Half tribe want one; half tribe want other. Father prove best warrior; he win Mother and chief's bonnet. Rebecca returned to uncle."

Joe put aside his empty plate. "I was wondering how the youngest son became chief while his older brother was still alive. Now I understand. I knew about the ambush and Silver Hawk's treachery from the reports by Colonel Sturgis and Major Ames. The Army let me, Stede, and Tanner read them to learn what happened here thirty-one years ago. You eat while I tell you about my meeting with Captain James Thomas. I've kept you talking until your food is probably cold."

"It fine. Tell of soldier you met," she coaxed.

Joe had promised to help her with her English, but hadn't corrected her because he didn't want to interrupt her interesting revelations. There was plenty of time for lessons along their journey. As she ate and observed him, he related his meeting with Spotted Tail and with Jim.

Finished with her meal, Morning Star set her plate on the ground. "Can Joe and Morning Star trust him?" she asked.

Joe reflected on the meeting. "I hope we can; I think so. I didn't sense any dishonesty in him."

"Joe have sharp wits, so must be good man."

"I'm glad you have so much faith in me, Morning Star. I don't want to do or say anything to hurt or mislead you. I'll always tell you everything . . . when I can," he qualified his vow.

She understood. "I think and do same. We keep riding, looking?"

"Yes, but from now on, I don't cut my hair or shave my face. If I'm going to play a trader or trapper, I have to look like one. You'll have to excuse my unkempt appearance until we finish this task."

"Part of disguise?" she used another favorite new word, then laughed.

"Yep," he concurred, then smiled at her.

"I tend hand before wash things. Not want wound to go bad."

He grinned. "English lesson time. I will tend your hand before I wash the dishes. I do not want the wound to get infected."

Morning Star ran the words through her keen mind, then repeated them twice to stress the correct order to herself.

"Good," he complimented. "You're smart and fast."

"Thank you. I . . . will work hard to be good . . . partner."

"You're more than a good partner, Morning Star." Catching his lapse, Joe added, "Let's get these dishes washed and turn in."

"We will wash these dishes and go to sleep," she jested.

"Before I know it, you'll be teaching me a thing or two," he teased in return. "I'll help with the chores." He halted her refusal by saying, "In the white man's world, sometimes we help with women's chores. This is one of those times. We're both tired and we both need sleep. If I help, you'll be done sooner. There's no need for you to work harder than I do."

"You are kind and generous, Joe Lawrence. You do as you want, but it does not hurt your pride as a man. That is good. It pleases me."

It was dark by the time they finished the task and lay on their sleeping rolls. The fire had burned low, and would be allowed to go out to guard their safety. They didn't want any flames or smoke showing at a distance to entice trouble. The location was quiet. There were not many frogs or crickets; they heard an occasional owl hoot and the running of the stream. A slight breeze stirred the leaves and grass, but it carried along very few scents from wildflowers.

"Good night, Morning Star," he murmured.

"Good night, Joe." She refused to let the bittersweet memory of what had happened between them earlier come to her mind. It would only create a troubled spirit as she reminded herself why it shouldn't happen again. She remembered she hadn't tended his hand and started to remind him, but she decided it was best if they didn't touch again today. He had used Payaba's medicine and wrapped it in a clean cloth this morning anyhow. Yes, it was best to check on it after the sun chased away the romantic shadows.

As they ate and prepared to break camp, Joe asked, "Why did Night Stalker name his son Bloody Arrow? That seems strange for a baby."

Morning Star related the custom of her people. "Child is named when born. Most come from nature or something happening when enter life. When Night Stalker born, tribe traveling to summer camp. He called Trail Son. When boy reach flap to manhood and seeks vision, he takes new name, one given to him in vision-quest. Sometimes, but few, names not changed. Sun Cloud and Bright Arrow named by Gray Eagle. In vision-quests, Grandfather not give them new names. Grandfather name sons in Gray Eagle's visions."

Her English suffered as she related a terrible raid by their enemies two years ago. "When brother's son born, camp attacked by Pawnee. They big enemy like Crow and Shoshone. Wife shot by warrior. Bloody arrow removed from her arm as son enter life. Night Stalker use sign to give son name. He say it will be as with Father and Grandfather, and Great Spirit will not change when he become man. That bad; name and sign rule man and life. No place for bloody arrows in peace." She told Joe how strange was Touched-A-Crow and how bad Bloody Arrow. "I not want mate, child, or tepee like brother have."

"One last question before we ride out," Joe said. "Why did Buckskin Girl compete with you in the contest? You told me you girls are best friends." He had perceived her distress over that episode as she told of the contest.

"I not know. It strange." She repeated what Buckskin Girl had told her, which wasn't an explanation, only a promise for a future one.

"I do have one more question. Will you teach me the bow and arrow?" Joe asked.

"You steal surprise. I bring one for you. They silent, not loud like guns. I good with bow. I teach you. I must tend hand before we ride."

"I took care of it while you were downstream bathing. It's already healing and doesn't hurt. But thanks. Let's go."

It was late that afternoon when they came upon a Crow hunting or scouting party. Every member was dead. After checking to make sure no enemies were still in the area, they approached the bloody scene and dismounted. The five Bird People had Red Heart arrows protruding from their bodies, the red stripes on the shafts assessing to her people's guilt.

"See with eyes, we no do! All in camp!" she shouted, angered by the unknown foes who were trying to provoke a war to get her people killed.

"It's clear to me your people are being framed."

"Bad men have good . . . scheme. Soldiers and others blame Red Hearts. They attack and destroy for evil man. See tracks," she said, and pointed to them. "Some shod and some not. They use Lakota moccasins. Nations have different moccasins and tracks. They steal, use to fool. See broken armband? It Red Heart." Her eyes enlarged as she retrieved it and looked closer. There was no mistaking its meaning, and she was angry.

"What's wrong?" He questioned her reaction.

"It have marks, symbols, of Man-Who-Rides-Wild-Horses; he put on *wicagnakapi wiconti,* death scaffold, in sacred hills in past winter. Warriors buried with possessions. That where enemies get weapons and possession to use in . . . frame. It bad, evil, to steal from death scaffold. Crow would not do. It work of evil whitemen. I check tracks and trail."

Joe followed as the woman moved from place to place, bending here and there to study signs upon the ground. She tested the dryness of broken blades of grass and horse droppings. She checked to make certain the depth of the tracks revealed that all horses had heavy riders and none were pack animals or hauling raid booty. That and other clues, which she explained to him as she did her examination, told her how long the attackers had stayed in this location and when they had departed. He was impressed by her many talents.

"Seven men. Three on shod horses. Four not. Crow killed on last sun. Men ride that way," she remarked, pointing north. "They leave before sun sink into chest of Mother Earth to sleep. They not go far before camp; it soon dark. They less than one sun ahead. We follow. Must get Red Heart possessions and return to *wicag*—scaffolds. They must die."

Joe observed Morning Star's expression during her last two statements. Her eyes were squinted and her lips drawn tight. Her aura seemed as chilled as her dark gaze. "If we can capture one, Morning Star," he reasoned, "we can take him to the fort to be questioned. We need to convince others of what we've learned. If we kill all of them, we have no proof for the Army."

She protested his plan. "We get other proof. Morning Star know guilty. They must die for bad deed; Red Heart law say this. Must obey."

Joe studied her expression which exuded determination to see justice meted out under her laws. "Under white law, we arrest and jail thieves," he explained. "If the crime—deed—is very bad, the law punishes them by taking their lives. We can't gun down men just for stealing Indian possessions. That would make us as cold-blooded and wicked as they are."

"Not *just Indian possessions!* Sacred possessions. They dishonor dead and insult my people with this very bad deed. Warrior must have things on Ghost Trail, or he be naked and helpless. Evil spirits can attack before he reach Grandfather. It more . . . crime than *just stealing.*"

Joe wasn't certain how to argue against her religious beliefs without offending her, so he took a soft path. "The whites believe," he clarified, "when a man dies, he goes straight to our God. It is an insult to desecrate a grave and body, but the spirit is safe from all harm. Perhaps your Great Spirit saw the evil and He protected the warriors on the Ghost Trail. If He's kind and powerful, He won't let evil spirits attack His people. I promise we'll try to get their possessions back and return them."

Morning Star realized that part of his words were meant to appease her, and to obtain her agreement to his capture plan. "They murder Crow, and Crow friends of whites. That very bad crime. No white law here to . . . arrest and punish. We law here. We must punish."

"The Army's nearby, and they're white law."

"They far away, many suns' ride. How we carry evil men that far without trouble? If we seen or they talk, others learn our scheme and it over. They become too careful to find and punish. To do white man's law is not good trade to expose sacred vision task. It bad strategy."

Joe admitted she had a good point, a disturbing one. To take men in for questioning might expose their actions to Snake-Man. The only crimes the men had committed that he could prove were to wear moccasins, to steal burial treasures, and to kill Crow with stolen arrows. Those didn't tie them to Snake-Man, and they surely wouldn't confess to being his hirelings. Men on the payroll of such a clever and powerful villain would be more afraid of their boss than the law. Still, Joe was too civilized to gun men down without valid reason. He must find a way to capture one of the men, make him talk, then turn him over to Captain Jim Thomas without exposing his mission. "We have to do this the legal way, the right way under white man's law, Morning Star, or we'll be in as much trouble as Snake-Men and his boys when they're captured."

"If we make mistake, Joseph Lawrence be in big trouble. If Snake-Man learn of us, he try to kill to stop task. If he no can find and kill Joe, he kill men who sent Joe. If they slay soldier, agent, and Tanner's father—they can say you side with Indians against whites. You be framed. If we killed and Snake-Man leave Red Heart clues, Army say my people guilty and they attack. If we exposed, they frame Joe. Big trouble."

Joe comprehended that her main concern was for him. "I'm safe, Morning Star. The President knows about me and this mission."

"What if they tell President lies like false words they tell soldiers? What if they say Joe killed and buried, and Tanner lives and sides with us?"

He smiled and caressed her cheek. "You worry too much."

"What is worry?" she asked, locking her gaze to his.

"To feel uneasy, shaky inside, tormented by bad thoughts and feelings, a troubled spirit. Too much worry steals your peace of mind. It makes you think the worst will happen."

Her dark-brown eyes roamed his face, and she felt herself warm. "Morning Star have reasons to worry. If we defeated, big war come. Many of my people slain. Worry keeps tracker on alert. Some worry is same as instincts. If worry, not get reckless, make mistakes. Stay alive."

To ease her tension, Joe chuckled and said, "You're right. I'll stay a little worried, too. Right now, woman, let's get rid of these Red Heart arrows and moccasin tracks. This is one crime your people won't get blamed for. Let's see how we'll do this," he murmured.

"I teach you. Come, do with me."

Morning Star and Joe pulled the falsely incriminating arrows from the Crow bodies. Together they dragged the dead men to a spot, where she cut a sturdy branch from a tree, then roughly brushed the area clear of moccasin tracks. She checked to make certain no other clues were visible to the trained eye of an Indian or Army scout.

"You walk here to make boot tracks," she instructed, motioning for him to stomp around the area. When he finished, she told him, "Do same with horse with shoes. White men do; white men take blame."

When everything was arranged to her satisfaction, they mounted and rode northward. Morning Star kept a little ahead of him to read the trail signs. Joe stayed on alert, apprehensive about catching up with seven dangerous men. They tracked until it was too dark to continue.

As they made camp, Morning Star said, "We safe. Signs say they half sun more than us. We ride fast on new sun and catch."

"We are safe. The signs say they are a half day ahead of us. We will ride fast tomorrow and catch up with them," he corrected with a smile.

"That is best English?" she queried as she worked on their meal.

"Yes. Or, you can say: We're safe. The signs say they're a half day ahead of us. We'll ride fast tomorrow and catch up with them."

"How do you know when to use best English?"

"In an important situation, in company with many people, in

197

a formal setting."

"What is formal?" she asked.

Joe stroked his stubbled jawline and knit his brow. "That's a hard one. Let me think a minute." He did so. "Mercy, it means to be proper, and that means to be right at the right time."

Her expression was quizzical. She grasped all but one point. "How do you know when . . . it is the right time?"

Joe stretched out his legs and leaned against the tree behind him. "That's something you learn while you're growing up and going to school. Your teachers and parents tell you the right things to do."

"I did not go to school. Joe will me teach such things?"

"I'll try my best, Morning Star. It sounds easier than it is."

"It sounds . . . simple," she jested with a cheerful smile.

Joe laughed and nodded. "See, you have learned some good words. I'm not such a bad teacher after all."

She lowered her gaze to her task. "You are not bad in all ways. I change to. You are *good* in all ways. Is that right?"

"The English is right, and I'm grateful, but I'm not perfect." He laughed and quickly said, "Perfect means there's nothing wrong with me."

"Why is Joe not perfect? What is wrong with you?"

Joe couldn't take his eyes from Morning Star. Her allure was potent, nearly overpowering. To break the hold she was gaining over him, he jested, "Plenty, but I'll let you discover the truth for yourself." Joe was unaccustomed to any female other than his mother and sister being so honest. He liked that trait in Morning Star, but sometimes it caught him off-guard. He knew Annabelle Lawrence and Sarah Beth Lawrence Readon would like his Morning Star, and the Indian maiden would like his family. Joseph Sr. would take to this female easily and quickly. If—

"If Joe is not perfect, tell me one bad thing," she challenged as she broke into his reverie.

He said the first thing that came to mind, "I think like a white man."

Puzzled, she said, "You *are* white man. You must think white."

Joe crossed his legs at the ankles and drew them close to his buttocks. He leaned forward to rest his elbows on his thighs, letting his hands dangle toward the ground. "To you that's bad, because I have to do things the way I was raised, the way I believe. The same for you, Morning Star; you'll want to do things the way you were raised and believe. At times, we'll think the other is wrong or stubborn. We'll have to compromise; that's do it your way sometimes, and do it my way sometimes."

"Compromise," she echoed. "That is fair."

"Another thing — I lied to your father; that was wrong."

She shook her head. "It was . . ."

When she faltered in search of the right word, Joe said, "Necessary."

"Neces-sa-sary. Yes, it was necessary to get help."

"But it was still wrong, and I feel badly about it."

"Grandfather understand and forgive us. He knows all things."

"But I made you lie to them, too. I'm sorry."

"How is true?" she asked, looking dismayed.

"You knew the truth and you didn't expose me. By holding silent, you lied, too. We're in this together, partners. Until this danger is conquered, we can be honest only with each other, no one else. Understand?"

In a serious tone, she replied, "I understand and will obey."

He abruptly changed the subject, "When we're in your camp, be careful of Hawk Eyes and Knife-Slayer. I don't like them cheating — doing wrong — at something that's supposed to be sacred to them. If a man can betray himself, his people, and especially his God, he's dangerous."

Morning Star handed Joe his evening meal. As if revealing a crucial secret, her voice was a near whisper as she related, "Hawk Eyes may not be shaman long. Running Water went on vision-quest and saw elk. He member of Elk Dreamers. Payaba teaches him. Payaba say his vision powerful medicine. Big bird ride wind, then land on elk's head. They speak; they tell Running Water he to become Wind Bird and shaman. It good, yes?"

Joe realized she was excited by that possibility because of the change in her speech. "Yes, that will be very good."

Her food waited as she rushed on. "Night Stalker sides with his friend, Knife-Slayer. When truth comes soon, his eyes will clear. It make me happy. Brother cannot become chief until he is better man. He make Father sad with bad ways. I will make Father happy and proud with victory."

Darkness had closed in on them. Flickers from the fire danced wild and seductive patterns on their faces. They finished their meal in silence, as each felt the strong currents pulling them closer and tighter together. The area they were in was secluded, intimate, and intimidating. Each was thinking too much about the other, and trying to discourage such forbidden emotions.

Reacting to the strain and wanting it to lessen, Joe suggested, "Why don't we get to sleep? We had a long day, and it's late."

"That is best," she murmured in agreement.

The dishes were washed hurriedly and put away. Their sleeping mats were unrolled and placed at a safe distance apart. The fire was doused. They lay down, both breathing deeply in an attempt to relax.

"Good night, Morning Star."

"Good night, Joseph Lawrence."

Fatigued and well fed, they finally drifted off to sleep.

It was nearing dusk when the Oglala maiden lifted her hand to halt their progress. "Not far ahead. We leave horses and walk."

They dismounted and secured their animals' reins to bushes. Sneaking from tree to tree, they made their way forward to the enemy camp. Only three men were present, all palefaces, who were drinking, talking, and playing cards. Their horses were tethered by a stream.

Joe cupped his mouth to her ear and whispered, "Where are the others? We've been trailing seven. See or hear anything of them?"

Morning Star leaned close and replied, "Tracks of seven enter camp. If four leave another way, I not see from here."

Joe strained his eyes and ears to pick up any clues as to the location of the other men. He didn't like this. He prayed they hadn't been exposed and they weren't walking into a trap. "They could be farther ahead in another clearing. Maybe they're Indians, and they don't camp together. If we make too much noise, they'll come running to help. I wish I knew how to use a bow for silence. I can't risk using my guns. We'll have to wait until dark to attack. What is it?" Joe asked as he saw Morning Star's eyes suddenly widen, then just as suddenly narrow.

Morning Star glared at the sight of a white man laughing and holding up on Oglala religious object. She watched him pour whiskey into one opening while drunkenly asking if the buffalo wanted a drink of firewater. The more the man laughed and jested, the angrier she became. When the men began playing toss with the sacred item, she was consumed by ire. They had no respect or understanding of her people and their ways. It was the same as if an Indian dishonored one of their holy Bibles! "They have sacred buffalo skull whose spirit guards burial ground. Spirits angry, restless. Must get it back. That very bad sign. They much evil."

Joe knew they were in for another disagreement as to the men's fates. He could read it in her grave expression and deadly tone. If there were only three left in the area, they had a good chance of capturing at least one to question. "Don't worry; we'll get everything back. Just stay calm until dark. Two against three aren't bad odds. I just hope those others are gone permanently. They could be off hunting or scouting. No risks, Morning Star; I promised your father."

She looked him in the eye and said, "They must die. Die this moon."

Chapter Nine

Dusk closed in on them at a slow pace, but time for action would arrive soon. Morning Star's words to Joe kept echoing through her head. She realized she had sounded cold and hostile. When she had battled Clem, she had not tried to slay him, despite the white men's wicked treatment of her. Presently, she was facing another test of her ways and beliefs: foes were to be killed for such evil deeds. But, she asked herself, could she obey the laws of her people?

Morning Star had been given time to settle down and to think. Unless their lives were threatened, could she slay those scaffold robbers in cold blood? she fretted. The Indians those men had killed were enemies of her people, so their murders should not trouble her, yet they did. Added to that, the men had tried to blame her tribe and get them massacred. The most important tasks to her were to retrieve the sacred objects and falsely incriminating clues and to prevent the men from doing such a thing again. Did they have to die? Could they be frightened into not repeating that foul deed or into leaving Oglala territory? She doubted her last thought.

Together she and Joe had battled three-to-two odds in Zeke's camp. They could do the same here. These men were not on guard and might be weakened by whiskey. Perhaps it was best not to sneak up and slay them as animals during a hunt. Too, she didn't want to appear a bloodthirsty, wild savage to Joseph Lawrence. As his past words traveled through her mind, she knew it was compromise time.

Morning Star glanced at her handsome companion from the corners of her eyes. His azure gaze was locked on the enemy camp, and his expression was one of intense concentration. The events of the last few weeks filled her mind. Joe was so unlike any man she had known. He was kind and gentle, yet so strong and self-assured. He possessed a fox's cunning, a wolf's daring, and a hawk's speed during a strike at its prey. The color of heaven lived in his eyes; the golden sun reflected on his head; the shade of a tanned doe hide spread over his muscled body. He had all the traits and skills of a highly trained warrior, ones that would require a great force to defeat. His voice could be as soothing to a troubled spirit as rippling water in a stream or as powerful as a strong wind that blew where it willed. It was as if many forces of nature touched, honed, and controlled him. As one who lived in a world of nature, that pulled her closer to him.

So why, Morning Star mused, was it so terrible to desire such a special man, a man chosen and sent to them by the Great Spirit? Her wits responded that desire wasn't the main problem; yielding to it was. They warned her she must retain the strength to avoid dishonoring her family by surrendering to a forbidden situation. They demanded she be true to her parents, traditions, and people. If only, she worried, that task didn't become harder by the day! Resisting Joe was difficult, particularly when she didn't view it as wrong, as her people and laws did. Her grandfather and uncle had met, loved, and joined white women. If warriors could capture and bond with female enemies, why was it so wicked and shameful for an Indian maiden to do the same with a white man? It was unfair! With more and more whites entering their territory, the two cultures could not remain separate long.

A breeze from the north picked up in pace and strength. It ruffled Joe's tawny hair, but lacked enough power to have any effect on the maiden's heavy braids. It brought the campfire smell to them. It enticed tranquil nature to life. Grass bent southward, as if too lazy or weak to stand tall against such a force. Leaves moved as if trembling with cold. Fragrances of wildflowers drifted on the air currents. The breeze felt refreshing on their skin. It was a peaceful time of day. If only they did not have the dangerous chore awaiting them, they could relax and enjoy it.

Joe inhaled the mingled odors of simmering beans and perked coffee that wafted in the wind. He was glad his hungry stomach did not growl aloud. It was almost dark, and the less-than-half-moon would help conceal them. The men had eaten, then settled down to more cards and whiskey. To Joe, they seemed in no hurry to turn in, as if they had no tiring ride ahead tomorrow. He speculated that they were waiting for somebody or something. He'd like to spy until he learned the answer to that puzzle, but it was too risky. Their prey could be awaiting a Crow party to spread lies about the Oglalas, or Snake-Man's hirelings and a delivery, or the return of their four friends. He couldn't stay and chance overwhelming odds; nor could he retreat, because he needed some questions answered and a starting point to solve this task.

Joe sensed Morning Star watching him, and it played havoc with his concentration on the camp. He sensed she had mastered her fiery emotions. Being near her was like sailing into the tropics, sultry and invigorating. It inspired suspense about what one would discover in that paradise. She was so alive and full of energetic fire that he could almost warm himself in her glowing essence. Morning Star was sensual, earthy, an innocent child of nature, a woman of provocative and entrancing spirit.

As she lay on the grassy incline beside him, Joe glimpsed lovely legs that were exposed from the way her buckskin dress had hiked up itself from wriggling movements during her observations. The well-fitting garment did more than hint at her shapely and taut figure. The short fringe at elbow-length sleeves grazed coppery skin on her arms; longer fringe at the tail caressed matching flesh on her legs. The beadwork — red, light and dark blue, and yellow — was in the Arapaho design, in line with her alleged identity. It was the same with her matching moccasins with their red mountain symbols rising into blue sky and the double-pointed yellow arrow to indicate the span of Arapaho territory. Her ebony hair, parted down the center, was braided, the ends decorated with colorful rosettes of skilled beadwork on small circles of buckskin. Her features were soft yet defined, giving her a unique beauty. He wanted to stroke her silky flesh, but dared not.

When Morning Star teased her lower lip with her top teeth, Joe had the urge to pull her into his arms so he could do the same. He yearned to feel her mouth against his once more, to taste her sweetness, to coax her response. His loins came to life, and his breathing quickened. He scolded himself for his lapse in attention to their peril and for his carnal cravings for Sun Cloud's daughter. He must keep reminding himself of that truth, of that and all the other many obstacles which stood between them, including his implied promise to Sun Cloud.

Joe focused on the still-active camp and frowned. His tension increased by the hour. He wanted this hazardous matter settled soon. It wasn't good to let anxiety build, as it stole alert and it dulled wits. He studied the location again. It was impossible to sneak over safely without a cover of darkness, which was slow in arriving. He waited.

Morning Star perceived Joe's attraction to her; it made her happy and worried. She needed his strength of denial to help her retain hers. If he leaned her way, how could she ever resist him? A fierce longing for him mounted within her each day, and she did not know how long she could control it. His warning about the emotional peril of them riding together was accurate. Yet she wanted to be no other place except in his arms. He was so close that she could reach over and touch him, and was tempted to do so. *No*, she ordered. *Always hold your distance or all is lost.*

At last, night blanketed the area, but the men added wood to the already dancing flames to brighten their campsite. Joe and Morning Star lingered on the embankment for the right moment to attack and prepared themselves. They removed anything that would make noise and prevent stealth. They covered anything light or shiny that might reflect the moon's glow or firelight, including Joe's blond hair. They also discarded anything cumbersome that might slow their pace. When all was ready, they observed with heightened alert, eager to make their move.

When one man stood, stretched, and told his friends he was going to be excused, Joe reacted with haste. "Stay down and quiet," he whispered into the woman's ear. "I'll work my way over and get rid of one of them. Don't move until I return or signal you," he ordered in a tone of protectiveness.

After he vanished into the shadows, Morning Star smiled, delighted by his concern. She listened and watched. Joe moved in complete silence, and she was proud of his prowess. She nocked her weapon to be ready to fire an arrow when needed.

205

She almost held her breath in suspense. This was the first test of their skills during the sacred mission. She prayed that everything would go right.

Time passed. All she heard were muffled voices from the two men near the fire, a pair of owls calling to each other, and the thudding of her heart within her ears. The large fire illuminated the clearing and provided a perfect view of the site. She wondered why they wanted such a big one, when only a slight chill was in the air tonight. Besides, it revealed their number and positions to any foe who happened by. It wasn't a smart action for men who had gotten away with so many clever deeds! Why were they so reckless—or so confident? Surely it wasn't a trick to lure them into that trap Joe had feared. If the other four were still nearby, wouldn't her keen senses detect them? She concentrated on the scene. Her ears strained to catch any warning sound and her eyes searched the shadows for a sign of trouble lurking in them. Nothing. She cautioned herself not to allow her worry over Joe to cloud her judgment and skills.

A man in camp stood and called to the one who had left the lighted area, "Hey, Coop! Wot's takin' so long?" When no response came, he called louder, "Coop! Anythin' wrong?" Nothing, so he yelled again, "Coop, where are ya, man?" then retrieved his rifle.

Morning Star saw the missing man appear at the edge of the campsite, and she froze in panic. There had been plenty of time for Joe to reach and conquer him. What had gone wrong? Where was Sky Warrior? If he'd been unable to attack, why hadn't he returned to her side?

Joe, discuised in the first man's jacket and floppy hat, walked closer to his target with a lowered head. He ignored their questions, as his voice would expose him. He hoped to get near enough to clobber the one with the rifle hanging loosely in his grasp and get some answers as to why he and the others had slain that Crow band and framed the Red Hearts. He wasn't sure how far he would go to force out information; only time would answer that for him. Joe did not reach and overpower the armed man before the other one became suspicious of his behavior and shouted a warning.

"Sompin's wrong! He ain't got Coop's limp! An' his beard's

too short!"

The man's friend turned fast for someone who had been drinking for hours and stared. He comprehended the trick, especially when Joe didn't refute the warning and identify himself. He yanked up his rifle to shoot.

Joe had no choice but to shove open the jacket, grab his Colt Walker, and fire it. He did so with speed, agility, and accuracy, his lethal bullet striking the shocked man. Before he could turn the nine-inch barrel of his .44 caliber on the last man, who also had lunged for his weapon, it was over. His astonished gaze traced the path of the deadly arrow that struck home with a thud, but it was too dark to see her. He knocked off the hat and shouted, "It's me, Morning Star! Don't shoot!"

Guessing the clever ruse unfolding in camp, Morning Star had jumped to her feet and hurried forward to level ground. She had braced herself, aimed, and sent an arrow into the last man's heart to save Joe's life.

She rushed forward to his side as he discarded the jacket. "I know is Joe. I see trick. Very cunning. When take long time, I worry." Her gaze raced over him from head to foot to make certain he was all right. She gave a loud exhale of relief, then watched him check the men.

His blue gaze met her brown one as he reported, "All dead. Thanks for saving my neck again. I'm glad you didn't panic and that you jumped in when I needed help. That was a good shot. Don't forget to teach it to me later." Impressed by her quick reflexes, he smiled and explained, "I stepped on a branch in the dark and exposed myself to that land pirate. He pulled a knife and came at me. Thank goodness he didn't shout a warning. I knew I had to silence him fast before he did. When I heard another one call to him, I was afraid they might have heard our struggle. I still thought it was worth the chance to get the drop on them with that disguise."

"Disguise cunning. We make good partners, yes?"

"Yes, we do. I just wish I'd noticed Coop's limp, but I was talking to you and didn't see it. He was easy to find in the dark; he wasn't trying to be quiet. I figured I could get close enough to take them before I gave myself away. I'll have to work on my sneaky skills. In the cave you said that is was good to be friends with the dark, but I guess I haven't learned enough yet. I'm happy you're here with me, Morning Star."

"You not angry we kill them?" she asked, looking concerned.

His hand lifted to caress her flushed cheek. "We had no choice this time. Let's get what we came for and move out fast. I'm still worried about those other four returning. That big campfire makes me suspicious. If they're still around, that gunfire could bring them running." Joe didn't want to risk a shootout with four men who knew of their presence and probably were well armed. During such a battle, it was doubtful he could capture one of the villains to question, and he didn't want to get pinned down until more culprits arrived. Even if an ambush worked in their favor, leaving too many bodies around would create suspicions in the wrong man—their boss.

"It's too dark to locate and follow their trail," he murmured, "and we can't hang around to see if they come back at first light. They might not be alone. Hopefully they're long gone and didn't hear those shots." Joe glanced at the grim sight they would leave behind. "It's time to put my other plan in motion," he told her. "Let's return these relics to their scaffolds, then ride for Orin McMichael's trading post to see what we can learn. Don't forget your arrow; we don't want innocent Arapahoes blamed for this."

Morning Star agreed with Joe. Together they collected the stolen Oglala possessions and sacred skull. Joe searched the men's saddlebags, but found nothing that could aid his mission. While Morning Star packed up the things she wanted returned to the tribal gravesite and recovered her arrow, Joe freed the men's horses. They returned to their mounts and rode five miles southwestward before making camp.

Exhausted, they ate the dried meat called *wasna* and bread pones called *aguyapi* and washed them down with fresh water. They did not build a campfire, as the area had not been scouted for enemy presence. Morning Star put away their supplies, and Joe prepared their bedrolls. He placed only a short distance between them tonight. Both lay down.

Since their lethal task in the white men's camp, they had spoken little. Each seemed to be adjusting to the gravity of the episode. Killing men, even in self-defense, did not come easy for

208

either one. The incident had stressed how serious their mission was and what it would require of them. Many things would be difficult to do, but surely peace was worth that price. Each knew it was wrong to view the situation as a pretense, and each knew they had to do their best not to kill more than necessary.

They lay in silence and gazed at the stars overhead. The night seemed too peaceful to hold a deadly confrontation so that reality moved to the backs of their minds. Soon, both drifted off to sleep.

Morning Star and Joe entered the Black Hills by late afternoon. The path that she took was not an arduous one, so their ride was easy and steady. Joe had no problem keeping up with his beautiful guide. As they traveled to the area she sought, his gaze took in the wonder of the setting, as hers had done many times in the past. They journeyed through color-splashed meadows, between towering pinnacles of obsidian rocks in many shapes and sizes, into and out of cool forests of spruce and pine and hardwoods, and beside running streams whose water played around stones and twigs. Everything was green and alive and fragrant. A refreshing breeze and frequent shade prevented the sun's heat from affecting them too severely. Though the sky was a deep blue, snowy clouds were turning gray in the distance. Several times they spooked deer, elk, antelope, and smaller creatures and a few times they encountered small herds of buffalo who were grazing on lush grass or lazing upon the verdant surface.

Joe understood why this area was so valued. Timber was abundant and sturdy, when much of the adjoining territory lacked a wood supply. Water was fresh and plentiful, as was lush grass for grazing. Lovely valleys offered sheltered surroundings from the harsh northern winters. The Plains could feed numerous cattle or other stock, and no clearing was needed for farms. It was perfect for civilization and exploitation.

They reached a clearing that was enclosed on three sides by tall rock formations. Bushes and trees grew at the edges and the center was filled with scaffolds that looked like beds of wood on lofty stilts. The flow of wind and tightly wrapped bodies prevented heavy odor of death that Joe had expected to find there; that was also the reason why no scavengers were drawn to the sacred site to feast.

Joe experienced a sensation of awe, as if he were in a holy place or church. He heard and saw no animal or bird to rend the tranquility, but it did not give him an eerie feeling. It almost felt as if be were on hallowed ground, as the Indians believed of their burial sites. If the Great Spirit existed, or was God in another form and He did watch over a special location, this had to be one. It sent home the Indian's belief in the sacred Circle of Life, from Great Spirit and Mother Earth at birth to their return in death. Morning Star had told him the bodies and possessions remained on the scaffolds until the forces of nature reclaimed them. Sturdy and built with love, the eternal sleeping beds lasted as long as they were needed.

Joe and Morning Star dismounted and secured the reins of the three horses to bushes at the natural entrance of the clearing. A tall cottonwood post was in the middle of the path. Eagle feathers and rawhide pouches were attached to the top. A large stub at head height caught his attention, and he watched the maiden slip the weather-bleached buffalo skull onto it, then he saw her retrieve items from the ground and replace them: religious tokens and special grasses and herbs that the white thieves had snatched out and discarded.

Morning Star glanced at her companion and said, "Natahu Wakan guards fallen warriors until journey to Grandfather is done. It warns enemies not to enter this sacred place. Most do not. Grandfather guided us to evil whites to take back Natahu Wakan. It is good. Come, I return warriors' possessions. Their spirits will be happy with our great deed."

As Joe followed her around the area, he carried the bundle and helped her replace the stolen property. Morning Star was tall, but many of the scaffolds were beyond her easy reach. He watched her to use markings on the eastern posts to identify from which ones the items had been taken, as the belongings were also marked with ownership. While they worked, he kept glancing at the signs of a storm heading their way.

Morning Star noticed nature's warnings, too. The sky displayed puffy white clouds whose faces were quickly turning a dark gray, as if anger were building inside them. The rapid change in colors told her the weather's temper would explode soon in a violent storm. The wind's force increased steadily, tugging at feathers on lances, shields, and bows. It teased across her flesh, and it raced through leaves and grass. Her skin detected moisture in the air; her keen nose smelled it.

The maiden studied the heaven once more and said, "Must hurry. Bad storm come soon. *Wakinyan,* Thunder Birds, live inside *tipi* clouds. When Grandfather say Mother Earth need water, He tell *Wakinyan* to leave *tipi,* to flap wings and make thunder, to open and close eyes to make lightning, to spill water from big lakes on backs. Eyes not see Thunder Birds. They fly fast and high, and hide in sky mist. Thunder warn people to seek shelter."

Joe was amused by her explanation of thunder, rain, and lightning, yet, he did not smile or chuckle and offend her for those erroneous beliefs and superstitions. It was the way she had been reared. Even if he explained science and weather to her, she might not understand it or believe him. He could not tell her she was mistaken or ignorant about so many things. But, as time passed, he would educate her with respect. For now, he continued his task.

As they moved through the burial site, they collected Crow beads, bits of red trade cloth that the Bird People favored, a tribal exposing arrow here and there, and a few other falsely incriminating clues dropped around to inflame the Oglala against the Crow. Just as the slain Crow party would appear the work of the Red Heart Band, this "evidence" was meant to frame the Oglalas' foes. Since Joe and Morning Star knew who was responsible for both incidents, both comprehended they were right in presuming someone wanted to provoke an intertribal war.

"We need to make certain the Crow and your people learn about these two tricks, Morning Star. There's no telling how many frames we won't find and halt, or how many old ones weren't genuine. I know they're enemies of your people and have been for generations, but these tricks can cause a bloody war. I hate to think of how many innocent people have died in retalitory raids for crimes their tribe didn't commit. When war-

211

riors go into battle, they aren't the only ones at risk. Their camps and families are in danger of attacks — children, women, and old people who can't defend themselves. If we don't open everyone's eyes to the truth, this entire area will become a blood-soaked battlefield." His mind wouldn't let him forget that Morning Star and her family — Tanner's kin — would be trapped in the middle, as would blameless white settlers and soldiers.

"Grandfather will guide us and help us, Joe," she encouraged. "He works with us for peace. Can you not see this truth in all that has been?"

"We'll keep talking to our gods, and pray they listen."

She tugged at his arm. "Come, I know place to hide from storm."

Joe lifted the bundle, this time filled with enemy items, and followed her to the horses. At the burial site entrance, he waited for her to pray to her god, then mount. Joe closed his eyes and sent a prayer to his, then pulled himself into his saddle. "You're the leader, Morning Star; guide on."

The maiden returned his smile and kneed her Appaloosa. Joe's gaze sent warm tingles over her body. She pushed that thought and the desecrated burial ground out of her mind. She must reach cover before bad weather overtook them.

The storm was approaching fast, but Morning Star knew her way around these hills. She headed for a place she remembered where the lower part of a black cliffside suddenly jutted outward near the base. The outthrust was sufficient to create an overhang with enough height, depth, and width for them to obtain protection from rain and lightning. It wasn't large enough for the horses, too, but animals were used to being out in the weather and would be safe in a copse of hardwoods.

Joe eyed the spot she chose. Beneath the ledge was a space of five feet by five feet, with a ceiling of four feet. The smooth rock seemed to form a slate roof to cover the inviting location. By then, thunder rumbled and lightning slashed overhead. "Let's get our supplies and bedrolls under cover," Joe shouted. "You grab some wood and I'll tend the horses. That rain'll be coming down in barrels soon."

They worked with haste, and had everything prepared within a short time. A small campfire heated the beans that Joe had taken from the dead men's supplies. Along with the dried meat and bread pones from Singing Wind, the couple ate a quick and satisfying meal. Joe set their empty dishes on a ring of inky stones around a cheery blaze. Drops of water struck his body and the surroundings, then rapidly became larger and heavier.

"Hurry, it's here. Leave the dishes. The rain will wash 'em."

Sounds of wind and thunder were joined by a noisy deluge of water. The campfire just beyond the rock overhang was doused within seconds. Joe and Morning Star laughed as they wriggled to the back of the snug area to keep dry and warm. They sat on Joe's bedroll to watch nature's drama unfold. Supplies, stored at one side and covered by his slicker, compelled them to sit close in the gradually darkening hideout.

Brilliant flashes of lightning frequently illuminated the cozy area. A few times, both jumped as startling thunderbolts boomed nearby. After each reaction, they exchanged glances and shared laughter. Heavy rain flowed down the cliff face that rose upward to a towering spire with a rounded top. It poured over the extended ledge, but there was enough of an incline to send the flood of liquid the other way. Except for earth-dampening splatters, their area stayed dry. They kept their feet tucked close to their bodies so they wouldn't get wet. They leaned their heads against an inky wall and gazed at the partition of water that obscured the outside world.

Trapped between the downpour and rocks, they were enclosed in a setting that reeked of intimacy. When vivid streaks of lightning blazed across the sky, it sparkled on the watery flap to their romantic tepee. During one lengthy bout of lightning that split into many branches and seemed to hang in the sky a long time, Joe looked over at his companion. She was so beautiful and desirable, so close, so out of reach.

Morning Star returned Joe's lingering gaze. The whiskers on his face had grown during their days together, and, for a man with golden hair, the short beard looked dark against his tanned face. In the dimness with only nature's flashes of light, she saw how blue his eyes were. Her shoulder touched his, and the contact was pleasing and arousing. She was glad the space was tight and forced them to sit close. The shadows of their present world and the sounds from beyond it created an aura of mystery and anticipation. She realized she was apprehensive about their impending journey into the white settlement, but felt safe and strong knowing Joe would be at her side. With him, she felt as if she could do almost anything. She watched him remove his boots and set them aside; she did the same with her moccasins. They shared a sleeping roll, keeping their weapons within reach. When a burst of dazzling light came again, Joe was still watching her with that bittersweet look.

Joe observed Morning Star as she unbraided her ebony hair and withdrew a brush to work on it. Soon, it lay silky and sensual around her shoulders. When she started to replait it, his hand stayed hers and he coaxed, "Don't. Leave it free. It's as shiny and black as a raven's wing. It's beautiful, like you are, Morning Star."

When she trembled at his stirring words, he assumed she was chilled, as the temperature had dropped. He retrieved a blanket and tossed it over their legs, then drew it up to their shoulders. He put his arm around her to settle the cover into place on her distant shoulder, then left his arm there. It felt warm and strong to Morning Star and she could not resist snuggling against him. Joe responded by moving his arm across her chest, near her throat, and clasping her nearest shoulder with his fingers. Morning Star leaned her head back to rest it against his cheek and neck. Her hand lifted to cover his. She felt Joe lean his head into hers. It was delightful to be snuggled together in the serene setting.

Joe told himself to enjoy this brief moment of weakness and contact but to go no further with his yearnings. Yet a fierce longing to kiss her galloped through his body at breakneck speed. He seemed unable to restrain that runaway sensation. "I've never met a woman like you, Morning Star," he murmured. "You make me feel so good inside. I missed you when I rode to the fort. I couldn't get back fast enough. I was afraid you'd become my helper—but more afraid you wouldn't. I want to be with you all the time. I want to hold you and kiss you. I'm sorry you think I'm stronger and more trustworthy than I deserve."

Sun Cloud's daughter rashly turned her head and body until their faces were within inches of each other. She raised her hand and stroked his cheek. As dusk had dimmed the light inside their rock dwelling, she could barely see him. She wished each burst of brightness was longer, as she couldn't look at him enough. "It is same with me, Joe. I am weak and cannot be trusted. What we do?"

The desire in her voice was evident to him. He seemed to tremble with yearning as much as she did; that was unusual for him, as he had learned self-control. He had to kiss her, he had to! Joe's head bent downward and his mouth sought hers. With her assistance, he had no difficulty finding her sweet lips.

Morning Star was staggered by the potency of the lengthy kiss. She thrilled to the way his mouth explored hers, and was surprised by the instinctive way hers responded. She heard him moan at the same time she did. She felt him tense and shudder at the same time she did. Her heart told her that a little kissing and hugging wouldn't do any harm. If her mind argued, she didn't hear it. She twisted her body until she was lying in his arms and facing the back of the shelter. She nestled closer. She felt his embrace tighten and his kisses deepen. Her arms clung to his body, wanting no space between them for a short time.

Joe had the same good intentions of only enjoying a few kisses, hugs, and caresses. His fingers wandered into her silky hair, then trailed over her satiny skin. She was so soft and sleek. He ached to have her completely, just once. It would give him a beautiful memory that he would never forget and probably never find again. His body burned with flames of desire. His spirit hungered to feast on her.

Morning Star was lost in a rapturous world of spinning desires. As her lips teased over his face and nibbled at his mouth, she murmured, "We fit like pair of moccasins. We match like petals on flower." She had been told that most men were not good with romantic words, that most used actions to show their feelings. Joe was different; he did both.

Soon they were inflamed beyond clear reason. Her hands traveled under his loosened shirt for her eager fingers to feel the hardness of his supple frame. She wore a two-piece buckskin outfit today, and Joe's hand slipped beneath her top and closed over one breast. Surges of pleasure stormed their bodies as fiercely as the weather was storming the world outside their secluded dwelling.

"I want you so much, Morning Star," Joe almost growled against her responsive mouth. "I know I shouldn't, but I can't help myself."

Before she could tell him she felt the same, his lips captured her and sent her mind to reeling. She loved him and wanted him. How could such powerful feelings be wrong? So many forces had tried to keep Gray Eagle and Alisha, Bright Arrow and Rebecca, apart; they had all failed, because the Great Spirit had brought both mixed couples together and given them a love too strong and tight to be broken or denied. It was as if she had waited for this tender ecstasy all of her life. A savage and bittersweet longing swept through her. Her mind and heart were too ensnared to resist this stolen moment. Her grandfather and uncle had surrendered to mixed love, so it could not be so terribly wrong for her to do so. They were honored legends, as she hoped she would be when this sacred task was done. She could not summon the will to refuse what she wanted with all her soul. Tonight, she and Joe could not help themselves; their match was irresistible, was fated, at least this much of it was, no matter what happened later.

Joe was lost in a whirlwind of emotions and sensation. He drew her to him with possessiveness. His breathing was ragged, his heart drummed within his chest. He seemed to quiver like a feather in a strong breeze. The storm outside ravaging the land was nothing compared to the one assailing him. He had no choice but to submit to whatever fate had in store for them tonight. He shifted his weight, which allowed them to sink to his bedroll.

Morning Star went along with him, willing and eager. His masculine scent filled her nostrils. His touch was tantalizing. Her deft fingers freed the buttons on his shirt and her fingers traced the smooth and hard surface of his chest where no hair grew but where muscles rippled like water over rocks. She explored the wonders of his compelling physique. Her head rolled to one side as his tongue trailed down her throat, then with titillating leisure returned to her mouth.

Their lips meshed with fierceness and urgency. The emotions they had tried to deny and restrain for so long burst free and galloped away. There was no way to recapture the innocence they

216

were leaving behind.

Morning Star savored the way Joe's hands felt on her pliant body. Her breasts did not want him to leave them. Yet she longed for so much more, and she had a suspicion where their new trail would lead.

Joe was as spellbound by the blissful moment as she was. His lips brushed over her face, halting at each feature to explore it in detail. His experiences with women had never prepared him for this rare one. He didn't want this to end. He wanted to keep her forever.

They continued their discoveries of each other, and reveled in the joys of them. Each knew their destinies were being forged into one, and they must find some way to help fate along. Each burned with desire. Each knew there was no turning back.

As their mouths clung together, Joe, with her help, wriggled out of his shirt. Morning Star, with Joe's assistance, removed her top, their lips parting only long enough for the garment to pass between them. When their bare chests touched, they seemed to cling to each other with wills of their own. While Joe caressed a breast with one hand and showered the other with ecstatic kisses, Morning Star loosened the ties of her breechcloth, as her skirttail had raised itself long ago during her writhings. She did not pull away to remove her skirt, and was only half conscious of it being between them. After Joe's seeking hand covered the distance between her breasts and abdomen, she arched and moaned when it made contact where she had never been caressed before.

Joe stroked and caressed his love until both could no longer stand the denial. His hand halted only long enough for him to work the fasteners of his pants. He moved atop Morning Star and slipped between her parted thighs, lowering his pants as he did so. He did not have to ask her if she was sure about continuing, her actions told him she was as willing to proceed as he was. With caution, he lowered his body to hers and entered the paradise he had dreamed of for weeks. Her response told him he had not hurt her.

Morning Star was consumed by the wonder of becoming a woman, Joe's woman, of surrendering to love completely. She had been right; they fit as perfectly as the best matched pair of

217

moccasins. It did not feel strange to have him within her; it felt right, wonderful, as if it should be.

Joe experienced those same thoughts and feelings. They were joined as one, as it was destined to be. Perhaps he had sensed that truth the first night they meet. He accepted the fact that he loved her. In all ways but one—under white law—she was his wife. He vowed to keep her for as long as possible. She was his, so that had to forever.

Morning Star's fingers halted their trek at the wound Joe had gotten while rescuing her. Even when they were strangers, he had been willing to die for her. Whatever it took, they had to find a way to stay together during and after this sacred mission. Surely Grandfather would not put such love in their hearts only to force them apart later.

As the most glorious moment of this new and rapturous experience burst upon them, they kissed and clung together as if promising nothing and no one would ever come between them. There was no retreat, no restraint. They savored the final destination they had reached together. For a time they were aswirl in a glowing mist that shut out all reality except for this blissful ending to something both had craved. Pleasure melted into contentment as they snuggled together, sated for now.

The thunder and lightning had ceased, but heavy rain continued to fall. It was music to their ears and relaxing to their spirits. Both sighed deeply as the they rested after their lovemaking. Without meaning to do so, each allowed the reality of the world outside to enter their minds. Perhaps it was the darkness of their surroundings which denied sight of each other's face that reminded them of their grim situation.

"Morning Star—"

She covered his mouth with her quivering hand. "Do not speak bad words. We joined in hearts and spirits. We have much this moon. We can have nothing more. Do not bring sadness and pain to our hearts."

Joe understood what she was saying and feeling. This was her world and her culture. His were far away; they could not join or overlap. He agonized over that truth, as neither could give up who they were. Her world would not accept him, and his would not accept her. They were too smart to say that nothing mattered

218

except their love. And he knew he did love her. Those words were hard for a man to confess the first time he truly meant them. Surely she guessed it from his mood and actions, as he knew she must love him to surrender tonight. If he spoke his innermost feelings aloud, it could frighten her and cause her to withdraw from him. People could not survive by love alone. Having everyone and everything against a union could damage it severely. But he was not ready to face that challenge yet. For as long as he could, he had to hold on to her. He embraced her tightly as he tried to accept what his heart refused to believe: that he would lose her.

Morning Star tried to halt any dream of a future with Joe from forming. It was futile, hopeless, and forbidden.

When she started to tense, he asked, "What is it?"

"I wash while rain still comes." She freed herself from his arms and, finding her way with her fingers against the stone roof, she crawled to the front of their shelter. She moved outside and stood in the pouring rain, naked, chilled, and heartbroken. The rain flowed over her slender, shapely body and washed away the traces of their lovemaking.

Joe finished removing his pants, then joined her and did the same. He lifted his face skyward and allowed the cold water to cool his hot body and remove his sweat. His heart felt heavy inside his chest. He raged at the obstacles that stood between him and the only woman he had ever loved. More so, he raged at his helplessness, his inability to overcome them. Despite his father's strength and Joe's respect for him, Joe had left home against the elder Joseph Lawrence's wishes. Something within him had demanded he seek the man he was inside, the man hidden by his father's shadow. He had been compelled to do something on his own, not just take over a business handed to him through an inheritance. He had hungered for adventure and excitement, and couldn't be blamed for seeing shipping as unfulfilling. He loved his parents and had obeyed them until his restlessness had forced him to walk away from home. One day he would return and take the place expected of him. By then, he would be mature and his wild thirst would be quenched. He would be confident and content, a man of his own. At least he had felt that way until meeting the woman beside him. Now, what would his life be without her?

As they stood there in anguish and silence, the rain slowed and halted. Clouds drifted westward, and the partial moon offered scant light. Joe gave a loud sigh then fetched a blanket. He handed it to Morning Star and watched her dry her flesh. Neither could see much of the other's unclad body, but neither shielded themselves. She returned the cover, and he did the same. Joe hung it over the ledge to dry if the sun came out in the morning. They ducked and returned to the bedroll, but they did not redress in the cramped darkness.

Joe took another blanket and lay down on it. "Let's get some sleep. We'll talk tomorrow," he suggested, and tossed the cover over them.

Morning Star snuggled into his beckoning arms and her chill left. For now she would enjoy his embrace but, she cautioned herself, there was no way to remove the stone wall separating them. When morning came, she must concentrate only on the dangerous task looming before them. "Sleep, Joe. A hard task rides before us."

The white man's arms pulled her more closely against him. He smiled when she nestled into his embrace. She fit perfectly in his arms. If only, he agonized, she could fit as perfectly into his life in Virginia. Even if she studied and worked hard for years, she could not change herself into an aristocratic southern belle. And even if by some miracle she did, she would no longer be Morning Star. He could not alter her into something she wasn't just so he could have her forever.

Nor, Joseph Lawrence the younger realized, could he remain here in Lakota Territory for the rest of his life. His family, work, friends, and life were back in Virginia. He had responsibilities and duties to his family and to his father's shipping business. He loved this wild and carefree existence but, he admitted, he would miss civilization eventually. It was just as cruel to let Morning Star think he would remain here after their task. A world and breed apart — that said it all and he must accept it.

Morning Star was not sorry she had yielded to Joe. Her problem was forcing wild thoughts and dreams from her head. She had heard many tales of how life was in the white world: eating at big tables, having wooden tepees with furniture, dressing in long gowns, behaving in strange ways, working away from your home to earn money, having slaves—servants—to tend your chores, getting food and supplies in stores. To think of going there was intimidating. She could imagine how the whites would treat her, and how they would treat Joe for bringing her into their "society." No, she could not be happy in the white world, just as Joe could not be happy here. She must not hope for more from him than he had given tonight. She could no more expect him to live in her strange world than he could expect her to do so in his.

After an hour of each telling themselves a permanent bond between them could never come to pass, their troubled hearts found appeasement in sleep.

Joe eased from her side and grabbed his clothes. He slipped away to excuse himself and dress. He knew he had awakened her, so he gave her time to do the same while he checked on the horses. When he returned to the shelter, Morning Star had the sleeping mats rolled and tied. She was clad in the same buckskin outfit she had worn yesterday, and she looked as fresh as the spring day in progress. She glanced at him and smiled. Relieved, he returned the gesture.

She focused on her chore. "Wood is wet and no burn. We eat little and ride. We eat more when stop to rest and wood is dry for fire."

"Morning Star . . ." he began in a hesitant voice, kneeling near her.

Her chocolate gaze met his blue one. She caressed his bearded cheek. "No need to speak of last moon. Let it sleep in our hearts until best time to speak of it. That not today. We friends. We partners."

"When the time comes for both of us, we'll have to talk about it."

She gazed deeply into his eyes. "That is so," she said, grasping how dismayed he was. She believed he loved her as she loved him, but it was too soon to expose such strong feelings. They needed more time together. If their Life Circles were meant to cross or to mingle, they would discover that wonderful truth

221

when the Great Spirit willed it.

"Thanks," he said, his gaze softening and glowing.

She knew what he meant. "Eat, and we ride."

It was midafternoon and they were out of the Black Hills. The sun was radiant and the sky was clear. Everything smelled fresh and was vivid green following the drenching rain. In four days they should reach Orin McMichael's trading post on the Missouri River, about forty miles north of the settlement that had come to be known as Pierre, pronounced Peer.

Joe lifted himself in his saddle and stared beyond them. He locked his eyes on a rider he recognized and studied him. His mind went to work quickly. He related his daring plan to Morning Star, who nodded her agreement with apprehension. "Let's ride. There's our chance to put a good plan into motion. Remember, you're my squaw, so behave like one," he jested and grinned. "We don't want to get ourselves shot."

Morning Star summoned her courage to face this challenge.

Chapter Ten

Joe and Morning Star realized they were about twenty miles from the site where they had met weeks ago. They had just crossed Elk Creek and left a treeline, after watering their mounts and pack animal. The man Joe had spied was approaching their location slightly to their left, coming from the northwest and heading southeast. As they were riding from the southwest to northeast, their paths would intersect soon. The stranger had seen them leave the trees and was continuing his course, obviously unafraid of them.

As the two traveling parties neared each other, the sunny-haired man and Oglala maiden noticed that the man with two loaded mules was dressed in a buckskin shirt and pants with lengthy fringes. The closer they rode, the more Joe and Morning Star took in details about him. The stranger's appearance and possessions told the couple he was a mountain man who was coming out of the wilderness to sell furs and pelts.

Joe told Morning Star to rein up and await the man's arrival, to see what they could learn from him. When he reminded her of her deceitful role, the maiden lowered her head and began her part as a submissive squaw to fool their company. She recalled how she had lost that part of the vision contest and how she was expected to behave. She cautioned herself to do and say nothing to endanger their task.

The trapper joined them. He removed a pelt hat and used one hand to mop perspiration from his brow. "Whar you headin'?" he asked Joe.

The blue-eyed man leaned forward and propped his arms on his saddle horn. Smiling, Joe replied, "For McMichael's post on the Missouri. You're the first person I've seen in days. Name's Joe Lawrence. This is my Arapaho squaw, Little Flower. Where you heading?"

After sending a spit of tobacco-filled liquid to the ground, he replied, "To Lookout. First trip since last fall." He rested a Hawken rifle across his thighs and adjusted the bullet pouch hanging around his neck that had shifted positions during his ride. A powder horn dangled from his pommel, and a large knife was secured around his waist in a decorative sheath. A man in this territory and in his occupation never went anywhere without being heavily armed.

"Have any trouble on the trail? Any of those Indians acting up?"

The man replaced his hat on a head of long and wavy hair that was thick at the base and thin on top. "Nope. Ain't seen narry a soul since I left my trappin' grounds, 'ceptin' a few Crow huntin' parties from a distance. I know whar they camp, so I avoids 'em. Ain't no need to tempt 'em to steal my winter's catch," he jested.

"I know what you mean. I keep a sharp eye out for them, too. Aren't you coming in a mite early?" Joe inquired, knowing there were two trapping seasons. One was in late autumn after furs and pelts had thickened for protection during the impending winter and the other was in the early spring after the snow and ice had cleared enough and before the quality of a trapper's targets had lessened when the animals shed their excess hair for comfort during the coming summer.

"Pete—he's my partner—Pete and me take turns gettin' our catch to Columbia Fur. I comes down firs' and sells our prime batch; then, he comes down second and sells our last batch. One of us always stays behind to guard and work our trap lines. This late of year, we're in need of supplies,

224

and I git there afore the others. Columbia pays the best price to private trappers, but all them tradin' posts are too high on supplies. I leaves there and rides over to the suttler at Fort Laramie to stock up and visit friends. I git back sometime in late June; then Pete takes off to do the same. He gits back sometime in August. That leaves us time to work on our traps and cut firewood and git dryin' frames built. This year we need to repair our cabin. Mighty cold this past winter."

Joe caught the clues in the man's words. "Why don't we sit and talk a spell? Little Flower can prepare us some supper."

"That sounds temptin' to me. My name's John Howard, but most folks calls me Big John. I'll tend my critters firs'." He dismounted and headed for the creek to water his horse and two mules.

From beneath her lashes, Morning Star noticed how large the man was; his name suited him. His hair was dark on top, then steadily lightened to medium brown as it flowed from its roots. He looked to be about forty years of age. His jawline was thick with whiskers and they surrounded his mouth as thirsty grass did a pond. His eyes were small and squinty, but the expression in them was gentle and trustworthy. She was relieved by that, as she didn't want any trouble from the stranger.

Joe and Morning Star dismounted. She took their reins, as an obedient squaw, and secured them to bushes. She whispered to her man that she would gather roots and wood then prepare their meal while the two men talked. She left to carry out those chores.

Big John hobbled his horse and mules where they could drink and graze. He didn't seem to pay much attention to the beautiful Indian maiden with the genial stranger. He sat down to converse with Joe, unmindful of the earth still damp from yesterday's rain.

"Where do you trap, Big John?"

Following another stream of brown spittle over his left shoulder, John replied, "Along the Yellowstone and Pow-

225

der rivers. It's a prime area most years. This past winter weren't so good, though. Too many com'ny boys encroachin' on the Stony and Missouri these days, tryin' to get rich fast. Last year, Pete and me made nine hunnard dollars. We'll be lucky to git five to six hunnard this season. That don't sit well with either of us. We came here from Kintucky to trap for five year; two of 'em's gone. I tol' Pete I was comin' in early to beat them Crow and Sioux afore theys go on the warpath. We don't want them furs and our hard work to rot 'cause we cain't git out."

"What makes you think new trouble is brewing, John?"

"It's been comin' nigh unto two year. Ever' time we git a visitor, that's all we hear, that a big war's a comin' soon."

"You and Pete ever have trouble with the Crow or Blackfoot?"

John spat again. "Nope, they leave us be. We respect 'em and stays outta their way, and they do the same with us. Me and Pete shares a Crow squaw; she's a good worker, right purty, too. Injuns ain't bad if you treat 'em right. Trouble is, they don't give some men time to treat 'em any way afore they kill 'em. I don't want to be 'twixt warring Injuns. When trouble comes, you best ride clear of them Plains," he warned.

"I will. Tell me, John, isn't it a long ride to Lookout, then to Laramie and home? That's a lot of days in the saddle."

"Yep, but, like I said, Columbia Fur Com'ny pays the best price for prime furs, and I git the cheapest supplies at Laramie. Laramie's where I have my fun. Them tradin' posts got too many men lazin' around, drunk and overusin' them pleasure women. They cheat you at cards, nearly charge you for the air you breathe, rob you while you're drunk or asleep, and fight all the time. I don't like to spend my relaxin' time at them crazy posts."

"That makes it sound worth the time and saddle sores," Joe jested.

The sun was low on the horizon, so John's gaze, as he faced west, was narrower than usual. The big man stroked his scraggly beard and mustache as he eyed the younger male.

"What you doin' way out here?" he questioned.

Joe pulled out a bottle of whiskey that he had taken from the burial-site robbers; he offered the man a drink to loosen his tongue even more. Big John beamed with pleasure, thanked him, and took a long swig. As the bottle was held out in return, Joe smiled and said, "Keep it, I have one more." John thanked him again, then took another long drink. Afterward the big man licked his lips to catch every drop.

As the trapper drank, Joe pondered asking him to take word to Tanner's father. He decided, since John would be a long way from there soon, his message wouldn't enter the wrong ears. He took a chance and asked, "Would you mind delivering a message to a friend of mine at Fort Laramie? I'd be much obliged. His name is Stede Gaston. I want to let him know I'm safe and heading to McMichael's post."

"No trouble," the other man agreed. "What work you do?"

Morning Star had tensed when her companion exposed a connection to Stede. Yet she assumed he must know what he was doing. She continued with her preparation of the evening meal and listened to the conversation.

Joe invented an explanation. "I've been a trader between here and Texas for years. A few months ago, I decided it was time to try a new area, see something different, learn some new things. I sent word to Stede and he checked out this territory for me. He said McMichael's is the biggest and busiest post. I'm heading there to try to make a deal with Orin McMichael. I think I can convince him he can sell more supplies if he hires me to travel around the territory taking and delivering orders to white and Indian camps. You know how people hate to leave their settlements and cabins to shop, even when supplies run low or give out. They also buy more things if you make it easy for them. Orin can make more money, and I can make a nice share. It's a perfect partnership. I sold all my goods last month and headed this way. I'll be there in five or six days."

"Sounds like a good deal to me," John remarked. "You can sell plenty of salt, sugar, coffee, ammunition, and flour. Folks will be happy to have stuff brought to 'em. Save 'em lots of time and ridin'."

"That's what I'm counting on to make my plan work. If Orin doesn't accept, I'll try at Pierre or Lookout. If none of them agrees, I'll just have to go into business alone. I'll do that later. For now, I need to be connected with someone who has supplies and knows this area."

Morning Star, with lowered head, served the two men their evening meal. She was careful not to look at either one and to assume an air of subservience. She would eat later. She busied herself about the fire and paid close attention to the conversation.

The men feasted on stewed meat with wild roots, heated beans, and johnnycakes and washed the food down with coffee and whiskey.

Joe halted a moment to suggest, "If you want to head on to Laramie, John, I'll be glad to buy your furs, then sell them at McMichael's. I hear the price this season is two to three dollars a pound. Looks like you have about a hundred pounds," he guessed, from years of weighing cotton and goods for shipping. "I have that much from the sale of my goods. I'd just as soon travel with money in pelts as in my saddlebag. Showing Orin I can make a good deal before I reach him should be impressive."

"You got a sharp eye, Joe. I figured it at a hunnard pounds, too. I been gittin' three dollar a pound for prime grade at Lookout. I plan to sell my mules for twenty dollar each, and buy new ones at Laramie."

Joe added up the price of that response and compared it to the money he possessed. "I can pay you two-fifty per pound, John, and forty for the mules; that makes two hundred and ninety dollars. I only have three hundred with me. That would cost you fifty to trade with me, if Columbia is paying three this year. I could," Joe murmured aloud, "give you the whole three hundred and some supplies. I'll reach Orin's in a few days, so I won't need much. That way you'll

228

be out less than forty dollars, and you'll save lots of aching bones and two to three weeks of travel. Then I'll sell the furs and mules for three-forty, so I'll make forty. Less replacement supplies."

The weary mountain man contemplated Joe's offer. He didn't care about visiting Lookout and having to face the many aggravations there. In all honesty, his mules weren't worth twenty dollars each. He could save two bone-jarring weeks in the saddle; he could be back to his trapping grounds two weeks early or spend that extra time in Laramie having fun and be out of this potentially dangerous area in a few days. Avoiding enemy bands as they moved to the Plains, which he'd have to cross twice, and all the other reasons compelled him to say, "You got a deal, Joe."

"It'll be a good one for both of us, John."

Morning Star was pleased with her partner's cunning. Now, they could head to the trading post as a trapper and his squaw; the furs and mules would make their pretense look real. When he had suggested the plan to the man to obtain pelts, she hadn't been sure it would work. She was relieved he had enough white man's money to make it come true. Surely the Great Spirit was guiding them. She experienced anxiety again when the conversation continued.

"You know a big man named Zeke?" Joe asked in a casual tone. He described the villain's hireling, then added, "He travels with two fellows called Clem and Farley. Clem's a drunk, and Farley has a knife scar."

"I seen 'em together last season at Lookout. Don't know 'em good."

"I learned that Zeke and his boys haul goods for some of the posts. I figure he'll be my biggest competition for a deal with McMichael. I know they travel around out here, so I thought you might have run into them."

"Nope, and hope I don't. I didn't take to 'em. Bad, if you ask me."

"From what I've heard about them, I can't blame you. If you do cross trails with them, don't mention our deal. I don't want them hurrying to McMichael's to save their jobs and cost me mine."

When the men finished eating and took a walk in opposite directions to excuse themselves, Sun Cloud's daughter ate a quick meal. She washed the dishes in the stream and straightened the campsite. Taking a hatchet, she chopped off leafy branches to place on the ground, over which she laid the bedrolls to keep away the earth's dampness. The men returned to find everything ready for turning in for the night. She was surprised when the visitor spoke to her.

"Thank you for a wonderful meal, Little Flower. You do a good job."

Morning Star nodded gratitude, but did not lift her head and lashes. She excused herself in the woods, then went to her mat and lay down.

To avoid raising John's suspicions, Joe said nothing more than "Good-night, woman." He curled on his mat and closed his eyes, congratulating himself.

Shortly after sunrise, the happy couple watched Big John Howard head southwestward with the message for Stede Gaston.

When the also happy trapper was out of sight, Joe scooped Morning Star up in his arms and swung her around while laughing in merriment. "We did it, woman," he bragged. "You were perfect."

As her feet touched the ground again, Morning Star smiled and said, "We have good disguise now. Joe plenty smart and clever." Her hands rested on his broad chest and she gazed into his blue eyes.

They talked about the deal Joe had made before he said, "We make a good pair, woman. I'm proud of you. I almost hated to fool him," he admitted. "He seemed like a good man."

"Not too good," she refuted with a grin. "Mules not worth much. You say you pay too much."

He chuckled and stroked her cheek. "That's right, but it wasn't worth arguing over, because we both knew he was

230

losing money by trading with me. I'll probably get about ten dollars each for them. I won't lose any money, and I wasn't looking to make any off him, but I'll get twenty more than I spent. I might even do better. I've heard some of the posts are paying four dollars a pound this year. In a way, I tricked and cheated him, but it couldn't be helped. We need those furs, but I only had three hundred dollars. All the supplies I gave him are the ones we took off those grave robbers. I just hope he doesn't find out about the better price, and come looking for me."

"If mad, he tell others Joe's name. He tell about message to Stede."

"I had to take that risk, Morning Star, to let him know I'm all right."

"Tanner's father be happy you safe. If man called John tell him you with squaw, he catch clue and know plan working."

"I hope so. After what happened to Tanner, I know he's worried."

"What Tanner and Stede look like?" she inquired.

Surprised and curious, Joe responded, "Why?"

"They family. Want to know how look."

Joe sensed there was more to her question. "They both had black hair, brown eyes, and dark skin," he answered. "They both looked Indian, if that's what you mean, but everyone thought they were of Spanish blood. Stede's hair has some white now. I was told he favors Powchutu. Those who knew his father will recognize him as the son." He wanted to explain that Stede looked Indian because he carried little white blood, but he had promised Sun Cloud to withhold that secret. As for Tanner, his mother had possessed brown eyes and hair, so her coloring hadn't affected his. Tanner . . .

"You look sad. What wrong?"

"I was thinking about Tanner. God, I miss him," he confessed with deep emotion. "How can he be gone forever, Morning Star? He was like a brother to me, and I'll never see him again. Damn those bastards! I'm going to find

231

them and kill them," he swore. "Just like they killed Tanner!"

She caressed his cheek. "I understand and help. I sorry ask about him. Pain still great." She explained why the answer was important to her and related her confusing conversation with her brother.

"He's wrong, Morning Star. Babies come from both parents. I do believe that God decides when to give you one, but the child is part of the mother and father. As I said, Stede and Tanner look Indian. Some blood is stronger and affects a child's looks more, but neither parent is ever totally overpowered. He's wrong, too, about it not mattering who the father is. If Powchutu and Alisha had married, they would have had their own child, not Bright Arrow and Sun Cloud. The two of them are part of Gray Eagle and Alisha. You and Night Stalker would not come from a child by Powchutu and Alisha. Gray Eagle's blood flows in you, and you would not be the same without it."

"It is how I believed, but Brother make good points and confuse."

"That's only natural. That's how people learn and grow. They search for answers and ask questions, then fit all the pieces together to make their own picture of understanding."

"You plenty smart. You teach me all you know."

Joe smiled and said, "I'll do my best, but I'm not very skilled in that area. We'll do lessons every night in camp. Right now, let's get those mules packed and head out. It's adventure time, Little Flower," he teased.

Together they loaded the bundles of pelts onto the scrawny mules. Joe saddled their horses while she secured their supplies onto their packhorse. The fire was doused, the campsite cleaned. They mounted and rode toward the Missouri and Cheyenne rivers conflux.

At the next campsite, Joe answered her questions about his life and family in Virginia. He related his years growing

232

up between the plantation near Richmond and a town-house in Alexandria. He told her about his years at school and about going to work with his father in the shipping business. At first he sailed with his father, and later he sailed alone, unless Joseph Senior had a reason for going along. "I guess I can captain a ship as good as the next man," he admitted. "Father did business with Stede; that's how I met him and Tanner. When I took over most of the important runs, Tanner was my first mate, meaning he was my best helper. Stede didn't mind; he had his brother-in-law, his sister's husband, to run his firm. She was named Alisha after your grandmother. When Powchutu came here years ago, Stede ran his firm. When Stede came, he put Wesley, that's Alisha's husband—in control of his company. Alisha and Wesley have four children. She hasn't been told about her nephew's death yet. Stede won't do that until we return home. I haven't sent word about it to my family, either; I don't want them to worry I'll get killed, too."

Joe took a deep breath. He waited a moment, but Morning Star didn't make any comments. "Tanner and I shared a lot of adventures. We visited many exciting and strange places. Then Wesley got sick, and Tanner had to help his father in their shipping business. Trips weren't any fun with Tanner gone. It was all work and too much dull time on water. I received a letter from Tanner last July, telling me about his father's plans to come here. He invited me to ride along. Father was upset, but I had to accept. Before winter arrived, we were at Fort Laramie."

"You have sister. Tell about her," she encouraged a happy subject.

"Her name is Sarah Beth. She's older than I am and is married to Andrew Reardon. He works for Father, and loves the shipping business. They have one child, a son, age four, named Lucas, a boy I'd be proud to have. He's a wonderful child, Morning Star; you'd love him."

"What if Great Spirit give Joe girls?"

As Joe envisioned a tiny replica of the woman beside

233

him, he smiled. "I'd love them and raise them the best I could."

"When return home, you go back to shipping business?"

"I'd prefer to run our plantation, or the business office. I wouldn't mind a few trips a year, but I don't want to be sailing every week." He gazed into her eyes as the reality of his eventual departure struck him. "I'll miss you."

"Morning Star will miss Joe, too."

He drew her into his arms and pressed his lips to hers. She responded. The kiss was sweet and mellow. Their spirits soared with the pleasurable contact. The ensuing kiss was more ardent. Their emotions were so powerful that they were alarming, and caused them to seize control before it was too late to prevent what would take place if they continued to kiss in this heated manner. Their talk of babies had warned them of the consequences of fusing their fiery bodies once more. They knew they must not allow those feelings to take command and run wild. As if passing an unspoken and necessary message between them, they kissed lightly, then cuddled until self-control returned.

The next morning, Joe set a pattern he would continue daily during their months together. He related facts about America and the world: geography, history, laws, customs, religion, and more. He worked with her English, verbs and pronouns in particular. He helped her practice numbers, times—hours, days, weeks, months, years—and seasons. When he came to training her in the use of his weapons, she was reluctant, telling him it stole their magic and power for a woman to touch them. Joe finally convinced her that was part of her tribal customs and laws, but it didn't apply to his rifle and pistol, and there might be times when their lives depended upon such knowledge and skill. He was delighted when she learned quickly. Each lesson was enjoyable, yet, somewhere deep inside his mind, he knew what he was trying to prepare her for, even if he couldn't admit it to himself or suggest it to her.

In return, Morning Star taught Joe how to use a bow and arrows, how to become more skilled at reading tracks and trail signs, how to find his way around the territory in case they became separated, and how to speak more Lakota. She pointed out which plants were edible. Later she planned to teach him use of the lance and more. She daydreamed that perhaps there was a way to keep him here, keep him in her life and arms.

Their work together was challenging and fun. It drew them closer and tighter each hour. Their friendship, respect, and trust increased; and their love became stronger and deeper.

In camp that evening, after he scouted the east and north and she scouted the west, they knew it was safe to practice with his weapons. Aware of how the echo of gunfire traveled across the land, they were assured no one was close enough to hear it.

Having acquainted her earlier with his Colt Walker .44 pistol, Joe felt it was time to educate her about his other powerful weapon. He showed Morning Star how to handle and fire his Sharp's rifle, a '48 breech model that used a self-contained paper cartridge. He kept his ammunition in a leather ammo pouch that was faster to get to, rather than in an awkward cartridge box which could cause a man to fumble for bullets in a rush.

As the sunny-haired man helped her hold and aim the rifle, Morning Star remarked, "It easier to use than heavy pistol. I need stronger hand."

Joe knew the nine-inch barrel and over four-pound weight of his six-shot cylinder Colt was more difficult to control and master than a long rifle that distributed its weight in two hands and was supported by one shoulder. "The thing is, you'll know how to use either one if trouble arises."

The white man stood slightly to her left and rear with their bodies touching. One hand steadied her left arm and his other supported her right. Both became overly conscious of the contact and heat between them.

Morning Star turned her head to look at Joe, who was staring at her. "I please Joe with my new skills?" she hinted.

"You please me in every way," he heard himself respond.

Their gazes met. They gazed at each other as if mesmerized, captive in an enrapt world neither wanted to flee. They felt the emotions rising between and within them. Their hearts pounded.

With Joe's assistance, Morning Star finished turning to face him. The rifle butt slid to the ground, and she unknowingly released her loosened grasp on the barrel; the weapon fell harmlessly to the grass. They caressed each other's faces and bodies as their mouths joined in sheer delight. The smoldering embers between them burned brighter and hotter until they felt engulfed by a roaring blaze. Swept away by a surge of hungers, they were helpless to do anything except be carried along in the swift currents.

Soon, the enticement of heady passion prevented any thought of the consequences of their joining. They wanted and needed each other; for the present, nothing else mattered. Their kisses were greedy and stimulating. Their arousing caresses took and gave exquisite delight. Discarding garments and shoes, they sank into the bed of grass beneath their shaky legs. The past and future did not exist, only this moment and themselves.

Their appetites for each other did not need whetting, but nature seemed to guide them in that direction. They embraced and nibbled and savored each other.

Joe's lips roamed her features, and his hands journeyed her supple flesh. His fingers trekked down her neck and teased over her breasts. As if a lost traveler, they wandered everywhere, searching for hidden treasures instead of a path of escape. They did not worry about finding their way home, only about making this trip a blissful one.

Morning Star adored the feel of Joe's sleek frame against her skin. She loved the way he held her, touched her, kissed her, and tantalized her beyond resistance. She was thrilled by the way he shuddered with need for her and the way sensuous groans came from deep within his brawny chest. It seemed as if his feelings came from the depths of his soul, as did hers. The maiden's hands reveled in the ripplings of his muscles. His body was perfect, hard beneath a surface of soft skin. His hands were strong, but more than gentle. He was so special, so unique, and he was hers.

Joe was drawn to everything about the maiden with him. She possessed so many strengths yet none detracted from her femininity. She was beautiful. She was exciting. She was fulfilling. She was perfect for him. She belonged to him, tonight and forever.

They pressed closer together, their hands roving wild and free. Their mouths met and their tongues danced the ritual of desire. Their bodies worked as one, laboring with joy and eagerness. As they explored each other and their still budding love, passion burst into vivid bloom, unfolding one petal of pleasure after another until a rosy blossom filled their senses with fragrance and beauty. Sweet, fierce ecstasy washed over them, first as powerful waves which they rode urgently, later as ebbing ones which lapped gently at them. Ever so slowly, love's flower closed its petals like a morning glory going to sleep, to await its next burst into bloom.

Both sighed peacefully and nestled together as their contented bodies returned to normal. Each realized their actions had been unstoppable; their oneness on the trail was fated. It was dishonest to say it meant nothing, or was only physical lust; it was foolish to ignore their emotional attraction; it was futile to resist it. Whatever the future held, they could not change what was between them.

As they lay cuddled together, Joe realized this was only the second time in his life he had made love, not just enjoyed sex. The key part in lovemaking was *love,* and he knew beyond a shadow of a doubt that he loved the woman in his embrace.

He had seen many females in the past; he had had fun with most of them. Some had been sweet and nice, some smart and polished, and some pretentious. He had known he would marry one day when the right woman came along. He had been told that real love grabbed you and never let go; or that was the way it should be. He had taken women to bed around the world, but none compared with Morning Star. She was the woman he had waited for and craved. He wasn't certain yet if he could win her, or how to do so.

Morning Star nestled closer to Joe. She recalled what her cousin — her uncle's youngest child — had told her last summer: "When spring arrives, all eyes and hearts think of love and mating; It is the way of nature to inspire hungers to renew old life and to birth new life. Warm and scented nights cause stirrings in young bodies. Such fevers are as old as Wakantanka and will continue forever." Tashina had been told that by their grandmother long ago, and it was still true today. Alisha/Shalee had also said, "Life is not easy, and neither is love." That was true during Alisha and Tashina's battles for true love. It was true of her own situation.

During visits to her father's band, Tashina had told her many things about their grandmother and about life. Sometimes she wished her cousin were closer for more talks, but Tashina was the Cheyenne chief's wife. Yet, Morning Star reminded, she had her mother, and they were close. If only this matter was something she could discuss with Singing Wind. But it was not.

Morning Star reflected on their customs. When a girl joined, it was usually arranged by her father, and hopefully she approved of the choice. The man or his family mentioned the subject first, so it was best for a girl to let an interested pursuer learn her feelings before that happened. Even if she didn't approve of him, a well-raised maiden normally accepted her father's wishes. Morning Star knew she was lucky her father had not chosen a man for her or shown interest in Knife-Slayer's pursuit of her. Fortunately the offensive warrior hadn't made an offer for her. Not that a brave purchased a woman for a wife, but he offered many gifts to the girl's family to prove his depth of love and his prowess as a hunter and provider.

Thankfully it was rare for a warrior to pursue or ask for a female who made her dislike for him known publicly. It was just as natural for a husband not to hold on to a wife who wanted to leave him. What the white man called divorce was simple in Indian life for a woman: as the tepee was hers, either she tossed out a husband's belongings or she packed hers and left. No man with any pride would return to her or beg her to take him back. For a man, all he had to do was announce his intentions, then leave the tepee.

One thing of which Morning Star was certain was that her husband would have one mate, not several as was acceptable in her society. Many from her bloodline felt and behaved that way. It was not mocking the white custom of one wife to one husband but *love* that prevented a need for others. She could not accept sharing her love, her husband, with another woman or women.

Among her people, a girl's purity was guarded carefully by her family and herself and was honored by her tribe. A girl was taught she must not give away her future husband's treasure.

But was it not hers alone to give to the man of her choice? Morning Star asked. When she was with Joe, she forgot the importance placed on virtue. He stirred feelings to life within her which she knew must be love. Even if it were wicked of her to feel and behave as she had with him, she could not help herself. She could not convince herself such beautiful emotions and actions were wrong. She loved him, and surely that made it all right. In the eyes of their gods, they were mates. True, they had performed the joining ceremony as a pretense, but both accepted it as real and meaningful, as a commitment to each other.

Having been raised with little privacy in a tepee by two parents who were much in love and who shared fiery passion for each other, lovemaking was no secret to her. It was a part of love, the sharing of all you are with your chosen one. It was obvious Joe felt the same. She also knew that a baby did not come from every mating. Joe had said one came when God said it was the right time. Since the all-knowing and generous Great Spirit knew this was not the time to bless them with one, she would not become heavy with child while riding this sacred mission.

Morning Star recalled that three days ago her people broke camp to journey to their first camp on the Great Plains to hunt buffalo. She prayed their hunt would be safe and successful, as would her impending task.

For four days, the terrain was a mixture of flat lands and low, rolling hills. Tall bluestem grass added color to that of gray-green needle and buffalo, as did the purplish hue of scattered bunches of switch. Pasque, the harbinger of spring, decorated areas with blue, lavender, and white faces. A few clumps of prickly pear displayed buds and un-ripened cactus fruits. Morning Star told Joe that Indians used the red fruits for food, as they did with the bulb of the creamy white segolily. An array of other wildflowers snuggled amidst the mixed grasses to dot the solid blanket of green.

The landscape altered to higher hills with lengthy plateaus — up a steep incline, across a pancake surface, and down into a valley with lumpy waves. The cycle was repeated over and over. Visibility was excellent, and a good safety factor. When they saw trees — usually cottonwoods — that indicated a water source was nearby: a sign any greenhorn had better learn fast, and Joe had done so under Morning Star's skilled tutorship.

About four o'clock, the couple neared the trading post of Orin McMichael. Noticeable apprehension chewed at both.

"What if Zeke and other man here?" she asked.

Joe didn't hesitate before replying, "We hit the trail fast. If anything looks or sounds strange, flee. If we get separated, head for our last campsite. I'll join you there. We can't take any chances of both of us getting captured. If anything happens to me, get word to Captain Thomas. If you get caught, stay calm and I'll find a way to rescue you.

4 FREE BOOKS

TO GET YOUR 4 FREE BOOKS WORTH $18.00 — MAIL IN THE FREE BOOK CERTIFICATE T O D A Y

Fill in the Free Book Certificate below, and we'll send your FREE BOOKS to you as soon as we receive it.

If the certificate is missing below, write to: Zebra Home Subscription Service, Inc., P.O. Box 5214, 120 Brighton Road, Clifton, New Jersey 07015-5214.

FREE BOOK CERTIFICATE

4 FREE BOOKS

ZEBRA HOME SUBSCRIPTION SERVICE, INC.

YES! Please start my subscription to Zebra Historical Romances and send me my first 4 books absolutely FREE. I understand that each month I may preview four new Zebra Historical Romances free for 10 days. If I'm not satisfied with them, I may return the four books within 10 days and owe nothing. Otherwise, I will pay the low preferred subscriber's price of just $3.75 each; a total of $15.00, *a savings off the publisher's price of $3.00*. I may return any shipment and I may cancel this subscription at any time. There is no obligation to buy any shipment and there are no shipping, handling or other hidden charges. Regardless of what I decide, the four free books are mine to keep.

NAME

ADDRESS   APT

CITY   STATE   ZIP

(   )
TELEPHONE

SIGNATURE   (if under 18, parent or guardian must sign)

Terms, offer and prices subject to change without notice. Subscription subject to acceptance by Zebra
Books. Zebra Books reserves the right to reject any order or cancel any subscription.   069102

GET
FOUR
FREE
BOOKS

(AN $18.00 VALUE)

Keep your eyes and ears open. Don't trust anybody. Anybody," he stressed.

Morning Star did not insist for them to stay together at all times. It might not be possible. Confident that Joe was clever and careful, she would follow his orders, whether or not she agreed with them.

Joe spoke his thoughts aloud. "It's been three weeks since our run-in with Zeke. He's had time to get here, if he was heading this way. This is a big territory; he could be anywhere. I don't see his wagons—that's a good sign. If he's been here, I doubt he told anyone about his trouble with us; it would be humiliating to expose his defeat."

"You right. I try not to . . . worry much."

The sunny-haired man reminded, "Remember, we don't want to do any private talking here. I don't want us overheard in case somebody decides to spy on us. We will play our parts as if they're real."

"I obey, do my best to play good squaw."

The alert couple studied the settled area as they entered it. Everything faced south, instead of the Missouri River and rising sun as one might expect. The Cheyenne River was behind, its many watery fingers pointing northwest, which created an excellent rear defense to prevent being flanked by attackers. The surging "Big Muddy" did the same eastward. Joe told Morning Star the purpose and power of two cannons—one aimed west and the other south—that asserted this settlement had little vulnerability and that the owner was determined to be safe. The undamaged landscape told them the weapons had not be used.

Orin's trading post was large, well-constructed, and rustic. A porch ran the full length of the front, with wooden poles supporting the roof. There was a small house to its right, probably the owner's home. It, too, looked strong and well suited to the wilderness that surrounded it. To the left was an oblong building with a door at each end. Joe suggested to his companion that it was half for storage and half for guest quarters, as he'd seen elsewhere. Between the two structures, they saw a stable and corral and through

241

one open door, they sighted a flat-bed wagon for hauling goods from the nearby river. The corral held six horses and seven mules. They noticed a worn trail snaking eastward, which indicated in which direction the boat landing was located. There were scattered copses of hardwoods around the clean settlement, and a dense tree line along most of the grassy bank of "The Misery" that joined the Cheyenne not far away.

They rode to the trading post, dismounted, and secured their horses' reins to hitching poles with metal loops. Joe did the same with the mules' reins. It was late afternoon on the seventh of June. Sunset would arrive in a few hours. It was time for serious work.

A tall, burly man with red hair and matching burnsides left the post and joined them. His brows were wiry, with hairs growing in all directions over hazel eyes. His complexion was flushed, but from natural coloring rather than results from any kind of exertion. The sparkle in his eyes and the broad smile on his face alleged him to be good-natured and friendly.

"Good tae see ye, friend," he greeted the stranger, barely glancing at the woman. "I'm Orin McMichael, tha proud proprietor of this fine establishment. I see ye've come tae sell 'r trade furs. Ye made ae wise choice." He rubbed his clean-shaven chin, finger-flicked his whiskered jawline, then stroked his thick mustache.

Joe grasped the large, strong hand extended to him and shook it. He noticed Orin's voice was deep and mellow with a Scottish burr. "The name's Joe Lawrence. Glad to meet you. It's been a long, hard ride." If Orin recognized his name, it didn't show. He had seen only one other man with the similar facial haircut, who had said he shaved his chin to keep food bits and grease out of his beard. From his attire and manner, Orin seemed to be a man inclined toward neatness. The redhead was dressed in a dark coat with matching trousers, a white shirt, patterned vest, and a bowtie. Orin looked as if he belonged more in an office in a large city than in a wild area like this one.

The Scotsman smiled. "Time for drinking, talking, and having fun, Joe Lawrence," Orin said, as if stressing the man's name to brand it into memory. "I have e'er'thing ye need 'r want here. Ye can set up camp o'er there in tha trees," he suggested, pointing to a shady area that faced his home. "Ye can stay with yer woman 'r stay in me fine lodgins. Either way, she'll be safe in Orin's shadow. She speak English?"

Joe removed his hat and held it by the brim at his left leg. "A little. I bought her last year. She's been a good helper. She's Arapaho."

Orin looked her over as he replied, "I recognized her markings. If ye don't learn tae do that fast out here, ye don't survive long."

"With so many forts within a few days' or weeks' ride, this area should be settled soon. That'll make it safer."

Orin chuckled. "Not soon enough tae suit most folks. Come inside. Meet tha others. Have ae drink, loosen ye jaws, and rest. Me woman will be serving ae good meal in about an hour. Ye be welcome tae buy ae plateful for twenty-five cent. If she likes white food," he added, nodding at the woman, "ye can buy her ae plateful, too. I don't mistreat Indians."

"Little Flower likes to eat her own cooking, but thanks." He looked at the Indian beauty, whose head and lashes remained lowered. "Woman, set up camp there," he ordered in a pleasant tone, motioning to the copse Orin had pointed out. "Tend the horses, then stay there. Don't leave camp. You eat. Don't cook for me. I'll return after dark."

Without lifting her head, Sun Cloud's daughter nodded in understanding and obeyed swiftly. She loosened the reins of his roan and her Appaloosa, and guided their animals to the river to drink. When they finished, she led them to the wooded area and tethered them there. She began her chores of setting up camp.

"Will these mules and furs be all right here for a spell?" Joe asked.

Orin pulled his attention from the beautiful maiden back

243

to Joe. "Naebody bothers anything around here, Joe. She's ae pretty one. Ye best keep yere eyes on her, 'r she'll be stolen by some hot-blooded buck. Follow me. I have some friends for ye tae meet."

Joe hoped his tension didn't show, but he was nervous about entering the confined space before him. He prayed Zeke and Farley weren't inside. He had left his rifle on his saddle, but was wearing his pistol. He flexed his fingers to be ready for action, and he summoned all his senses to full alert.

During the previous two days, Morning Star had experienced her woman's flow. She had come prepared with trade cloth for it. Whenever necessary, she had excused herself behind knolls to tend the task. Now she wanted a cleansing bath.

Watching Joe from a distance, Morning Star whispered the same prayer he had. From their assigned location, she could see the fronts of all structures and she was in plain view of anyone inside of them, so a bath had to wait. Although she looked to be busy with chores, she remained ready to spring into action if Joe needed her help. Her eyes and ears had never been more focused on something than the door through which Joe vanished.

Protect him. Great Spirit, she prayed again. *I do not like this white man's world. Help us to find what we seek and to leave here soon.*

Chapter Eleven

Joe glanced around the interior of the trading post; it was stocked heavily with anything a man or woman could need in these parts.

"It was rowdy here two days ago," Orin said, "but it's quieted down now. Had ae boat stop by tae unload supplies. It was heading upriver tae Union and Benton—American Fur Company posts. Had several company fur buyers along and ae few men seeking thrills in tha wilds. Only have three guests now; I'll introduce them tae ye soon. They're in tha back room, drinking and gambling and running their mouths. I sell good aged rye whiskey, not that rot-gut 'r watered-down stuff. I don't sell it tae Indians because it makes them crazy; that's why tha boys drink in the back room. If ye tell them ye don't have any, ye best not show it around and cause trouble. Where're ye from, Joe?"

"I've been trapping northeast of here for the past nine months," he alleged. "That area wasn't too good for me, so I decided to try my luck farther west this next season, along the upper Yellowstone and Missouri. If I don't decide to do something else before then," he amended with a grin to set his strategy into motion. "I've been a sailor and a soldier, and I didn't like either job. Too many rules and demands. You could say I haven't found the right opportunity to suit me yet."

"I doubt ye want tae be heading up that way. I hear trouble is coming this year between tha Crow and Dakotas."

Joe sent the observer a displeased frown. "If that's true, it could mess up my other plan," he muttered, then scowled in feigned displeasure.

"What is that?" Orin questioned as he leaned against the counter.

"I thought about starting a traveling trader business. I figured if I could join up with someone who owns an established post, I could travel around taking orders and delivering them for a nice profit for both of us. I think people — Indians and whites — would buy more goods if they're brought to their doors. I thought I'd try it out until fall; if I found I didn't like it, I'd go back to trapping. You interested in such a proposition?"

The red-haired man didn't take time to think before answering, "That idea sounds as dangerous as yer first one."

"A man don't make much money playing it safe. Since you're sitting in the middle of Indian country, you know you have to take risks to get rich."

Orin grinned as he fingered his smooth chin. "Ye be right, tae ae point. It's an interesting idea, but I don't think this is the season for it. Yere plan will be safer in ae year or two."

Joe decided to be bold, especially before he entered that back room. "You know a big man named Zeke? Hauls goods in these parts."

"E'er'body knows Zeke. Why ask about him?"

"I hear he transports most of the supplies in this territory, so I figured I'd better not infringe on his territory without checking him out first. Maybe he'd be interested in having a partner. From what I've been told, he knows this area and these people better than anyone."

"I haven't seen him in weeks." He glanced to his left at the closed door before saying, "I'll warn ye about Zeke: he's ae loner. He can get mean and odd on ye. I doubt he'll want tae share earnings with ye 'r anyone. He's high-priced, but I've used him many times because he is dependable. Zeke isn't scared of anything 'r anyone. I can't blame him for charging so much; his job is dangerous, especially with those Indians acting up."

"You have much trouble with them? I noticed your cannons."

"None sae far. Ne'er had to fire ae shot. They're tae scare off thieves and renegades. Robbery is ae big threat in ae wilderness. No big problems with the Indians. Tae be honest, I don't like or dislike them. They're paying customers like anybody else, sae I'd be foolish tae offend them. And stupid taw rile them. Sometimes they'll try tae cheat ye, 'r intimidate ye into giving them ae cheaper price 'r goods for free. They know they're welcome here and I treat them fair. Best way tae get along with one is tae treat him like any other man, if he'll let ye. That's why I don't let them know about tae whiskey; they don't take kindly ta being lied tae 'r cheated. 'Course, it's against tha law tae sell whiskey tae Indians, e'en though it's done all tha time." Orin changed the subject. "Let's get our business settled, then ye can join tha others for cards. I pay three dollars ae pound. That suit ye?"

Joe smiled and said, "That's fair. You want to buy those two mules?"

"I'll have tae take ae look at them." He headed for the door.

Joe followed, then watched Orin examine the furs and animals. He glanced at Morning Star, who appeared busy with camp tasks. Yet he sensed her eyes on them, and had to suppress flashing a smile in her direction.

"I can pay ye seven dollars ae piece, and three hundred for tha furs."

Joe looked at the laden beasts, pretended to think a minute, smiled again, and said, "It's a deal." At least he would recover his investment.

"I'll make ye another offer: if ye decide tae buy ae wagon and supplies tae trade on tha trail, I'll make ye ae good price on both. If ye live tae see September and ye make good money, we'll talk about ae partnership then."

"After I leave, I'll look around and check out the area and any brewing trouble. If it suits me and appears safe, I'll return and deal with you. If I'm not back in four weeks, you'll know it

247

didn't look good and I moved on."

"Ye be ae smart man, Joe Lawrence. Let me introduce ye ta tha boys before I unload these furs and corral these mules."

Joe followed Orin back inside the trading post. The big man halted at the counter; and he took some money from a metal box and paid Joe the amount due. Joe pocketed his earnings and took a deep breath as the older man opened the door to the other room. As soon as Orin's large frame was out of the way, Joe's gaze rushed around the area. He was relieved to find that none of the three men present was familiar.

"Tha Army scout is George," Orin said. "He likes ta take his leave here with tha best women and whiskey." The soldier nodded, then returned his gaze to his cards. "George doesn't talk much. I suppose he doesn't want civilians getting worried about this trouble brewing." The scout didn't look up or respond to Orin's genial remarks. The red-haired man moved on, "That's Ben; he's ae prospector. He's been searching this territory for several years for ae lucky strike."

"Gonna find me one, too, you'll see," the gold seeker declared, then smiled through several missing teeth.

"Not if ye head into them Black Hills like ye're planning."

"Don't be worryin', Orin. Them Injuns are headin' fur the Plains as we jaw. Soon as they git outta them hills, I'm takin' me a look-see. You kin bet yore britches they's gold in there somewheres. I'm gonna find it."

"What ye're going ta find is yer hair missing," Orin jested.

Ben chuckled and stroked the thinning strands that needed a good washing and brushing, as much as his body and garments needed scrubbing. "Hell's bullets, them Injuns think I'm crazy! Theys don't bother no crazy folk. I'll be back here, rich as a king, afore the leaves are fallin'."

"I wish ye luck, Ben, but ye best be careful of those Lakotas. They're real protective and selfish with their territory. Ask George; he'll tell ye tha straight of it." Getting back to the last introduction, Orin said, "That's Ephraim; he's ae trapper like ye, Joe. He's down early this year. He might know more about tha western area than any of us."

"You 'tending to trap over my way?" the buckskin-clad man

asked, squinting his already beady eyes to examine Joe from head to foot.

"Haven't decided yet. Trapping sure isn't good east of here. I came by to sell my furs to Orin, then take a look around. I may get into trading."

"You wuz smart to come here. Orin's got the best prices. Them American Fur boys at Benton and Union don't pay as good as him. I has to haul my pelts further, but Orin makes it worth me while."

Orin smiled and thanked Ephraim. He motioned to the last person in the room, a woman with blond hair and green eyes. "She's Mattie Lou. I only have one girl at present. Three more 'r coming by tha fifteenth. Most of tha boys don't come in until tha end of June or first of July. Mattie Lou is ten dollars for one service, twenty-five dollars for all night. She's tha best trained pleaser I've e'er hired. She can give ye any treat ye want. Right?"

The pretty prostitute sent Joe a seductive smile and agreed with her boss, "Anything you like or want, I'm best at it."

"I'll get ye ae drink, Joe; first one's on tha house. I'm sure tha boys would like ae fourth hand in their card game. Relax. I'll finish me chores and join ye boys later." Orin made eye contact with the woman before he served the newcomer a glass of aged rye whiskey. He asked the other customers if they needed anything, and everyone shook their heads no. He left the room and closed the door.

Joe caught the interaction between Orin and Mattie Lou, but did not comprehend its meaning. He sat in the empty chair at the square wooden table. "Good to meet you boys. Don't get to see many faces when you're trapping. Right, Ephraim?"

"Nope, but it don't trouble me none when I'm working. How much pelts did you bring in?"

Evening shadows were dimming the three-window room, and Joe saw the prostitute light two lanterns. "A hundred pounds of beaver, otter, and muskrat. Prime quality, but not enough critters in that area. How is it over your way?"

"Not as good this year as most. Thick and healthy, but slim takin's. Too much work to keep going. Figured I'd come on in and have some fun."

Joe noticed how Ephraim eyed the pretty woman nearby and assumed the trapper was whetting his appetite to enjoy her later. He sipped his free drink as he studied the men.

"Any trouble over your way this spring?" George asked.

Joe wondered why the Army scout didn't look up at him, but just kept staring at his card hand. "Nothing that I saw or heard about. Did my trapping on the upper Minnesota and James rivers. Those woodland tribes are pretty friendly, if they come around at all. What's the trouble between the Lakotas and Crow that Orin mentioned?"

"Same as always: old enemies, and too many whites settling in."

"What about that rumored treaty the Indian agent is working on?"

George didn't look up to respond, "It'll be summer here all year long before those two nations make peace. Longer before whites are accepted."

"Sounds as if you don't care much for Indians or treaties," Joe hinted.

The scout looked him in the eye. "I don't care for anybody who ain't a friend of mine or anything that makes my life harder," he revealed. "Out here, it's risky to accept strangers fast. Too many men who'll put a bullet in your back or slit your throat while you sleep just to get your horse and supplies, or to empty your pockets, or to take your winter's catch. If you stay here, you've got to keep your eyes and ears open to survive. Don't trust anybody until you know for sure he's worth your time. You playing?" he asked, his tone gruff.

Joe was surprised by the amount of words George spit out. He nodded. "If you boys don't mind, I'll join in on the next hand."

"Be happy to take your money," Ephraim said with a lop-sided grin.

Joe waited patiently while the three men finished the game in progress. Mattie Lou came up behind him and rested her ivory hands on his shoulders. She pressed her body against the chair and him. He felt the heat radiating from her like a blazing sun. Her open overture made him uncomfortable.

She bent forward and murmured into Joe's ear, "You've been in the wilderness a long time. I'm sure I can help you relax between supper and bedtime. Ephraim has me later."

"I got her all night, Joe," the trapper boasted.

"She'll wear you out in an hour," the crusty prospector jested.

"Ain't seen the day or night any female could tire me, Ben."

"He ain't had a go at you, has he, Mattie Lou?" the prospector refuted as he leaned over and playfully patted the woman's buttocks.

She laughed throatily and tickled Joe's ear. "I've never left any man awake, hungry, or without his money's worth. I promise you'll never forget me, Joe. You'll be hanging around for days just to get stocked up on me before leaving."

"You don't git no free sample of her, Joe, like whiskey."

Joe felt the woman rub her ample breasts against the back of his head. Her skilled fingers drifted over his shoulders to his chest where they caressed the flesh through his shirt. He smelled her cloying perfume in the air. He was repulsed by the provocative invitation to hire her.

Ben nudged the scout and jested, "Only person who gits it free is George there for keepin' Orin up on news around this ter'tory."

"That's not true," she refuted with a giggle. "George has to pay like everyone. Isn't that so, George?"

The scout spread out a winning hand as he muttered, "If I'm in the mood for a woman, I pay for her, if she ain't for the taking."

Joe was unconvinced that Orin didn't give Mattie Lou to George anytime he desired in exchange for scouting information. That didn't strike Joe as being too suspicious, as Orin had a profitable business and his life to protect. But Corporal George Whatever, he was a man to check out with Jim. Joe grasped that the scout didn't like attention and questions, so it was best to avoid both until tomorrow after they had gotten friendly.

The prostitute's forefingers began to make erotic circles

around Joe's nipples. He jerked in surprise at her vexing boldness, and captured her invading hands and pushed them away. With a genial chuckle, he discouraged, "Sorry, Mattie Lou, but I have my own woman with me. I won't be needing your fine skills." When the female made a noise of displeasure, Joe assumed it was because few men had refused her charms.

"You have a wife with you?" she questioned.

"Nope," Joe replied, picking up the cards passed to him.

"A squaw?"

"Yep, perfect in obedience, and skills. I'm sure you are, too, but one woman is plenty for me," he added to soften his rejection.

"Men need variety. Wouldn't you enjoy bedding me for a change?"

"Thanks, but no. Little Flower provides everything I need. You open?" Joe asked Ephraim, displeased with the personal topic. It was common for men to talk and joke about conquests, but it left a foul taste in his mouth for his beloved Morning Star to be discussed openly this way.

Mattie Lou left the handsome newcomer and stood at one window to watch the dark-haired beauty in Joe's camp while she sulked.

The four men played cards for a time and talked only when betting. Joe pretended to concentrate on the game, but he was closely observing each man. More drinks were ordered, and the quiet female served them. One game drifted into another and another, with Joe winning two of them. Small talk ensued by all except George, who remained distant, sullen. Even Mattie Lou calmed down and joked with the men, particularly her customer for later.

When Joe felt confident enough to query the men, he asked, "Any of you know a man named Zeke?"

Ephraim and Ben nodded, George shrugged, and the woman grinned.

Joe tried again. "Where I can find him? I have a deal to discuss."

"What kind of deal?" George asked. "Zeke don't like strangers."

252

With a smile and in a genial tone, Joe related the traveling-trader story he had told to Orin. "Zeke and I could make good partners."

"Zeke works alone. He's real strange," George remarked.

"If he isn't interested, at least I won't get him mad at me by working his territory. I'd be obliged if you can tell me where to find him."

"Don't know. Zeke's all over the place all the time. If I run into him while scouting, I'll give him your message. Just hang around any of the trading posts, he'll ride up soon. Zeke stays on the move this time of year. Everybody knows him, so he won't be hard to locate."

Ephraim finally got to speak. "He's gitting furs from them Crow west of here. Ever' spring he travels around buying up all he can, real cheap. He takes 'em to a boat at Lookout to send downriver to St. Louis. Gits a better price than anybody here, 'cluding Orin. Costs him a mite to boat 'em out." He asked for two cards, then continued. "I saw him in the Powder River country when I wuz coming down. Said he wuz joining some friends at Rake's Hollow; they wuz to ride as guards across them Plains. Redskins are on the move this time of year. Been . . ." He thought a moment, then said, "Two weeks past, so he ain't had enough time to git back. Don't know where he's heading after that. He was in a bad mood, wors'en usual."

"Probably ridin' to Lookout on the 'Souri," Ben guessed. "If you head downriver, you should run in to him along the way."

"Maybe, but it could be a waste of my time. Zeke might head in any direction from Lookout," Joe surmised. He assumed the reason for Zeke's bad mood was his recent deceit and Morning Star's escape. He could envision an even worse mood after he discovered his cohorts slain.

From the trapper's words, Joe deduced that the men he and Morning Star had attacked must have been the escort Zeke was to meet. It was a good thing they hadn't waited around that area! The news told him that Zeke was trading ammo, weapons, and whiskey for furs. But, Joe speculated, for whom? Surely buying Indian pelts was only a cover to get arms and supplies to the Crow with which to battle the Lakotas. He

253

also wondered if Zeke had ordered his hirelings to rob the Oglala burial ground for possessions to use as falsely incriminating clues, and if Zeke had been using those men to rile each side against the other. There was no doubt in Joe's mind now that Zeke was working for Snake-Man.

From then on, Joe had trouble keeping his mind on poker and lost two games. He finished his second whiskey to the other men's fifth drink. He was about to dig for details on the Indians and brewing conflict when Orin McMichael returned.

"If ye boys're ready tae eat, clear tha table. I have ae fine meal acoming. Good timing; yer game just ended."

It was dark outside, so only lanternlight brightened the room, adorned only with several tables and two sideboards. Through open windows, crickets, frogs, and nocturnal birds made music in the darkness they loved. George collected and stowed the cards. Mattie Lou cleared away empty glasses. The men stretched and sighed.

A hefty Indian woman entered the room carrying bowls of food. The prostitute fetched plates and utensils, then set two tables. Each man, including George, reached into his pocket for money to pay for the meal.

Joe saw the silent Indian woman go back and forth as she brought in more platters and bowls whose delictible odors filled the room. He wondered how his love was doing, but he must eat before joining her. He was past ready to leave this tension-inspiring chore for a night's rest.

"I call her Lucy," Orin told Joe, " 'cause her Indian name is ae foot long. She does me cooking, cleaning, and washing. She's Pawnee. I traded ae horse-load of goods for her. She's tight-tongued, but she's a good worker. If this isn't tha best meal tae pass yer lips, ye don't have tae pay."

Joe tasted the roasted meat and vegetables. He took a bite of a cat's-head biscuit with butter and honey. Orin had not exaggerated. He licked his lips and complimented, "Delicious."

"Lucy is tha best cook anywhere. I have vegetables and fruits sent up from downriver. My guests eat better than at any trading post. She's made apple pie for dessert. Mattie Lou, pour tha coffee, woman, afore tha men choke tae death and I lose good customers. Help yeself tae all ye want."

The men feasted on the wonderful meal. Orin and Mattie Lou sat at another table. The Pawnee servant came and went from a kitchen in the other house to replace empty bowls and platters with full ones. Another pot of steaming and aromatic coffee arrived, along with the apple pie. Joe had to admit to himself that it was the best food he had tasted since leaving Fort Laramie, and he wished Morning Star could enjoy it with him.

Joe finished eating. He bid the men good night and headed to his camp. A gentle breeze gave the air a soothing freshness that was effective medicine for settling his taut nerves. A new moon was overhead, so it was dark outside. With the aid of a lantern, Joe strolled toward the dying glow of a small fire. In the shadows beneath several hardwoods, he saw Morning Star on her bedroll. As he removed his boots and pistol, Joe whispered, "We'll talk tomorrow when we can see our surroundings."

To let him know she heard and understood his precaution, Sun Cloud's daughter gave a soft, "Hum." She wished they could talk, as she had things to tell Joe, but they must wait. She had worried about his safety all evening and was relieved to have him nearby again. She was eager to hear what he had learned, and was eager to leave this intimidating place.

Morning Star watched three visiting men leave the post with lanterns lighting their path and faces. A golden-haired female clutched the arm of one white man and she pressed against his body in a way that needed no explanation. The maiden observed them until they entered the west end of the oblong building. Laughter and voices came her way, but their words were not clear. She saw Orin and the Pawnee squaw go into his home. Light flickered against curtains for a short time, then was gone. Yet she sensed a powerful gaze in her direction. She heard occasional noises from the horses and mules, and heard the rushing of the adjacent river. Soon, she calmed her anxieties enough to go to sleep.

When Joe awoke, he saw Morning Star sitting beside a fire. He hadn't heard her rise, so he knew he had been in a deep sleep. It was unusual for him to drop his guard so low, even during slumber. He smiled when she turned her lovely face to him. No matter how many times or how long he watched, he never tired of seeing her and having her close. He wished they were closer, but embraces had to wait until they were alone. That time could not come soon enough to please him.

Morning Star noticed how Joe looked at her and realized what trail his thoughts rode—the same one hers traveled. Every day she came to love and want him more; every day she had to remind herself it was impossible. Being around whites and in one of their settlements impressed that reality deeper into her mind. Even though these men were nothing like Joseph Lawrence, other whites were like them. There was no place for her in his hostile world. If only he could—

"Don't think sad thoughts, love," he murmured after witnessing the glow in her eyes fade. "No matter how bad things look, there's always a path to escape."

Morning Star did not disagree with him at this time. But later, they must speak the truth and accept it. For now, being and working together, and having each other was all that mattered, all they could ever have.

Dawn lightened the landscape and their campsite. Birds sang or took flight to begin their daily chores. Horses neighed and mules brayed in the corral to signal it was feeding time. Smoke rose from the chimney on Orin McMichael's home.

Morning Star glanced at Joe. She was afraid to look too long in case anyone was watching them, but found it difficult to pull away her gaze. She loved how the early light played on his sunny locks. His hair was longer and thicker than at their first meeting. She yearned to stroke the wavy golden mane. The increasing light seemed to darken his blue eyes. Sometimes she believed she could stare into those sky-colored depths forever. She wasn't sure if she liked his short beard, as weeks of growth caused it to conceal too much of his tanned, handsome face. She wanted to spread kisses over it. She craved to flee to a place where their differences didn't matter, where peace and love ruled.

"If you keep looking at me like that, woman, I'm going to burst into flames. You have me kindled good already," he teased in a husky whisper.

Morning Star lowered her head to hide her amused grin from any watchful gaze. "I cannot kiss and hold fire," she whispered back. "Jump into the cold water to save and cool yourself."

"I'd love to share a bath with you, but not here," he responded.

"As a good squaw, I will scrub you clean in our next camp."

Joe caught how well she spoke. Their many lessons on the trail were working. He was delighted and proud. "Your English improves, grows better, my love. Your victory warms my heart and enlarges my pride."

Morning Star grinned once more. He always made her feel so happy. "I make a good squaw?"

"You make a good anything. I wish you did belong to me. Then, when this task here ended, I'd take you home with me. We'd—" Her head had lifted and she was staring at him, dismay written in her gaze. He inhaled deeply and apologized, "I'm sorry, Morning Star, but you make me forget myself."

"You make me forget myself. That is bad, wrong, Joe. We have nothing more than many days on the trail together. And many nights."

He grasped her meaning, and it pained him. He almost declared his love for her, but restrained himself. Yet it was something he—they—must deal with sooner or later.

"I must go into the forest," she hinted, her look clarifying her words.

Joe explained about the outhouse behind the oblong building. "It gives privacy. I'll walk to the edge of the building with you. I need it, too."

He guided her in that direction, then waited while she excused herself. She lingered while he did the same. They returned to their camp.

Just as they reached that area, Orin came out of his home. He stretched his healthy body. "Good morning tae ye!" he shouted.

Joe returned the cheerful greeting, but Morning Star remained quiet.

"Breakfast in one hour, if ye be eating with us. I bet it's been ae long time since ye had ae real breakfast," he said as he joined Joe near the trees. "Scrambled eggs stirred just right, crisp fried pork strips, biscuits with butter and jelly, steaming coffee, grits that slide down yer throat like honey," he tempted. "Join me while I hay tha stock?" Orin invited.

As they walked toward the corral, the proprietor disclosed, "I get me eggs and milk from farmers downriver, some vegetables and meats, too. I don't like grubbing in tha dirt, 'r like hearing chickens cluck and leave their droppings all o'er. Ye want some sweet feed for yer horses?"

"I think they'd like a treat," Joe replied. He took the bucket Orin handed to him. He lingered to inquire, "You do all your chores? Surely you don't work and live here alone when you don't have guests."

Orin lifted a board in a slanting trench to allow water to flow from the river into a sunken trough for the animals. He tossed hay from the barn into a corner of the corral. As he worked, he related, "I have two men who do me work. They're delivering supplies, tools, and furniture tae local farmers and home-steaders that came on tha boat. They rarely leave me alone, but tha money was tae good tae refuse." He brushed off his suit and smiled.

"It's ae good thing they don't venture far and wide, or you wouldn't need to consider my proposal. If thunder is in the wind like you said, I don't blame you for keeping them close."

"They'll be back later. They know Mattie Lou is here. She keeps me boys happy when they aren't busy. She be a good piece of property. She would have worked ye good last night, Joe, but I understand ye didn't want tae offend yer woman. If ye get tired of her, bring her here. She can help Lucy with me cooking and cleaning. Sometimes it gets very busy. I'll make ye ae good offer for her, and she'll have ae good home here."

"Thanks, Orin, but I doubt I'll ever sell or trade Little Flower."

"When it comes time for ae good-looking lad like ye ta marry and settle down, remember me offer. Just don't bring no babies with ye."

Joe laughed, because he couldn't think of a clever or guileful retort to terminate the vexing talk. "I best feed my horses and get washed up for that tempting breakfast. I'll see you later, Orin."

He barely finished treating the three horses when Ephraim, Ben, and Mattie Lou left the oblong building. The two men sent greetings his way, which Joe returned in a genial manner. The blond prostitute headed toward him. Joe warned his love about the bold woman.

Mattie Lou eyed the Indian beauty from her glossy black hair to moccasined feet. "This your woman?" she asked the obvious.

Joe didn't give the nosy female a smile. "Her name is Little Flower. She's Arapaho. She's kind of shy, but she's the best worker I've seen."

Mattie Lou ruffled her curly hair and placed her hands on rounded hips. With pouty lips, she asked, "She speak English? Understand it?"

"A little of both." Joe was careful with his words, knowing they would no doubt be repeated to her boss. He didn't like this intrusion, but there was little he could do at the moment. He wanted things to stay calm here.

"Don't you get bored without talk?" the whore asked in an almost hateful tone. "You need a woman with fire and spirit."

Joe had to suppress his irritation to reply in a passive tone, "Little Flower has everything I need. She never gives me a hard time."

"All men need a hard time in some areas." She licked her mouth in lewdness. "I can give you an unforgettable one today. These hands and lips have skills to take you to heaven. Why not give me a try, Joe?"

"A beautiful and talented woman doesn't need to rustle up reluctant business, Mattie Lou. I'm just not the kind of man who needs more than one woman. Why don't you work your magic on George this morning?"

259

"George left before sunup. He stayed here a day longer than he should. He had to ride fast and hard to make up lost time."

Joe controlled his reaction to that news. He wondered if Mattie Lou was telling the truth or if she even knew it. He didn't like hearing that the strange scout had left so early, especially since George knew Zeke. "I have to get finished here, so I won't be late for breakfast. See you inside."

"I'm leaving," she snapped, his words more than a subtle hint.

Joe watched the annoyed woman stalk toward the post. He compared her to his love. Mattie Lou was tough, deceitful, and worn. Morning Star was gentle, honest, and fresh. One was a fake; the other was genuine. Both were strong; both were survivors.

"Lordy, Morning Star, she's worse than fleas. I'm sorry she came over," he apologized.

Joe's interaction with the white woman had not caused any jealousy in Sun Cloud's daughter, but she was angry with the wanton creature who lusted for her man. She would never suggest he act receptive to her just to glean clues for their mission! As a distraction, she asked, "What are fleas?"

Joe grinned and explained, "Those little blood-sucking bugs on dogs."

Morning Star laughed and nodded agreement, then added, "She is bad. I do not like her."

"I don't, either, but I was trying not to cause trouble here."

"I understand."

"I'm going to get us something to eat so we won't have to make a fire and cook. I'm uneasy about that scout leaving before dawn. After breakfast, I'll buy our supplies, and we'll ride soon."

"Scout wake me when leave," Morning Star revealed. "He ride west."

Her manner of speech told Joe she was anxious. "The same direction Zeke is in. Don't look in a hurry, but let's get moving as fast as possible."

"I work while you get food. To hurry, I eat white man's this day."

260

He chuckled at her amusing frown. "It isn't bad, I promise."

When Joe returned with two filled plates, they sat down and ate the tasty meal. Morning Star smiled and licked her lips in enjoyment.

"Good, right?"

"Plenty good. I surprised," she admitted.

They finished in silence, then, Joe returned the plates to Lucy.

Morning Star packed their belongings while Joe was gone. Having enjoyed the paleface meal, she didn't dread future ones during their journey. She realized she had much to learn about his ways.

Inside the trading post, Joe selected their trail supplies: flour, meal, sugar, salt, cured meat, canned goods, and ammunition. As he and Orin gathered his choices, Joe told the three men, "I'm not much on gambling and drinking, and we rode in slow and easy, so we don't need to laze around or catch up on rest. I like to stay on the move. I'm eager to check out this area before any trouble starts."

"Keep your eyes and ears open, Joe," the trapper cautioned. "Them redskins are on the move. They can be sneaky devils."

"Thanks, Ephraim, I will," he replied as he paid the owner.

"I'll be leavin' in a few days meself. Maybe I'll see you on the trail."

"That would be nice, Ben; I'll watch for you. I plan to head west today. I'll stop at those homesteads and farms you mentioned, Orin, to see if they're interested in my plan. I'll probably camp near one of them tonight. If things look promising, I'll be back for trade goods soon."

"Ride along tha Cheyenne and ye'll find them easy."

Joe and Morning Star mounted and headed west from the post. As he turned and waved, he saw Orin and Mattie Lou observing their departure from the porch. Ephraim and Ben weren't in sight.

The couple rode for miles until they were out of sight and were certain they weren't being followed. They did not talk until they halted for their first water and rest break.

Morning Star listened as Joe explained the new plan.

"We'll ride about fifteen miles toward the setting sun before we turn southeast to Pierre. We'll make a few stops at homesteads and farms, just in case Orin checks on us. Once I'm sure he—or anyone—will be fooled, we'll enter the water and set a false trail. That'll give us about sixty miles to Pratte's. I want us to travel easy, Morning Star, so we and the animals won't get there too tired to make an escape if necessary. With this terrain and taking time to establish our cover, it'll take three days."

"Plan is good. I am glad we ride from Orin's. I do not like him."

"Tell me what happened while we were there," he coaxed.

"When you gone, he put furs in big tepee, building. He put mules in fence. He look at me many times. When task finished, he stand at post and watch me. I worry. Afraid I not being good squaw. Other times, he stand in door and watch our camp. I not like to be afraid. I see Pawnee squaw take food from house to post many times. She not visit me. That strange."

Joe noticed how her English suffered during the retelling of her uneasiness at McMichael's post. "Orin called her Lucy. She didn't speak any, but she's a great cook. Maybe he told her to leave you alone."

"Lucy strange. She walk as if not see me. Maybe she afraid of man with fiery hair. He come to camp and bring me food. I not like his eyes. I not speak to him. Take food and nod thank you. He ask questions, but I no answer. He look at our supplies. He go inside where you are."

Joe was displeased to learn of Orin's visit. "What kind of questions did he ask you, Morning Star?"

"If I speak English. If I be happy with you. Where I come from? How you buy me? Where we going? If I need help or goods. When I no talk and no look at him, he go. I think he mad at Morning Star. I no like, no trust."

Joe assumed Orin was annoyed because she refused to talk with him while he was practically wooing her. Now he understood why Orin wanted Mattie Lou to enchant him—to help effectuate a sale of his woman! Such transactions were common out here, and he understood Orin's lust for this beauty. "You're a beautiful woman, Morning Star. He asked about buying you. He said to help Lucy with cooking and cleaning, but I doubt that's why he wanted you. I can't blame him for craving you. His desire was what you sensed and made you nervous. He seemed all right to me."

"When he go home at night, I feel eyes watching our camp. Strange."

"He was wishing he was in my place with you. I didn't see or hear anything to make me suspicious of him. We can't let his lust confuse us."

"What is lust?"

"Strong desire, a big craving, usually the bad kind. It's when you see someone you want badly, even without knowing or wanting to know her. All you want to do is take her or him to your mat and join your bodies. You don't care about having more than sex. Understand?"

Morning Star knew it was not like that between her and Joe. They shared desire. "I understand; lust can be good or bad, but most times bad."

Joe grinned and nodded. He wanted to pull her into his arms, kiss her, and sink to the grass with her beneath him. He dared not make a single move toward the enchanting creature or his control would vanish.

He knew this was not a safe time and place to make love. "Let's ride."

When dusk arrived, Joe and Morning Star halted their journey. As a precaution, they had stopped at two homesteads where Joe talked with the husband and wife. They had eaten a noon meal at one, with Joe inside and her— a squaw—outside. They had traveled fifteen miles westward along the wide and muddy Cheyenne. They had weaved around cottonwoods, bushes, and underbrush, and had crossed many creek and stream offshoots. Tomorrow, after setting a fake trail, they would head southeast for Pierre.

As they prepared the evening meal together, Joe said, "We need to take turns sleeping while the other stands guard. We don't know who's in this area, Indians or whites. We can't take any risks of being surprised."

"That is good." She glanced at him and asked, "What about big guns at post? Will Orin fire against my people?"

"Don't worry; he can't risk using those cannons against any tribe. The Army would know where they came from; they'd be furious."

Recalling their power as Joe had explained it, she was relieved.

They completed their meal and ate it. Both knew they could not make love in this area, so neither made romantic overtures to the other.

It was dark; the tiny sliver of moon gave off only dim light. "We'll let the fire die so we can't be seen," Joe said, "I'll put the safety matches and a torch here. If any noise sounds threatening, it can be lit fast."

Morning Star liked his keen wits. She smiled.

Joe took the first guard shift. He watched Morning Star settle herself on her sleeping mat. He did not get to observe her long before the firelight was gone, and darkness soon engulfed them like an impenetrable black fog at sea. He listened to various sounds and guessed what made them. He remembered what Morning Star had told him about being friends with the night. He practiced that skill until it was time to awaken her.

Morning Star awoke quickly. She and Joe exchanged places by using their hands to feel their way. His touch was warm and encouraging. She wanted to kiss him and to talk with him, but did neither. She wished she could see him, watch him sleep. The moment she imagined his tanned and chiseled features, she scolded herself for her lack of attention to her task. She returned to full alert, listened to noises and absorbing scents. She detected nothing unusual, but she kept herself on guard against another lapse. Hours passed, and she awoke Joe for his turn.

They followed the same routine for two days and nights. As they traveled, they continued their lessons. Morning Star's English improved, as did Joe's use of the bow. She did not practice firing his weapons, as they didn't know who was within hearing range. At one location, they had to journey close to a wide bend in the river to avoid adding numerous extra miles. As they rode, they skirted homesteads, farms, Indian camps, and "woodhawks"—men, Indian, white or mixed—who cut and sold wood along the bank to passing boats. A perilous and hard job, the men charged high prices and received them. When they did approach the Missouri River to water their animals, they were careful. Once they saw a keelboat heading northward. Another time they almost rode into a woodhawk camp where two men were resting, their axes silent.

Tuesday, following Joe's advice about entering Pierre in a rested state, they halted early. They camped behind a cluster of dirt-topped hills between them and the post. Many trees near the river also helped obscure their presence.

Morning Star was nervous about visiting another white area, but she promised herself she would remain brave and helpful.

Joe was anxious, too, for other reasons. Tanner had been murdered in Pierre, and was buried in the graveyard there. It was where his best suspect to date worked and lived: Simon Adams. On the last visit, Simon had been too busy to talk and reveal much. Joe knew he would have to work harder this time to withdraw information.

Pierre was a large and busy settlement, one of the oldest posts in the territory. It was situated at the mouth of the Bad River where steamboats and keel boats docked and traded. Joe recalled a large stable, small boardinghouse that served meals, several cabins, the trading post, and a house used as a saloon for drinking and gambling, with rooms in the back for prostitutes to ply their trade. Unlike Fort Laramie and other western posts, none of the three posts along "The Misery" had Indian tepees around them.

The only good thing Joe could think of was that there had not been enough time for Zeke to reach Pierre, if Ephraim had his timing right . . .

Chapter Twelve

Morning Star stayed close to Joe as they entered the settlement. She longed to hold his hand, as she needed his comforting touch. If she were alone or still Zeke's captive, she would be terrified surrounded by so many whites who mostly hated her kind. With head lowered in a servile manner, she glanced at the setting from the corners of her dark brown eyes. She realized that Joe had described it with accuracy and had prepared her well for this intimidating adventure. She recalled that he had admitted he was tense about this place where her cousin had been slain. She wished she could have met Tanner, and presumed he had been like Joe, as most best friends were a great deal alike. That belief was one thing that alarmed her about her brother's close and long friendship with Knife-Slayer.

They reached the stable and dismounted. Both tried to behave naturally. Without being obvious, both studied the busy area. Each noticed that Zeke's wagons were not in sight and were relieved.

Joe asked the liveryman if he could leave his horses tethered at the corral while he took care of business. If he decided to stay longer than a few hours, he said, he would return later to make arrangements for the feed and care of the animals. Joe wanted them ready to depart if they had to move fast. He didn't hesitate to leave the three horses and supplies there, as few robberies occurred in daylight and in an occupied area.

Morning Star followed Joe inside the trading post in a meek manner. She was glad Joe wore his pistol and was skilled with the weapon. They had arranged two signals — *danger* and *move fast* — before entering Pierre, as they could use neither English nor Lakota as a warning if a perilous situation arose. Her heart pounded, her mouth was dry, and her hands were cold and damp. A strange sensation gripped her stomach. She wondered if her apprehension showed, as she seemed aquiver all over. If anyone guessed she was the daughter of Sun Cloud and granddaughter of Gray Eagle, she would be in deep trouble. So would Joe! She worried over his safety more than her own. Coming here was a big risk, but one that must be taken. The lives of her band and other tribes were at stake, as was peace with the whites. She was relieved Joe had been more afraid of hiding her somewhere to wait rather than of bringing her along. She wanted to be here to help him if the bold plan failed.

Morning Star felt eyes on her, many eyes. She dared not lift hers to look around or to return gazes, as that was considered brazen and offensive conduct for a lowly squaw. Joe had told her not to worry about stares, that her beauty was the reason for them. She knew she was pretty, and knew it was not vain to admit it. Denying the truth, even about oneself, was the same as lying or being a coward.

Morning Star waited nearby while Joe chatted with the men and picked up a few items. She was careful not to get caught studying the man who worked for Bernard Pratte, the post's owner. Simon Adams was tall, the same height as Joe. His hair was as dark as a moonless night, and his eyes were as green as spring leaves. He looked strong, and appeared about ten years older than Joe. Her companion had told her this man hated Indians, especially her nation. She tried to envision him in the costume Knife-Slayer had described. She paid close attention to details so she could question the warrior about them when she returned home. She saw Simon leave by the back door.

Joe approached the short man behind the long wooden counter. "Simon returning soon? I need to speak with him?"

As he continued his work, the man replied, "Outside resting and smoking. Been busy this morning with that keelboat in."

"Can I go out the back door?"

Without looking up, he replied, "Sure, just close it."

Morning Star followed Joe outside. She went to stand near the corner of the building. She didn't want her presence to hold the man's tongue, but still she listened to their words.

"Hello, Mr. Adams. Joe Lawrence, remember?"

Simon released a curl of smoke from his cigar. "You were in a few months ago with your friend who was robbed and killed. You report it to the Army at Fort Tabor?"

Tanner had not been robbed, but Joe didn't correct him. "Didn't think it would do much good. Anything like that happen here again?"

Simon lazed against the wall with his back to the Indian woman. He took another drag on his cigar before replying, "Not that I know of. If anyone's been attacked, no body was left behind to alert us. Such things rarely happen in Pierre. Pratte doesn't like trouble and a bad reputation."

Joe watched the man flick ashes off his long sleeve. He noticed the sizable brown birthmark on his right hand. "That's good news for everybody except Tanner! If we'd arrived a day later, he'd still be alive. I was the one in a stupid hurry to get off the trail," he invented with hopes Simon would respond to a guilt-riddled man. "We were like family, like brothers. We always took care of each other. I should have been more alert in a strange place. I figured we'd be safe here and get some needed rest; I was fatigued from keeping on alert day and night for renegades. I'm alone now, and I miss him. All our dreams were slain with Tanner. It twists my gut for him to die like that and for me to be powerless to avenge his death. That's no way for a man to die; it's as bad as Indian slaughter. If you've ever lost a best friend and nobody was punished for it, you know how I feel."

Simon stood straight and stiff, with a scowl on his face. "I do. I've lost people to those infernal Sioux who got away with murder. Riles me. They sneak around doing their dirty business without getting caught and punished, but they leave enough behind to show who's guilty. I'm surprised the Army hasn't shoved them into hell where they belong. They won't have much choice soon but to retaliate."

Joe witnessed the coldness in Simon's voice and eyes and how the man's body was now taut with pent-up rage and hate. "What do you mean?"

Simon leaned back once more. "The soldiers know who's to blame; they'll have to chase them down — and soon, with more incidents happening all the time. I don't understand what's taking them so long to react. They're supposed to be here to protect us."

"And to keep the peace," Joe amended, keeping his tone genial.

Simon tensed and straightened. He shot back, "Peace, hell! Whites can't have peace with bloodthirsty savages. Truces, either. They forget we own this territory. Our government purchased it, with *our* taxes. We have a right to settle and work here, and to be protected while we do. Let those savages fight. We'll wipe them out and conquer this area like we did the eastern half." He settled back again, drawing deep on a cigar. "The Crow ain't no better, but at least they know their place and don't attack their betters. I wish they'd wipe out those Sioux for us. Then the Army could get rid of them. Indians are nothing but a pack of wild animals. All they know is raiding and killing. White or red targets, it doesn't matter to them. This territory would be a wonderful place without them."

Joe also leaned against the wall to appear relaxed. He didn't refute Simon's opinions of Indians or argue over who had a rightful claim to this territory. "I haven't been here long enough to know much about either tribe," he alleged. "They were still holed up in winter camps when Tanner and I rode through. They as bad as you say?"

"Worse. I wish we could sell them rot-gut whiskey to eat up their minds and spirits. They love firewater, but the law stops us. A man could make a fortune in a territory like this if those Sioux were pushed out or cowered. Never trust an Indian, Joe; they'll turn on you in a minute and slit your throat without feeling a thing."

270

Joe saw Simon glance at Morning Star and frown. He headed off trouble by explaining, "She's Arapaho. I bought her off a trapper heading south. He said he couldn't take his squaw home because his wife wouldn't like that at all. Little Flower's shy, but she's been a good worker."

"Bedding and doing chores are all they're good for, if you don't mind Injun smell on you."

"I make sure she bathes every day and doesn't use any fat on her skin. I'm inclined to cleanliness myself. That trapper told me lots of men in these parts have Indian servants. She was real cheap, and he was in a hurry. Gave me a good deal, so I figured, what the heck? Let her take care of me and my chores." He chuckled, then continued. "I didn't realize my having her would offend some folks. Maybe I shouldn't keep her. What do you think, Simon?" he asked. Joe knew how powerful giving advice made some people feel. He knew he'd guessed right about Simon when the man grinned and leaned close to respond.

"Most men around here don't care if you have a squaw, Joe. I'd keep her and use her good, unless she's trouble. Those savages have certainly stolen and used plenty of white women. It drives bucks crazy when we take their woman, particularly the pretty ones." He glanced at the raven-haired woman again. "She is a good looker, and seems to know her place. Since those bastards are greedy and cruel enough to sell or trade us their females, why should they care what we do with them? If I had the money, I'd build fancy brothels along the river and stuff them full of young beauties like her. I'd be rich in a month, because I'd train the little creatures myself on how to please a white man." He chewed the cigar butt a minute while his eyes glittered strangely. His attention returned and he asked, "Where you been since your last visit? Where you heading from here?"

Joe used the same traveling trader story he had told Orin McMichael. He noticed that Simon's interest was captured by it. "Since my friend is dead and I want to stay here a while longer, it seems a good way to earn money and see this territory. Of course, I didn't know the Indians would be acting up

271

soon. That could mess up my plan."

"Don't worry; the Army will slap them down before summer's over."

"This territory has promise, Simon, if trouble can be averted. A man could carve out a nice ranch here. Plenty of water and grass. I'm sure more forts will be coming soon to provide more protection. All I need is some money for building and for buying stock. I think I can earn it by selling goods on the trail — if those hostiles don't start a war and interfere," he muttered, trying to sound as if his opinion of the Indians matched Simon's.

"It'll come to a fight, Joe, but we'll win. The Army will be like a boa constrictor; it'll wrap around those Sioux and squeeze the life from them. Nobody will be happier than me to witness that glorious day." Simon grinned as if envisioning the heartless massacre he admitted he craved. "Those Crow are like coyotes; they run when wolves appear. I'd like to see their nasty dens cleaned out, too. It's a shame we can't put them all in cages and train them like the wild beasts they are. We'd make a fortune displaying such intriguing specimens around the world. Yes, sir, Joe, we'd make a fortune if this territory was conquered and real settlement began."

"Speaking of displays, I saw a war shield and headdress on the wall inside. They for sale? I'd love to mount a souvenir collection in my ranch. I was almost hoping for a run-in with a highly decorated warrior so I could snatch a few treasures when the Army and his band weren't watching. No such luck yet. Haven't caught or see one alone in his finery."

Simon's eyes gleamed. "Those were gifts to Pratte," he whispered, "but I can get you some, for a good price. You can't say how or where you bought them, though. Pratte would have my scalp for sure if he heard about it."

Joe feigned a look of delight and complicity. "Don't worry, Simon; I'll stay quiet. I'll be back through in a few weeks. I'll see what you have then and ship them to my family back South to hold for me until I get that ranch house built." Joe grinned as an idea came to mind. "I bet Papa would like a set, too. We'd want Sioux artifacts, fierce warriors, with plenty of symbols

272

exposing their prowess. As you said, Crow aren't that brave. That makes Sioux souvenirs more valuable."

"I know the different colors and markings of tribes, so don't worry about getting the wrong ones. I buy them off a man who comes across plenty. He roams all over this area. Isn't scared of anything or anyone."

"Sounds like Zeke," Joe remarked.

Simon looked at him. "You know Zeke Randall?"

Joe shook his head as he replied, "No, but I've heard plenty of tales about him. Seems he's becoming quite a legend."

Simon laughed heartily. "Zeke will love hearing that news. He deals with Indians, mostly Crow, but he hates all of them."

"Why?"

"Like me, he has his reasons. Nothing a man likes to discuss."

When Simon didn't explain, Joe let it pass. "I'm sure he does. I'd like to meet him one day. I bet he could teach me plenty about Indians and this territory. He probably knows the perfect spot to place a ranch. I might hire him to help me claim it."

"Zeke's here every month. Maybe he'll be around when you return." Simon stretched his tall frame. "I'd better get to the privy and back inside. We're busier than a lion in mating season. Too many orders to hump."

Joe shared laughter with the other man, and made a mental note to remember Simon's constant references to animals. Simon dropped his cigar and mashed it beneath his boot, but Joe had already registered that he was right-handed; that and the birthmark could be valuable identification clues.

"You guard your hide out there, Joe. I'll mention you to Zeke. Maybe he can use a partner and help you with your idea. It's a clever one. Could make a lot of money if handled right. Wish I'd thought of it. If I had the money to finance it, I would be tempted to steal it from you, or even join you."

"I bet we'd make good partners if we could afford to join up."

"You might consider hauling around a wagonload of delicious white whores. You'd tempt starving white men to empty

273

their pockets faster than they could drop their pants. And some of those Injuns would love a little taste of creamy white meat. If you do, better get blondes and redheads; braves hunger for women different from theirs."

Joe was astonished by the man's suggestion. He wondered how a man who hated Indians so much could want to have sex with *any* white woman. "Thanks, Simon. I'll—"

Morning Star caught Joe's eye and gave both the signals they had arranged. She looked frightened. His hesitation caused Simon to turn and look her way. Quick-witted, his love lowered her head.

"Something wrong, Joe?"

"For a minute I thought she was about to run off. Must have been a bug bite. I haven't had her long, but she might not like me or being a piece of property. Or maybe she needs to use the privy, too. I'm a stranger to traveling with a female, so I don't know their curious ways."

Simon chuckled. "There's a public privy behind the boardinghouse," he said, implying she was not to use his.

"Thanks. I'll be going now, but we'll talk again soon."

Simon went into the outhouse, and Joe joined Morning Star. She was peeking around the wall she had jumped behind moments ago.

"What's up?"

"Zeke and other man come!" she reported. "They go in that building! They no see me."

Joe looked around the corner and saw a wagon in front of the structure used as a saloon. "Let's get out of here before he spots us or our horses. Hurry, before Simon finishes and stalls us."

They walked around the other way, careful not to use a suspicious run. He casually checked for safety, then they went to their horses. They mounted and rode out of the settlement in the other direction—north.

Later, they skirted Pierre and headed south. They didn't talk, as their pace was fast to put distance between them and peril. They crossed rising and falling slopes, avoided gulches, and galloped over grassland.

When they finally halted to rest, Joe gave a loud exhalation of air and said, "Damn, I didn't expect to run into Zeke this soon. I was hoping he was still a long way from here. Once Simon tells him about us, that will get him to thinking. He'll know I'm not anxious to meet him and that you're still with me. Simon will realize I lied to him, so that'll put Pratte's post off bounds. Worse, when Zeke goes to Orin's and they talk, Orin will know I tricked him, too. That makes another visit to his post risky. Damn!" he swore again in frustration, as it was evident Zeke's return would lock them out of much of this area that held clues to the mystery.

Morning Star touched Joe's arm and smiled to calm him. "Not worry so much. What if Zeke think you ask questions to . . . avoid him?" she asked. "What if he think he captured your woman and you tricked him to rescue me? He learn by now we here, so he must wonder if we cannot be ones who killed friends far away. Maybe he believe Oglala warriors attack friends to punish, to take back stolen possessions. Why he think, on many moons later, we do that deed? What if he believe you trapper and believe clever story you tell Orin? What if Zeke think you travel here only to seek friend's killer? Why he think you think he . . . villain and you seek to defeat him with only a woman helper? He think he smart and careful, so give others no reason to be . . . suspicious." She finished her reasoning with, "Why he worry over one man and his squaw?"

Joe was impressed. She was perceptive and intelligent. He didn't point out the loopholes in her speculations, such as his being here earlier with Tanner, without her, and not as a trapper, but he sent her a broad smile and caressed her cheek. He fused his gaze to hers and wanted to fuse their lips. Her expression exposed matching emotions. But danger was too close for them to halt for loving play. He sailed to another island of concern. "I wish we hadn't had to leave so suddenly. I wanted to get a look inside Simon's place for evidence, and maybe get a look at his arms for tattoos. He raises my suspicions; I'd like to know if I'm riding the wrong trail and wasting time." He drew in a deep breath, then added, "I wish we'd had time to visit

275

Tanner's grave. I don't like leaving his body there."

Morning Star knew his friend—her cousin—had been on Joe's mind since yesterday. "Do not worry; he is safe," she comforted.

He knew she was right. "You have a kind heart and gentle spirit. You and Tanner would have liked each other." To prevent renewed grief from distracting him, Joe returned to their task.

They went over what they had learned from and about Simon Adams.

"Smart . . . villain would not say so many bad words to stranger. He talked much. Is not smart enough to be Snake-Man," she concluded.

"Maybe that's a trick, a disguise, a cunning scheme. He might figure no one would suspect a man like him who's so open about his ill feelings."

"He . . . pretend to hate Indians?" she asked, misunderstanding him.

"No, he hates them all right, especially the Dakota Nation. What I meant was, he could be making sure everybody—especially strangers—knows he hates Indians, and he could be assuming nobody would become a loudmouth and make himself a suspect. If I were Snake-Man, would I pretend to like or hate Indians?" he reasoned aloud. "I think leaning too far in either direction isn't smart. Whatever, that villain is very smart and very dangerous."

"It confusing, Joe. If I have enemy, I not hide it. But I not trying to start war between sides. I say, smart man not hide it or show it."

"I agree, but sometimes desperate or greedy men don't act smart. They make mistakes, and that's what finally defeats them."

Morning Star thought of how her brother and Knife-Slayer behaved sometimes. Soon, they would make mistakes and be entrapped by them.

"With Zeke around, we can't do much in this area," Joe said. "By the time he learns we've been to Pierre and Orin's, he'll be searching for us, probably with more hired men. If his boss doesn't suspect us by now, he will as soon as he and Zeke add up the facts, then suspect we're up to something. They'll be out to stop us any way they can."

Morning Star grasped that he didn't accept her speculations and still believed they were in great peril. She had to concede to his thoughts, because Joe knew whites better than she did. "We be careful and alert."

"Since we don't know who or where this boss is," Joe decided aloud, "we should get out of sight and reach for a while. Let's try to get information from the Indians, the Crow. We'll need trade goods. Let's risk going on to Lookout to buy them."

"Zeke come from Lookout," she reminded.

His blue gaze locked with her brown one. "I know, but we have no choice. We can't go back to Pratte or Orin's and we need trade goods. We can't give up, Morning Star. But we have to get out of this boiling kettle for a while; I just hope we aren't jumping out of it into a roaring fire out there." He caressed her cheek and urged, "Don't worry, love, we'll be careful." His tone altered as he said, "I want you to lead me to the first Crow camp, then hide until I finish my business and return to you."

Her sunny smile vanished. "I go with you!"

Joe shook his blond head. "Crow won't harm a white trader with gifts. I've put you in too much danger already."

Determination filled her eyes. "I go, too, or I not lead you there."

Joe eyed her raven hair spilling over her shoulders and how it swayed when she tossed her head in defiance. He had to keep her safe! He decided there would be time on the trail to persuade her to stay behind at the last minute, so he didn't argue. "Let's ride, woman."

"I see fox sneak into Joe's body. Eyes expose you. You not fool me or leave me behind. I part of sacred vision, too. Must go and help."

"You know me too well, Morning Star. I yield, but I don't like it. I couldn't stand for anything to happen to you. We take no risks, woman."

Sun Cloud's daughter smiled. She was happy Joe possessed the self-confidence to concede when necessary. She loved looking at him. His hair grazed his broad shoulders like a golden mane. It waved like rolling hills and gleamed when the sun kissed it. And she could lose sight of reality when she stared into his blue gaze, as beautiful as the sky above them. The sienna buckskin garments enhanced his dark tan and clung to his muscled frame. His features were bold, perfect. Joe was irresistible in looks and character, though she did not care for the white man's beard that grew thicker and darker each day. She adored being with him; she loved him beyond control.

When Joe sent her a quizzical look for her long and silent study, she grinned and teased, "Very good decision. You plenty smart, Joe Lawrence."

They traveled as fast as possible for two days. At night, they took guard shifts once more. Early Saturday morning, the apprehensive couple rode to Lookout, a trading post owned by the Columbia Fur Company. It was not busy, as the keelboat had stopped here first and trappers hadn't arrived yet.

This time, Morning Star remained with the horses while Joe went to purchase "gifts" for the Crow. She was tense the entire time he was gone, and strove to keep herself on full alert. This was their last stop in a white settlement, at least for a while. She was glad. She wanted to return to the Plains and forests and hills where she felt at home and safe. She struggled not to think of the people who were depending upon her to guide their destinies in the right direction and who were depending upon her to remain true to her heritage and customs.

Morning Star confessed she had tried but failed to keep to the last part. By now, being with Joseph Lawrence was as natural and vital as breathing. Their love was the food upon which her spirit survived and grew. Her life would never be the same after his inevitable departure. She could never yield to another man after being with Joe. Without that part of life, she would bear no children. Perhaps, she ventured, the loss of a true love was why Buckskin Girl had never joined another! But her friend had never mentioned a lost loved one.

Lost . . . Forever . . . Those words cut into her soul with a white-hot knife that seared her from head to toe with burning wounds. It was a fact she could not leave with Joe. It was a fact he could not remain with her. But it was possible to have him and love him until this sacred mission ended, one way or another. Payaba's vision had claimed that would be in glorious victory, so she must not be so afraid. Yet, her faith lagged on occasion. She felt that surely the Great Spirit understood and forgave human frailty. Surely He would not allow her weakness to endanger—

A mule brayed loudly in the corral, jerking Morning Star back to reality. She scolded herself for such a terrible loss of attention. Her dulled wits could get them killed. She commanded herself back to full alert.

Inside the trading post, Joe chatted with Harvey Meade. He had met the perky fellow on his visit with Tanner. So far, nothing looked or sounded suspicious. Joe used the same strategy as at the other posts; it appeared to work again. He was told Zeke headed for Pierre on Monday.

"I must have missed him on the trail. I think I'll do some looking around before I try to catch up with him again." Noticing the manager's reaction, he took a risk by adding, "Or maybe I won't try to herd up with Zeke. From what I hear about him, that could be a mistake. I just thought I shouldn't work this territory without checking him out first, as most folks act like he runs it. I'm not a coward, but he sounds like the kind who'd be riled and dangerous if pushed." Joe was delighted when Harvey responded favorably to his deceit.

"You'd be smart to avoid him, Joe. He's trouble, the kind we don't need here. You mentioned ranching and settling down," the post manager began. "Didn't Simon tell you about the Pre-Emption Homestead Law?" When Joe shook his head, the short man explained, "It's been in effect since '41. You can purchase up to one hundred sixty acres of land at a dollar-twenty-five per acre in many locations of this territory. Best place to check which areas are for sale is at Fort Laramie. That's where most territorial business is carried out and where the Indian agent stays. I know Simon's purchased a tract and bought a couple off other fellows. If you asked me, he used them as go-betweens to get his hands on more land. After this area opens up, they'll be worth a lot more money. Others have bought up tracts, too. Me included."

"Our government claims they own it," Harvey continued, "bought it from the French, so I guess they have the right to sell parcels. They've even paid more dollars to some tribes to avoid conflicts. I guess I shouldn't feel guilty over the Dakotas' claims they still own it. If I hadn't bought my parcel, some other man would. It's on the James River, east of here. As soon as I'm sure of a real treaty, I plan to build on it and farm the land."

"Sounds like a good opportunity to me. I'm surprised that Simon didn't tell me about the Pre-Emption Law. I'm also surprised he's buying up land. It's odd he would stay here since he makes no secret of his hatred for Indians. Must have been something real bad to cause such feelings."

Harvey glanced around to make sure no one was coming inside the post. "It was," he confided. "When Simon first came here a few years back, his keelboat was attacked by marauding Indians; his wife was killed and he was robbed clean by Oglalas. He intended to open a trading post, but lost everything. He survived by slipping over the rail, swimming underwater, and hiding in bank brush. Everybody aboard was killed; even three women were raped and murdered. That was strange, because Indians usually take them captive. Law figured they were in a hurry and didn't want to be slowed by prisoners. Evidence said they were Red Heart warriors. I don't have to tell you that Simon was consumed by hatred and a hunger for revenge; but there was nothing he could do to find and punish the guilty ones. I was sure they were only renegades, but he wasn't. Still isn't. He had to go to work for Pratte for survival money. Believe me, he didn't take to being a hired hand instead of an owner and boss. Sticks in his craw; so does running away and leaving his wife to suffer and die. I can't fault him there; wasn't anything he could do to save her or the others. I think he's only working Pratte's until he earns enough to get out on his own again. I bet that land he bought is for a post. Sad how cruel fate changes a man. 'Course, I don't know what he was like before coming here. But now—"

Harvey listened and looked for arrivals once more. "I hear he sells bloody souvenirs behind his boss's back. Bernard Pratte would be furious; he's a good and honest man. It's the worst thing any man could do to cause more trouble. All it does is provoke scoundrels to rob scaffolds and ambush Indians for goods to sell him. I hear he sells Indians guns and whiskey, too, but I've never witnessed it with my own eyes, just overheard trappers whispering. It's wrong, and it's against the law. If everybody would take it slow and easy, we could have peace here. If we give the Indians time to get used to us, expand real slow and careful, they'd accept us."

"You ever mentioned this to your company or the Army?" Joe asked.

An expression akin to sheer terror filled Harvey's face and enlarged his eyes. In a quavering voice, he vowed, "I don't interfere because I don't want Simon riled at me. He's the kind of man who would make a bad enemy if you crossed him. He's tight with that Zeke Randall."

"Don't worry, Harvey, my mouth won't open to the wrong ears. I don't want Simon and Zeke gunning for me, either. It'll be our secret. I'm going to skip looking up Zeke and head on to the Plains. I'll need plenty of gifts to make friends with the Indians. I want to see for myself if trouble's brewing. If it is, I bet Zeke has his hands in it."

"You can win that bet, Joe. I'll get the usual trinket sack ready. You can check it over and pay me."

"Thanks, I'm sure you know what the Indians like." As Joe waited and looked around, he sighted an interesting object. He questioned Harvey Meade about it, then purchased the enchanting item.

It was dark, as they had ridden as long as possible before stopping to camp. Without wasting time and energy, they tended the three horses, prepared a hot meal, and settled down to rest.

"You think Meade say — said — those things about Zeke and Simon to point eyes to them?" Morning Star asked. "Take eyes from him?"

Joe mused on her question. "I don't think so. He's too short. In all honesty, I'm not sure whom I trust. For all I know, Zeke could be doing a side business with Simon on those souvenirs. In view of what happened to Simon years ago, it's not unusual for him to be filled with bitterness and hatred."

"My people do not slay women and children."

He smiled at her and said, "I know. I'm just wondering if Snake-Man was here and working before Simon's arrival or if it was only renegades. It could be that our villain has no connection to any of the trading posts."

"Where would villain live?"

"Could be on a farm or homestead. Could be a camp along the river."

"Could be at fort," she amended, looking worried.

"Perhaps, but I doubt it. I think it's too big a plan for a soldier."

"You look good at fort when arrive . . . tomorrow," she cautioned.

"I think it's best if we stop by Tabor and see Captain Thomas. We're close, and it's been a while since I reported my finds to him. I can send a message to Stede and the Indian agent at Laramie. I'll write it up at first light. I'll send my family a letter, too. Let them know I'm all right."

"Our families worry about us."

"At least you'll get to see yours soon. It's been a long time since I saw mine. I miss them, more than I realized I would. I hope my father's settled down by now. He was against my coming here. I'm sure Mother's done plenty of talking to him; she has a special way with him. With luck, he'll listen to her this time; she understood why I had to leave. So did my sister. You'd like my mother and Sarah Beth." He smiled. "I bet Lucas is growing like a spring weed. Little boys change fast at four."

Morning Star didn't want to discuss or think about the strong family ties that would soon take Joseph Lawrence from her side and life. Nor did she want to ponder her own. She wished she and Joe were a family and had a future together. That could never be, and it tormented her.

Joe sensed her warring emotions and let the melancholy topic die. "We'd best get to sleep. Tomorrow is a busy day."

Joe's report and letter home were finished. Breakfast was over, all chores were done, and the horses were saddled. Their weapons and supplies were loaded and their canteens were full. They would reach Fort Tabor by midmorning, if they left within a short time. By noon, they could be on the trail toward the first Crow camp.

Joe went to Morning Star and held out the gift he had purchased at the last trading post. "Remember when I told you white men can do tricks to fool people who don't know about them?" he reminded. "This is one of them. Hold it up like this and look into that hole," he instructed, assisting her. "See, magic can be created with tricks and skills. Keep it pointed toward bright light and turn it slowly."

Morning Star did as he said. Her breath caught in wonder. Her hands trembled as she clasped the gift.

"It's called a kaleidoscope. The first one was invented, created, by Sir David Brewster about thirty-five years ago. My mother loves them and collects them. Every time I sailed someplace, she'd ask me to look for a new one. She has them with beads, colored glass, pebbles, dried flowers, shells, insects, all kinds of things. Every time you move it, the pattern and colors change. It's amazing, isn't it?"

Each rotation offered a different design and hues from the tiny specks of glass inside it. "How does it do such magic?" she asked. When she stopped turning the long tube, her eyes filled with awe.

"I'm not sure I can explain in words you'll understand, but I'll try. It's an optical—that means anything to do with eyes and seeing—optical instrument. An instrument is something like a tool that does a certain task." He motioned to areas as he explained, "There are two small mirrors at each end of the tube. Glass or whatever is used is put into a space at one end. The mirrors reflect them like water does your face when you look into a pond or river. This is the peephole, because you peep—that means, look—into it. I wish you could see my mother's collection. The one with flowers is breathtaking, and the one with insects in almost unbelievable."

"You give this one to me?"

"Yes."

"What of your mother?"

"She would be happy for you to have such a special treasure." As she held it up again, closed one eye, and peered inside, Joe watched her with joy. She was as excited as a child at Christmas. She twisted the tube many times, almost squealing with delight at each new design it made. When she lowered it, she gazed at him with gratitude and joy.

Joe saw how the tears in her eyes sparkled like dewdrops under the morning sun. Their shade of brown reminded him of the darkest band of the stripes in the carnelian and onyx he had shipped from Brazil. Her skin was as soft as the cotton raised on his family's plantation, the color of a newborn fawn. Her hair was as black and shiny as the coal from mines back East. He recalled how, when they galloped across plains and meadows, her ebony mane spread out behind her in glorious splendor. She could not possibly know how beautiful she was, or how deeply she affected him. Being near her was paradise, and sometimes hell when he could not touch her. How, he fretted, could he return to an existence without this woman who had become a vital part of his life?

"I will protect it and love it always," she said in her best English.

When she leaned against Joe and kissed him, his body shuddered with longing for hers. He was relieved but dismayed when they parted. If he knew they would not be distur— He warned himself not to lose control. They were too near the fort for privacy. "Let's go," he urged tenderly.

Morning Star comprehended his reaction, and knew how she felt, too. It was unwise to remain here any longer. "I am ready."

Captain James Thomas was standing on the porch of his office when Joe and Morning Star rode to the hitching post before it. He looked surprised to see them, and eyed the beauty with undisguised curiosity.

The couple dismounted and secured their reins. When Joe greeted the soldier, Jim returned it, but looked rather hesitant.

"We need to talk. I have plenty to report," Joe hinted.

"You best leave her here. It might look odd to anyone watching if she goes inside with us. No offense intended, just a precaution."

Joe explained to his companion, who nodded. He followed Jim inside. He was a little intrigued when the officer closed the door, as the June day was warm. "What's up?" he asked.

Jim took his seat and told Joe to do the same with the chair before his desk. "So that's the legendary Sun Cloud's daughter," he remarked. "She's beautiful. She understood you, so that means she speaks English."

"She spoke some when I met her, and I've been teaching her more on the trail. This is the first chance I've had to report to you what I've learned."

"What have you learned?" Jim propped his elbows on the desk.

"I wrote out a full report to Stede Gaston and Tom Fitzpatrick and asked them to check on a few things for me. I'd be obliged if you'd send one of your fastest and most dependable men to deliver it to Fort Laramie."

"I have the perfect man for the job. He's never failed me. What's in here?" he inquired as he accepted the sealed packet Joe passed to him.

Joe told about the slaughtered Crow hunting party, with Red Heart arrows in the bodies. He revealed how they had tracked the men responsible and attacked three at Rake's Hollow and how four others had escaped before they arrived. He explained about recovering the sacred possessions and returning them to the Oglala burial ground, and of how Crow arrows had been left there to incriminate the wrong people. He told

Jim about meeting the trapper, buying his furs, then visiting Orin McMichael's trading post. He halted his report to ask who George was.

"I don't recall an Army scout named George with that description. Maybe he's from Fort Laramie or Ripley or Snelling. He's a long way from wherever he's posted. I'll check on him. I wonder why I wasn't informed of his mission in my area and why he hasn't contacted me. That's strange, unless he's on leave. You sure Fort Laramie or Tom didn't put someone else on this investigation besides you?" Joe shook his head. "A corporal, you say?" Jim murmured. "No doubt he's military?"

Joe found Jim's lack of knowledge dismaying. "That's what the others told me, and the stripes he was wearing verified it. The men at Orin's seemed to know him. Said he visits there frequently. Implied he shares his scouting reports with McMichael. But if Orin was our man and that scout's one of his hirelings, he and George wouldn't be so open about his visits. George knows Zeke, but so do plenty of people. Simon said Zeke is there every month, so they have a connection. That scout puzzles and worries me; but if somebody else was on this case, I'm sure they would have told me. George didn't seem to guess who I was, but he left fast and early the next morning. I was afraid he was hooked up with Zeke and was going to warn him of me." Joe was puzzled as to why the scout, said to be in this area often, was unknown to the officer before him.

Jim's thoughts seemed to stray a moment as he commented, "I knew about Orin's cannons; they're a scare tactic. He'd never fire them. You sure those men Ephraim mentioned were the ones waiting for Zeke's arrival?"

"I don't know, but it made sense."

"You best not mention them to anyone," Jim warned. "It could appear an unprovoked attack. You only have your word about their foul deeds, which no white law considers a punishable crime. You don't want to get into legal trouble. If I were you, I'd do my best to prevent any more attacks and killings; murder's a serious matter."

Joe thought Jim's choice of words and reaction were strange. "It was all self-defense, but I can't prove it." He related how they visited Pierre and what was said by Simon Adams; that brought a scowl to the officer's face. He revealed how Zeke had arrived and they had fled.

"I've heard rumors about Adams' dirty dealings, but have no proof against him. I can't act without evidence or a witness. I sure wish one or the other would step forward. That kind of thing is dangerous. If I questioned them, they'd deny it. All they'd do is be careful for a while. If you buy that stuff from Adams, you'll be partly responsible for how he got it."

Joe finished his report by telling Jim about his visit to the Columbia Fur post with Harvey Meade. On gut instinct, he decided to keep Harvey's confidence about Simon and Zeke, as he'd already told Jim about his "souvenir" talk with Simon. "That report to Stede and Tom has a few questions I need answers to. After I spend a few weeks with the Crow and Dakotas, I'll be back for them. Get your man to wait for their replies. I'd like to know more about the Pre-Emption Homestead Law and who's buying up land. That issue can make for trouble and provide clues. I'll be playing the white trader for a while. I might luck out on an Indian who drops clues about Snake-Man or Zeke. So what have you learned so far?"

"To be honest with you, Joe, I haven't done much investigating. I was afraid I'd endanger you if the wrong person discovered I was nosing around. We don't actually have a formal case yet, just suspicions and rumors. If we can just get some proof documented, I'll open one, secret, of course. Then you'll be protected from any recriminating charges. Until this is official, our necks are stretched out for chopping off. Frankly, I need a letter of authorization from Tom, and from the President on behalf of Mr. Gaston. I'll request them when I send this over. I like my rank, Joe, and I don't want to risk losing it and my hide if you're on your own."

"I understand, Jim. Get the papers you need. No problem."

"You realize that once you and I are connected, your cover is destroyed. That could be today. That beautiful girl outside won't go unnoticed. It wasn't smart to bring her along. She'll draw attention to your visit."

"Sorry, Jim, but I couldn't leave her alone out there. I figured she'd pass for a squaw. Plenty of men have them."

"But not men who keep visiting my office regularly."

"How else can I report information?"

"There's a hollow tree about two miles from here. From now on, I think we should leave our messages there. I'll draw you a map. That's where I'll put the answer to this," he said, tapping the missive to Fort Laramie, "when it arrives." He sketched a map and explained it.

"You're right, Jim. We have to be careful from here on. Zeke is no doubt searching for me. He's probably reported to his boss by now. We could be in big trouble if they come after us."

"You already are in big trouble, Joe. I haven't told you what's been happening while you were out of touch. It's bad, for you and your Indians. For one thing, Zeke Randall has accused you of the murder of Clement Harris, made formal charges. He turned in evidence—a scrap of your shirt—and listed witnesses against you, and he demanded I use a patrol to hunt you down for arrest and trial. Then, there was a payroll theft by Red Heart warriors last Wednesday. The entire unit was wiped out." Jim took two items from his drawer as he talked and placed them on the desk between him and Joe. "From what my best scout tells me, these possessions belong to Knife-Slayer and Night Stalker. Know them? The last one is the brother of the girl outside, right? The Red Heart chief's son?"

Chapter Thirteen

Joe's mind whirled. Jim hadn't done anything to help him this time. The officer alluded to the storm ahead of recriminating charges, murder, evidence, witnesses! During their May meeting, Jim hadn't mentioned the 1841 Pre-Emption Law, needing letters of authorization, or Simon and Harvey. Jim had said only that Bernard Pratte and Orin McMichael were good men and doubtful suspects. Joe worried over why Jim had waited until after receiving a full report before putting him in a vulnerable position.

Joe couldn't allow this important task to blow up in his face. He had known such a mission would be perilous, but he had expected more help than he was receiving. He recalled Morning Star telling him that Payaba's sacred vision prophesied both whites and Indians would work against him. Joe didn't want to believe that James Thomas, Fitzpatrick's friend, also a man who knew their every move, was his nemesis. He couldn't help but glance at the captain's long sleeves as he thought furiously.

The evidence against his Morning Star's brother and her people was mounting. He must decide if Jim was trying only to protect himself from problems over this explosive matter and protect the mission or if the officer had other motives . . .

Joe prayed that Morning Star hadn't overheard the two shocking charges. "Zeke Randall has the gall to accuse me of crimes!" he scoffed. "He's the one hauling illegal goods to the Indians. He's the one who captured an innocent girl and planned to have her abused by his evil boss. Can you imagine what Sun Cloud and his band, and probably all his allies, would have done if anything like that had happened to his daughter? If nothing more than preventing their retaliation, it justifies Clem's death. But I told you, we didn't kill him. Zeke did because he was becoming too much trouble. By now the vultures haven't left me any proof."

"Don't get heated up, Joe. Of course I didn't believe him. I didn't even make out a report and haven't investigated his so-called evidence. Frankly, I'm baffled by why he came to see me about it. If he's working for Snake-Man, it seems as if he'd want to avoid drawing attention to himself and his boss. And I doubt Zeke would take such a step without asking his boss first. He said he'd be checking back with me soon, so I'll have to tell him something. If I refuse to act on his accusation, he'll get suspicious of me, too. Once he thinks the Army's involved, he'll alert his boss and they'll probably halt their crimes for a while."

Jim locked his gaze with Joe's. "But if you don't come around again, I'll have a reason to not pursue you. I could say I've checked and that you're gone. That's why I suggested exchanging information through that hollow tree, and why I'm dismayed about having you here today. I have to cover myself, Joe. Whatever happens with this matter can either get me promoted or court-martialed. It can get you hanged, if you can't prove you're acting under legal orders. You've killed several men without evidence to back those slayings. You're riding with Sun Cloud's daughter and working for the Oglalas, the very Indians incriminated in so many foul deeds. This can get out of hand fast if we aren't more careful."

Joe realized the officer was making valid points. "I do have the authority to work on this mission, Jim — from Tom, Stede, and from the President himself."

"Authority to kill suspects? By your own admission, you entered camps and attacked men without proof in your favor."

"They're guilty!"

290

"You know it, and I believe you, but what about the law if their friends push for justification? What if this Snake-Man is rich and powerful? What if Zeke and his boys aren't working for him? Zeke said he was hauling weapons and supplies to trappers and customers in Powder River country. He has receipts to back those sales. Can you prove he did otherwise?"

"He met with a Crow party. Morning Star overheard him say he was carrying them guns and whiskey."

"Did you actually see the goods exchange hands? No. It's your word against theirs. You're the blood brother of the infamous Sun Cloud, son of the infamous Gray Eagle. You're traveling with the chief's beautiful daughter. Your best friend was Sun Cloud's cousin, whose death you want to avenge. The Indian girl as a witness, Joe? She's from the same band accused of most of the attacks."

Joe grasped the full seriousness of Jim's words.

The officer continued. "You could be asking men who think they have good reasons to hate Indians, particularly the Red Hearts, to judge you innocent of slaying white men while aiding and befriending their enemies. You know how Zeke is either feared or revered. Would you want a jury of those men to decide your fate? If I allow you to carry on without approval and at least a few shreds of proof that you're riding in the right direction, I'm in trouble."

"If I get Snake-Man and Zeke, neither of us will have to worry."

"*If,* Joe, that's the hazardous word."

"After you receive word from Tom and President Fillmore, will we be safe from backlash?"

"Yes. If you remain within the law," Jim amended. "*Nobody* can break it, Joe, for *any* reason."

Joe nodded his understanding. "What's this about a payroll theft by Red Hearts?"

"A unit was coming from Fort Laramie with it. Fifty miles south of what's called the Badlands, the unit was attacked, robbed and slaughtered. There was one survivor. He exposed the Red Hearts."

Joe remembered that Jim had said the entire unit had been

291

killed. At full attention he asked, "When?"

"Last Wednesday. The wounded man got here yesterday. Isn't the Red Heart band camped on Sunday in or near the Badlands, hunting buffalo?"

"Yes, but they're not responsible for the slaughter. Sun Cloud promised no attacks, only self-defense. I trust him. You would, too, if you knew him. What made this soldier think it was Red Hearts?"

"The matching symbols on their chests. You probably haven't seen them prepared for a raid. They paint a red shape like a human heart on their upper left shoulders to show unity or to boast of who they are."

"Can I question him? Or can you do it for me?"

"As I said, they're all dead. Dawes, the soldier who made it here, died last night. It took him four grueling days to get here. He might have survived if he'd made it sooner. He lost too much blood along the way. He lived long enough to give a detailed account of the raid and to hand me those items. I had to file a report, Joe. It was a military defeat and other soldiers heard it."

Joe motioned to the headband and necklace. "How did he get those?"

Jim lifted the knife charm and explained. "This was torn off an attacker's neck while he was killing a soldier. Dawes pulled the headband off his killer during their struggle. He was left for dead. When he came to, he and the others were missing small scalp locks. I guess you know by now," he interrupted his answer to say, "Indians don't cut off the whole head of hair; they just carve out a button size piece to use for decoration. Anyway, Dawes still had Night Stalker's headband when he awoke. He noticed that *wanapin,* as those charms are called, and figured it could help identify the warriors responsible. I don't have to tell you how bad this looks for Sun Cloud's band. That dying soldier had no reason to lie or to aid Snake-Man's plot."

Joe glanced at the talisman, so like one he'd seen on a thong around Knife-Slayer's neck. He fingered the headband with a brown stick figure holding a bow in one hand and a knife in the other on a black background of artistic beadwork, also so like one he'd seen on his love's brother. "This leaky boat has bailers, Jim; it isn't holding the poisoned water Snake-Man tossed in to sink it. Those two warriors wouldn't be so careless, and they'd never leave behind something so valuable to them; *wanapins* are sacred objects. The band wasn't under attack from a rescue party and didn't have to get away fast, so they had time to recover them. It's part of the frame."

"Let me take these along," Joe suggested. "Maybe the Indians can tell me who made them. From what I've learned, they each have their own colors and patterns and use certain specific kinds of beads."

"I can't give you the evidence, Joe."

"Just let me borrow them. I'll return them in that hollow tree soon. I need to see if the Red Hearts recognize these imitations — and they need to see how cleverly they're being framed, in addition. This way they'll understand what we're up against, let them know why the Army has reason to doubt them."

Jim mused a moment. "All right, but make it quick," he agreed.

"I can assure you the Red Hearts aren't involved, and I'll prove it."

"I hope so, Joe. I agree that so-called evidence was left there on purpose to make them look guilty. But what if it was other Indians, another Lakota band? Not many white men can pass for Indians. Getting that many who can fool a soldier is doubtful. Timing proves it wasn't Zeke or George."

"Maybe they were Crow; they're siding with Snake-Man. After we leave, we're checking some Crow camps and we'll visit Sun Cloud. If the Red Hearts were involved this time, I'll be honest with you."

"What about her?" Jim asked, motioning toward the closed door.

"Whoever is to blame, we'll report it. She wants peace, too. If her brother and other warriors secretly attacked soldiers, she won't agree with those actions and she'll make sure they're punished."

Jim watched him. "Sounds like you trust her completely."

Joe strained to keep his real feelings from showing. "I've gotten to know her well, Jim, so I do. She's taught me all she could, and she hasn't led me on any wild chases. What about this Corporal George Whatever?" Joe ventured, wanting to change the subject. "If he's from Fort Laramie, maybe he knew about the payroll. Maybe he was over here to report it to his boss. The timing is perfect for his treachery. We need to learn who he is."

"I'll handle that when I send this report to Tom. Check the tree in a few weeks. I know Simon Adams is from New Orleans. I plan to send a trusted man downriver on the next boat to do some checking on him."

"New Orleans?" Joe echoed, and Jim nodded. "We might have answers sooner than that. Stede Gaston lives in New Orleans. He might know something about him. If he does, he'll put it in his response to my questions. I strongly implied Adams is our man."

Jim leaned back in his chair and kept his gaze on Joe. "You told me everything you've learned about him, didn't you?"

"One point I didn't stress to you is his feelings about women." Joe went over Simon's words again, then related what Clem had said concerning Morning Star's fate at the hands of their boss. "Those two patterns match, Jim. See if you can find out if he keeps Indian girls around and how they're treated."

Jim stroked his smooth face. "That'll be tricky, but I'll try."

Joe glanced at the missive to Tanner's father that revealed all the facts and clues he had gathered. It listed questions about Simon, George, and land buys. In a few weeks, he would have more pieces to this puzzle, hopefully enough to begin solving it. Then, he would be going home soon. That thought reminded Joe to ask Jim to mail a letter to Joseph and Annabelle Lawrence in Virginia.

"That's all for now, Jim. Thanks," he said as he concealed the borrowed items.

"Ride carefully, Joe," the officer said, then walked him outside.

Both men looked at Morning Star, whose expression was

impassive. Jim nodded to her, and Joe joined her. The captain watched as the couple mounted and headed for the gate, then he returned to his desk.

"Hide fast!" Morning Star warned, pulling her mount's reins to the right. She walked Hanmani around a stable, Joe and the packhorse behind her.

When they were out of sight, she explained her behavior. "I look out big door. See Zeke coming. He not have time to see us."

They hid until Zeke and Farley halted their wagon at the sutler's store and went inside, then at a pace that wouldn't attract unwanted attention, they left the fort at the mouth of the White River and rode north. Within a mile, they had to conceal themselves again when they spotted the suspicious scout named George heading for Fort Tabor.

"That's strange. Zeke and George arriving at the same time," Joe observed. "As soon as that snake learned we'd been in Pierre, he headed straight here; probably came to see if we're reporting to the Army. Then, that dubious scout shows up flying in his tailwind. Could be they're in this area to collect that stolen payroll from those hired renegades. Damn. This eliminates Orin McMichael as our villain; Snake-Man is too smart to be connected so easily to his hirelings."

Morning Star asked Joe to explain the words she did not understand, then advised, "Too soon to e-lim-min-ate Orin. He give me bad feelings."

Joe knew why the man's undisguised lust made her uneasy, but he took her suggestion to heart. "We can't go back; it's too dangerous. And if we hang around to spy on them, it'd be our luck they'd stay for days or leave by boat." Joe didn't tell her that if he were alone, he'd do just that. Knowing the open range they would have to cover while trailing those bastards, she would be in too much danger of exposure and capture. Besides, those men might do nothing more than visit, then leave and he'd have wasted days, energy, and supplies. He was eager to get moving to find hard evidence. "I'll have to depend on Jim to observe them. At least he'll finally get to meet that baffling scout. Let's put some miles between us and this place. I'll tell you everything when we camp tonight."

They camped before darkness would cover the land, choosing a shady grove on a calm river.

Joe noticed how silent Morning Star had been along their journey; yet, he hadn't talked much, either. He was deciding if he should tell her everything and, if so, how. If she didn't know about the homesteading law, it was best not to mention it this soon. Her people felt that the Great Spirit owned the land and it was created for their use. To reveal that his government believed they owned her territory and was selling off parcels would only anger and distress her.

Only their chores drew forth words. Soon, a fire and hot meal were underway.

As they ate, Joe asked, "Did you have any problems at the fort?"

"No. I watch soldiers, but they no come near me."

"Did you overhear anything we said?"

"No. I stay with horses. I did not want men to think I listen. I know you tell me all when we camp."

Suppressing a pang of guilt, Joe began his revelations. He explained about Jim's worries and precautions and related he had told the officer everything they had done and discovered. He knew his tone altered when he talked of Jim's not knowing George and of the captain's speculations. He saw concern fill her brown eyes when he exposed his and Jim's peril if they didn't get written approval for their actions and eventual proof to back them up. He realized she was as shocked and confused by Zeke's murder charge as he had been.

"You warned me of danger in killing men we chase. I not want you hurt for helping my people."

"Don't worry about me, love. I won't get into any trouble. But we'll be more careful from now on. I suspect Zeke was either trying to learn if the Army's on our side or wants to get the law after us to slow down our tracking. It won't matter, because Jim believes us. I was suspicious of Jim for a time back there," he admitted. "But I understand his points."

When Morning Star queried his talk of arrests, trials, court-martials, judges, and juries, Joe explained them to her.

"You sure you trust soldier? He say not know scout, but scout come to see him. Zeke come same day. That plenty strange, Joe."

"Maybe just a coincidence, love."

"What is co-in-ci-dence?"

"Something that happens at the same time and at the same place—but one isn't a part of the other. If they were there to see Jim, it was about Zeke's wild charges and George's mission or his sneaky work for Snake-Man. He must realize he can't keep his presence in this area a secret, so he's covering his tracks. I'm sure he isn't working for Tom or the Army."

Morning Star observed Joe as his mood became hesitant. She sensed there was more to his meeting with Jim, something bad. His blue gaze exposed an inner conflict that she waited for him to reveal. He scratched his beard and took a few bites of his food as he seemingly stalled the remainder of his talk. "What is so hard to tell me?" she asked, dread chewing at her.

"Jim asked me if we would expose whoever was guilty, Morning Star, even if it's your brother or anyone from your band. I told him we would, because we both want peace. I was right, wasn't I?"

"You know you do not have to ask. Yes, I will do it for peace."

Joe let out a loud sigh of relief and smiled, his gaze filling with love and gratitude. "I was sure, Morning Star, but I had to ask. I had to make you realize what this mission can demand from you and your people. If anybody from your band commits a crime, we can't protect them."

"Father gave his word for no attacks. Did you not believe him?"

"I trust Sun Cloud. I trust most of your people. But I worry over what men like Knife-Slayer, Hawk Eyes . . . and your brother might do."

Morning Star grasped how difficult the last name was to mention, but she understood why Joe had that feeling. "They will obey Father and the council. It is our way, our . . . law."

Joe pulled the two items from inside his shirt. "This is w̶ asked and why I'm worried." He related the payroll rob̶ and massacre of the soldiers and told her how Jim and he ha̶ gotten these possessions.

Morning Star put aside her plate and took them in her hands. The tiny knife seemed identical to her pursuer's. "When we reach my camp, we will learn if he has lost his." She examined the headband, closed her eyes, and breathed her own sigh of great relief. Smiling, she looked at Joe and said, "This not my brother's. I help Mother make Night Stalker's headband. Touched-A-Crow cannot bead good. Bow and knife in wrong hands. It not long enough for brother's head. Thongs not same as we use."

"I didn't think they would be so reckless with sacred possessions."

"But you think they be so reckless to raid in secret?"

Joe glanced at the ground, then returned his gaze to hers. "Yes. Sometimes men do what they want, not what they should do. Sometimes they think that once a glorious and daring deed is done, others won't be angry with them for defying orders. Sometimes they just do as they please and keep it a secret to avoid trouble and punishment. I'm sorry, Morning Star, but I think Knife-Slayer is that kind of man; and I'm not sure he couldn't talk your brother into helping him. You know Night Stalker's feelings about whites and war, truce and the Crow. With Knife-Slayer pushing and pulling at him to prove his prowess . . ."

"I sad to say, you right. But brother stop bad journey when he see wrong trail for people. Knife-Slayer talk and push much, but brother not jump on wild horse without much thinking. He not want to get hurt so cannot become chief after Father. I not believe brother do raids to now. But if trouble grows, he talk to council for war."

"With luck, he'll realize peace is best for everyone."

They finished their meal and clean-up task in silence. Each took a turn being excused in the shadows, then each did the same for a quick bath to remove the day's grime. By then, night surrounded the site. Crickets chirped, frogs croaked, owls hooted, water babbled its way around obstacles, a coyote howled in the distance and received no answer, and nocturnal birds called back and forth: all giving sounds that relaxed the couple. A cooling breeze wafted over the Indian beauty and the sunny-haired white man. The sky was clear above them, with only twinkling stars and a crescent moon to adorn it. They breathed deeply of the scents of grass, wildflowers, and burning wood. They felt far removed from civilization, basking in the glow of the campfire.

As Morning Star used a brush of blunted porcupine quills on her unbound hair, she said, "We ride on grasslands for many days. Not many trees or water. I know where to find and make camp each day. We see many bands and tribes hunting buffalo. Many be Dakotas; some be Oglalas. In five suns we reach Bird People. Most tribes use same hunting grounds every season. We be safe with Dakotas, but Crow . . . It be dangerous to enter enemy camps. We be brave and do sacred mission."

Both realized that peril and possible death lay before them. Both wanted and needed each other before confronting either one.

Joe watched the raven tresses shine more and more from her brushing; the firelight seemed to sparkle off the glossy hairs. She looked so feminine and delicate with ebony hair flowing around her shoulders and framing her exquisite face. He was too aware of the fact she had not removed the damp blanket around her freshly scrubbed body and put on clean garments, just as he was sitting opposite her with only the dying flames separating them wearing nothing but a doubled blanket around his hips.

Morning Star felt Joe's gaze and thoughts upon her, as if they gave sensuous caresses to her tingly flesh. The tenderness in his eyes gradually waxed to smoldering desire. It was evident he wanted her as much as she craved him. So much stood between them and would forever keep them apart. For them to have a life together they must prevent a war, expose the true villains, overcome the hatred and suspicions each side had for the other, understand and accept each other's people, and compromise on their beliefs and customs. Yet, if they solved or lessened any of those obstacles, more would arise and others increase. Surely there could never be more for them than what they could steal along their journey, for neither side could be changed very much. And as long as things remained the same, he could not live in her endangered world and she could not enter his hostile one.

Joe stood and went to her. "Let me do this," he entreated, urging the brush from her hand. He stepped over the cotton-wood trunk she was sitting on, which had fallen from age. As he passed the bristles through her silky strands, he murmured, "Your hair is beautiful, Morning Star, like you are. I love the way it feels around my fingers; it's as smooth as water."

She closed her eyes and savored the unique pleasure. "Only Mother do this task before you. I like. I make your task every night."

Joe felt her warm laughter flow over his body. "Fine with me," he replied, and heard how husky his voice sounded.

After a time, she said, "I do Joe now," and sent forth giggles.

He was about to decline, but didn't. He exchanged places with her. She stood behind him, as he had done with her. With gentleness and care, she brushed his wheat-colored mane. He was surprised it felt so relaxing.

"You like, too?" she asked, her tone merry.

"Yep," he murmured. Her body touched his and the shape of it filled his mind. The blanket tickled his bare flesh, but he would never tell her to step away.

Morning Star delighted in the various sensations that teased through her body. The way her breasts rubbed against the blanket and then against his body tantalized her. She thought of soft rabbit fur as her fingers traveled behind her brush strokes. She felt as if this were a new and exciting adventure. Her heart raced fast and seemed as if it filled to a bursting point. The power of her feelings washed over her like a raging river that carried her away, beyond the bank of retreat.

Joe experienced contradictory sensations of tension and serenity. It was as if tiny, invisible flames from the fire before him licked at his tanned flesh. Mercy, how he yearned to turn around, pull her into his arms, cover her mouth with kisses, then make blissful love to her! *Why not?* his hear demanded. They were in a safe and private location, and soon, the open Plains would take away both. Soon, their life together would be broken apart, as his heart surely would be, too. How could he face life without her?

Morning Star perceived the change in Joe as his calmed and happy body became taut and troubled. She decided his thoughts matched hers. If only they could remain tranquil and together forever, but he knew, as well as she did, that was forbidden. Her warring heart warned, *You have only the passings of a few full moons with him, seize all of them. Store them in your heart.*

All day, each had fantasized about the other and their next joining. They had daydreamed of being in each other's embrace with emotions unleashed and passions unrestrained. They had imagined their hands traveling over each other's body—stimulating, pleasuring, sating.

Before Joe could act on his impulse to yank her into his arms, the brave Morning Star dropped her brush, stepped over the large log, and stood before him. She gazed into his eyes with obvious longing. When she saw him return that look, she maneuvered into his lap. Without boldness, she rested her legs over the cottonwood and shifted close to him, her knees hugging his hips on either side and her hands wrapped over his broad shoulders. Still, his lips were out of reach, until her fingers journeyed into his hair and pulled his head downward to mesh their mouths.

Joe's arms encircled her blanket-clad body, and he held her against him. His astonishment quickly faded, replaced by urgent desire. His lips worked ravenously at hers. He felt intoxicated by the nectar his mouth gathered from hers. His mind reeled from her nearness.

When their lips parted, Joe's trailed over her face and down her throat. Morning Star leaned her head back and let him do as he pleased. She was his willing captive, his prisoner of delight. She thrilled to the way she felt as his mouth tasted the pulse at her neck. Her mind was awhirl in a mixture of sensations, as she let herself go completely.

Her long raven hair teased over Joe's hands at her waist. He felt the heat radiating from her womanhood to his groin. His tongue played in the hollows of her throat and trekked over her collarbone. Her flesh was like Oriental silk; no Parisian perfume could smell sweeter than she did. His teeth gripped the blanket, tugged at the thin covering that kept him from this hidden treasure, and loosened it to explore the depths of her surrender. He stroked her breasts with his cheek, then tasted the sweet flesh. He didn't know who moaned with delight, he or she, or both.

Morning Star was glad when Joe eased them downward to the grass but didn't change their position. It was bliss that he had freed the blanket around his hips as he did so. Nothing was between them now. Her knees rested on the ground at his sides. While he kissed her with greediness, she eased him inside her. As they shared endless, countless kisses, she rocked upon his lap.

The campfire was dying, but the entwined couple seemed to give off more heat than a hundred flames could. Their passions burned brighter and hotter until the greatest blaze of all ignited and consumed them. It melted their wills, then forged the molten liquid into one bond.

"I love you, Morning Star; I love you," Joe confessed.

Her heart flooded with overwhelming emotion. *"Waste cedake,* Joe; *waste cedake."* She murmured the same words in her language.

Joe understood them, or prayed he did. "We belong to each other forever," he vowed, and it was not the result of the rapture he experienced. It was true, and time to act on his feelings.

Morning Star rested her head against Joe's shoulder. She felt limp and content in his possessive embrace. She liked the way his fingers teased up and down her spine and the way his head nestled against her hair. She was at home in is arms, more at peace there than anywhere. But when he spoke, his words dissolved the golden aura that encompassed them.

Joe said in an emotion-strained voice, "We have to talk,

love."

Morning Star heard the seriousness in his voice. She lifted her head and read it in his gaze. She sensed what was coming, and wondered if she were ready to confront that awesome truth. "I must bathe and dress. We talk when I return." Joe did not try to stop her as she rose. She retrieved her blanket, gathered her garments, and headed for the river. *Medicine* it was called, but could it heal what wounded her heart and diseased her life? Could anything or anyone, even her beloved Joe? She dreaded testing its powers when she left its water.

Joe bathed not far away, deep in thought. If he couldn't persuade her they belonged together and must find a way to share one life, his future existence would be as dark as the night closing in on them. To chase away those depressing shadows, he tossed more wood onto the glowing coals when he finished rinsing off and had donned his garments. Too, he wanted to be able to see her face when they talked.

Morning Star returned, dressed in a buckskin top and skirt with swaying fringes. Her feet were bare, and her flowing mane was braided.

Joe tensed. He feared the plait was symbolic of her restraining her emotions. He spread their bedrolls, took a seat on his, and motioned for her to join him. Instead, she sat on hers. "I love you, Morning Star. I need you," he vowed in earnest.

Never had anything been harder than to not fling herself into his arms, cover him with kisses, and repeat those beautiful words. It took more strength than Sun Cloud's daughter knew she had to reply, "We do not know what Grandfather will bring on the new . . . tomorrow. We must eat the joys of today which He allows. Tomorrow or another sun, they may not be."

"I want you every day, Morning Star, for the rest of my life."

"It cannot be," she responded, her gaze exposing anguish.

"We'll find a way to stay together. I love you. I want you to become my wife. I can't lose you, woman. I can't get enough of you during the next few months to last me a lifetime. We've tried to love day to day. I want more. I want to marry you. I want to have children with you. I want to grow old with you at my side. I want to share every day with you."

"It cannot be. The path between us is filled with brush; it stops us from riding together. My trail is here. Your trail is . . ."

"I love you and must have you, Morning Star. I'll burn any brush tossed in our way. I'll fight for you, woman, any way necessary."

No matter what happened, Joe loved her and wanted her, Morning Star knew. She was no redskin, no savage, no wild animal to him. He considered her worthy to become his wife. But it required sacrificing her life here and her loved ones and entering the enemy world. She tried to halt the painful talk. "Some forests are too large and thick to burn, and some rivers are too deep and swift to cross."

Undaunted now that his decision was made, Joe argued, "I'm a good swimmer. I'll keep moving through the water to remove any obstacle between us. While we're finishing this mission, I'll teach you everything I know. When we reach my home in Virginia, my mother and sister will teach you all I don't know. My family and I will make certain you don't have any trouble adjusting to our world. My family will love you and accept you as I do."

Anxiety attacked her so forcefully that she trembled. "It cannot be! Do not hurt us with such words," she entreated.

Joe crawled to her, took her quivering hands, and refuted. "It can be."

Morning Star worried over his persistence. In her dilemma, she rushed her arguments and her English suffered. "We not the same. I die in your world. If I change to live, I not be Morning Star. If I choose Joe, I betray family, people, ways, and Great Spirit. I break law! I be banished, dishonored. Never see family and lands again. You ask Morning Star to go to enemy land where Indians hated. Where I not know how to survive. Tha destroy Morning Star, destroy love we share. It not . . . simple as to speak words. For Joe, perhaps it sound simple. For Morning Star, it mean denying all she is and possesses; it mean shame and separation for me and family. It mean banishment, dishonor," she stressed.

Joe realized what he was asking her to give up, or thought he did. In his culture, women always left their homes and families to go with their husbands. He would keep her safe in his world. She was too intelligent not to learn everything necessary in order to fit in perfectly. He would find a way to persuade Sun Cloud and the Red Hearts that he loved her and would treasure her always. Both the sacred vision putting them together and his success at earning peace should work in his favor. He would make certain she got to visit her people and lands. Love wasn't something that caused anguish and shame; fighting it was. Joe explained his thoughts to Morning Star. "We can make it work, love."

"No, it not possible. Whites hate Indians. They insult and push away. Whites laugh at Morning Star, laugh at Joe. You not stay here. My people not accept you. Joe family need him. Work there. Friends there. When time come, you go, Morning Star stay. We be one until that moon."

Joe used the Colonial and British wars as another argument. "We battled long and hard two times, but we're friends and allies now. One day, it'll be that way between your people and mine. My grandparents were from different sides, but they found love and happiness. So did Gray Eagle and Alisha. So did Bright Arrow and Rebecca. It can be the same for us, Morning Star. Let it happen. You know how we'll feel when we're separated. We'll both be miserable. I need you in my life. I love you. Why do we have to suffer because our peoples can't accept each other?"

Morning Star could not endure any more pressure tonight. She told him, "If it meant to be, it happen. Must not force it to happen. You like breath to me, beating of my heart, food for my body. I pray you be my destiny. If Grandfather say you not, Morning Star cannot have you."

"How will you know his answer?" Joe inquired. He was thrilled by some of her words but disappointed that he could not convince her entirely.

"When it come, I will know," she replied with careful words.

Joe studied her for a while. He hoped he had time to weaken her will, time to convince her they were matched by fate, time to teach her so much about his world that she would be eager for them to face it together. The challenge confronting him was exciting and hopefully would be rewarding. "That doesn't mean I can't do my best to convince Him to say yes. I'll prove I'm worthy of you, woman. I'm going to fight for your love and acceptance."

Morning Star comprehended how hard this rejection was for both of them. In tonight's dreamy shadows, he was snared by love's magic. Tomorrow's bright sun would dispel it and he would realize she was right. There was no need to sting him more, so she attempted to soothe his emotional wounds. "You have my love," she said softly. "You have acceptance in my heart."

"I know. That's why not winning you because of other people's feelings makes me angry. Love like ours is too rare and precious to lose. It's meant to grow, to create happiness, to birth children. If Alisha and Rebecca could live with Oglalas, why can't you live with whites? It worked for them; it can work for us. It wasn't any harder for those white women to join your Indian world than it will be for you to join my white one."

Morning Star concurred with most of what he said, but that didn't change their predicament. "Women do as men say," she murmured. "Father is boss until marry. Husband is boss after joining. That much is same in both worlds. Grandfather and uncle take captive white women they want; is way of raids and wars. Whites have slaves, too. Whites steal, trade, and sell people with brown skin. I am Indian woman and must obey Father. It different for warrior to take white captive than for Indian woman to reject people and go with paleface enemy. It bad, forbidden. Hurt many. You must understand and accept our ways and laws."

Joe caressed her cheek and whispered a mischievous threat. "Then I'll just have to steal you as my captive when I'm ready to leave."

She didn't realize he was trying to joke to lighten the situation. Her gaze widened with distress. "That worse than bad! Father and warriors come after me to rescue. They slay you!"

Joe was enthralled for a time by the idea. Why not do as the Indians—as her legendary grandfather and uncle—and seize

306

the woman he wanted? "We'll be too far away. They'll never find us."

"Gray Eagle tracked Shalee to place called St. Louis and take her back after Powchutu steal her," Morning Star refuted. "He follow trail many weeks old. We cannot escape Oglala warrior skills. They best trackers."

"You're as skilled as they are," Joe pointed out. "If you hide our tracks, they'd never find us."

In a sad tone, she responded, "If I betray, I never return to family and lands again. Do not ask me to choose between you and my people."

"But you *are* choosing, Morning Star—them over me. Why can't you share the rest of your life with me? Think of all you've done for your people and what you're doing now for them. How could they dishonor and be cruel to She-Who-Rode-With-The-Sky-Warrior? How could they refuse to let you follow your heart and seek your true destiny?"

"Joe part right, but what can Morning Star do but duty teached her since birth? You not know how hard it was for Alisha and Rebecca, even if worked in time. You forget they not have families in white world to return to. Grandmother and Wahea not have to worry over dishonor and rejection by their people. Wahea not chief's daughter. I yield little; perhaps love strong enough to conquer enemies. We must wait, see if that powerful."

"That's the best thing I've heard you say. It gives me hope."

"I want hope. It hard. You not lived in my land long enough to know how big is the battle we face. We must pray for strength and courage."

"We will, because the battle for you is as important to me as our task."

"Sacred mission must come first. If we do good—"

"Our prayers may be answered," he finished for her.

They gazed at each other a long time, then exchanged smiles.

After breaking camp on Tuesday at the White Clay River,

Morning Star gazed beyond them at the seemingly endless Great Plains. The rangy land they crossed was almost treeless and scrubless, except for a few cottonwoods and chokecherries near a water source. The ground was covered with a mixture of thick grasses in shades of green: short, tall, sweet, tender. Cactus and wildflowers were sighted at some points. Antelope, deer, and buffalo were abundant, so, too, jackrabbits and prairie dogs. Every now and then, gusts of strong wind yanked at their clothes and hair.

A few times, at a distance, she noticed what whites called sod houses, or rock homes, or dugouts. She knew sod helped defeat the summer's heat and keep out the winter's chill and winds. They were strong dwellings, with most having a combination raid-root cellar nearby. Soon, only grassland stretched before them once more; white encroachment was left behind.

Morning Star guided Joe and the animals at a steady pace. It seemed as if the land went on forever, then vanished into the blue sky far beyond any distance they could ever ride. She led Joe across a few streams and creeks and past the Bad River that flowed toward where Simon Adams's lived in Pierre.

As the day moved on, so did the hot sun across the sky. Any clouds above them were small and white. Morning Star kept on constant alert, as did Joe. She was amused by his astonishment at the number of buffalo in her territory and the size of their gatherings.

He was amazed by the size of the herds which often traveled for miles in several directions. At some points, the earth was covered by a dark blanket as far as he could see even with his fieldglasses. Antelope and deer intermingled with the buffalo. Though the huge beasts grazed contentedly and appeared sluggish, Joe knew they were dangerous and unpredictable, and anything but slow. The sizes of their horns and bodies exposed an accurate warning of how deadly the animal could be.

Joe scanned their surroundings. He had not imagined the Plains to be so immense. After a while, he realized the scenery was repetitious, with every five miles repeating the last five and the many miles before it. At least, he thought, they didn't have to use a tiring jog trot as much today.

Before dusk, she pointed to an Indian camp at the end of Plum Creek. She took Joe's fieldglasses, as he had taught her how to use them, and focused them on an area outside the encampment of numerous tepees. She checked symbols on the lance and markings on a large buffalo skull surrounded by a circle of smaller skulls. *"Mahpialuta wicoti."*

"What?" Joe asked, staring at the nomadic village of countless tepees outlined against the gradually darkening horizon.

"Red Cloud camp," she translated. "His father Brule; that one of Lakota tribes. His mother Oglala. He become Oglala. Lead mother's people; they called Old Smoke Band. He plenty smart and brave. He tell Father he want peace, but he hate white takeover of lands. If whites push, Red Cloud fight. It important he speak and vote for new treaty. Come."

Morning Star perceived the many stares given to she and Joe. From years of celebrations, Sun Dances, trading, joint raids and talks, she knew the Oglalas recognized the daughter of Sun Cloud. She halted at the largest, most beautiful tepee in camp. A rainbow was painted on each side. She remembered red circles on the back that represented *Wi*, the sun, and the figure of a buffalo. Yellow rings encircled the tepee with a black top for the night sky and a green bottom for the earth. The colors and markings symbolized Red Cloud's medicine and vision signs and were evocations to the Great Spirit. Morning Star related those meanings to Joe and told him the chief was a member of the White-Marked Society.

Joe comprehended how important this chief was to his mission and to Tom Fitzpatrick's new treaty. He observed the man who left the artistic home and greeted Morning Star with a smile and obvious affection. He listened to them talk a while in their tongue, but he hadn't worked on his grasp of Lakota as much as they had on hers of English.

Morning Star told Joe to dismount, then introduced him to the chief. She was relieved when her love was offered friendship and hospitality. Red Cloud invited them inside his home to eat and to spend the night.

Joe quickly learned from the sage Indian that he wanted peace, but doubted it was possible. Joe explained the treaty, his mission, and his problems so far. He told Red Cloud of his plans to spy on the Crow, and promised to warn the Oglalas of any threatening intents. He sensed that the chief believed him, even liked him.

Morning Star drew the same conclusions. She related Payaba's sacred vision, the contest, Joe's alleged identity, and their task to him.

"It is good. Sun Cloud will know great honor and pride."

After a restful night and a successful visit, Morning Star guided Joe from Red Cloud's encampment on a journey across more prairie land to the lovely location of Sinte Geleska and his band on the tree-lined Cheyenne River.

Spotted Tail greeted them with a genial and courteous manner. He said it was good to see Mahpiya Wicasta and the daughter of Sun Cloud again.

Joe liked being accepted as Sky Warrior, and the Indian name, with all it represented, made him feel proud.

Morning Star was elated by their reception and honored treatment. She was glad Joe was learning that the Lakotas wanted peace. She listened as the two men talked, and was impressed by both.

The evening passed in a pleasant way with Chief Spotted Tail and his friendly band. Then the couple enjoyed another restful and safe night.

At dawn, they mounted, bid the Brules good-bye, and rode for their next camp on an offshoot of the murky Cheyenne River.

As they traveled, even sounds — what few they heard — were repetitious: the hooffalls and breathing of the three horses, the sound of their own breathing, the squeaking of leather saddles and reins, the movement of canteens and rifle sheaths, and the shifting of trade goods on the pack animal. They couldn't talk all the time to divert their attention from the almost eerie quietness, for that dried their throats and encouraged drinking too much water that had to last from water source to water source.

Joe came to look forward to the areas where hawks soared overhead, their shrill cries renting the silence. He missed the music of songbirds, singing of crickets, and croakings of frogs. The rocking pace and unvaried scenery made it hard to stay alert. He couldn't imagine any white man choosing to spend a lifetime homesteading in a barren and lonely place like this when there was so much good land elsewhere for farming.

"I wish you could see where I live," he told Morning Star. "It's so different here. We have lots of trees. They change colors between summer and winter. Some years it looks as if the forest is on fire with reds, purples, oranges, and yellows. And in the spring after winter, flowers grow everywhere in every size, color, and shape you can imagine. We don't have places like this that are so barren. Empty," he clarified. "Our winter isn't as cold and long as yours. Our summer isn't as hot and dry. Friends live around us, not miles and days away like here. We don't have people separated into bands who attack and kill each other. It's peaceful and beautiful."

She was so attentive and interested that he went on. "During the day, men do their tasks, then spend the evening with their families. Life isn't as hard there. Men work for money, then hire others to do certain chores for them. Women don't have to work as hard, either; they have easier ways to cook and do dishes in stoves and sinks in big kitchens. They don't have to sew clothes if they don't want to or don't know how; they can buy them ready-made or hire a seamstress. Anybody who doesn't want to grow food or have the ground to grow it on can buy it in stores or at open markets. It's safe there. It's . . . I'm rambling," he said with a chuckle.

"What is rambling?"

He grinned. "To talk on and on about anything, everything, nothing."

"I like to hear you talk on and on. I learn much about you and your land. Rambling more," she coaxed. Before she let him begin again, she queried unknown words he had used during his talk, such as kitchens, seamstresses, and markets.

She listened and learned.

They shared laughter and journeyed onward, chatting frequently.

Another night of safety passed as they took turns standing guard at Cherry Creek. Both were in good moods following their visits with two Dakota chiefs but fatigued by their long and tiring ride. Yet, each avoided the bittersweet subject of their forbidden love and uncertain destiny.

The vast range continued to spread before them. It was hotter and drier in this area. The ground covering was now a blend of green and tan. Winds blew in from the west at regular intervals, waving grasses to and fro in a mesmerizing motion. The sky was a mixture of pale blue and white, with few clouds having real definition. Soon, unusual formations intermittently loomed from the earth: buttes, mesas, hillocks, and rocks. Trees called attention to any waterline present. They crossed the shallow Moreau River. Ecru ground showed a pebbly surface more frequently. Then, at last, the familiar terrain returned.

Joe and Morning Star made their last camp on Rabbit Creek before entering the Grand River area where many Crow bands were doing their seasonal hunts. The couple did their chores in silence as each pondered the great peril they would confront on the next day. Both realized that before the sun was high or set on that day, they could be dead . . .

Chapter Fourteen

"Will you wait here for my return?" Joe asked. "I don't want to put you into more danger."

Morning Star caressed his cheek, smiled, and said, "The danger we face is not following Grandfather's vision. I am part of it, so I must ride with you. To change it brings trouble. You do not know much sign language." She reminded Joe of one of the main reasons she was with him.

He knew it was futile to argue. He'd probably need her assistance, and besides, he couldn't leave her alone in enemy land. "I'll hide those things I got from Jim and retrieve them after we leave the Crow camp. They would be hard to explain if we're searched. I'll also leave most of our trade goods here, so the chief won't insist on taking all of them."

They covered the last miles at a slow pace to keep themselves and the animals rested in case a speedy flight was necessary. As they looked ahead, it was as if odd formations suddenly leapt from the grasslands and rolling hills to expose the biggest change in landscape they had seen for days. The beautiful terrain had bushes and trees — cedar, spruce, pine, and hardwoods — and water and countless rocks. They almost rode into a distant semicircle of mesas and buttes. Various-colored grasses encompassed the lovely site. Most of the formations looked like castles and pinnacles grouped around an enormous one that reminded Joe of a giant fortress. Animals and birds were abundant.

The first camp, like an evil spirit in a nightmare, loomed before Joe and Morning Star. She read the markings and told him it was the camp of Black Moon; the once feared leader normally used Slim Buttes for his big camp and had again this season. She explained how small groups of hunters and women went in several directions to shoot and slaughter for days. Then, those weary groups returned with loaded travois to this location where some waited to cure the meat and others to take over the task while they rested.

Again her apprehension took a toll on her speech. "He sly, mean, and greedy. In moons past, he kill many Oglalas and steal many horses. Men who own many horses best warriors and most honored. They called Bird People because hands and feet small like birds. They have many groups; some for honor and some for battle," she told him, then explained the social and military societies. "They call best warriors Big Dogs. They not have shirt-wearers to do council's work; Big Dogs in command. They most important, like Sacred Bows in our tribe. Careful of all words you speak. They . . . pretend not to listen, but ears open big. They use tricky words to fool. Believe nothing you hear and see." After those final cautions, Morning Star fell in behind Joe in a squaw's humble position and they rode into the camp. She sent up one last prayer for their safety.

Joe observed the warriors who gathered around them, and was relieved no weapon was brandished. As if by order, the women and children moved out of sight behind or into tepees. Dogs barked, ran forward, and sniffed at the newcomers. This camp did not seem as active as Red Cloud and Spotted Tail's had been. Of course, the Crow traded with the whites for many goods that the others made.

Joe took in all the details he could while he reined in and dismounted. The Crow were indeed a people who loved finery. He knew they were hunting buffalo as all Plains Indians did this time of year, because he saw countless meat-drying

314

racks, fresh hides, and unhitched travois. He noticed they favored beading onto red trade cloth or blanket cloth. Morning Star had told him lavender was the most valuable bead color, and he saw few of them in that color. The Crow seemed to lean toward pastels of pale blue, yellow, and green; they rarely used dark shades, particularly blue and red—colors favored by the Lakotas. He noticed tufts of horsehair attached to coup feathers, which she had explained meant added prowess during the earning deed. He also noted how many warriors had coup feathers. Some wore highly decorated cuffs with a fringed side, similar to cavalry gauntlets. He wondered if that had become popular after the Army's arrival. Headdresses were numerous; several were made from owl feathers that were fanned out like a Tom turkey's tail. Intricate breastplates were wore by most men, and eagle-bone whistles by a few. They used more elaborate necklaces and armlets than the Dakotas. Their regalia was striking, and Joe wondered if they were clad for a special ceremony or if they did this every day.

Joe hoped it was true that an Absaroke prophet had warned them not to battle the whites and that all tribes believed that vision. He also hoped his ruse would be effective and that his enemies had not sent warnings about him to this place. He watched the chief come forward, scowling. As taught by his love, he gave the sign for *peace* and *friend*.

"What you want?" the Indian asked in a belligerent tone.

"I come with gifts for Black Moon and his chosen warriors." Joe saw suspicion gleam in the older man's dark eyes. "They are gifts from Snake-Man and Zeke Randall." That announcement got a reaction of more suspicion. Joe went to the packhorse and removed the bundles he had purchased from Harvey. He spread a blanket on the ground and emptied the cloth sacks. He watched the chief join him and eye the tobacco, pastel beads, knives, hatchets, mirrors, bells, fancy buttons, and trade cloth.

He glared at Joe and said, "This not what Black Moon want."

Joe smiled and pulled a smaller sack from the packhorse

Sun Cloud had loaned him. "These are special gifts for Chief Black Moon."

The leader withdrew two cigars, a decorative can of safety matches, a pocket knife, a packet of lavender beads, and a bottle of whiskey.

Joe motioned to the other goods and said, "Those are gifts for Black Moon to give to his best warriors and wives. These," he said, tapping the woven sack in the man's grasp, "are for you." He learned why the chief was annoyed when the leader glared at him and spoke again.

"Where guns, bullets, whiskey? How we kill Sioux with trinkets? They coyote droppings. They kill, raid like rabbits. No more great warriors. No more good battles. They want white-eyes to not trust Crow and slay. They speak lies. They must die. Snake-Man say he help. Zeke his warrior. Why they break promise to bring guns in . . ." He halted to hold up ten fingers, ball his fists, then lift one finger. "Moons from one in sky."

Joe leapt on the clue that revealed a July second rendezvous in eleven days. "They don't break promises, Black Moon. The weapons and whiskey will come on the day Zeke said. I was sent to bring these gifts. You still want to meet him in the same place?"

"Yes, same place, mountain like sleeping bear."

Joe knew the site. As he repeated the numerical signals the chief had used, he stressed, "You'll be there after eleven moons cross the sky?"

"We come. No tricks," he warned with a scowl meant to frighten.

"Snake-Man said he would supply you. Don't you trust him?" Joe asked, seeking a weak spot.

"He have powerful magic. We must trust. We help kill Sioux as he wants, but need guns and bullets."

"What do you tell the soldiers who come to ask about him?"

"We say no words to bluecoats. We say Sioux lie. That Spirit's order."

Joe sensed the chief hated but feared the masquerading

316

villain. He took a risk to say, "Don't fear him, Black Moon; spirits have weaknesses like men do. If you want to meet him, look inside his wagons while the magic smoke burns and he leaves to rest. If you find him and remove his mask, the mask and his magic will belong to you. It takes a brave man to challenge a spirit; that's how you win his strong medicine."

Black Moon pondered those astonishing words. His eyes glittered with curiosity and envy. "How man find and defeat spirit?"

Joe sensed he had the man almost ensnared and pushed to get him all the way into a cunning trap. "By being as clever and brave as the white spirit. Snake-Man would be happy to share his secrets and magic with the great Black Moon. But you must be sure to face him while his magic is weak, after he has used it and while he rests in the wagon. He must roam Mother Earth until a glorious warrior earns his medicine symbols. When he passes them to that warrior, he can join the Great White Spirit and live forever in the heavens. That is what all white spirits want."

"He white spirit?" the chief asked, looking shocked.

"Yes. Didn't you see his hands and hair?"

"Hands hidden. Hair like night."

"I've seen them; they're white, like mine," Joe claimed, extending his hands before the chief to drive his point home. "That's why he uses Zeke and white men as his helpers. But only an Indian warrior of prowess can challenge and conquer him. Think what you can do with such power."

"I ride brave trail, become great leader."

"When you become that great leader, I will bring you all the supplies you need. I must warn you, bad white men ride in this territory. They kill Oglalas, rob their burial grounds, and leave Crow arrows to make the Sioux and Army think Bird People seek war. They try to trick Crow by doing the same. I saw seven men attack a Crow hunting party and kill them. They dropped Sioux arrows and beads to anger and fool the Crow. A bad white leader provokes you against each other before it is the best time to fight. I removed the arrows and beads, tracked them, and killed them. In their camp was

317

Oglala possessions to do the same in your territory. That's bad."

Black Moon was furious. "What man do bad tricks?"

"I don't know, but he wants the Crow and Sioux to kill each other so he can take this land for himself." Joe hoped that got the chief to thinking in the right direction. "When I defeated them and asked questions, they said Snake-Man was their boss. Surely that cannot be true."

"We not raid Sioux burial grounds. They not raid Crow. Spirits, fallen warriors be angry. Plenty bad medicine to wake them from death sleep. Always been this way. Bad to change, plenty bad."

"You speak good English, Black Moon," Joe complimented.

"Learn tongue to stop lies, to trade with white brothers."

Joe put in one last word to cause trouble. "If Black Moon takes the power and magic of spirit man, Zeke and all white traders will bring you all the weapons and whiskey you want. Even the Sioux will fear Black Moon."

"Why you not defeat spirit man and steal power?"

Joe reminded him of his earlier fabrication, "I'm not an Indian warrior, and I'm not allowed to get near him or his wagons. If you can sneak up on him in his wagon while the magic smoke fills the air, you can conquer his power. Then, no white man or Indian can defeat Black Moon."

The chief went silent in thought. "If Black Moon come near spirit man, he bring snakes to life." He motioned to his arms. "They strike, kill."

Joe did not laugh or mock the superstitious man, but played on those irrational notions. "Not if Black Moon holds a knife in each hand and puts them into the snakes' heads before they move. This territory will belong to Black Moon with such power and magic in his possession."

"Why you tell Black Moon?"

Joe hoped his answer sounded truthful. "Snake-Man punishes me when I do not do all he says. He orders me and others to steal Sioux possessions to leave where we attack whites so the Army will blame Sioux. He tells us to take tokens off trees on sleeping bear mountain. He wants the Sioux destroyed. I don't want to cause a war between the whites and the Sioux. If Black Moon becomes leader of this territory, he will honor peace with whites as your shaman saw in the vision. The Sioux will flee your magic. All will be good."

"Bad to rob Great Spirit at sacred mountain," he scolded.

Joe feigned a contrite expression. "I believe you," he said, "but I have to follow Snake-Man's orders or die. When you meet Zeke for the guns, don't tell him what I've told you about the spirit's weakness. If they learn you know the truth, they'll guard him close, and you won't be able to get near him or his wagons to steal his power and magic." Joe hoped those seeds would sprout mistrust and desire and would entice Black Moon to double cross Zeke and his boss. If so, his task would be over soon and his beloved would be safe, hopefully back home with him in Virginia. From the chief's expression and next query, Joe assumed his clever ruse was working.

"Why spirit tell you to kill whites and blame Sioux?"

Joe shrugged and faked ignorance. "I don't know. Do you know why he tells you to kill Sioux? Why does he hate them so much? Why does he want them all killed or driven out of this territory? Does he want it for himself? Is that why he supplies you with weapons to do the job for him?"

Black Moon pondered those discoveries, but said, "We enemies with Sioux more winters than Black Moon lived. You fear white spirit?"

Joe faked his discomfort. "He has lots of men and can have me killed if I don't obey him. But he's not all powerful, not really a spirit like Indian spirits. He's more like your shaman, a clever medicine man. He makes that smoke with balls of powder from far away, like the powder inside bullets. Snakes are his medicine sign like the black moons on your possessions. They're painted on his arms like you paint your symbols on your shield and tepee. Painted snakes can't come alive and strike, if he can't use his magic. That takes time. He wants people to think he can bring them to life fast only to scare them into not challenging him."

"Black Moon think on words. Come, we eat. We have Sacred Arrow Ceremony. You see bravest warriors in land."

Joe wanted to get them out of camp fast, so he smiled and alleged, "I was ordered to bring these gifts, then return quickly for another task."

"You sleep in Black Moon's camp. You friend. You leave on next sun."

Joe dared not refuse the chief's hospitality, so he was trapped into accepting. "Thank you, Black Moon."

"Woman stay with you?"

"Yes, she's my wife," Joe laced his arm around his cherished love in a possessive manner.

Black Moon eyed the beauty, particularly the tribal symbols on her garments and accessories that said she was Arapaho—neither enemy nor ally. He shrugged and motioned for them to follow him.

While they ate a hearty meal of rabbit stew, roasted antelope, boiled roots, and fry bread, Black Moon showed Joe a pocket watch and told him that Snake-Man had given it to him as a gift. He opened it to let Joe hear the "magic" music it made, something that amazed Morning Star.

Later, Joe and Morning Star sat with the chief on buffalo mats to observe the Sacred Arrow Ceremony. It was a test of bravery and skills, the rite to select which warrior was to lead in the next battle, with the winner achieving the highest rank of honor and power next to chief in the band.

The couple watched as three warriors took positions in a row, in a clearing for the safety of observers. At a signal, they rapidly fired seven arrows each overhead, then did not move as the deadly shafts fell downward with sharp tips coming straight at them. Any man who moved to avoid a wound or death was a coward and was banished. Any warrior who chose to enter the contest would rather be slain than dishonored and exiled. If he was a skilled shot, his arrows would pierce the earth around him to form a fence of great prowess. By the time the ritual ended, one participant was dead, one was injured, and one was unscathed: Matohota in her tongue.

Morning Star hoped she appeared calm, but she was apprehensive in the midst of a tribe who had warred with her people for generations. She did not want to imagine what the Bird People would do to her if they discovered her secret or Joe's cunning tricks. She presumed the winner spoke and understood English, as he had listened with great interest to Joe's words about Snake-Man. As the fierce warrior returned to the chief for acknowledgment, she prayed the victor's name wasn't a bad omen. She knew few creatures or medicine signs were stronger than the Grizzly Bear.

After spending a restive night in the chief's tepee, Joseph Lawrence and Morning Star left Black Moon's camp after the early meal. They retrieved the hidden goods and clues to the payroll attack, then headed for the next Crow camp of Talking Wolf at South Folk River. Along the trail, they discussed what they had learned in Black Moon's camp.

Joe related seeing a half-burned crate with letters *PR* still readable, and he speculated it had come from where Simon worked. "Since he runs the post and Bernard Pratte isn't around to catch him doing mischief, he could be having guns and ammunition sent to him to pass along to Zeke. Simon does have black hair. If Simon isn't Snake-Man, he probably works for him. He's in an excellent position to receive illegal goods without anyone catching him. I wish I could have taken that board as evidence, but I couldn't figure a way to do it without Black Moon getting too curious. With luck, they'll be more when we reach Zeke's rendezvous point."

After questioning the unfamiliar words, Morning Star said, "I hope Black Moon or Grizzly Bear kills them for us."

"And does it fast, before Zeke exposes us. I just hope Snake-Man doesn't have more so-called magic up his sleeve. If he fools Black Moon again, that sneaky bastard will spill his guts about us. That means to tell all he knows. Then we'd have Zeke, his boys, and Crow chasing us."

A rush of anxiety charged through her and tainted her English words. "Why you think Black Moon believe you and attack spirit man?"

"Men like him live in both worlds, love. They're sly, greedy, and evil. They want power, and they'll do almost anything to get it."

"It not matter if you not catch Snake-Man and kill?"

Joe caught the clue to her apprehension. "All that matters is getting rid of him and his plot," he soothed. "Once he's out of the way, things will settle down. Then Tom can make his treaty work. That will stop Black Moon from attacking your people again."

She glanced at him in concern. "You wish to hurry this task?"

"Yes, to prevent more people from getting hurt and killed."

His answer delighted her, but it made their separation even more imminent unless something powerful intruded and helped them. She didn't know if it was right to pray for such divine intervention. Perhaps it was best to wait and see what happened during and after the sacred mission.

On Sunday, they visited with Talking Wolf and his band, who were much less showy and aggressive than Black Moon's. Joe used his same ruse, and it worked again. That chief also had met Snake-Man and believed in the villain's magic. He, too, wanted more guns, bullets, and whiskey, and to kill Lakotas. Yet Talking Wolf did not have an impending appointment with Zeke for additional illegal supplies; they didn't know how to take that information. But, unlike Black Moon, Talking Wolf was afraid to attack "the spirit who come and go in smoke." Wisely, Joe didn't entice him to do so.

They spent the night in the chief's tepee. It rained hard until dawn, a heavy deluge accompanied by awesome thunder and lightning. Yet the sturdy conical dwelling protected the inhabitants from the fierce powers of nature and barely disturbed their slumber.

Shortly after sunrise and a hot meal, the couple departed.

On Monday, they camped on the Grand River beneath a full moon with Two-Bulls. As he spoke little English, Morning Star used her skill with sign language to interpret for the men. Two-Bulls said he would accept the gifts, but he had told Snake-Man and Zeke he did not want war with the Lakotas. He explained he did not want guns, bullets, and whiskey found in his camp by the Army, their friends, but revealed he had accepted one load long ago for his warriors to use while hunting buffalo. He said he had told Zeke and the spirit man he would not take guns with which to attack and slay Lakotas and asked why they had sent Joe to him with another plea.

Joe explained how he didn't want war or trouble, and how both would come if those evil white men were not slain. He alleged he was leaving the area and not working for them anymore. That seemed to please the chief.

Two-Bulls vowed that he did not fear the spirit man and his white warriors. He related he would kill them if they caused him trouble.

Joe was thrilled, as Two-Bulls was the most influential and powerful Crow leader in the territory. He took great delight in telling the chief how to defeat and expose the villains. That news seemed to interest Two-Bulls, but he didn't say whether or not he would attempt to destroy them.

Joe was caught off guard and worried when the chief asked if he could buy Morning Star, who still called herself Little Flower. He had her sign that she was his wife and he loved her very much so he couldn't part with her.

When Morning Star translated, "You good white man to love, accept Indians. She have good man," Joe smiled and thanked him.

Through her, Joe asked why Two-Bulls didn't report Snake-Man and his mischief to the Army, as they were "friends." He was surprised and dismayed when the chief responded that he wasn't sure he could trust soldiers and the white laws completely, so he always denied knowing anything to prevent trouble. Two-Bulls didn't want the Army to think he knew the villains so they wouldn't suspect him of lying about receiving illegal goods.

Joe and the daughter of Sun Cloud were impressed by the good and wise leader. It relieved her to learn not all Bird People were bad or hated her people. Both made certain the renowned chief knew they respected and liked him, as Two-Bulls could be a big help with the peace treaty.

Tuesday morning, they rode to locate Zeke and his wagons at Bear Butte. They prayed he had panicked at their intrusion and come early with his delivery and to warn the Crow. They hoped he didn't have many men with him and they could accomplish the crucial task of destroying the weapons before they fell into the hands of the wicked Black Moon. If they rode fast and hard, they could be in position to wait and work in two days.

Joe told Morning Star that Stede and Fitzpatrick should have his and Jim's reports by now. He was eager to discover who George was, if the scout had a military reason for being in this territory, if Stede knew anything about Simon Adams, and to learn who was buying land here.

The last mention drew a question from Morning Star. She listened as Joe explained the Pre-Emption Law but did not argue its power.

To get her mind off the alarming matter, Joe asked, "How do you know your way around such a big territory? Women don't leave camp much."

Morning Star related the joint meetings at many times, places, and seasons that took her across this land. "Long ago," she added, "Bird People lived and hunted far away. Lakotas lived and hunted in these lands. When summer grows too hot, buffalo travel longer." She pointed to the cooler north. "We go after, must ride where they go to hunt. Crow come, and we must fight to hunt over the Cheyenne River. To save lives, Red Hearts come here no more if plenty of buffalo where we live. There is more ways."

"*Are* more ways," Joe gently corrected, then asked, "Like what?"

"Trail signs. I see, read. Marks everywhere if you know how to find and read. Black Moon, he come to same place; easy to find him. I use where *Wi* in sky for that season, where stars glow and how they move."

Ex-Captain Joseph Lawrence knew about using the sun, moon, and stars for charting courses, and he knew they were in different positions in the sky during each season.

Weeks ago, he had shown her his compass and explained how it worked. He had laughed and told her it was useful only when you knew which direction to follow, and it was particularly helpful on a cloudy day and moonless night. He had made notes, measurements, and drawn a map. He had told her it would be informative later about their journey for the authorities, but both knew it was also for a time when or if he had to travel alone.

When they neared the Belle Fourche River on Thursday, Joe sighted two men heading north. Using his fieldglasses to watch for approaching peril, he made out Zeke and Farley. At that distance, he knew they had not been seen. The couple hid themselves behind the nearest knoll. They rested and chatted until the villains were gone.

"Why he not take guns to Black Moon camp?" Morning Star asked.

"He's too clever and cautious. He doesn't want to get caught near an Indian camp with illegal goods. He has to go fetch them because he's six days early, and I doubt he wants to hang around here longer than need be. His little trip should give us about five days to do our task and be far away when he and those Crow return and find the damage we'll inflict. This time, we'll get some undeniable proof to unmask him and to protect us."

At over four thousand feet, Bear Butte — Mato Paha to the Lakotas — was highly visible long before they reached the sacred mountain as it rose in majestic splendor from the surrounding plains. Fortunate for the couple, treelines, ravines, and the Bear River were nearby to help with concealment and stealth.

With hopes Zeke had chosen the same spot, they left their horses near the water, at a distance where their noises couldn't be heard by the wrong ears. They discarded anything that might make sounds, and carried only knives for weapons. Morning Star took the initiative to check the wind direction to make certain their scents would not be detected by a guard's keen nose. They stepped with caution to avoid crunching twigs or anything that might create a telltale noise. They kept watch for animals and birds that could give away their approach and location if disturbed. They heard the "to whitcha, whitcha, whitcha" cry of one bird and the sound of another that reminded Joe of a gosling. They halted to let a deer move along so they wouldn't spook it. Another time, they stopped to allow a skunk to amble on during his forage for food.

Joe was wearing moccasins to aid his silence on the ground and to avoid boot tracks that would cut or break grass blades rather than bend them as the soft leather shoe did.

More acquainted with the signs of her land, Morning Star led the way. Abruptly she halted Joe once more. When he leaned close, she pointed to a bear trap someone had attempted to conceal. Joe smiled, impressed with her sharp eyes. After they came upon the third one, she warned Joe the traps were set to snare anyone coming close to Zeke's campsite. Joe realized he may have missed the deadly traps if he was alone or leading them, so he was even happier she was present and in control. As dusk was nearing, she told him they should slip into the river and spy on the area from it. She told him to remove his moccasins, as bare feet were quieter in water.

They neared a place where they could see and smell smoke from a campfire. Morning Star warned Joe about swatting at insects, about mastering control over his breathing, and about jerking his bare foot if a fish, weed, or rock made contact with him. In the fading light, Joe nodded understanding.

Suddenly, a trap sprang and a snared creature thrashed wildly to obtain freedom. Morning Star grabbed Joe's wrist and yanked him toward the bank, having already planned this strategy if trouble struck. She covered her mouth and nose with one hand to indicate for him to hold his breath. The wet beauty pushed Joe's head underwater, ducked, and pulled him beneath tangled debris. She pushed his face to the surface where there was only enough space in the bunched branches for catching air.

Joe was careful not to gulp air or to move a muscle. She did the same. They heard two men rush over and talk.

"What is it, Billy?"

"Justa muskrat or otta. We'll git him out in the morning."

"Zeke put out them traps along the bank to catch two nosey people. Think we best reset it?"

"I ain't sticking my hand in that water. He'll bite it off. Ain't nobody coming around herebouts tonight. Iffen they do, it'll be in the woods. Zeke's got traps all over. Come on, Murray, let's go take a drink and play cards."

The two men left, but the couple remained motionless for a time.

When they believed it was safe, they returned to their camp downriver.

"We can't make another move until daylight, woman," Joe said worriedly. "I don't want either of us stumbling into a trap in the dark. We've got time; it'll take Zeke five to six days to get back with the Crow. Let's get dried off and change clothes, then eat and rest. We're safe for now. The men won't come looking around in the dark with those traps everywhere. At least we know we have two guards to defeat. We want to capture witnesses and take evidence this time."

Morning Star concurred, even knowing that action would bring them closer to the end of their task — and separation from each other.

After they had changed their clothes and eaten, they lay on the same bedroll and snuggled together to sleep. The meal had been eaten cold, as they couldn't risk a campfire. Both savored the warm contact with each other, but knew this wasn't the time or place to make love.

As she lay curled in Joe's embrace, Morning Star's mind roamed for a time. The longer she was with him, the harder it was to imagine a life without him. She had watched him with Indians and whites. Each day her respect, trust, and admiration increased, and she had come to love and want him even more. Everything he had told her that night at Medicine River seemed right and possible. How could she give him up for any reason?

Joe's white world, from how he had described it, was different, much better than the one here that conflicted with the Indian's. Her grandmother and aunt had adapted to the Indian way and, with the help of Joe and his family, surely she could adjust to theirs. She had proven she was not a coward. Surely she possessed enough courage and wits to conquer his world to live at his side. Didn't she? her heart asked.

Qualms troubled her. Maybe she had been with Joe so long that she was blinded by love and desire, and was sleeping in the Dream World. Could she risk her family's love and respect by choosing a white man over them?

As soon as enough light permitted inspection of the ground for perils, they left camp. Morning Star had a knife in her sheath and a nocked bow in her hands. Joe had a rifle cocked, a knife at his waist, and two holstered pistols. They sneaked to the small clearing where the wagons were located. Two men sat near a cozy fire, eating and talking.

Joe had hoped the villain would sleep late so his attack party could get the drop on them without endangering anyone's life. This morning, he was attired in unbeaded Indian garments: moccasins, breechcloth, leggings, and vest. An unmarked leather band was around his head to keep his long blond hair from interfering with his vision. He asked God to help and protect them.

Morning Star implored her Great Spirit to do the same. And she implored herself to keep her eyes and thoughts off

Joe. Her heart had raced with love and her body had burned with desire as she watched him dress earlier. He was indeed a well-honed and skilled warrior, the most tempting and irresistible one she had met.

Joe gave the signal to attack, bringing both of them to full alert. He focused on the man to the left, she on the one to the right. They stepped into the edge of the clearing. "Put up your hands and don't move, or we'll shoot!" Joe shouted.

The men, with cocked rifles at hand, seized them as they jumped up and turned to defend themselves against what they feared was certain death.

Joe wounded his target in the shoulder; Morning Star placed her arrow in almost the same place on hers. They dodged simultaneous fire, but the injured men, as hoped, didn't surrender after being spared. The hirelings yelped in pain and surprise, but drew pistols to save their lives.

"Give it up! You don't have a chance to escape!" Joe shouted.

They were the ones with no chance to survive if they didn't take the culprits' lives. The reluctant couple did what they must.

Afterward, they approached the campfire and dead men. "Damn," Joe swore under his breath. "I wanted a witness. To protect our cover with Jim, we could have taken him to Fort Laramie."

"They fear capture more than dying," she remarked.

He exhaled audibly, then suggested, "Let's get our work done and get out of here. We can't do anything for them."

Joe collected weapons and ammunition as gifts to Sun Cloud for hunting. He yanked off a board with *PRATTE AND COMPANY* stamped on it. "Here's proof this load either came from or through Simon Adams. One way or another, this will help trace it. When Zeke and the Crow find this mess, all they'll see are moccasin tracks. Hopefully that'll confuse them for a while."

"I have Crow possessions in pack. We put some here to fool them?"

"That won't work, love. If Crow attacked, they'd take the

supplies, not destroy them as we're going to do."

"But we take some," she reminded, "many as small band can carry. They will think others destroyed so Lakotas and Army not find and take."

"You're right. As usual," he amended with a broad grin. "It's worth trying. I'll start here while you fetch them. Be careful of those traps."

By early afternoon, Joe and Morning Star had used hatchet butts to ruin the rifles. With broken or bent hammers, breechloading covers, or crushed barrels, the weapons were useless. Gunpowder was spread over a wide area and kicked into dirt and grass; it was too perilous to fish and animals to dump it into the water. It was also too hazardous to set aflame and risk igniting the forest and prairie with an explosive blaze. The whiskey was poured out for the earth to drink. Identifying boards for company and contents were taken from the ammunition and whiskey barrels. Everything possible was completed, including the false clues.

At twilight, Morning Star and Joe made camp miles away from the site of their daring ploy. After the horses were tended and they had eaten a hot meal, they settled down to talk before bedtime.

"I can't figure why Simon would incriminate himself by not removing the marked boards before giving Zeke those shipments," Joe wondered aloud. "I keep thinking that he might be Snake-Man or that he's working for him. Then I get a gut feeling that says he isn't involved."

"He is a bad man, but I do not think he is the man we seek."

Joe glanced at her and smiled, noticing how good her English was these days. "I'm proud of you, Morning Star; your parents and band will be, too. I couldn't have done all I have without your help and friendship. I hate putting you in danger, but you've proven over and over how much I need you with me."

330

Her expression revealed her joy at those words. "Thank you."

Just looking at her aroused Joe, but he knew they were both too tired to enjoy lovemaking to the fullest. He didn't want a fast joining only to release his pent-up tension. It was best to wait until tomorrow night when they were rested and farther away from Zeke's camp. "I think I'll shave. I don't need this beard any more, and it scratches like wool on a summer day."

Morning Star observed as Joe heated water in a shallow basin and placed soap nearby. She watched him sit near the fire with a mirror resting on his knees and a sharp razor in his grasp. "I will help," she offered, knowing the job would be difficult at night. "I cut shorter first," she suggested, then used the scissors he gave to her. When she finished, she held the mirror up for him to take over the chore.

Cognizant of her tender gaze witnessing his every expression and stroke, Joe felt lucky not to have cut himself.

"Shaving is like small Sun Dance," Morning Star remarked. "All a man owns is his body to offer pieces to the Great Spirit. You grow and cut off hair for sacred mission; that is part of Joe's body. Great Spirit is happy." She didn't include that a clear face made his appearance seem more Indian. He was shirtless, and she looked at the scar on his arm where Zeke's bullet had passed through it when he rescued her. Yes, that night had been destined between them.

Morning Star prayed there was also a bright future destined for them. She hated to think of their imminent separation. She had agreed to part with Joe for a short time for three reasons: first, two tasks needed tending before they could journey again together, and she wanted to accomplish them soon. Second, she wanted to see her parents and friends. Third, she wanted to have her "woman's flow" in the privacy of her tepee. She had completed one just before her capture by Zeke, another just before reaching Orin McMichael's, and the next was due in three or four suns. She thought she had been able to conceal her female condition from Joe last time, but a man reared around a sister knew

331

about such things. When he had purchased supplies at Lookout, he had bought her a length of white cloth and only said, "This is for you when you need it." His expression had made his meaning clear.

Joe finished and put away his things. "Better?" he hinted.

"It is bad to hide face like yours" was her merry response. She wanted to caress the hairless surface, but something halted her. She suddenly realized what it was, that the skin was white against the rest of a face that had been darkly tanned by the prairie sun. It was as if the recently concealed flesh beside the dark flesh pointed out the differences in them.

"Something wrong?" he queried her altered expression.

"No, just tired," she had to reply.

Joe didn't question her. "Me, too. Let's get to sleep."

After a steady ride, they halted on Elk Creek. They tended their chores and ate, then bathed in the refreshing water.

While Joe made more notes and marked his map, Morning Star did some serious thinking. Tomorrow they would separate, and she dreaded not being with him. She was so confused and tormented, and she feared that visiting her people would increase her dilemma. She knew what she wanted, but deciding to take that path would cost her much. Yet, by nightfall on the next sun or at any time, either or both of them could be dead, out of the other's reach forever. Life was often short and dangerous. It should not be spent in misery. Was there a way for them to remain together after this sacred task? Could she convince the Great Spirit, her parents, and her people that she belonged with Sky Warrior? And if she did, what would it be like for her, for them, in Joe's world?

Surely there are many whites like Joe, she reasoned — Alisha Williams, Rebecca Kenny and her parents, Bonnie Thorne, wife of the past Cheyenne chief Windrider — Stede and Tanner Gaston, and the friends her ancestors and band had made in the past. As with the other women from her bloodline, to have her man surely she could adjust to another type of life. There must be so many wonders she didn't know about, added to the ones her lover had related during their long journey. There were so many things to experience with him. More, she admitted, than she could do here where her life was simple and often hard, where death stalked with each new and closer encroachment by whites or raids by Crow. To live in a place surrounded by safety sounded wonderful. Could she—dare she—choose Joe and his world over hers?

The sunny-haired man wrapped his arms around the beauty with such a serious expression on her face. "Stop worrying, woman; I'm not going to chase you down and carry you off like I teased. I'll let you make your decision about us when you're ready. I realize how hard it is for you, and a future for us might indeed not be possible. From now on, we live and love day to day. We'll expect nothing more than that from each other. Agreed?"

Morning Star tensed in Joe's embrace and wished she could see the expression in his eyes. He had been so loving and tender, so compassionate and understanding of her feelings. She prayed her last rejection had not stung him so deeply that he had lost hope for them, had changed his mind about pursuing her. Perhaps she should discuss the matter with him this moment. Yet she did not want to give him false hopes they could overcome all the obstacles between them. He could be wrong about his family and friends. His father had not wanted him to come here. They might not be happy about him taking an Indian as wife.

Joe knew, as well as she, there were good and bad whites and good and bad Indians. Surely he understood her trapped position by now. Surely he had been telling her so much about his world and teaching her so many things to persuade her she could fit in there. Every day he whet her appetite for what was beyond her territory—that had to be an intentional ploy. She had witnessed how quickly and easily the Dakotas accepted and believed Joe. His arguments held much truth not long ago. Once this great mission succeeded and he was honored by her people, the Red Hearts couldn't think too badly of her for wanting to remain with the glorious Sky

Warrior. Surely they would realize the Great Spirit had put them together and wanted them to remain together. Joe had worked for peace in her world; perhaps she was destined to work for peace and understanding in his.

Morning Star asked herself how Sun Cloud could say it was wrong to marry a white-eye when his father and brother had done so and had been very happy with their choice of mates. She wondered if her people could resist this union when the Red Hearts knew what Alisha/Shalee and Rebecca/Wahea had done for their band. When peace was within their grasps, how could anyone call Joe an enemy? How could her family and people not want her to return for visits to relate all she learned about the whites? Even if she left in banishment and dishonor, how long could it last? Surely time would bring understanding and forgiveness.

For all her dreamy hopes and desperate prayers, Morning Star knew it would not be that easy to leave with Joe or to enter his world. It troubled her that he was having doubts, was retreating from her. No, she decided, it was a clever and necessary move for their safety and peace of mind.

She turned and gazed into his eyes. "My choice is made, Joe. I—"

"You don't have to explain," he interrupted in a sad tone.

She realized he anticipated the worst from her strange mood. She smiled, caressed his cheek, and said, "I love you. If possible, we will find a way to be together when our task is done."

Joe stared into her softened gaze. He was afraid to trust what he was hearing. "Are you saying . . . Do you mean . . ."

Morning Star grinned, then laughed. "I will marry you after our mission is completed."

"You aren't teasing me? You aren't saying this to clear my head?"

She realized that her own was as clear as it could ever be. No matter what anybody said or did, they were destined to live as one. "It will not be simple," she said slowly, trying her best to speak correct English, to show him how much she had learned about fitting into his world. She related to him all she had been thinking and feeling. "I love you," she finally concluded.

Joe scooped her up and swung her around, laughing with joy as he did so. "You just made me the happiest man alive. I promise, Morning Star, I'll make you happy and I'll protect you from any harm."

She believed him, but cautioned, "We must say nothing to others before our sacred task is done. It will be hard to win acceptance of our joining . . . and my leaving."

Enchanted by her, Joe suggested, "Would it be best to start dropping hints about our feelings when we visit your family?"

She shook her head. "You forget you are Tanner Gaston, of our bloodline. To reveal the lie now will bring much harm to us and our task."

"You're right," he conceded. As he held her in his arms, he confessed, "The hardest thing I've ever done will be to pretend our love and bond don't exist when we're in your camp."

"If we reveal it," she warned, "how can Father, Mother, and others believe any words we speak after lies and tricks are exposed?"

"You're one of the smartest women I've known. No, *the* smartest. And the bravest," he added with a wide smile.

"Some will cause trouble for us," she alluded.

"Knife-Slayer. Does Knife-Slayer mean anything special to you?"

Morning Star traced his lips with her finger. "You are the only man I have loved. He desires me and chases me. I do not like him or trust him. But he will battle us with all his skills. So will Night Stalker. I do not know what Mother and Father will . . ."

Joe tightened his embrace a moment. "We'll find a way to make everyone understand and agree. After our victory and the new treaty, they'll see why I had to trick them. They can't deny I'm Sky Warrior. I look and behave like the man in Payaba's vision; it's sacred. It's meant to be."

She smiled. "I pray you are right. We must not fail in our

335

mission. If we do, my people will say it is punishment for our deceit, and they will not allow me to leave with you." *Even if I must die to be halted or punished* . . .

"We won't fail, love; I swear it."

Morning Star decided there was no better time than *anpetu tonpi,* her birthday, to make her choice and to receive the gift of a future with Joe.

The happy white man and nineteen-year-old beauty sank to his bedroll and made passionate love before sleeping entwined in each other's arms.

Joe watched Morning Star head south while he continued east. He was glad she was going home for a visit. He knew she could make the half-day trip alone. He hated being apart from her, but he felt he would be safe stopping near the fort to retrieve the messages from Stede, Fitzpatrick, and Jim. If anything went wrong, he could always expose his identity as a government agent. As soon as he had answers from them about troubling questions, he would head for Sun Cloud's camp and his love. He wanted this mission completed so he could marry the woman of his heart.

Morning Star followed the trail signs to her people's second location of this nomadic season and rode into the Red Heart camp. It didn't take her long to make several shocking discoveries. She was relieved Joe wasn't with her or he might be slain before she could reveal the good news and clear up one particular and dangerous mistake.

Chapter Fifteen

Morning Star gaped at her best friend, who had left her tasks and rushed to meet her. Her dark-brown eyes were wide and her mouth agape as she took in the thirty-six-year-old woman's shocking words.

As if she hadn't heard them, Buckskin Girl repeated, "He has come, the true vision warrior. Did Tanner learn this news and flee for his life?"

Confused, Morning Star replied, "Tanner has gone to the fort to speak with the soldier who helps us. I returned to tell Father and the council all we have learned and done. *He* is the true Sky Warrior. I do not understand your strange words."

With glowing eyes, Buckskin Girl caught her breath and explained, "Sky Warrior returned two suns' past to help us defeat the evil whites. Sky Warrior, Notaxe tse-amo-estse, son of Windrider and his white mate, Bonnie Thorne. I can tell you all that lives in my heart now, Morning Star. When you won the contest, I feared I was wrong. I was not. Tanner Gaston is not the Sky Warrior in Payaba's vision. The son of Windrider is. All forgot about him, for he has been gone sixteen winters. He was driven from his band by dishonor and anguish. He was stripped of his chief's bonnet by evil. He—"

"Soul-of-Thunder followed Windrider as chief, not his half-blooded brother; Morning Star interrupted. "Your mind is confused. I will seek Payaba to tend you." Before she could leave, the woman's grasp halted her.

"No, you must hear my words. Sky Warrior was war chief.

337

The sacred vision did not say what chief's bonnet was lost. He has been in the white world. He is half white and half Cheyenne. His grandmother was Oglala, Red Heart. He is of our band." She stressed the connection. "I do not doubt Stede Gaston is the first vision man, but my love is the second. His looks and Life Circle match the vision words. I believed the Great Spirit would call him home to find his true destiny. He has done so. I tried to warn you Tanner is not the vision warrior," she reminded. "There is another bond to our band, to Gray Eagle's bloodline: his brother, the chief, is mate to Bright Arrow's daughter, Tashina."

All of this was news to Morning Star, but it didn't change what she and Joe had done and must continue doing. But now she knew what had driven her friend. "Such things do not make him the Sky Warrior in the sacred vision."

"Do not be blind, my friend," Buckskin Girl urged.

The kind-hearted daughter of Sun Cloud did not toss those words back into the woman's face. Suddenly she thought of how her brother and Knife-Slayer might try to use this unexpected event to cause trouble for her and Joe. To learn everything about the past episode, she entreated, "Tell me why he was banished."

The daughter of Flaming Star assumed her friend accepted her words, so she complied with eagerness. "Sky Warrior's mate and children were slain during a Shoshone raid. Before his heart was healed, he sought another mate. He chose the shaman's daughter, a beautiful girl. But she was evil. She let no one see her entice him. She sneaked into the forest and lay upon his sleeping mat many times. She desired him as a man, but did not want a half-breed as a mate. She did not want her children stained by his blood." Buckskin Girl's eyes filled with anger and hatred.

"He did not know she tricked him, as his mind was clouded with pain. When a warrior lay claim to her, Sky Warrior saw another woman being taken away, so he challenged for her and fought to the death of the other man. The slain warrior was a Dog Man, the highest-ranking sash wearer. Many were troubled by his death over a woman. She refused to join him. She lied to her father and people."

338

Buckskin Girl's tone became colder as she related the tale. "She told them Sky Warrior wanted her so much he threatened her and her family if she did not join him. Her father, the shaman, was fooled and he spoke for her. He spoke against Sky Warrior, the half-breed. He claimed his daughter had not shared a blanket with my love or listened to his flute music. He demanded my love be banished. The tribe was aroused against him. The words of Windrider, Bonnie, and Soul-of-Thunder were not heard above the shouts to dishonor him. Shamed and hurt, he left the Cheyenne camp and he entered our camp to stay with us, his grandmother's people. Many offered him a place in their tepee. I came to love him and desire him, but he feared such feelings because he was in great pain. He went into his mother's white world to learn if that was his destiny."

Morning Star was touched by the tragic story and listened to more.

"I have longed for his return. I love him. That is why I have not joined another. I believed the Great Spirit would answer my prayers, and He has. When Sky Warrior came to us sixteen winters past, no one thought of the vision of four winters before it. There was no war, and he was not returning after a long absence, as he is this season. His hair is the color of the sun and moon, and his eyes match the blue in the sky. My heart was knifed when I challenged you in the contest, but I wished to ride with Sky Warrior. I believed he would come soon to take Tanner's place. I do not care if his blood is mixed. I love him and want to join to him. I loved him long before I even knew of those feelings. Our fathers were best friends. You were three winters old when he rode away, so you did not remember him. Tanner's coming was strange. I feared I was mistaken; I had waited for nothing. Something in my heart and mind said that was untrue. Do you understand now why I challenged you and why Tanner is not the true Sky Warrior? Others believe my love is the vision warrior. They wait for Tanner to return to be challenged on his claim."

"Only those who wish to cause trouble, my friend," Morning Star contended. "Open your heart to the truth: I am rid-

339

ing with the true Sky Warrior."

"Here comes your father and mother returning from the hunt. My love is with them. He rides next to Knife-Slayer."

There was no need for Buckskin Girl to point out the handsome half-breed in the party. Morning Star eyed him with intrigue and dismay: his appearance did match the vision words! She prayed the son of Windrider would not become trouble for her and Joe, but she feared he would, especially if he believed he was Sky Warrior more than in Cheyenne name.

Knife-Slayer leapt off his pinto and hurried to the woman he desired. "Where is Tanner?" he asked, glancing about for his rival.

Eyes on her parents, she replied, "He has gone to the fort to share our news. He will return soon for me. We ride again in a few suns."

"No! It cannot be. He lies. Stede Gaston and the son of Windrider are the vision men. Only one true medicine warrior; Tanner is false! He heard of Sky Warrior's return and is gone to betray us."

She protested the accusation, "Your words are foolish! You speak as a man who knows and feels nothing. You seek to cause trouble again."

"Silence!" Sun Cloud ordered as he joined them. "You fight as children," the chief scolded. "Morning Star, a woman does not speak to a man and warrior this way."

Before he could be reprimanded in public, Knife-Slayer charged, "It is the evil white man's doing. He teaches her to behave as a woman of his kind. He steals her heart from us and her eyes from me. He is bad."

Morning Star was angered. "He steals nothing! He—"

"Silence! We will hear my daughter's words when the council meets after we rest and eat. Say no more harsh words," Sun Cloud told both.

Singing Wind had joined them. She embraced her child and whispered, "Hold your words until we are in our tepee."

Morning Star nodded. She saw Knife-Slayer, who was wearing his *wanapin,* join his father. She noticed how Buckskin Girl edged her way to the stranger's side. Before she fol-

lowed her parents home, Morning Star quickly studied the
newcomer. He was almost as tall as Joe, but was many winters older: forty-six, Buckskin Girl had told her. His skin was
the same color as her own. The hard and toned muscles of his
body were as defined as those on a skinned deer. His bare
chest exposed Sun Dance scars, marks attesting to his great
prowess. Another scar ran along his left jawline; as if following her line of vision, the man stroked it. His stormy blue eyes
had not left her face since dismounting. A breeze swept
through his hair and lifted strands of moonglow and sun-
light. Notaxe tse-amo-estse was a man, a warrior, to steal a
woman's eye and heart — as he had done with her friend.

"Do not worry over him," Singing Wind whispered.
"Come."

Sun Cloud walked with his wife and child past the meat-
laden travois that would be unloaded and cured tomorrow.
Covered by hides to protect the hunks from insects and spoil-
age, they would be fine tonight. He was anxious to hear of his
daughter's adventures and to prevent dissension.

Inside the dwelling, Morning Star pointed to the rifles and
ammunition. "They are gifts to you and Night Stalker from
Tanner. We defeated men hauling them to the Bird People.
We destroyed all others."

As the chief lifted one to study it, Singing Wind said, "Our
fear was great for your safety. It is good to see you home."

"It is good to be home, Mother, but we must leave when he
returns. Father, do you wish me to speak all things to you, or
wait until council?"

"There is no need to weary you with speaking two times."

The council began with Knife-Slayer charging that "Tanner" was not the vision man, that Notaxe tse-amo-estse must
replace him in the mission.

Morning Star had been given time to think and plan during the meal and rest period. Having been given permission
to speak freely, she pointed out that "the sacred vision said
two men, different men. It did not say the vision warrior with
Oglala blood *lost* his chief's bonnet or *returned*. It said he

341

was *denied* his rank, land, and people. The man with sky eyes, white blood, and sun hair is not the same as the man with Oglala blood who was *denied* such things. It cannot be Windrider's son."

Hawk Eyes, shaman and father of Knife-Slayer suggested, "It may be only one vision man. Two may be a symbol: the man before leaving and the man after returning. Payaba saw no faces. All words match Notaxe tse-amo-estse. He was a great warrior, a cunning chief, and will be so again."

"No, it is two men," Payaba refuted, "not the same man."

Wind Bird, who was training under the old shaman, ventured, "What if there are two Sky Warriors? What if the Great Spirit called the son of Windrider home to help him with the sacred mission?"

"The vision did not show three men," Hawk Eyes argued.

Morning Star leapt on his words. "If two can be a symbol for one warrior as you believe and reasoned, Hawk Eyes," she contended, "why do you say one cannot be a symbol for two? Is it not strange two men come who match the vision? I say one does not come to prove the other false. I say let both work to help us. We must halt the trouble before buffalo season ends and the Bird People raid with guns from the evil white man. We have traveled far and much and our faces are known to enemies and those we doubt. His is not. He can do tasks at white posts we cannot enter. He was sent to join us, not to take Tanner's place. The vision said our helper would have hair that blazes like the sun. Tanner's hair is of the sun, but Sky Warrior's has the light of the sun *and* moon. Tanner's eyes are as blue and calm as the day he came to us; Sky Warrior's are dark as a sky before a storm. We have ridden the vision trail. How can you say what we have done was not meant to be? Many bad things would be past if Sky Warrior came this late to help us."

"Tell us what *great* things he has done" came Knife-Slayer's words in a sarcastic tone.

Morning Star used patience and self-control as she related their adventures for the past thirty-two suns. She observed the men as she talked, to interpret their feelings and reactions to her news. As was their way, none interrupted. She noted worried looks when she exposed the incriminating Red Heart arrows at the massacre of Crow hunters. Smiles and nods greeted news of their tracking of the attackers, their slayings, and the return of sacred possessions to the burial ground. Dismay was obvious when she told them of the Crow false clues left there and suggested the evil whites were provoking the tribes against each other. More smiles and nods came her way when she spoke of the fur-trapper ruse. She saw the men listen intently to information about Orin McMichael, the strange scout, Simon Adams, and Harvey Meade. She explained about the murder charge against "Tanner" and their visit to the fort to see Captain James Thomas. She told them how much they trusted this white soldier and how eager he was for peace with them.

Morning Star watched Knife-Slayer almost jump up to argue, but his father's hand stayed the scowling warrior. She revealed how Zeke and George had arrived as they were leaving and explained that matter. She related their pleasant visits with Red Cloud and Spotted Tail and saw her pursuer's scowl deepen and his eyes chill to hear of how her love was accepted by those two respected chiefs. Knife-Slayer's envy, anger, and doubts increased as she spoke of their daring visits to three Crow camps as a trader, hireling of Snake-Man, and Arapaho squaw. When she asserted that Chief Two-Bulls was a good man who wanted peace, the tense warrior could not contain his fury.

"He was sly and tricked you! We cannot have peace with Bird People! He trails you this sun to attack our camp to slay all Red Hearts."

"If so, he and his warriors would be here by now. There has been time for such a dark deed, Knife-Slayer, but it has not and will not come to pass." She saw Hawk Eyes prevent another outburst from his son.

Morning Star continued her revelations with a detailed description of the destruction of the wagons with guns, ammunition, and whiskey.

Once more, Knife-Slayer interrupted. "Why did you destroy the supplies? We need them to protect our lives and camp."

Her patience was tried and strained, but she replied calmly. "I brought some to Father and Night Stalker and others, but it was all I could carry. We could not steal the wagons and reach camp before the evil ones caught up and slayed us; heavy wagons travel slow and leave a big track. We destroyed them so Black Moon's band could not use them against us."

"It was a brave and wise decision," Sun Cloud remarked. He hoped his words would quiet the intrusive and belligerent warrior before he was compelled to scold him in front of the council. He was relieved when others concurred and Knife-Slayer silenced himself.

"Tanner goes to the fort to speak with our helper there. He carries proof of where the crates came from. He tells the soldier of the treachery of Black Moon and Talking Wolf. He goes to retrieve a message from Stede Gaston who gathered answers elsewhere for us. He will return in nine suns to ride the trail again. There is other trouble," she alluded and withdrew the *wanapin* charm and headband from a parfleche. She told them about the payroll theft, massacre, and clues found.

"It is not mine!" Knife-Slayer shouted.

Morning Star smiled knowingly, "That is true," she replied. "We told the soldier these are not Red Heart possessions; he believes what we tell him. But things like these and the false attacks on Crow and whites point to our band. We told the soldier how possessions are stolen from burial grounds and slain warriors, or made by others like these I hold. We do not know who leads the bad whites, but we are tracking him. We defeat many of their evil deeds. We have the Crow doubting them. We have the Army alert and suspicious."

Proud and impressed, Sun Cloud asked, "What do you do now?"

"We will see what the messages say and what the soldier has learned since our visit there. That will tell us what trail to take."

"The Crow do not raid yet. All are busy hunting for winter food. When it is done, they will come with guns from the men you track to defeat."

"The soldier will warn them and prevent war. Soon we will have the proof needed to bring Stede and the agent here to make treaty."

Sun Cloud looked forward to the visit of Powchutu's son and said so.

"Knife-Slayer," Morning Star asked, "will you tell me what you saw when you spied on the one called Snake-Man? Did you see his hair and hands? Was his voice strange from other whites?"

The warrior liked the way she spoke to him this time. He smiled as he responded, "He is tall like Tanner. Hair is like night. I could not see his hands and eyes. His voice was the same as other whites. Why do you ask?"

"A man we suspect has a strange voice, but his hair blazes as a fire. It cannot be Orin McMichael. Another we suspect has black hair, is tall, and has a mark on his hand the color of a buffalo hide. He is Simon Adams. He works and lives in the post called Pratte's at Pierre. Many clues point to him, but something tells us he is not Snake-Man. The one called Harvey Meade is at Lookout; he gave us no reason to doubt him. The soldier has our trust, but there could be another in the fort we have not seen."

"You have worked hard and done much, Daughter."

"Thank you, Father. Is there more you wish to hear?" she inquired, glancing around the many faces who nodded agreement with Sun Cloud.

As no one had more questions at that moment, the council ended.

"The journey has been long," Morning Star told her father. "I will bathe and rest. Tomorrow I will help the women with their chores."

Buckskin Girl joined her at a stream near camp. It was almost dark with the moon waning to half, so they had to hurry their task and talk.

As she washed away trail dust and perspiration from her body, Morning Star coaxed, "Tell me more about your love."

Flaming Star had related news of the council meeting to his daughter, so she said first, "They did not vote who was Sky Warrior in the vision. Father says both men could be the vision helper; that would be good."

Morning Star smiled and agreed, glad her friend was happy.

"My heart is filled with joy at his return. He has not found another mate. His looks say his past feelings for me still live. I let him see I love him and want him. I do not care about his bloodline and white looks. If I must be dishonored and banished to join a half-breed, I do not care. Great love is rare. Some Life-Circles are small. I must win him this time."

"I hope he loves and wants you, too, my friend. It is smart to show your feelings. Men cannot read women's heads and hearts as they read tracks. I do not believe his bloodline matters. It is the man who matters. You would not be shamed and sent away for joining to your true love. I will pray for Grandfather to help you win him."

"I must hurry before he returns to his tribe."

"Why that, when he was dishonored and banished?"

"The shaman's daughter bore his son. She killed it, for he favored his father. She became ill. Her head burned with fever; she revealed many things. Before she died, the truth was learned: my love was innocent. But he was gone and did not know they wanted his return. I have told him that news from Tashina, but he is not ready to return home. He wishes to help us because we did not scorn and reject him. We did not think him guilty. He wants to be a great warrior again, to ride home in honor and victory. He must be a part of the vision-quest to do this."

"What does he say and think of the vision? Of you?"

"He says he will help with the task, but he is not the vision warrior," the older woman admitted. "I do not know how he feels for me."

Before Morning Star could begin her chores with the other women, the stranger approached her near her father's tepee. She watched his self-assured gate and looked straight into his secretive eyes. He was attired as an Indian, with a leather band around his sunny head of shoulder-grazing hair. His features were strong, his hairless chest broad, and his abdomen flat.

"I figured we should get something settled up front, Morning Star. I know about the vision, the contest, and your work with Tanner Gaston. I told them I wasn't the man in Payaba's words, but I do want to help you two. I think I can; and you do, too. Let me explain why I'm here."

Morning Star didn't halt him as she listened to him.

"I've been all over the place since I left here years ago. I already knew English from my mother, so it wasn't hard fitting in with my white looks. Stop me if I talk too fast or say something you don't understand. Buckskin Girl told me you speak English." After she nodded, he went on. "I use the name Clay Thorne, after my mother. My last job was in St. Louis, loading and unloading boats. I kept hearing bad tales of what was happening here and what was expected to happen soon. I saw Red Heart and other Lakota possessions sold as souvenirs. I realized crates were bringing too many guns and too much ammunition to these parts. I knew the charges I was hearing about had to be wrong. When one trapper joked that the Army was going to 'whip Sun Cloud and his redskins all over the place,' I knew I had to come help."

Morning Star watched the play of emotions in those secretive eyes. His tone and conduct were under his control, a result of his Indian upbringing and years of practice in the white world. He was strong and healthy, hard and sleek. He had a habit of stroking the scar on his jawline every so often, as if reminding himself it was there and why.

Aware of her gaze, Thorne/Sky Warrior disclosed, "Got it in that fight before I was banished. He was going for my throat, but I wasn't ready to die."

"I am sorry you knew such pain for many years. Buckskin Girl told me your story; I had not heard it before. You are welcome here always."

"You speak excellent English," he noted with undisguised surprise. To win her confidence, he sent her a lopsided grin and softened his gaze.

347

Morning Star was intentionally careful with her speech. She grinned before explaining, "My parents taught me. Tanner taught me more on the trail. We practice much. I teach him skills and things I know. It is a good trade. Where do the crates of weapons come from? Who sends them?"

He shrugged powerful shoulders as he replied, "I don't know. They ship to Lookout, Pratte's, and McMichael's in this area. A few go farther upriver, but not enough to draw suspicion. I do know the man's name on the slip to pick up the suspicious crates is always Zeke Randall. From what Buckskin Girl told me, you've already had run-ins with him."

Morning Star went over those episodes quickly. She liked this man and felt he could be trusted. "You are much like your father and brother," she observed. "They are good men, great warriors."

Clay thumbed his scar. "You're right. I've missed them."

"Will you go home after you help us with the mission?"

"At least for a long visit, probably stay the winter. After that, I don't know. I'll have to see how much I've changed, and them, too. It was a bad time for everyone before I left home. When you've been done wrong by your own people, sometimes it's hard to switch from resentment to forgiveness and understanding," he confessed with a wry smile. "I didn't know what happened in my camp after I left until Buckskin Girl told me. That was sixteen years ago to them, but only a few days for me to deal with it."

"Buckskin Girl will be happy if you live with your grandmother's band."

The blue-eyed blond looked uneasy with that subject. Obviously, Morning Star deduced, he was one of those men who had trouble expressing feelings, or had trouble trusting women. She was glad it was not that way between her and Joe.

Finally, Clay replied, "She's a fine woman. We were close before I left. I guess I'll have to wait and see what changes there are in that area, too."

"I will not speak of it again." She changed the topic back to the vision. "Tanner will return in nine suns. He will like you; you will like him. We will speak and make plans for your

348

help." Morning Star realized that meant she would no longer be alone with Joe, and prayed that coupled with Clay's arrival were not signs from the great Spirit about their forbidden relationship. Yet she grasped that she could learn more about white existence from this half-Indian who had spent sixteen years among Joe's kind. With Clay's help, they could finish this task sooner, then work on their personal challenge.

Morning Star had to get to her chores. "We will talk more later," she said. "I want to hear about your life in the white world."

"We'll have plenty of talking time on the trail."

"Do you wish to be called by your white or Cheyenne name?"

"Here, by my Indian name. Out there, by my white name."

"On the trail I am called Little Flower, Arapaho squaw."

"That's smart. The Crow would die to get their hands on Morning Star, daughter of Sun Cloud. Tanner's protected you well so far."

"He is a good man. I must go."

As she worked, Morning Star knew she could not expose her true feelings for Joe or drop any hints he was not Tanner Gaston. That shocking discovery would give Knife-Slayer and others the right to challenge her love as Sky Warrior. They would say it proved the Cheyenne warrior was the vision man. She prayed Joe would return fast so they could depart soon.

She watched Clay leave to join the hunters miles beyond and above camp on the prairie land. The tepees were situated in a safe canyon with no fear of frightened buffalo racing headlong over people and dwellings. Most whites thought the area wild and forbidding, but it was beautiful to her. It was a location of oddly shaped and colored rocks, ridges, ravines, spires, buttes, gorges, lush grass, and streams.

As Morning Star scraped a hide to remove fat and bits of flesh, she recalled past hunts she had witnessed and worked. Brave and skilled men rode around and into a large herd and

349

shot the number that could be handled that day. Women in the small group skinned and gutted the animals where they fell and loaded meat onto a travois. After the needed number was brought down, the men traveled back and forth to the site as they hauled their kill to camp to be divided and prepared by all families. Beneath the hot summer sun it was a long, hard, and bloody task. Exhausted workers returned near dusk, to be replaced the next day.

In camp, countless wooden meat racks held strips while they dried beneath the sun: *pa-pa* to the Oglalas, and jerky to the whites. Some meat was packed in parfleches, to be eaten as was. Other portions were pounded almost to a powder, mixed with berries and hot fat and sometimes nuts, allowed to cool, then formed into rolls of *wakapanpi:* pemmican. The rolls did not spoil for years, and they could be transported easily.

Other women labored on preparing hides, as Morning Star and her mother did today. Once they were free of all unwanted specks, they were stretched on a frame to dry. Their final use determined the remaining treatment. Some would remain furry, while others would be stripped of all hair. The ones Morning Star and Singing Wind prepared were for warm winter robes.

When the seasonal hunt was completed, tribes met for a great feast and to observe the Sun Dance before heading for their winter camps in the sheltered valleys, canyons, and meadows of the Black Hills. Morning Star wondered if this would be her last buffalo hunt and Sun Dance.

As they worked in silence, Singing Wind wondered almost the same. Though her daughter had said nothing alarming about Tanner, she suspected the girl's feelings. At least, the worried mother concluded, her daughter was being virtuous, as her woman's flow revealed this morning. For that much, the wife of Sun Cloud was grateful, as she recalled how hot and dangerous desires could burn for the man you loved and wanted.

When the women took a break to eat and chat, Morning Star showed them the kaleidoscope Joe had given to her. The gift passed from one eager hand to the other for the tube to be turned and enjoyed.

While she strolled about camp to loosen her back and neck muscles, Morning Star visited Waterlily. The young woman felt the older one was too good and kind to be the wife and mother of two men as awful as Hawk Eyes and Knife-Slayer. She noticed what the woman was working on and questioned, "Where did you get this hide?"

Waterlily looked up. "Knife-Slayer and Night Stalker found a herd of spotted buffaloes. They brought one to me. They wished me to see how it cures and the meat tastes. If it it good, they will slaughter the others."

Morning Star was alarmed. "They are white man's cattle. We will be accused of stealing them. Kill no more, Waterlily. They must be returned."

The woman was upset by those remarks, but she nodded in compliance.

Morning Star knew she must discuss this discovery with her father. How, she scoffed, could a herd of steers get lost from its paleface owner? Doubts about the two men shot through her panicked mind. If they could steal cattle, could they steal an Army payroll and massacre soldiers? Could they be doing other things without her father and the council's knowing? If so, they could bring down the Army's and white man's wrath.

The July days in camp seemed hotter and longer for Morning Star. She busied herself with preserving meat, scraping hides, gathering buffalo chips and scrubwood for the fire, cooking, sewing garments, and washing clothes in the stream. She missed Joe and worried over his safety. The markers were out for him to find his way along the White River to their second seasonal camp. She was eager to share news of the events here. Her brother and his untrustworthy friend had sworn to the chief and council they had found the herd on the Plains, but the cattle had not been returned yet. She fretted over the steers being found in the Red Heart camp, but she had said and done all she could to warn them.

The time she spent with Clay Thorne was enjoyable and

enlightening. He had revealed many exciting things about his years far away, and she related details of the sacred mission and recent council meeting. If he suspected the reason behind her many questions, he said nothing. She was happy to see him taking up time with a glowing Buckskin Girl who had blossomed like a spring flower under his gaze and attention. She also noticed the longer Clay stayed, the more he relaxed. But as with her, he was waiting for Joe's arrival and the continuation of the great task.

Soon, Joe would return and their search for peace would resume. If all was fine, he had reached the message tree and retrieved helpful clues. Surely he was on his way back to her this very sun. Also by now, Zeke and the Crow had found their destruction. She wondered, though she had used all her skills and knowledge to conceal their tracks, could those villains be heading for her people's camp, and some be trailing Joe? Her love was to leave a note telling Jim where he had hidden the gun/board evidence nearby. She must not doubt that proof would aid their cause. She prayed for his protection and a painless solution to their personal predicament.

On the afternoon Clay calculated the white man's return, he suggested to Morning Star that they ride to intercept Joe to chat privately. As her chores were done, she eagerly accepted. A few miles away, they halted to wait for him. They would remain there until dusk left only enough light for returning to camp.

When "Tanner Gaston" was sighted, Clay said, "I'll wait here. You ride to meet him. You'd probably want to speak with him alone first."

"Does it show?" she asked, dismayed.

"You hid it well, but I know the truth now," he responded.

To win his confidence, she said, "You are of two bloods and worlds. You understand why I must say nothing to others until the task is done."

"I understand, but waiting won't make any difference. If you were of my tribe or not of the chief's bloodline, it wouldn't matter. It will, Morning Star. Be ready to face dis-

352

honor and banishment. It's your law."

"It is not fair or right, Clay. I did not choose to love him."

In a bitter tone, he murmured, "Not much in life is fair or easy."

"You will not speak to others?" She pressed for secrecy.

"No, it isn't my place. Just be careful how you act around him."

Morning Star rode to meet Joe, who was watching her with a quizzical gaze. She smiled, allowing her eyes to roam him.

"Who is that?" he asked, nodding toward the lingering male.

"Much has happened. We must talk fast." She dismounted and Joe followed her lead, but glanced at the stranger once more. When she asked him to report first, he obliged. "I didn't see Jim, but I left him a report and that evidence we gathered. He'll know that Black Moon and Talking Wolf are getting illegal supplies from Zeke. I told him what you said about those clues found at the payroll massacre not being Red Heart. I left him answers to his questions, and sent another letter home to my family. Jim said Harvey Meade has been acting strangely, but he doesn't thinks he's involved in this mess. I don't, either."

He took a breath. "George visited him and claimed he was following a marauding band of renegades into this area, said he was headed back to Fort Laramie. But Jim suspects another officer of working with them, Sergeant Bartholomew Carnes. This Bart hates Indians; he's mean and tough, and Jim doesn't trust him. He said Bart didn't meet with George and Zeke because Bart was recovering bodies from that attack; that means he didn't see us visit Jim, either. He said Zeke wanted to know if he was pursuing me to arrest me. Jim told him he'd made a search, but couldn't locate me and couldn't venture farther from the fort. He warned us to be more careful."

Joe glanced at the stranger again who didn't seem to be paying them any attention. "Stede's letter has some interesting information. It seems that Simon Adams talks about animals so much because he collected them around the world and exhibited them in cages. I've already told you why he

353

hates Indians, especially Dakotas, so much. Stede said his zoo—that's where animals are kept— included snakes from many places. Simon's traveled as much and as far away as I have. He's been to the Orient, where those magic balls are from. The last Stede heard of him was when he sold his property and business in New Orleans and left town after trouble with another man over stealing his wife. Jim said Simon didn't have anything to do with Indian girls like we heard Clem say his boss did. I just can't decide what Simon's role is. So many clues point to him, but I keep thinking they're coincidence or intentional false clues."

Joe sipped water from his canteen and mopped sweat from his brow. "Stede said they'd question George when he returns to the fort; he's supposed to be scouting in the Powder River area. They also want to know what he's doing over here. Tom sent a list of names for land buyers. It includes Zeke, George, Farley, Orin, Harvey, Simon, Bart, and some trappers who trade with all three posts. That ties a lot of names together, but doesn't give us too much more to use."

Joe looked at the other man again, but didn't stop his report to question her further. "Things are getting worse along the Missouri River, love. Homesteaders and farmers have been attacked. They left Red Heart and other Lakota stuff again. Jim isn't failing for those tricks, but he can't keep holding off his men and the complaints much longer. He needs something done fast. One of the worst things is another attack on soldiers. They were bringing cattle to the fort, and they were massacred and the herd stolen. A patrol couldn't trail them because their tracks were covered by a buffalo stampede. I can't guess why those villains have changed their strategy, but they must be killing whites now to provoke the Army into attacking the Lakotas. They must think the Crow aren't doing much to push the Oglalas out fast enough. Jim suspects they're enticing an Indian against white war now, not just an intertribal war. Jim's doing all he can to stall things to keep from exposing us and our mission, but the settlers are demanding protection and retaliation. You realize what this means, love: Snake-Man wants Lakotas out badly enough to use the Army and innocent whites to do his dirty work. The last thing is, Zeke is spreading lies about us. We can't be found in your father's camp, love, and neither can those cattle."

Morning Star was distressed by Joe's news, and concurred with his precautions. "We must leave at dawn. We cannot let them win."

"You want to tell me about him?" Joe hinted, eyeing the stranger who was toying with his reins while he watched the couple.

Morning Star told Joe all she had done and learned since returning home. He reacted strongest to Clay's arrival and to the news of the stolen cattle being near their camp.

"We have to move those cattle tomorrow. If this was a deadly plan, soldiers could be here any day. They'd never believe us with all that's been happening. I'm not sure Jim could control hot-headed men; if this Bart comes, he won't even try. This incident could begin the war, love."

"Sky Warrior will help us; they do not know him."

"*You* know him?" Joe probed, still uneasy about the development.

"Only since I returned. He left when I was three," she reminded. "Others know him. He can be trusted. My people accepted him and helped him long ago. He would not betray us or harm us."

Joe wanted to test that for himself. "Let's talk to him." As they walked to join Clay, Joe asked, "How much have you told him?"

Just above a whisper, she responded, "I told Father, the council, and Sky Warrior all things. He is the only one to see my heart is weak for you. He will tell no one. I did not tell him you are not Tanner."

Joe saw how the man, whose description matched his, observed their approach. He prayed Clay Thorne didn't feel bitter and vindictive toward his Indian blood, as he knew all their secrets.

Clay half-smiled and extended his hand in the white custom to shake Joe's. The two men quickly sized up each other.

"Morning Star said she filled you in. We can sure use your help, Clay. We're too known in Crow camp and at posts. We have to move around carefully. If you can spy for us in settlements, we'll do the field work. First, I'd like to get that herd near Fort Tabor before soldiers come looking for it."

"You think you can prevent a war and help make a treaty?"

"We're doing our best," Joe answered to the unusual query. "I hope so."

Clay's hand casually drifted to his pistol and he had the weapon leveled on the other man before Joe could blink. The startled couple gaped at the half-breed with a narrowed gaze and a cocked gun on Joe.

Sun Cloud's daughter inched closer to her love, and Clay frowned. "You tricked me," she accused. "Why do you do this bad thing?"

Clay didn't smile as he told her, "Sorry, Morning Star, but I have no choice. He has to be stopped. I have to kill him."

Fear consumed her. Her heart raced with panic. Her gaze widened. She felt betrayed. "You must kill me, too," she vowed in honesty.

Clay shook his head. "No, you're coming with me."

Morning Star was near him, but Joe knew he couldn't draw and fire his weapon before Clay's bullet struck home. He was angered by his helplessness and his love's peril. This traitor would defeat their mission and take their lives! He would help provoke a bloody war. No doubt Jim, Stede, and Tom would be in danger, too. He raged at himself for letting down his guard and for dismissing any suspicions about this man.

To stall Clay's attack while he attempted to think of a way to rescue them, Joe scoffed, "Don't tell me the famous Sky Warrior, ex-Cheyenne war chief, is working for Zeke Randall and Snake-Man."

Chapter Sixteen

"I'm not," Clay replied in a cold tone, "but you probably are." He glanced at the frightened woman and said, "I told you I wasn't the vision warrior, but I guess I am. He surely isn't. I have to kill him."

"Do not do this, Sky Warrior," she pleaded.

"He has you and your people fooled, Morning Star. He isn't Tanner Gaston; I've met Stede and his son. This man isn't him."

Joe exhaled in relief. "That's all? You know I'm not Tanner?"

Clay ignored the man's question to ask, "Did you know the truth, Morning Star? You hesitated over his name like you weren't used to calling him Tanner. I know love can blind you, but don't let this liar trick you into betraying yourself and your people."

"Tanner was my best friend, Clay," Joe hurried to explain, "I came to this territory with him and his father. He was murdered at Pierre by the gang I'm after. We were scouting for Stede and Tom Fitzpatrick, the Indian agent at Fort Laramie, when Tanner overheard something they didn't want him to. One of the men killed him. He gave me a clue before he died. I was tracking Zeke when I met Morning Star, but she's probably already told you that part of our story. When I learned she was Tanner's cousin, I told her everything. Of course the Red Hearts didn't trust a white stranger and things were going badly for me. I had to use Tanner's name to win Sun Cloud's confidence and help, and to save my hide. Morning Star knows the whole truth, and she agreed it was necessary to keep my identity a secret. They've let her travel with me as a translator and guide because they believe we're blood kin and nothing physical can happen between us. As for that sacred vision I matched, I don't know about mystical things. All I know is it seemed to be a prophecy coming true and it won them over."

He extended his hand again, this time in an offer of friendship. "I'm Joe, Joseph Lawrence, Junior, from Virginia. My family owns a shipping firm like Stede's. That's how we met and became friends. I've been honest with Sun Cloud about everything else. How do you know Stede and Tanner?"

Clay studied Joe a minute, holstered his weapon, and accepted the man's amiable offer and explanation. "I was fifteen when Gray Eagle's half brother returned home to make peace. I rode with my father's warriors when the Cheyenne helped retaliate after their ambush. When I was banished, I remembered how Powchutu had survived in the white world. I figured, with my looks, I could, too. My father had told me many things about Bright Arrow's uncle. Windrider was best friends with Gray Eagle's oldest son, so he knew many stories about Gray Eagle's bloodline. When I left this territory, I worked many jobs and places. Three years ago, I worked for Stede Gaston in New Orleans. I met his son twice."

Joe was curious, not suspicious, when he asked, "Stede and Tanner have never mentioned you to me. Why not?"

"I never told them who I was. I was still denying my Indian blood, and I wasn't sure how much they knew about Powchutu's history. From what Morning Star's explained, they pretty much know it all."

"You guessed the truth," she ventured, "when they told you Sky Warrior was Tanner Gaston. You knew he did not have sun hair and blue eyes. To slay him is why you rode to meet him."

"That's true," Clay admitted with his wry grin. "I'm glad you're an honest man, Joe. I would have hated to kill the man Morning Star loves, and I would have hated to tell the Red

358

Hearts how they'd been deceived. I was also worried about exposing you and taking your rank in the sacred vision. It's been a long time since I was war chief."

"You're mighty handy with a gun," Joe remarked with a grin. "Thank goodness you listen before you gun down a man."

"I've had to be good with guns and fists over the years moving around so much. Some men are determined to be dangerous."

"You planning to stay here after this trouble is cleared up?"

"Don't know yet. I've missed my family, people, and the way I was raised. I guess my Indian blood's the strongest. We'd better get back to camp before a search party comes looking for us."

They rode into camp as dusk approached. Sun Cloud and Singing Wind came to meet them, both looking worried about their daughter's lengthy absence. The chief and his wife greeted "Tanner" and queried his success.

Joe briefly went over his journey alone. Then, Sun Cloud called for a council meeting of the Big Bellies and any warriors available.

As soon as everyone had eaten, the Red Hearts gathered to hear Joe's words. The meeting was interrupted by a late-arriving Knife-Slayer and Night Stalker. The shaman's son challenged Joe's rank once more and demanded Joe and Clay battle to the death to decide which one was the true Sky Warrior. Most Indians were dismayed by the man's wicked behavior.

Joe and Clay refused to fight and insisted on working together on the mission. The chief and council agreed that was wise.

Joe handed Sun Cloud two flags from Jim — white truce and striped American — to fly over the camp to ward off Crow and white attacks until the trouble ended and peace ruled the territory.

"We are not weaklings who need enemy cloth to protect us!

We are warriors!" Knife Slayer proclaimed. "We will battle and slay any man who attacks us!"

"A good and wise warrior knows when to fight, when to retreat, and when to compromise, Knife-Slayer," Clay told him.

"Your mind has been captured by whites!" the angry man accused.

"Your mind and heart live in the past," Clay retorted. "It is a new time. To survive, you must forget old days and make peace. If you care little for your life and safety, think of those of your people."

Hawk Eyes caught Knife-Slayer's arm and pulled him back to his sitting mat. "Forgive my son," he said. "His blood burns hot to punish those who threaten us. It is hard for a warrior to sit while others ride against his foes. Is there not a task he can do for his people?"

Joe leapt at the chance to appease the medicine man and his son. "Yes, Shaman, there is an important and daring task for Knife-Slayer, if he wants it. He can ride with Running Badger to the camps of Red Cloud and Spotted Tail to tell them all we have learned."

"How is that important and daring?" the warrior scoffed.

"The Army, Crow, and evil men are searching for me and Morning Star in that area. You'll have to use great prowess to sneak by them to visit and then to return. I know you're skilled at tracking and raiding. Are you also skilled at crossing open land without being seen and captured?"

Knife-Slayer took the challenge. "I will go."

"Why do you send Running Badger, not me?" Night Stalker asked. "Do you not trust us together?"

"The son of the chief is needed here, Night Stalker. If your father is slain or injured, you must lead your people and defend them."

Morning Star grasped Joe's ruses to keep the two warriors separated. She hoped the men would be too busy to get into trouble while the matter was being settled. The third — her opponent in one of the contests — was an excellent choice to accompany and control the headstrong Knife-Slayer.

Clay comprehended the ruse, too, and was impressed by

Joe's wits. He looked forward to getting to know Joseph Lawrence better.

Joe, Morning Star, and Clay departed with the cattle at dawn. They followed the White River toward Fort Tabor at a good pace. They used all of the daylight hours, then camped at dusk. But at night, the new moon offered no help with security and the three took shifts doing guard duty, allowing each more sleep and providing all with protection.

As they traveled, the three became close friends. Morning Star was taught more about the white world, her next challenge. She enjoyed the easy rapport and Clay's lessons. She thought he was an excellent choice as Joe's best friend, though no one could replace Tanner. She was happy that Sky Warrior agreed that she and Joe were perfect for each other, but he continued to warn them of serious obstacles they would confront soon.

Seven days later, they made their last camp of this trek, a third of a day's travel, with the herd from the fort.

Before darkness shadowed the land, Joe left them to fetch Jim's latest message. He was delighted to find a letter from home in the hiding spot, as he had told his mother in May to contact him through the officer. As instructed, she had addressed it to Lucas Reardon, his nephew's name, for secrecy and protection.

Joe thought that his family might not have received his mid-June letter yet, and surely not the one he had written in early July. Nor had there been enough time for a response to either one to reach him. Joe recalled he had related news in June about meeting Morning Star and her people and told a little about the work he planned in this area. Two weeks ago, he had revealed his love for the woman and his proposal to her. He knew his parents would be surprised by this, and would realize the task before all of them would not be an easy one. Yet he was certain they would be happy about his impending marriage and the thought of having grandchildren by their only son to carry on the family name. He wished he could have told them about his love in person, but he didn't want to arrive home with a fiancée about whom they had heard nothing.

Joe ripped open the letter from his mother. He knew he must hurry, but he wanted to read it in private. He covered the business, political, and social news, grinning at the way Annabelle Lawrence related some of it. His mother always tried to find something good or amusing in every situation. She possessed a special knack for lightening burdens, lessening tension, and getting to the truth of a matter.

Joe chuckled at humorous remarks about his nephew's recent antics. She said everyone was doing fine and missed him. She was praying for his safe return by Christmas. He halted a moment as he caught a change of tone in the letter that caused love and a smidgen of homesickness to swell in his chest and constrict his throat. He had been gone almost a year, but it suddenly seemed longer. He loved and missed his parents, and his sister and her family. He was eager for them to meet Morning Star, and for her to meet them. He was positive all of them would get along splendidly. Such thoughts called the Indian beauty to mind, and he galloped back to her.

Morning Star had their meal ready when Joe returned. The steers grazed near the water, as did the horses. Clay was standing lookout. As soon as his mount was unsaddled and tended, Joe approached the fire. They ate, then went over Jim's news.

Joe summarized the information as he read Jim's words. "Says Stede and Tom are checking on Orin McMichael, Simon Adams, and Harvey Meade. They've sent men to question the local authorities. I hadn't thought of suggesting that kind of investigation; it could be helpful," Joe commented, then went back to reading. "Jim's happy about that last message I left two weeks ago telling him about Red Cloud, Spotted Tail, and Two-Bulls' agreement for truce. He's upset that Black Moon and Talking Wolf have had illegal dealings with Zeke. Says he won't investigate that part yet and risk endangering us. He doesn't want the Crow coming after us, too.

Says he hasn't seen Zeke since his last message. He's visited Simon and Harvey, but nothing new there. He is keeping a tight eye on Sergeant Bartholomew Carnes. He's real pleased with the evidence I left for him and with our destruction of those weapons and whiskey. What's this?" Joe murmured, rereading the last few lines.

"Damn," he muttered. "It says Stede warned us that Corporal George Hollis shot a soldier and fled when he was questioned about being here. Says for us to be on alert for the deserter. They chased him northwest, but he got away. Stede and Tom think he'll make his way here to his boss."

"At least we know he's guilty," Clay surmised for all three. "If we could get our hands on him, we could *persuade* him to talk."

"Or get our grips on Zeke or Farley. We know they're in on this mess. We can't beat information out of Simon or Bart since we haven't fully connected them to the case." He related Jim's warnings concerning the necessity of acting within the legal framework.

"Tell me, Joe, if there are as many attacks and they're as bad as this Jim says, why isn't the Army over here doing more to check them out? With Red Heart and Oglala clues left at the scenes, why haven't white men banded together and retaliated? How is this Jim keeping the homesteaders and his soldiers under control?"

"I don't doubt the raids, Clay, but nobody can prove who did them. Even if they're tempted, I don't think there are enough men to mount an attack on a strong Indian camp. As for the Army, besides hanging back to let us work on this trouble, they don't usually intrude on Indian conflicts with each other unless it gets big and nasty. From the way it looks, those boys at Fort Tabor are happy not to ride out and challenge the mighty Lakotas. If it's Jim you don't trust, see what you think about him when you two meet. You'll need to return that evidence from the payroll massacre that I borrowed, explain again how it was faked. Give him Knife-Slayer's scanty description of Snake-Man, be sure to tell him what you learned in St. Louis, and let him know you're joining us. The return of the cattle should convince any hotheads there the Red Hearts don't want any trouble."

"What are you planning to do?"

"Morning Star and I will ride back to Bear Butte and see if we can pick up Zeke's trail. With luck, he's so mad that he'll head straight for his boss and leave us clear tracks to follow. While we're gone, you nose around those posts. If you see any of our suspects, watch them closely. We should be back near Pierre in . . ." He calculated the distance and timing. "Ten to twelve days. Meet us two miles upriver and two miles westward."

The couple and Clay Thorne parted at dawn. The half-breed herded the steers toward the fort and to meet with Captain Thomas. Morning Star and Joe headed northwest toward the site of their last victory.

Clay would reach his destination by noon. Morning Star and Joe would reach theirs after four days of long and hard riding across relatively flat prairieland.

Joe and Morning Star scouted the location, found it unoccupied, and camped in the trees near the sacred mountain. They planned to follow the wagon ruts tomorrow. They tended the horses, ate, and bathed.

The full moon and a glowing campfire brightened the clearing where the couple shared a bedroll and snuggled in each other's arms. As they kissed and caressed, the blankets around their bodies slipped away. Their love was so pure and real, that neither was embarrassed by their nakedness.

"You're so beautiful, and I love you so much," he murmured.

"We are mates in our hearts. One day we will join under your law. If my people do not battle us, we will become mates under my law before we leave. I love you. I must remain with you."

Joe stroked the raven hair that flowed like a river of ebony silk around her shoulders and spilled forth upon his bedroll. It framed the most exquisite face he had seen anywhere. He

364

gazed into the warm chocolate eyes that expressed her deep feelings. Besides his mother and sister, she was the most gentle and loving person he had known. If he made love to her every day, it would not be enough to feed his insatiable craving for her. She intoxicated him more than any liquor, and bewitched him as no other could. She was a part of him, a part he must not live without. He could not voyage through the rest of his existence without her as the gentle wind behind his sails, caressing him and being the source of his power. The months with her had proven he had made a wise choice in loving her and proposing to her.

Morning Star trailed her fingers over Joe's face. She enjoyed any contact with him, whether it was emotional or physical. She traced the strong jawline where two tiny nicks exposed his haste while shaving earlier. There was such joy in touching him and watching him. She guided her fingers down his throat, aware of the rapid pulse there. One hand halted for a time to feel the pounding of his heart, knowing she and their contact were the reasons for it. This was what Singing Wind felt with Sun Cloud, what Alisha Williams had experienced with Gray Eagle long ago. It was real, special, rare. It was the tight bond and true love that all couples should find and keep. It was wrong and cruel to deny such emotions, for others to prevent them. Yes, her heart concurred with what Joe was thinking, she had made a wise choice in loving him and agreeing to marry him, no matter what that decision demanded of her.

Joe's hands savored the tautness of her breasts, the flatness of her abdomen, the ridges of her rounded hips, the lithe length of her sleek legs, and those secret places only he had visited. For a time he wanted and needed only Morning Star to be his reality, to control his feelings, to engulf his heart.

Their bare flesh met and clung as they explored each other's body with leisure and skill. They had learned from experience what pleased the other, but found it difficult to prolong this wondrous foreplay. Their lips met and traveled on for a while to sample other delights. Their fingers roamed every area within reach until both writhed with heightened need. Each knew when the time came to join their bodies.

At first, they moved slowly, seductively. As their hungers increased and they embraced fiercely, tightly, possessively, seizing rapturous ecstasy, reveling in every moment it consumed them. Even when contentment and relaxation came, they did not separate. They held on to the satisfaction of this long-awaited joining. They never knew when another total sharing was possible, so they must drink every drop of nourishment from this one to sustain them to the next.

The couple examined the wagon ruts and horse droppings at the site. Joe arrived at the same conclusion as Morning Star. The Crow rode north; Zeke rode east; and one man on an unshod horse followed their trail.

"A big storm came. Zeke could not leave for two suns," she deduced from the amount of manure and ashes. "Mother Earth will not let him travel easy. She will pull at the wagon to slow him for us. Streams will slow and fight him. He left *ake zaptan* days ago." She held up that number of fingers.

"Fifteen," Joe reminded her.

She smiled and continued. "He travels . . . east. Much rain on Mother Earth does not hide his trail; it becomes deep."

"Deeper," he grinned as he corrected, knowing that's what she wanted him to do. "Let's ride to see how fast he's going and to where."

Before nightfall, Morning Star said, "More rain came. Hard. Zeke camped . . . one day. I cannot tell what day. Horse chips are wet and—"

"Scattered," he filled in as they looked at the disintegrating clue.

"I read how dry they are and how they fall apart to learn time."

"That's all right, love. At least we know he was slowed a little. Wherever he was heading, he should be there by now. We'll stay on his trail. We don't have to worry about that warrior; he rode southeast."

366

"It is Grizzly Bear," she speculated with instinctive accuracy.

Tuesday afternoon, Morning Star halted to study the ground and concluded, "Zeke moved faster, but he lost time. Streams were full, they were hard to cross in wagon. He is only . . . six days ahead."

"Yep, and riding straight for Pierre and Simon Adams."

"Or to get more guns and whiskey. Crow must be plenty mad."

"I suppose his direction doesn't tell us much, does it?"

"Yep," she said with a laugh. "If he is not gone, we can see what he does and where he goes. We can follow and spy, perhaps capture."

"If we get near him, we will. Clay and I can make him talk."

At six, they halted on the Cheyenne River. Before camping, they split up to scout the area and arranged to meet back there when done. Leaving their packhorse concealed in the cottonwoods, Joe headed to check north and east while Morning Star rode south.

She completed her part in thirty minutes, finding nothing and no one in that direction. While she awaited Joe's return, she made camp. She gathered scrubwood and arranged it, but would not light a fire until he said it was safe. She readied the supplies to cook their meal, filled canteens, and spread out their bedrolls. If he arrived and said the location wasn't a good spot, she could quickly repack everything. He would make certain that he would not let whatever threat he saw follow him here.

More time passed. The waning full moon appeared low in the eastern sky, a pale white ball against a still-blue backdrop. Morning Star scanned the horizon, straining her eyes and ears for Joe's approach. She paced as she waited and watched, and became anxious. She knew something was wrong; Joe should have returned by now. With dusk now blanketing the land, she realized daylight would be gone in half an hour, and tracking would be difficult by moonglow. It was vital to begin a prompt search for him and see what the problem was. She worried that he had been injured or had encountered enemies. As he was to ride only a few miles in both directions, she leapt on Hanmani's bare back with her weapons and fieldglasses. With wariness and vigilance, she trailed Star's hoofprints to find Joe.

It did not take long to locate the alarming spot where two men on unshod horses had apparently intercepted him: Crow, she fretted. It appeared they had been concealed in trees at the riverbank, then sprung upon her love. The condition of the attackers' tracks exposed the fast movement of a surprise attack, as did Star's prints indicating an abrupt halt and nervous prancing.

Morning Star sighed in relief at not sighting Joe's body or blood, which indicated he had been captured. She dismounted and walked to where the Bird People had recovered hidden horses, also unshod and probably stolen. She knew the other animals carried no riders, as their tracks were not deep enough to be bearing weight. Using her fieldglasses in the fading light, she moved with caution. As darkness arrived, she saw smoke rising from trees along the river. She left her Appaloosa and sneaked closer. When she could study the enemy camp without continuing farther, she halted, as she must not allow her scent or sounds to reach her foes. She had to prevent her capture in order to rescue Joe.

Two enemy warriors sat at a small campfire close to the water. They laughed, talked, drank whiskey, and went through Joe's saddlebags. Her love was bound to a tree, twenty feet from the men and blaze, edging the grassland. There were no other trees or bushes close to him to provide concealing assistance to carry out her rescue. He did not appear to be harmed. His horse was with the other five, to the right of the villains.

Morning Star studied the site. She couldn't approach from the water; with the river wide and the bank low and beneath a full moon, she would be seen swimming across or surfacing for air or coming ashore. She could not sneak in on the right, as the horses would catch her smell and expose her. To the left, there was nothing close enough to use for cover to begin a successful attack. Around Joe, there was nothing to use for freeing him, and his tree was too slender to hide her forward movement. She needed more feet to obtain an accurate shot at the warriors with either bow or gun. Under a bright full moon, she could not even crawl closer in the open on her belly. The braves had selected this location and Joe's confining post with great skill and caution.

She tensed as one man stood on liquor-shaky legs and staggered to Joe. The warrior looked the prisoner up and down. He laughed and pointed and poked while he made insults for his friend's enjoyment. She moved two trees closer to the scene, unable to get nearer without risking being noticed and captured or slain. She could hear one villain's words.

"You bad white man. You in big trouble. We capture for Zeke. He want you plenty bad. He give many horses, goods for trade. Zeke talk, kill."

Morning Star realized they were holding Joe for Zeke Randall to question — and inevitably, slay. But that meant he was safe for now. She could leave to prepare herself for his rescue, using the only desperate plan that came to mind. She retraced the path to her camp.

Morning Star lay on her stomach under a blanket covered with grass. She had captured several fireflies and secured them with blades to the disguise over her. Their flickers of light would imply to her foes that any movement they glimpsed was only grass swaying in the breeze; those brief flashes would say nothing could be near or under the insects, or they would take flight. Every few minutes, she inched herself and her weapons closer to Joe. The Crow were at their campfire, drinking and snooping through her love's possessions. It took a long time and great patience to cover the open distance from where she began the belly trek to her destination.

Finally she reached the confining tree. Using Joe's larger body as a shield, she eased from beneath the blanket and

369

stood behind him. "I am here," she whispered to prevent startling him, then touched his bound hands. "Do not move or speak. It is like my rescue long ago." She sliced through the rope, careful not to cut him, then placed his pistol in his freed grasp. "When I say *now*, kill the one on the right. I will shoot the one on the left," she instructed, glad she recalled the direction words.

After he cocked the hammer and she placed her arrow, she saw the warriors stand to be excused before taking to their sleeping mats. "Now!" She gave the signal, stepped from behind her love, and fired at her target.

Joe swung his armed hand around and fired at his. Both braves were slain. He whirled to sweep her into his embrace, kiss her, and praise her courage and wits. He listened to her explanation of how she had planned and carried out the rescue. "Thanks, love. I was so worried about you. I was afraid they'd retrace my trail and take you by surprise, too."

"Come, we must hurry. We will take your possessions and return to our camp. It is ready. We must eat and sleep, and go from here fast."

"It's almost like Zeke expected us to track him, so he planted these men here to stop us. He doesn't want us to know where he's going. That could mean it's straight to his boss, and he's riding for Pierre."

"We will know soon. We must stay alert. More Crow may be chasing us." Morning Star realized that caution meant no more nights of sharing a bedroll, of nights spent separated by guard duty. She dreaded the perilous suns and moons ahead. She craved a quick and successful victory that would allow them to be together again as lovers.

Thursday, they neared Pierre. Zeke's wagon ruts continued on into the settlement. They hadn't encountered any more Crow ambushers, nor had they found Red Cloud still camped on Plum Creek. They rode for the location where Clay was to meet them, but they were a day early from their swift pace and sunrise-to-sunset schedule. Two miles upriver and two miles west of water from Pierre, they reached the meeting spot.

Clay Thorne was waiting for them. "You're back early," he said.

As they dismounted, Joe remarked, "You, too. Learn anything?"

"I reported to Jim like you said. We got along fine. No trouble over returning those cattle. We told everybody I found them grazing on the river and herded them in. He's sending another report to Fort Laramie. Jim was worried about you two going back to Bear Butte and tracking Zeke. I told him you two would be fine."

"We almost didn't make it," Joe revealed, then related the events and findings of their journey.

Clay was amazed by Morning Star's skills and courage, and he praised her for them. "You're right about him coming to Pierre. Before I get to that part, I'll tell you about Farley. He was at Fort Tabor when I arrived."

"What was he doing there? Spying? Reporting to Bart?"

Clay shrugged as he replied, "Don't know. I followed him to Lookout. He talked with Meade, then left."

Joe was surprised by that news. "He visited Harvey Meade? Why?"

"Don't know, couldn't get close enough to hear anything. Looked to be just a friendly conversation and rest stop."

Joe didn't like this unexpected twist, as he trusted Harvey. "But Meade is out of the way between Fort Tabor and Pierre."

"Yep, but that's all I saw. I trailed him to Pierre. He met Zeke there."

Joe caught what he thought was a contradiction. "Wait a minute, Clay. Farley was with Zeke at Bear Butte. It must have been someone else."

"That was four weeks past, Joe," the half-breed pointed out. "He had plenty of time to get to Fort Tabor after he split up with Zeke. It was him."

"Zeke must have sent him ahead to report the trouble with us," Joe surmised. "But why would Farley ride to Bart instead of to Snake-Man? Unless Zeke's the only one who knows who their boss is." The blond argued against his own

371

speculation. "But if that were true, Zeke wouldn't need to report our mischief so fast to Bart. That's real strange. I didn't get to meet Sergeant Carnes and size him up. Did you see Farley talk with anyone else?" Clay shook his head, and Joe added, "Did you meet Bart Carnes?"

"No time." Clay responded. "I took care of business with Jim fast because Farley was getting ready to pull out when I arrived. Jim pointed him out to me, but he didn't know who Farley met or if he met with *anyone*. I hurried because I wanted to make sure I didn't lose sight of him."

"That was smart, but I wish one of us knew something about Bart."

"What does Jim say about him?"

"Not much more than he's mean, tough, tight-lipped, and hates Indians. His name on that land-buying list doesn't mean much if we can't tie him to the trouble. Talking with Zeke and Farley isn't a crime and can't be used as evidence. My gut instinct says there's an important reason why Bart was contacted so fast. Maybe he's the leader we're after. He's certainly in a position to know the movements of the Army and the Indians. He's also sitting in the right saddle to use hired soldiers to frame Red Hearts for raids he's investigating. Besides, who would suspect an Army officer of instigating an Indian uprising? Or of being Snake-Man? Damn," Joe muttered, "just what we don't need, another suspect as boss."

"What if Farley only went to fort to see if we go there to tell Army about the guns and our attack?" Morning Star speculated, and Joe nodded.

"Makes sense," Clay remarked. "Anyhow, Zeke and Farley took a keelboat upriver. I rode along the bank to make sure they didn't get off anyplace. When I reached Orin McMichael's, they were there. So was a man called George, but he wasn't in uniform. He stayed hidden except to sneak out at night to catch air, take a smoke, and use the little house. I watched the post for two days. It's real busy this time of year; lots of men were around. Those three were staying in Orin's house. They looked pretty settled in for a while, so I left yesterday to ride here to leave you a message. I was planning on

372

heading back in the morning to watch them. Seems to me they're meeting with their boss, Orin McMichael."

Joe pondered those facts. "But Orin has red hair," he told Clay, "Knife-Slayer said Snake-Man's is black. But if Orin isn't working with those villains, why would they be meeting there and staying in his home?"

"He looked at me as the boss Clem . . ." Morning Star reminded.

"Described," Joe filled in for her. "If Snake-Man has a craving for young Indian girls like Clem said, Orin would fit that. Simon Adams certainly doesn't keep any around."

"If Orin has magic balls to use," Morning Star suggested, "maybe he has a way to make his hair black to fool everyone. Snake-Man has many tricks."

"You're right," Joe said, excited and pleased. "It fits together perfectly. All three suspects are there with their boss. It has to be Orin. Zeke and Farley thought they'd throw any pursuer off their trail by using a boat to leave Pierre. They know we can't come around without being recognized. They think they're safe to come and go as they please now. As for George Hollis, that deserter has to stay hidden a while."

"It does fit, Joe. It must be McMichael. That means he knows you two from your visit there. But he doesn't know me. I'll head back in the morning and see what more I can learn."

"That's good, Clay. We'll ride to Fort Tabor and share our conclusions with Jim. As soon as we leave him a message, we'll sneak to meet you." Joe described the safest location to join up near Orin's post.

As the three headed out for their separate tasks, they did not know that the men they sought were in Pierre and plotting worse mischief . . .

Saturday, Clay reached Orin's, to discover all three suspects were gone. He surmised they had taken a boat downriver. He headed back to warn the couple of approaching peril.

By Sunday evening, Joe and Morning Star found a concealed location on the White River near the fort and made camp. At dawn, they would head for Orin's trading post to rejoin Clay Thorne in a few days.

Joe rode to the message tree, where he found a missive from Captain Thomas and another letter from home. Knowing Morning Star was safe in the dense treeline and on alert, he decided to open both there, in case either related bad news. Morning Star was sensitive to his moods and expressions, and he didn't want to worry her. He focused on the note first and smiled as he learned that Stede, Tom, and troops were coming from Fort Laramie. As the date for the proposed treaty council was approaching, they wanted to help settle the problem here as quickly as possible. They were expected to arrive in two weeks. Joe frowned as he read that Bart was acting strange and might suspect Jim of working with Joe. Jim warned the couple to be on guard until help arrived.

Joe hoped Jim would visit the exchange spot either tonight or early tomorrow so they could talk. If not, Jim would find his message soon and would mail the concealed letter to his parents.

After Joe ripped open the letter from his mother, he realized it was a response to his mid-June one about more news of Morning Star and his work here. When Annabelle wrote her letter, she hadn't known about his early July revelation of love and marriage. By now, his family knew everything, and probably another letter was on the way to congratulate him.

Joe was glad his mother understood the hunger in him, his search for something he hadn't quite been able to comprehend or explain. She grasped how exciting and fulfilling his mission was. Best of all, she had convinced his father of those truths. That made Joe happy, as he deeply loved and respected both his parents. He laughed aloud when his mother teased him about soon losing his heart to the Indian beauty who obviously had stolen his eye, especially since he had guarded them so well for twenty-eight years. It no longer amazed Joe that Annabelle was so perceptive and intuitive, as was Morning Star. He knew the two women, along with his sister, would become fast friends.

Yet Joe detected a subtle coaxing for him to return home

as soon as possible, and he pondered if something was wrong there. He was eager to see them all again. Those yearnings increased as he envisioned his parents. Their mental images revealed they were older than Joe had realized before this reflective moment.

Suddenly he was anxious to spend time with them before it was too late. Perhaps advancing age and declining health were the real reasons his father had urged him not to make this journey and to take control of the shipping business this year. Joe had not considered those possibilities before, and his proud father would never admit them. Yes, he needed to go home as soon as he settled matters here.

Those worries evoked a need to be near the woman he loved, who would share his life as the first Joseph had Annabelle's. He pocketed the letter and note, then mounted to get back to her.

Morning Star sensed her love's serious mood. When she questioned him, Joe told her about the letter from home and its effect on him. "It is good they understand why you came here and why you must stay until the sacred mission is done. It is good to love and miss family, to have a strong bond. It is good they do not warn you to not love me. I will learn fast and make them proud of me. I will not dishonor you or your family."

Joe pulled her into his arms to hug and kiss her. "I love you, woman."

"I love you," she responded before their lips meshed. Morning Star was relieved by the news from Joe's mother. She could relax now, knowing they would accept and help her. She prayed her family would be as kind and understanding, and feared they would not.

Joe and Morning Star did not break camp before they heard a loud noise—the sound of many horses galloping northward from the fort on a worn trail. He told her to stay hidden while he investigated. With his fieldglasses, Joe saw that Captain James Thomas was not with the troop; rather the man leading it was burly, brown-haired, and wearing sergeant's stripes.

A homesteader in a wagon came along, obviously leaving the sutler's store after spending the night at the fort. Joe halted him and queried the commotion so early in the day.

"Captain Thomas and a deserter were killed yesterday. Sergeant Carnes said it was the work of an outlaw named Joseph Lawrence and his renegade squaw. Woodhawks saw 'em canoeing upriver toward Pierre. He's gone to pursue 'em and capture 'em. I hope he catches 'em fast. We don't need no murderers and savages causing more trouble in these parts."

Joe concealed his shock. "Thanks, friend. Did Bart say what this Lawrence looks like? I don't want to run in to him by mistake."

"Nope, but he knows him. He's heading upriver, so this area's safe."

"Much obliged," Joe said, and watched the men leave.

He rejoined Morning Star and gave her the distressing news about Jim's murder, George's death, and the stunning accusation against them. He saw the panic in her eyes and cuddled her close to him. "I love you, woman. I promise I won't let anyone harm you."

"It is bad, Joe. What will we do?" she asked, worried.

"I bet anything Bart killed both of them, and he's using the Army and that fake charge to kill us. That's probably what Farley came to tell him. Nobody saw us going upriver, so that was a lie. But what's behind it? Bart has to be going to join up with Zeke and Farley in Pierre. George must have come downriver by boat after Clay left Orin's. I bet Zeke and Farley are on the move, too. That means Clay should be back near Pierre. Something's bad wrong, love. I have to follow that patrol to see who Bart meets. You'll go home while Clay and I settle this. I don't want you in any more danger."

Morning Star embraced Joe and refused. "No, I stay with you. If soldiers, Crow, and bad men are looking for us, I am safe with you."

Joe held her in his arms as they drew comfort and courage from each other. This mission was more dangerous than he ever imagined it could be when he started it with Tanner. The villains were determined to stop them any way possible. Joe wondered if they would be called upon to sacrifice their lives for peace. He asked himself if it was *his* duty to continue, if it was *his* war, *his* fate, a reason for both of them to lose their lives. They had given this task their best efforts. Why couldn't they just accept they were battling overwhelming odds and retreat? Why couldn't they just leave the perils and sacrifices behind and ride away to Virginia? He knew why not. Morning Star would never give up this sacred task and ride away at this point in time; she would never desert her family, tribe, and vision orders. That meant he could not leave her in danger or risk losing her. Besides, so much was at stake, and he had made himself a part of this situation. They couldn't quit now; they had come too far in solving this mystery. "All right, love, you come with me; it's safer. We'll free the packhorse here and get rid of any extra supplies. We can't be slowed down if we're sighted and have to run for our lives. First, we need to retrieve my message to Jim and my letter to Mother."

Joe and Morning Star hid the horses behind a hillock and lay on their stomachs at its crest. From their distant and lofty position, they had time to flee to safety and had a view of the trail to the post. They could see who came and went from Pierre after Bart and his patrol entered the settlement, if the men came by land. Suddenly, they were using the river for speed and for secrecy in movement. That worried him, because they could not track men in boats or keep up with crafts from horseback.

They waited and watched for hours. The late-July sun seared down on them. So vital was their task that they ignored their discomforts. At last, dusk appeared with its darkening and cooling shadows.

Joe continuously scanned the landscape with his fieldglasses. He sighted their new partner coming from Pierre. "It's Clay. Too far for shouting. I don't want to ride out and meet him. If anyone comes by, I don't want us seen together. How can I signal him?" he wondered aloud.

"Flaming arrow," Morning Star suggested.

"Let me see if anyone else will sight it," he murmured, searching the terrain through the fieldglasses. "Looks all right. Let's do it."

Joe used a safety match to light the cloth wrapped around the arrowhead. Morning Star fired it into the air at a southeast angle. Joe saw Clay's head follow the fiery shaft's flight, then retrace its path. He watched the man think a moment, then ride to where the arrow landed.

Clay poured water from his canteen onto the burning rag to prevent a prairie fire. He studied his surroundings and figured it was safe to check out the unusual message. He hoped he was right about who sent it.

When the half-Cheyenne warrior dismounted behind the hillock, he didn't smile. "Big trouble, you two."

"We know. We trailed Bart's patrol from Fort Tabor. The bastard murdered Jim and George and framed us. Did you see who he met?"

"Yep, Zeke and Farley. But you've got more trouble than that; Simon Adams is dead. Those snakes must have left Orin's while I was camped with you. Somehow they lured Adams away from the post and into an ambush. He was found shot not far away in a wagon with guns and whiskey— not many, just enough to make their point. Charge is, you came here after killing Jim and George at Tabor to silence your partner in crime."

"That's crazy! They can't prove I was anywhere near Pierre."

"Problem is," Clay informed them, "he had a letter on him to you, Joe, about how good your plan to provoke the Sioux against the Crow and whites was going. They were smart; they had Simon write it. They checked his script against the post's books. I don't know if they forced him or he worked with them or if he just joined up with them. Those are some powerful charges against you two. With Jim gone, you don't have any protection now. With Bart in control and working with the villains, you two should hide for a while, but not in your camp, Morning Star. If the Army finds you there, your people will be in great danger."

Joe told his new friend about Jim's message saying help was on the way. "All we have to do is stay out of their sights until it arrives. Now that we know who Snake-Man is and who's working for him, I have a scheme for entrapping that bastard and his gang. While we fetch something we need to make it work, you watch for Stede and the soldiers near Fort Tabor. Try to catch them before Bart and the others know they're in the territory. We need secrecy for my plan to work." He explained it to Clay and Morning Star. She smiled and nodded agreement.

But Clay ventured, "What if Jim never got his message sent? What if the soldier he assigned to deliver it is one of Snake-Man's boys? Or what if he never reaches Fort Laramie? Lots of dangers between here and there. Besides, what you've got in mind is risky. Crazy," he added.

Before dawn, Joe gave Clay a letter to mail home, addressed to his sister to pass through Pierre, changing his contact to Stede. He told his family he would finish his mission and leave here in six to eight weeks. The couple headed west to fetch an item needed to carry out their daring plan.

Clay, who would leave soon, watched them ride away. He shook his head. If Joe's plan didn't get them killed, the forces after them might. All they could all do was hope that help was on the way.

Chapter Seventeen

A week later at Slim Buttes, Joe and Morning Star spied on Black Moon's camp from a rock formation near the site. The invisible new moon allowed them to get close without being seen. Many campfires illuminated the Crow area enough to see what was taking place.

They had ridden fast and hard to carry out their hazardous task, the August days providing long hours of needed daylight. They had stayed on full alert, but confronted no peril during the arduous journey.

They were glad sunset had released them from the demands of the summer heat. The area needed rain, and they would welcome its cooling effect. The ground was dry and hard. Prairie grasses had changed to shades of yellow, tan, and gold. Some had withered, but most were of hearty varieties well suited to this climate. Animals were still abundant, as if no tribe had slaughtered many for winter rations.

The camp beyond them was busy and noisy. Two wagons stood to its right with four white strangers. Women and children rummaged contents of crates and cloth sacks. Indian men were in a section of trees to the left, guzzling the recently arrived whiskey and examining the trinkets.

"Must be those four men who escaped our attack at Rake's Hollow," Joe whispered. "Looks as if Orin has sent plenty of firewater and gifts to settle them down until more guns and ammunition arrive."

Morning Star concurred with his conclusions. She listened to the drumming that provided music for the drunken warriors to dance to. The braves moved about as they laughed, shared tall tales of past exploits, and boasted of future raids on the Lakotas. Such bloody plans had to be prevented, even at the cost of her life. She didn't know how either or both of them could get to the chief to steal the watch Orin had given to him, the bait needed to lure their foe into Joe's clever trap. She invoked the Great Spirit's help, guidance, and protection.

After two hours of drinking and merrymaking, Black Moon staggered to a fallen tree, sank to the ground, and rested his head against it. He appeared to be dazed or asleep. Every so often, a few women brought over food, delivered more whiskey in buffalo paunches, and obeyed other orders.

Morning Star recognized the opportunity the Great Spirit had placed before her eyes. As was common on such an occasion, where food and drink were in such wild abundance, the men paid little attention to the females serving their needs. "I will cover my hair and shoulders with a blanket to hide my face and Arapaho markings," she told Joe. "I can sneak to Black Moon, pretend to help him, and take the possession we need."

"It's too dangerous. You'll be in the middle of those crazy warriors."

Morning Star knew the risk she would be taking. She was scared, but confident. "I will be careful. He is away from the others. Women come and go. It is the only path to victory. I must walk it, fast and alone."

Joe studied the area as he recalled how cunningly she had rescued him and all she had done at his side. It was a big risk, but she could do it. Too, it was the only way to get their hands on that bait. If they could pull off his trap, war would be averted and their future could begin. He agreed.

Morning Star tossed a blanket over her head and positioned it around her face and shoulders. With the assistance of the dark moon, she crept toward the site. She lowered her head and casually went to where the chief lay, snoring and sprawled on the ground. She knelt and straightened his limbs, placed another folded blanket beneath his head, and lifted an empty water pouch that reeked of whiskey. As Joe had instructed, she unfastened the musical watch from the cut in Black Moon's vest where he wore it. She secreted it into her garments, then did the same with his knife as a raid gift for her father. She rose, with lowered head, and left the trees. She was quickly encompassed by dark shadows and ran with skill and caution to Joe's side.

"You did it," he praised her success, then kissed her.

Morning Star allowed herself to relax for the first time since leaving him. She returned the kiss, elated by her daring coup.

When they parted, he said, "Let's make tracks, woman."

"No, we must not. We do not wish them to follow us."

Joe chuckled softly. "That means, let's leave fast," he explained.

They rode ten miles in the darkness, traveling at a walk to prevent accidents. They camped on Antelope Creek, too weary to do more than take turns standing guard and sleeping.

Friday around five-thirty, they reached Spearfish Canyon. Morning Star told him the direction to take while she rode to the rear, concealing their trail to the lovely location. The valley near the northern boundary of the Black Hills was lush and green, smelling of spruce and pine and fresh air. It was sheltered from the outside world, but unused this time of year when the Plains beckoned nomadic hunters. Ebony peaks, spires, and rocks loomed beyond their gazes. Timber and grass were abundant. Deer, elk, and birds favored the enclosed area. A towering waterfall cascaded over a line of ivory limestone cliffs, its roar loud. The rush of liquid was so white that almost looked like running ice or snow. The clear blue creek it created journeyed for miles through the area, playing around rocks or twigs in its path.

Joe looked around and smiled. It was the perfect spot to spend what would probably be their last time together until victory was won and their love revealed. They could remain here only tonight and a short time tomorrow. It would require three to four days to reach Sun Cloud's third camp of the season, which Morning Star said he would be at by now. Their rest in this canyon would provide safety while Clay guided help to

Sun Cloud at Buffalo Gap. If all went as planned, they would be in her father's tepee only one or two days—hopefully not long enough to endanger the Red Hearts.

Joe tended the horses while she unpacked their supplies. As the two animals grazed, he went with her to collect firewood. As they foraged for fuel to feed the fire, Joe felt a thump on his back. He turned as Morning Star tossed another pinecone at him, then giggled as her eyes sparkled.

"A big coup to strike great warrior without slaying him," she jested.

"Is that so?" he replied with a broad grin. "I thought you had to touch the enemy without slaying him. Let's see if Sky Warrior can earn a coup."

When Joe came after her, Morning Star squealed, dropped the wood, and raced behind a spruce. She darted from side to side as Joe attempted to round the tree and capture her. They both laughed as they romped like children in the idyllic location, perils forgotten for a while.

"You're fast and clever, woman, but I'll get you," he playfully warned.

Morning Star dashed for the stream, thinking Joe would halt. She hurried to the waterfall. As she was splattered, she shrieked, "It is cold!"

Joe reached her, grasped her wrist, and pulled her toward him. "Let me warm you," he murmured as his mouth closed over hers.

They kissed with great need. Soon, the chilly water soaking them went unnoticed in the heat of rising passion. They removed their garments and flung the drenched items to the bank. They splashed and bathed themselves and each other. The water's temperature enlivened them as their bodies burned hotter with raging desires. They explored each other's flesh with hands and lips, removing clear drops in their paths.

Soon, Joe scooped her up in his arms and carried her to the lush grass. They rolled upon the soft surface as they tantalized and tempted each other beyond self-control. Grass tickled their skin, as did mischievous fingers and daring lips. Both were enthralled by the other and neither wanted to wait much longer.

Joe entered her body to join them together as one force striving for unity of hearts and spirits. He felt as if everything he was and knew was bound to this moment in time, to the love in his embrace. This woman tempted, sated, and completed him as no other ever could. He was eager for the day when everyone would know that truth, accept it, and abide by it.

Morning Star thrilled to the way Joe made her feel. He loved her fully, honestly, and thoroughly. She enjoyed giving him pleasure, and savored how his responses affected her. Just to touch him brought rapture. To gaze into his adoring eyes warmed her soul. To kiss him drove her wild. To feel his hands and mouth upon her evoked ecstasy. To mate with him was beauty and delight beyond measure and words.

They lay nestled as their bodies returned to normal. The grass made a soft bed. They gazed at the sky above and felt its tranquility within themselves. They listened to the rush of water over the cascade and to birds singing. They smelled clean air, evergreens, wildflowers, and the erotic scent of love. They were at peace in their verdant and romantic haven.

Finally, Joe teased, "If we don't get moving, love, we'll both be asleep. I'll wash off, then help you cook."

"I will join you, but it will be more cold. The sun goes to sleep. How do you say this?" she asked, knowing she had spoken wrong.

"I will join you, but the water will be colder. The sun is setting, or going down," he corrected, then he shifted to gaze to her eyes. As his fingers pushed aside stray hair from her lovely face, he murmured, "I love you, Morning Star. You've learned so much; I'm proud of you." His fingers caressed delicate features. "I want you and need you more than I realized. This will be over soon, then we'll leave to begin our life together. I can't wait to marry you and know you're mine forever."

Morning Star drew his mouth to hers and kissed him. She looked into his serene gaze and cautioned, "When we reach my camp, we must not reveal our feelings. We must wait until the sacred victory is ours."

A troubled look filled his blue eyes as a streak of panic ran through him. "Promise you won't change your mind about me," he urged.

Morning Star smiled and vowed, "I will not. I love you. We must be mates for life. But we must take no risk with victory."

"I understand and agree. We're too close to success to endanger it."

They made love again the following morning before they dressed. It was time to go home, to put their cunning plan into motion. They would camp tonight on Elk Creek; tomorrow night, on the southern branch of the Cheyenne. Late the next day, they would reach Buffalo Gap.

Monday nearing dusk, Joe and Morning Star walked their horses into Sun Cloud's last camp of the hunting season. Her parents and people halted their shared tasks to greet them. Both smiled and dismounted. Young braves took their mounts to tend them.

"Come, sit, rest," the chief invited the weary travelers. Sun Cloud's keen glance scanned both, but nothing seemed amiss. He did detect friendship and closeness, but that was not unusual for cousins and partners. He was glad they seemed to trust, like, and respect each other. The Great Spirit had brought them together and sent them on the sacred quest. Sun Cloud thanked his god for protecting his child and the son of Stede.

As they took places on the buffalo mats that Singing Wind spread for them, Buckskin Girl hurried forward to offer the couple refreshments. Morning Star knew her friend was anxious to hear news of her missing love, but both women realized that personal talk would have to wait until later.

"Tell us of your adventures," the chief encouraged.

People gathered around the seated group to hear news of their daring exploits. Elderly Red Heart males threw down mats for relaxation during the talk. Children pressed close to parents' legs. Warriors were on alert, eager to learn of any impending threat to their band. Women studied the handsome paleface with their leader's daughter. Night Stalker, his timid wife, and contrary son stood nearby, both parents grasping a hand of the unruly boy.

Joe related the events since their last report. He witnessed the awe and approval for Morning Star's participation, particularly her daring rescue of him from the Crow. He went over it in detail to give her all the credit she deserved. "She's out of danger now. Stede and Indian Agent Tom Fitzpatrick will arrive soon with help to finish the task. She will not need to leave camp again. You," he said to Sun Cloud, "will lead your band of warriors in the final battle, if there is one. I pray we can end the matter without a bloody conflict. We're certain Orin Mc-Michael is Snake-Man. After we send a brave warrior to him with the watch from Black Moon, he'll be forced to come and meet with the Crow chief and will be snared."

When Joe revealed how they had gotten hold of the token to be used in the trap, more praise was spoken for Morning Star. He watched her give her father Black Moon's knife as a raid prize. Joe saw the chief examine it, smile, then lean over to embrace her with pride.

"You have done as the sacred vision claimed, my daughter. Your coups are many and your legend will be great; they will shine as brightly as those of Gray Eagle. Songs will be sung and stories told of She-Who-Rode-With-The-Sky-Warrior. My heart feels much joy at your victories and safe return. I am glad you are home and your task is finished. Sky Warrior," he addressed Joe. "You have done well, my brother and friend. Bring me the gift I made for him to carry in the final battle," he instructed Wind Bird.

Wind Bird fetched the shield he had worked on for days.

Singing Wind was thrilled by her child's deeds and prowess, but was happy the girl was home to stay, out of peril's reach and away from the white man's temptation. Morning Star deserved a matching shield, but that was not their way. Yet, the girl's daring deeds would be painted on the tribe's and family's pictorial histories—buffalo hides that hung in the meeting lodge and their tepee.

Sun Cloud handed the gift to Joe and said, "It is the Shooting Star shield. It has big medicine. Few men have carried one. Only those whose signs are of the heavens—as are *Mahpiya Wicasta*—and who have earned the right to carry one may do so. My father was the last of our band to earn and carry such a powerful shield; Gray Eagle's was destroyed after his death to keep it from enemy hands. This one is yours, Tanner, for you have earned it."

Joe felt a twinge of guilt over deceiving the man who trusted and admired him, who rewarded him with their highest honor. He wished Tanner were here to share this moment, the past months, and the future. He handled and looked upon the object with gratitude and sacred reverence. It symbolized the essence of the powers of nature and their god. The sunburst that filled the center in blue, white, and yellow was of the colors of the heavens, the brown hide representing the earth. It was believed to protect its bearer from all dangers, physical and supernatural. A weasel pelt was suspended from the center, sign of the Great Spirit's messenger. Coup feathers, one for each of Joe's previous deeds, and good-luck tokens hung from the lower points between each peak of the sunburst. An eagle feather was attached with the weasel pelt, one from Sun Cloud's chief's bonnet. The shield was of tautly stretched buffalo hide on a willow frame. It would withstand arrows, lances, and even bullets.

Joe listened as the chief told him about such meanings and powers. "Thank you, Sun Cloud. I shall treasure it always, my brother and friend."

The chief noticed an emotional catch in the white man's throat that controlled his voice, and he was glad to find Joe so moved by the gesture, of which the Red Heart Council — with the exception of Knife-Slayer — approved.

The antagonistic warrior was so vexed by Joe's acceptance and great honor that he shouted, "We must not wait for bluecoats! We must ride to the post on the Big River and slay the one called Orin, as I killed Grizzly Bear who tracked Sky Warrior and Morning Star from Bear Mountain."

Night Stalker explained his friend's words to his confused sister and the white man. "He wears the scalp of Matohota on his war lance. He tracked you from the sacred mountain to slay you. Knife-Slayer found the camp where the Crow waited for you, and he attacked."

Joe thanked him, as did Morning Star, then praised his

skills. But he refuted the brave's suggestion, "We must ride with the Army and do this last deed by white law to stop the evil men."

"We cannot trust the whites and the white laws! We must not let soldiers ride into our camp. They will spy, return, and attack."

"Jim, Captain James Thomas at Fort Tabor, died helping your people, Knife-Slayer. He was a bluecoat, a white, a man of the white laws. If we do not trap Orin and his men with Black Moon's token, we have no proof he is guilty. Without proof, an attack will appear an act of war against whites. The Army will be forced to come here for retaliation instead of friendship. Surely Indians and whites can work together for truce this time. If Red Hearts lead the way at Bear Butte, all will know they want peace, not war. Everybody will know the charges against them are false, that they were Snake-Man's work. This is the great day all have awaited; do not spoil it now."

Sun Cloud and other council members spoke up before the warrior could argue. They agreed with Joe's clever plan. Blood rushed with excitement and suspense. Hearts pounded with eagerness. Mouths tasted sweet victory in the making. Eyes envisioned it upon the horizon. Hands knew all they had to do was reach out and seize it.

"Crow are sly, but we will fool them," the chief said with a chuckle. "It is a big laugh. A good victory. It will stop the trouble and prevent danger. We will ride with Sky Warrior and the bluecoats. We will follow the words of my uncle's son and the agent from Fort Laramie. We will have peace again. Men will hunt in safety. Women will work in safety. Children will play in safety. Old ones will sit beneath a safe sun to rest in their last days. This is what Grandfather promised in Payaba's vision. It will be so."

After a day and a half of rest and talk, a lookout galloped into camp to reveal that a unit of bluecoats was approaching. Joe seized his fieldglasses, mounted, and rode out with the warrior to see if it was the Fort Laramie troops or Sergeant

Bart Carnes with his men. He breathed easy when he sighted Clay Thorne, Stede Gaston, and Tom Fitzpatrick in the lead.

Joe rode to meet them. "Glad you finally made it. Sun Cloud and the Red Hearts are willing to work for peace and help with our trap." He reiterated what Clay had explained earlier, and the soldiers agreed. "Let's go work out the details. I want this settled before more incidents occur."

Sun Cloud and Stede Gaston eyed each other as the latter dismounted with difficulty after the long ride. They shook hands as Stede said, "It's an honor to finally meet you, Sun Cloud, and to be among my people. My father told me many great stories about his brother and kin. I'm only sorry it took me so long to visit you, particularly under such grim circumstances."

The chief liked his cousin's words and the sincerity of Stede's tone and gaze. He smiled in pleasure. "It is good to meet the son of Powchutu, Eagle's Arm, half brother to my father. We have many words to speak, many seasons to cover. First, there are other matters to discuss."

The white man was impressed by the chief's wits and command of English taught to him by his white mother. Stede liked this man, and he knew they would get along fine. "I'm eager to hear everything," Stede replied as he massaged his aching leg. "We've gotten excellent reports from him," he said, nodding to Joe. "He and your daughter have done a brave and fine thing for everyone concerned. You must be proud."

"I am proud of Morning Star and Tanner. Peace will come from their great deeds. Again, I will ride with a great warrior as I once did with your father. He died a brave man at the side of my father. When the war moon rises next, their sons will ride together and will survive the evil of their enemies. It will be a glorious day. Come, sit, rest, and eat. We will talk of past days and families after we have spoken of traps and peace with others."

Stede moved on a leg stiff from the past break that had prevented him from accompanying Joe after his son's murder. He was glad Joe had taken Tanner's place, but hated deceiving the great leader—his kin. He hoped the truth could be revealed soon, and that Sun Cloud would not feel used and betrayed by the deception. He sat down beside his cousin, awed by the dignity of the chief.

Morning Star and Joe took places nearby, each apprehensive about a slip from Stede Gaston or from one of the others with him. They knew the damage careless words could do, and both prayed to their gods to hold a tight rein on tongues. The moment of final victory and a treaty loomed before them, and nothing must prevent that.

Sun Cloud asked Thomas Fitzpatrick to join them. The ex-mountain man sat down, crossed his legs at the ankles, and cupped his knees with his hands. One hand—the reason for his Indian name, was missing three fingers from a gun accident. White hair, straight and thin, barely grazed his collar, as he favored a neat appearance. Deep-set eyes beneath protruding brow bones revealed a serious nature. He was still a hearty man at fifty-two.

Sun Cloud had met the past explorer, renowned wilderness guide, and ex-trapper several times in the past. Tom had worked most of the streams in the Dakota Territory, beginning in 1822. Tom was considered smart, brave, skilled, and self-reliant. He got along with most Indians because of his good character and pleasant personality. Sun Cloud believed Tom was an excellent choice for peacemaker between whites and Indians. He said to the agent, "It is good Broken-Hand visits the Red Hearts to prove the words he speaks on paper are wise and true."

Tom had talked with Indians many times during his thirty years here, so he knew the most effective words to use. He had sent messages to all the big tribes, but he stressed the important points again. "It is an honor to sit and speak with the noble chief Sun Cloud. I have asked the Great White Father in Washington to reward the Lakotas for allowing his people to cross your lands, to trap your streams, and to take animals for food; he has agreed. He desires all men—Indian and white—to live in peace. If the Great Plains are divided into hunting territories for each Indian nation and the Great White Father gives each many supplies, no tribe will need to invade another's land for survival. Your people will be safe from enemy raids and their needs will be filled. The chief of each tribe will sign the joint treaty; he will be responsible for honoring their part of it and for punishing any warrior who breaks it. Many nations are sending their leaders and warriors to Fort Laramie to discuss peace and to sign the big treaty. Some are your allies; some have been your enemies for generations."

Tom kept his gaze locked with Sun Cloud's, a sign to show he was being open and honest. "It is time to put aside raids, wars, and bloodshed. It is time to live in truce. Too many warriors, women, children, and old ones have died over hunting-ground disputes. Too many have died attacking white immigrants who cross your lands heading west, or from conflicts with soldiers over those raids. There have been too many fights between soldiers and warriors because each side feared and misunderstood the other. It is time for peace between Indian nations, time for peace between Indians and whites. It is time for learning, healing, and accepting each other. To obtain these goals, everyone must compromise; everyone must think of the good of their people. I have lived and worked in this territory for many years, so I know many wrongs have been done to Indians out of fear, ignorance, carelessness, or greed. The Great White Father wants them stopped. He wants our Red Brothers compensated for their losses and for their future generosity in allowing whites to travel through your lands and permitting some to settle on them. He wants peace now and forever."

"Broken-Hand's words are hard to accept, but they are wise and just. We know you to be a fair and honorable man. We have heard many tales of Broken-Hand's exploits and daring; your coups and prowess have made you a legend among Indians and whites. After we defeat the evil paleface who provokes the Crow and bluecoats against us, we will ride to Fort Laramie to make treaty. We do this because of Broken-Hand's promises and because of the sacred vision Grandfather gave to Payaba twenty years ago. The coming of Stede and Tanner Gaston have proved its magic and power. First we war against evil, then, we ride for good. We must share the pipe of friendship to bond our words to our hearts."

While the smoking ritual was in progress and no one spoke, Tom's mind drifted over the situation. It was known that whichever way Sun Cloud leaned—so did most Oglalas: the most powerful and largest branch of the Lakota Indians. In addition, most allies followed Sun Cloud's lead in crucial episodes. Tom was relieved and grateful Joseph Lawrence and Stede Gaston had helped bring about the chief's receptive mood.

Tom did not betray Joe's secret identity. His deceit could damage the treaty he and Colonel/Superintendent David Mitchell had worked so hard to achieve. He felt compassion and empathy for the Indians' plight—one he knew could only worsen in time—but he was not unduly emotional about it. He was not a glory-seeker in this historic mission.

Tom did not believe this truce would last, but it would be a life-saving reprieve for both sides for a few years. He had warned his superiors in Washington of "the consequences should twenty thousand Indians well armed, well mounted, and experts in war turn out in hostile array against all American travelers." He had suggested the annuity of fifty thousand dollars worth of supplies to be given every year for fifty years, and his government had agreed. In less than a month, redmen from most Plains nations would gather at Horse Creek to establish intertribal peace, and would unknowingly open the door for more whites to walk into the territory. That inevitable reality did not escape Tom's keen mind, nor did the grim consequences of it. He was certain Sun Cloud knew and felt the same way, and that increased Tom's respect for the Red Heart chief.

As Morning Star observed her father among the whites, she gained hope that their joint efforts for peace would inspire friendship and acceptance with their new allies. She noticed her father's rapport with the white agent and with Stede Gaston. Surely a shared pipe and battle and a treaty would mellow his feelings toward palefaces. While he was soaring on the wings of victory and peace and while her and Joe's great coups were fresh in his mind, surely her father would not stand between her and her love. As her gaze met Stede's, his gentle brown eyes seemed to read her thoughts. She returned his encouraging smile. She dared not look at Joe, as her expression could expose her forbidden feelings for him.

Morning Star glanced at Lone Wolf and hoped their war chief's rank would become only an honorary one. She looked at Hawk Eyes and prayed the deceitful shaman's influence over her people would rapidly diminish until it ceased. Her gaze sought Payaba, and love filled her heart for him. She studied her silent brother and wondered why Night Stalker did nothing more than watch and listen. Her roaming eyes jumped over the sullen Knife-Slayer, but she refused to worry about him tonight. They returned to her father as pride, love, and respect washed over her body. Her gaze met Singing Wind's, and they exchanged smiles. Morning Star grasped the meaning of her mother's nod and rose to help serve food.

Following the meal and a discussion in the meeting lodge where plans were made, Sun Cloud and Stede Gaston entered the chief's tepee to speak of the past, present, future, and their blood connection. Singing Wind served buffalo berry wine and listened to the genial conversation.

Soldiers camped outside the village, feeling at ease after their cordial reception. Most were surprised to find the Red Hearts so friendly, honest, and intelligent. When curious braves visited the area, they chatted amiably.

Knife-Slayer and Night Stalker went to the chief's son's tepee to talk privately of the disagreeable events controlling their lives. When the contrary Bloody Arrow became naughty, the men left to speak elsewhere.

Morning Star and Buckskin Girl took a walk with Joe and Clay near the river. The two couples laughed and talked. The women, best friends for years, had confided in each other about their loves for men of white blood. Both had decided to pursue their choices and to follow them wherever they led, no matter the consequences.

Joe and Morning Star noticed how Buckskin Girl and Clay Thorne glanced at each other, and knew a romance had been revived. Both were glad for their friends, and were eager for all to begin bright futures.

When Clay asked Joe what his future plans were, Joe grinned before answering, as the half-Cheyenne already knew the answer. Joe guessed his motive with accuracy, to give Clay a chance to speak his. "I'll be heading back to Virginia to help my family. My parents are getting old and need me to take over the business. I won't stay long after we're done here. What about you, Clay? What are your plans?"

Clay ruffled his blond hair and stroked his smooth jawline as he pretended to consider the query. "I'll stay here." he divulged. "This is where I was born and raised, where I belong. If I've learned one thing during my long absence and journey, it's that I have more of my father's blood and feelings than my mother's. I'll make certain the whites and Indians live up to their impending agreement. Your people have agents and soldiers to protect them; mine need me to do the same. I'll work closely with Tom Fitzpatrick to keep things fair and safe."

Joe smiled. "That sounds good to me. But where will you settle?"

"I plan to visit my family and people first to settle what happened years ago. Then I'm going to accept Sun Cloud's offer to live with my grandmother's people, here with the Red Hearts."

Buckskin Girl glowed with happiness at that news. "You will be welcome here, Sky Warrior. I will make a tepee for you."

Clay faced her and asked, "Will you make it for me and my wife?"

Buckskin Girl did not catch the humor in his tone and eyes, and she missed the meaning of his words. Her smile faded, but she replied, "Yes."

"Good, because I wouldn't want you to be displeased with your home."

Confusion was evident in the older woman's gaze. She glanced at Morning Star as the younger female giggled and covered her mouth.

"You will join to me, won't you?" Clay asked, caressing her cheek.

Buckskin Girl gaped at the half-white man who was grinning at her. She stuttered, "You ask m-me to be-come your . . . m-mate?"

Clay chuckled. "Yes. You loved me and wanted me years

394

ago. I hope you haven't changed your mind. It just took me a long time to realize that what I was seeking elsewhere was waiting for me here."

Those words flowed through Buckskin Girl as warm honey in her veins. Tears glistened in her dark eyes. Her cheeks rosed with joy. Without modesty, she confessed, "I love you and will join you."

Clay let out a loud sigh of relief. Only because Morning Star had assured him of the woman's love had he found the courage to take another chance with love and marriage. "I'll make you a good husband," he vowed.

Buckskin Girl forgot her friends' presence for a time. She gazed into Clay's dark-blue eyes and handsome face. She loved him with all her heart and soul, as Morning Star did Joseph Lawrence. At last, both of them would share true love. "I will make you a good wife," she murmured, "I have waited many years for your return. In my dreams, Grandfather said he would bring you home to me. It is so, but I feared it would not happen when Tanner appeared as the vision man."

"Morning Star, why don't we leave them alone to talk?" Joe suggested, "I think they have a lot to discuss."

The chief's daughter was filled with joy for her best friend. "That is a good idea. But we must not be alone together," she reminded. She hated to sacrifice any of the little time remaining with him. She was worried about the danger he would face soon without her help. She prayed the soldiers and Clay would guard him well when he challenged Orin alone.

Buckskin Girl and Clay/Sky Warrior looked at them with empathy. Their union would be easy to achieve, but it was not so with their friends.

"Don't worry, love," Joe said, "this won't be for much longer."

"He is your destiny; you are his," Buckskin Girl remarked. "Many will resist your mating, but let nothing and no one halt it."

"We won't," Joe responded for them, and Morning Star nodded.

He sent her an encouraging smile and whispered, "Soon, love."

As she left his side, Morning Star was plagued by Buckskin Girl's words. For a short time, she had deluded herself by thinking anything—including peace and her many coups—could change the laws and customs of her people or influence her father's mind about her intention. She must not allow herself to get wishful again, as it clouded the mind.

How she longed to be a part of the exciting final victory over Snake-Man, to be at Joe's side when the obstacle to their departure was removed. She wanted to ride to Bear Butte and participate, but her father and Joe had refused her request. She would not defy their order or display recklessness by sneaking there; that was the act of a foolish woman. She must not be disrespectful or dishonorable. She would obey them, even if she didn't agree with being left behind during this triumphant episode.

Later, Joe and Stede took a walk as dusk was yielding to night. The older man said, "I received a letter from your mother just before I left Fort Laramie. She's worried about you. She asked me to make sure you stay safe and return home soon. She also wanted to know all about Morning Star."

Joe related what he had written to his parents and when. "Did you write her back?" he inquired, a strange sensation gnawing at him.

Stede clasped Joe's shoulder with a strong hand. His gaze was filled with kindness and affection. Wind played through his graying deep-brown hair and ruffled the lashes around dark eyes: signs of his Indian heritage. At sixty-five, he knew his years were numbered, but he had accomplished his last wish. He had met his kin, found the missing part of his roots, and would help win peace for them as his father would have wanted. He felt complete, even thought a vital part of him was gone forever. But soon he would join his brave son, whose death had not been in vain. He would be with his beloved wife again, leaving only his sister and her family behind. It was the way of life. "Yes, but she'll worry anyway. Mothers are like that."

Joe had noticed the brief, faraway look in Stede's eyes, and suspected where the man's thoughts had fled. He loved and missed Tanner, too. Nothing could bring him back, but the memories of their years together would always live in his mind. As a distraction, he asked, "You don't think she and Father will reject Morning Star, do you?"

"No. They're fine people, Son. Besides, they know I'm part Indian and they like me. They have no prejudice against our kind."

"That's good, because I can't give her up for anybody."

"Tanner would be happy you're marrying his cousin. He would be proud of all you've done to help our kin. I am."

"Lordy, how I miss him. He was closer than a brother to me. Sometimes I think this is all a bad dream; I'll wake up, and he'll be there. His killer will be punished soon." He met Stede's gaze. "I'm sorry you're caught in this deceit of mine, sir, but it was the only way to help them."

"I understand, Joe. But I'll be glad when we can tell the truth."

"You think it will turn Sun Cloud against me?"

"Frankly, Son, I don't know. From what my father told me, Indians are taught to keep their bloodlines pure, and they're reared to honor their customs and laws. It's even more restrictive for chiefs and their families. You'll be asking Sun Cloud to send his only daughter into a world where some people want to conquer or destroy his culture. Worse, from some points of view, his bloodline is already tainted with enemy blood, and I'm sure he wants to get it back to its purest state. I'm sure he has no idea of your feelings and intentions for his daughter, nor hers for you. He knows what you've done for his people, and he likes you. But I can't venture a guess how he'll react to such news."

"I appreciate your honesty and candor, sir. Somehow we'll have to convince him of my love and persuade him I can protect her in my land. It will help, when the time comes, if you speak in our favor."

"I'll do what I can, Son, but I'm a half-breed and visitor, too."

Early the following morning, Wind Bird, who was being trained by Payaba to become a shaman one day, departed for Orin McMichael's trading post with Black Moon's musical watch and alleged message. A man with small hands and feet, he could pass more easily for a Crow than any other Red Heart. He was instructed how to use his wits, English expressions, and a white truce flag. If Orin wondered how a Crow knew to come to his place, Wind Bird was to say he was seeking Zeke Randall. That culprit had no doubt rejoined his boss while they awaited news from Bart of their blond intruder's death.

Joe was sure Sergeant Carnes would not search too far into the vast grasslands for him and risk confronting an Oglala war party. Bart was probably back at Fort Tabor, enjoying his stolen command. No matter, the traitorous officer would be arrested soon and be kept out of their way.

If things went as planned, Zeke would talk with Wind Bird, then report the message to Orin. The crafty Scotsman should respond without delay. While at Orin's long ago, Joe had glimpsed a wagon in the barn, but had not thought to check it for a false bottom and "magic" balls. Nor had he thought to ask Clay to examine it during one of his spying trips. Yet Joe was positive it was there and Orin was guilty.

Wind Bird was ordered to ride slowly to give the others time to reach Bear Butte to prepare for the impending trap and for Joe's party to carry out their additional task. The Red Heart brave was to tell Zeke the Crow would no longer follow, trust, or obey Snake-Man's words unless the spirit met them at the sacred mountain and commanded it. Snake-Man must again prove his magic and powers to them, or their truce was over. Wind Bird was to dangle another piece of bait before the heartless villain: Joseph Lawrence, whom they had captured for him as a gift. The meeting was set for six suns after the message was delivered. It would require that long for Orin to travel there by wagon, as he would need his special one for Snake-Man's vanishing trick. It would be good for Black Moon to see him unmasked and to be taught the error of his ways.

Joe and Morning Star were certain Orin and his gang would

398

fall for the ruse. The villains needed to retain control of the Bird People for their vicious scheme to work, and the blackhearts were eager to get their hands on Joe to question and torture him. The couple was sure Wind Bird could entice the culprits there for defeat.

That same day, Joe, Stede, Tom, Clay, Sun Cloud, Red Heart warriors, and half of the troop departed to set their part of the plan in motion. The other soldiers left for the fort, to arrest Sergeant Bart Carnes and to take command of the post to prevent any trouble during the final episode.

Miles northwestward, the forces would separate, with most journeying on to Bear Butte to make preparations there, while Joe and a few others continued northward to carry out Tom Fitzpatrick's added order.

Joe admitted it was a clever but risky scheme, and he wished he had thought of it. He envisioned Black Moon's reaction when he was issued such an ultimatum. It was a cunning coup de grace to the Crow chief's final treachery. Over the years, Tom had learned about good and bad Indians, and Joe was glad the agent had suggested this ploy.

Joe's only regret about this final confrontation was Morning Star's exclusion from it, as she deserved to be included, but it was best not to have a beautiful Oglala woman around so many men. Every mind had to be focused on their joint task. He wished he could take her in his embrace and kiss her goodbye. But soon she would be in his arms and life forever, and he eagerly anticipated that day.

As the large group rode away, women and children watched them take their leave, as did the warriors left behind to guard the camp.

Morning Star, Singing Wind, and Buckskin Girl watched until their loved ones were out of sight. Concern filled each woman.

"Come, we have chores," the oldest woman told the younger two.

"What if this plan fails?" Buckskin Girl worried aloud.

Morning Star murmured with undisguised trepidation, "It must not. But I fear the change the Indian agent made in it. Broken-Hand does not want Orin to know he walks into a trap. It is clever," she admitted, "to have Black Moon waiting for him to destroy any suspicions. It will be good if Sky Warrior can learn why Orin does this evil thing. But this deed has many dangers. Sky Warrior will be bound and helpless among many foes. He could be slain before soldiers or our warriors can help him. When Snake-Man sees he is trapped, he will strike at Sky Warrior before his capture or death. Broken-Hand wishes to prove enemy tribes can work together, but it is dangerous to let the Bird People share in this great moment. Black Moon has proven he is our foe and Orin's friend. Why must they ride to his camp to seek his help? It may defeat the sacred vision."

"No, my daughter, it is a good plan," Singing Wind refuted in a gentle tone, trying to conceal her own fears. "It will draw us together for future peace. It will force Black Moon to give up his bad ways. He does not wish to anger the soldiers and whites. He fears them more than he fears the false spirit. He will obey and help. When the evil white man and his men see Black Moon, they will approach and be trapped by forces working together."

"I understand such hopes, my mother, but I do not trust him, and it was not in Payaba's vision. Evil is strong this season and seeks to defeat all that is good. I should be there, for all know Sky Warrior rides with a squaw."

Singing Wind patted her shoulder. "Your tasks are over, my child. Women do not ride into battle with men. There is no need to risk your life again. Your presence would worry and distract others and it could anger Black Moon to learn the daughter of Sun Cloud tricked him many times. It is dangerous to walk on a man's pride; it make him behave bad."

"What if Black Moon slays them when they reach his camp? Do you not fear for Father's life? Do you not know what a great coup Black Moon will earn if he slays Sun Cloud and Sky Warrior? All he must tell other whites is they did not reach his camp. If he buries their bodies, Mother, who can prove he lies? If the agent is slain, there will be no peace. Snake-Man will pay many guns and supplies to stop the treaty. Black Moon's heart is filled with greed and evil. What is to stop him?"

Singing Wind had thought of such grim possibilities, but

cast them aside. "Grandfather will not allow such evil to win over good. You must believe the sacred vision, my daughter. You must learn to trust and accept past foes. It is the new way. What is more important than peace and survival?"

"Can you accept and trust past foes, Mother?" the girl probed.

"I must, for the sake of our people. But your words and eyes carry a different question. Speak it, Morning Star. What worries you more?"

Payaba had joined them during Morning Star's list of worries. "Do not fear, my child," he coaxed. "Victory will be ours. What you must say to your mother must be spoken to her alone; it is not for the ears of others on this sun. Go with her, Singing Wind. Listen with your heart and mind. Know what she says is the will of the Great Spirit, for I saw it in a vision. I did not speak of it because Grandfather held my tongue. Go, Morning Star, and tell the words in your heart and mind; this is the sun for them."

"You know what I must say and do, Wise One?" she queried with torment in her gaze and voice.

His eyes filled with wisdom, his mind controlled by insight, and his tone tinged with grief at her impending loss and sufferings, Payaba nodded. "Yes. It will be hard and much pain will come from it, but it must be done. It is your destiny, your sacrifice, your Life-Circle."

"Is there no way to make it easy, Wise One?" she fretted.

The gentle and tender-hearted old man shook his head of white hair. "No, little one. The path you must soon walk will destroy your old one. Do not lose courage and faith. It is the will of Grandfather."

"No," Singing Wind murmured in alarm and anguish, guessing what the two meant, what she had feared since the white man's arrival. "It cannot be. It must not be. It is wrong. Bad. Shame and dishonor. He is of your blood, Morning Star. Turn away before it is too late."

"No, Mother, he is not —"

"In your tepee," Payaba interrupted. "Nothing must destroy peace."

Singing Wind and Morning Star obeyed Payaba's soft or-

401

der, both noticing the way this matter affected their elderly friend.

Inside, Singing Wind faced her only daughter and urged, "Tell me what I fear is not so. Tell me you do not challenge a loss of face and dishonor."

Morning Star dreaded this confession, but it was time to make it. Now that Payaba had revealed it was part of the sacred vision, she had the courage to expose her feelings and intended departure. "I love him, Mother. I will go with him to his land and join to him when the mission is over. When Father returns, I will tell him of my choice."

Singing Wind's eyes enlarged with panic and disbelief. She had feared her child would come to love the paleface, but had believed she would remain true to her heritage. She imagined the effect of this news on Sun Cloud. "How can this be so, my daughter? He is of Sun Cloud's bloodline."

"He is not. His name is Joseph Lawrence, not Tanner Gaston." While her mother gaped at her in astonishment, Morning Star explained the ruse and the reason for it. She related Joe's true identity. "I am sorry I tricked my parents and people, but Grandfather commanded it. You said nothing was more important than peace and survival. Can you deny words you spoke from your heart?"

Singing Wind was distressed, but she tried to remain calm. She had to reach her daughter and change her mind. Her voice quavered as she reasoned, "That was before I knew of such lies and tricks, my daughter. You will be banished forever. The whites will not accept you among them. They will see and treat you as a wild savage; they will make fun of you, for joining with Joe. Have you not thought of such torments? You must be true to your blood and your people, to your ways and laws. We did not teach our child to shame herself and her family. How can you accept white laws, enemy ways, their god? How can you leave our land forever? How can you eat, dress, live, and behave as white? How can you raise the grandchildren of Sun Cloud, bloodline of Gray Eagle and Brave Bear, as palefaces, half-breeds? You will destroy a great bloodline; you will hurt and shame your father deeply. You will never see us again. Whites will insult you, hate you, reject you. How will

402

you feel when the new treaty is broken, as Payaba warned long ago? Which side will you choose then, my daughter — his or ours? You cannot take both."

"I have thought of such things, Mother. They trouble me, but I will face those challenges when they appear. Joe is the sacred warrior, Mother; he has done all the vision said. Did you not hear Payaba? This is part of the vision; it is my destiny. The Great Spirit put us together many moons ago when I was a captive of the evil whites. He would not do so if it was wrong to love and marry Joe, for He knows all things. He gave us special time together to work for peace and to yield to our love for each other. He has not separated us or slain us for such feelings. He has not punished us, so how can our love be wrong?"

"He allowed your weakness to continue for the good of our people." Singing Wind realized how much her daughter had learned from the white man. Morning Star was stronger and more confident now. "What if Grandfather proves to you this joining must not be? If He says you cannot go and the white man cannot stay, will you obey Him?"

"Yes, but that will not happen," she replied with certainty. "You say the whites will not accept Indians, but they did not reject Powchutu and Stede. They did not scorn Bright Arrow and Clay Thorne when they lived among them. The Great White Father, their President, commanded acceptance and friendship. We must do the same."

"Powchutu, Stede, Bright Arrow, and Clay were accepted because they all passed for white and none revealed their Indian blood in words or deed. Your face cannot fool the whites."

"Joe says they will think I am from a land far away. They will think I am a . . . bride he found while riding his ship over the big water. The ocean," she corrected. "You say I must be true to my Oglala blood. How will that be so if I defy Grandfather's sacred command? The treaty will be broken one day, if I go or if I stay; my actions do not control that bad deed."

Singing Wind knew she was losing the battle to save her child and to spare Morning Star from terrible wounds. If only she and her husband could have talked to Joe first, they could have made him realize he would destroy the woman he loved if he took her to his enemy land. Perhaps when Joe returned, she and Sun Cloud could convince him to sacrifice Morning Star and leave her here where she belonged. "How can you love and join a paleface, my daughter?"

"How could Grandfather love and join a white woman? How could Bright Arrow love and join a white woman? How could Black Cloud love and join a white woman? If it was not wrong for them, why is it wrong for me? Life can be strange, Mother; Life-Circles sometimes join with enemy ones. Your mother was to join Gray Eagle, but Grandfather chose a white mate for him. Your father loved her, too. If Chela and Gray Eagle had wed, you would not be here. That was His will. Grandfather sent Powchutu into the white world to find and marry the real Shalee, to have a son who could return to bring peace. That was His will. Bright Arrow desired you and the chief's bonnet, but Father won both. That was His will. The Great Spirit gave my uncle a white woman to love, to bear his children, to give one to the Cheyenne chief, son of a chief who joined a white woman. All of these Life-Circles have touched on some moon. Yet both sides said they were forbidden, wicked, shameful. How can that be when they were powerful and victorious? All found happiness with true loves that could not be denied, that were destined. It is the same with me and Joe."

Singing Wind felt her heart drumming in alarm at one sentence. "What do you mean, Powchutu joined the *real* Shalee?"

"I know the truth, Mother. Joe did not tell me. I heard Father speak it to him and ask him to tell no one about my grandmother. I do not care she was white; Alisha/Shalee was a great woman, an honored legend. I have told no one I know the truth; I did not tell Joe I heard those words. I only speak them now to you in secret to prove our union will work. You scolded me for using lies and tricks, but my grandfather and father did the same to win their loves and to keep peace. I cannot hate half-breeds; Sun Cloud, Bright Arrow, Night Stalker, and Morning Star are mix-bloods. Can you hate my child who will carry two bloods, as your husband does? Did the truth about Alisha change your feelings for her? Do you scorn Gray Eagle for joining a white? No, no, no, Mother," she answered the

404

three questions with accuracy. "Powchutu was full-blooded, son of a great chief, but he was forced to suffer the life of a half-breed. We must learn to feel with our hearts, not judge with our eyes against those who look different from us."

"Your words touch my heart, Morning Star, and make me proud," Singing Wind declared. "But change takes time. Love controls you, so you are blinded to many things. You think your choice will work because you want it to do so. Powchutu was raised half white, my daughter; Shalee/Sarah was raised all white, so they were accepted by the palefaces who did not know their secrets. Rebecca earned her way into our tribe by risking her life for Oglalas and Cheyenne, as did Bonnie Thorne. Your grandmother was believed to be half Indian, daughter of Chief Black Cloud, so she was accepted. Such is not true with you, my daughter. You are Oglala; you were raised Oglala. You cannot become and live as white."

"Alisha was born white and raised white," Morning Star countered, "but she became Blackfoot and Red Heart. She was worthy of Gray Eagle. The same is true of Rebecca Kenny with Bright Arrow. Why can I not do the same with their people? Why is it not bad for Sun Cloud's father and brother to have forbidden loves, but is bad for his daughter to love and join Sky Warrior from a sacred vision? Joe risked his life for Red Hearts, and he is blood brother of Sun Cloud."

"They accepted our ways and joined us. For you to join him, you must accept his world. How can a maiden with the bloods of Gray Eagle, Black Cloud, Running Wolf, and Sun Cloud deny her bloodline, people, and ways to love an enemy, to sacrifice all she is and knows?"

"He is not our enemy," Morning Star protested softly in dismay.

"But his people are, and a wife must go with her husband and accept his band as hers. Yes, there are many good whites, and we will make peace with them soon. But it will not last; they will not change. What then?"

"Can I deny what Grandfather places in my heart? Can I refuse to walk the path He has planned for me?"

"If it is His will, my daughter. I do not understand it. If such is true, I will not stand in your path. But it will be different

405

with your father. He is chief. All watch what he and his family do. He will not believe or accept this until the Great Spirit proves it to him."

"How will He do this, Mother?"

"I do not know. If it is, he must obey it; but he will never accept it, for it means the loss of his daughter. He will be forced to turn his back, to deny you, to banish you, as is our law. The Red Hearts yielded for Gray Eagle and Bright Arrow, but not until much suffering was endured. It will cause worse trouble to ask them to do so again for the bloodline of their chiefs. That will say Gray Eagle's line wants white mates."

"But Father married you, an Indian." Morning Star contended, "Night Stalker, the next chief, is joined to an Indian. Bloody Arrow, chief after him, has no mark of the white man on him; the bloodline is strong and pure again in my brother's son. I am a woman and cannot become chief. My sons are not in line for the chief's bonnet. Why must our people care if mine is broken? Why must they order me to stay here and to join an Indian, a man I cannot love? It is not fair or good, Mother."

"You are Oglala and it is our way. If you defy our law, your father will be forced to never speak your name again, to never look upon your face again. Can you shame and hurt him this way, our child? Many suns from now, will it not harm your feelings and marriage when your husband's people attack and slay Oglalas? When they steal our beloved lands? When they try to put us on reservations after our strength and will are broken, as they have done with other Red nations? When the people you have chosen kill or rule all you loved, what will you feel? That moon will come, my child, for Payaba has seen it. Do you love Joe this much?"

Tears ran down Morning Star's cheeks, but she did not brush them away. They dropped to her buckskin garment and made dark spots there. Her heart ached, and a heaviness burdened her chest. Despite what her mother had said about her being too blinded by love to see this matter clearly, such was not the case. She realized how hard a break with her life would be. She realized how difficult and intimidating — and perhaps painful — her new challenge would be. She had agonized over her decision; she had not rushed carelessly and selfishly into it, as she knew it affected many people.

Yet the full reality of her choice had just hit her. Hearing the things she had feared spoken aloud was different than when her mind gave those warnings in silence or gave them while Joe was near with his love and assurances. She considered the many challenges and sacrifices: a mysterious world far away, filled with strangers who might reject her, unfamiliar customs she must learn, an unknown religion she would be expected to embrace, the necessary demand of hiding her race and up-bringing, the strain of behaving as a paleface every day, accepting the fact she was dead to her family and this life. Banished forever. Live as white until she died. Never see her family. Hurt her loved ones. Never come—

Singing Wind intruded on her concerns. "Can you become white, Morning Star, *forever?*" she asked. "What will happen to you there if Joe dies before your training is complete? You will be alone in an enemy land. What if his parents do not accept you and they reject him for joining you? What if his friends leave his side? Will he remain happy with you? Is his love enough to receive in return for so many sacrifices? Does his love have the strength to help you win the many battles you will face? Think on this more. Once you choose, my daughter, your path leads but one way."

Chapter Eighteen

At Bear Butte, the lookout rode into the clearing to report that a wagon and seven men were sighted: six white-eyes and Wind Bird. The party had halted an hour away while two of the men rode toward them to scout the area. It appeared that Orin McMichael was taking no chances this time, though the red-haired man with an unusual half-beard had not been seen. It was presumed the trader was staying concealed in the "white tepee."

Everything was ready, every precaution had been taken. Black Moon and a few Crow were camped at the regular meeting site. Soldiers and Red Hearts were concealed behind trees, rolling hills, and bushes that encircled the location, but at a safe distance to avoid discovery by the approaching scouts. Horses, except for the Crow's, were tethered a mile away to prevent their sounds from alerting the prey to a cunningly baited trap. The signals were arranged — one by Joe and/or one by Tom Fitzpatrick. No one was to fire a weapon or make any movement until either or both was given. Then they were to fire only in self-defense, as they wanted all villains captured alive.

Joe's hands were bound behind his back and he sat on the earth before a tree. Clay's rifle was aimed on his spot for quick rescue if things went badly. Other sharpshooters had weapons trained on the scene to make certain no lawbreaker escaped, particularly the boss. Joe and the others would bide their time until Orin's motive was uncovered, if possible. Then the trap would close around him and his gang.

The scouts arrived: Zeke Randall and Farley. The husky man eyed his surroundings before he dismounted, and the towhead follow his lead. Zeke glanced at the blond captive, grinned, and turned to the Crow chief.

"What's the problem, Black Moon? Ain't we treated you fair?"

"Bad feelings come, Hair Face. We capture man you want. He say Snake-Man no spirit. He say use tricks on Crow. When Spirit come to prove white man wrong, prove great magic and power?"

"Farley's going after him now. We had to be sure this place is safe. Get him," Zeke ordered his companion, who obeyed without speaking.

"Why man with big medicine afraid? What can hurt spirit?"

"I meant, safe for his men; we ain't spirits. Nothing can hurt Snake-Man. You'll see. He'll reward you big for that gift." He pointed to Joe.

Zeke walked to the prisoner, but the others stayed behind. He looked down at the helpless man and chuckled. "I told you I'd get you, boy. You're gonna suffer good before you're dead."

"You didn't get me, Zeke; the Crow did. I've led you a merry chase for a long time. We both underestimated Black Moon; he's a sly devil. You and Orin won't fool him much longer."

Zeke stared at him, then snarled, "Shut up."

Joe read the threatening glare, but asked, "Why? Afraid Orin's tricks won't be strong enough to protect you when Black Moon learns the truth? When he does, he'll skin the lot of you. He'll feed—"

Zeke silenced him with a backhanded blow to the cheek as the bearish male growled, "Shut up. Talk again, and I'll take out your tongue."

Joe didn't provoke the enraged man to lose his temper. If he had to be rescued from a beating, the trap would be sprung too early. He was glad Clay and the others hadn't panicked when he was struck and come to his aid. Joe looked at his enemy with what appeared a contempt for danger.

"Where's the woman you took from me? She's been riding with you."

Joe didn't answer, just stared with an insulting sneer.

Zeke used his booted toe to kick the bottom of Joe's foot, several times and hard. "Answer me, dead man," he ordered.

"First you say to keep quiet, then you ask questions and demand answers. Which do you want, Randall, silence or talk?"

Zeke stroked his beard as he sneered, "Think you're real brave and smart, don't you?"

"I haven't done badly until now, and my trouble didn't come from you."

More fury glistened in Zeke's shiny eyes, so Joe cautioned himself to settle down. He couldn't be too cocky or Zeke would get suspicious. He was attempting to keep the burly man distracted from the Crow until Orin joined them; he didn't want any slips from the Bird People. "She's with Black Moon's wives. He decided to keep her and to trade me. I tried to bargain with him, but he thought I was more valuable to you than what I had to offer. I tried to convince him he's being a fool, but you two have him duped good. As to your question, you've got it wrong; you stole her from me; I just took back my property. If you'd harmed my wife, you'd be dead by now instead of just mad."

"Yore wife?" Zeke echoed in surprise.

"That's right. Little Flower was gathering herbs while I hunted. She was to meet me nearby at noon. You snatched her. You did a pretty good job of hiding your trail back to camp, but I'm an Apache trained ex-Texas Ranger, so I'm not fooled easy. If you'd let her be, we'd have been out of this territory the next day. Then you went and put a ball in my arm and roughed her up. That made me real mad."

Joe saw that he'd captured Zeke's attention with his tale, so he continued it. "I guessed what you had in your wagons and what you were up to. Being an ex-lawman and plenty riled, I figured I'd hang around a while and take a little revenge. Trouble is, Randall, you and your boys kept pulling me deeper into your business. I don't like being accused of murder—Clem, remember? I had a tough time convincing Captain Thomas at Fort Tabor I was innocent, but my Ranger badge carried more

410

persuasion than your claims. Your lie riled me more. I told Thomas what I suspected was going on, but he believed this Snake-Man stuff was Indian superstition. I could see you boys were going to get away with your crimes. It wouldn't have drawn me in if you'd left us alone. You didn't, so I destroyed your guns. We were heading out of this sorry area when the Army came after us for two more murders. That made me mad again. I had you, soldiers, and your Crow friends chasing us with blood in the eye. With Thomas dead and framed good, I figured it was smarter to ride west and forget about you and your dealings, but we ran in to some of Black Moon's braves."

"You saying all this trouble was over that woman, a squaw?"

"*My* woman, Zeke; that's a big difference to a man."

"Why didn't you ride into my camp and lay claim to her?"

"Texans aren't fools. You'd have killed me and kept her."

"Damn right," he admitted. "I shoulda hired you that night. You're good, Lawrence. You've been a wound in the gut to us."

Joe glanced at his bonds, chuckled, and said, "But I ain't perfect, or I'd be free and long gone. Standing too much guard and getting too little sleep dulled my wits." He realized Zeke was falling for his story and relaxing. The evildoer even seemed to expose a begrudging respect for his prowess.

"You'll get plenty of rest soon," Zeke jested.

"In a permanent bed six feet underground?" Joe retorted.

"Yep, so why you so calm?" he asked, glancing around again.

"A man has to die sometime. A Ranger stares it in the face every day; I got used to living on the edge of a grave. Once you accept the fact it's coming for you and you can't stop it, you learn not to fear it as much. In your line of work and surrounded by hostiles, I'm surprised you haven't learned that lesson, too; or maybe you have. Tell me, Randall, why do you boys want to provoke an Indian uprising?"

Zeke looked at Black Moon and his braves at the campfire. He turned to frown at Joe. "You're talking too much again," he warned.

"When a man's gonna die, he needs a reason for it. It isn't

411

because I riled you boys a few times. It's because of why you thought I was challenging you. I've guessed that much, but not the why behind it."

"Who are you? Who you working for?" Zeke demanded.

"Joe Lawrence, like I told you that first night. I've been drifting with my wife for about two years. Ever since the Apaches burned our ranch, killed our son, and captured our daughter," he said in an icy tone, with a frozen glare in his blue eyes. "They didn't like me using the skills they'd taught me against them. Trouble is, only an Apache can track an Apache, and even I'm not that good. Never could find where they took my little girl. Finally had to give up searching for her to make a fresh start. So, we've been drifting around and look-ing for a new place to settle. We want to stay in the West, we don't like crowded areas, but we've found Indian trouble everywhere we've looked, and we don't want that risk again. You boys stirring up Indians to go on the warpath was part of why I was so riled against you. Too many innocent whites get hurt and killed. Ever seen a real massacre, Zeke? Probably not or you'd think twice about what you're doing. I bet you don't have any family to worry about losing to hostile attacks."

"Nope, just have me. Why's an Injun hater married to a squaw?"

"Married her before all the trouble. Except for her skin color, she's as white as you and me. Speaks good English, so she heard all you said. Little Flower figured it was safer and smarter to stay silent."

"She was a real looker. Be glad she'll last longer with Black Moon than Snake-Man. He likes to use a strong hand with his women."

Joe scowled for effect. "I guessed that much from Clem's slips. You were smart to silence him; a man with a loose tongue and a weakness for whiskey is dangerous. Any chance we can make a deal? You get me back my wife and we'll clear out of your territory?"

"You ain't in no seat to deal. It's too late, Joe."

"I figured that, but can't you tell me why I'm dying?"

"So you can yell it to them Injuns?" Zeke jested.

Joe chuckled. "In my place, wouldn't you use just about any

412

trick to save your hide?" He laughed again as if resigned to his predicament.

"Wagon come!" Black Moon shouted and stood.

"Your last card's been played, Joe. Game's over and lost."

"Yep, I guess it will be over soon. Leastwise, I'll meet your boss. I'm real curious about a man with so much power and money. Clever, too."

Joe watched Zeke join the Bird People, who watched the wagon pull into place. He assumed the other four cutthroats, whom he'd seen at Black Moon's camp recently, were survivors from his Rake's Hollow attack. Their employer wasn't in sight yet, and Joe prayed he was with them. The riders dismounted and tethered their reins. Farley went to Zeke like a moth to a flame. Wind Bird made his way toward Joe, but they didn't speak or look at each other. Joe was relieved by the brave's safe return and success.

The tailgate was unbolted and lowered. The string closing the cloth-bowed top was loosened and flared, creating a large opening. A big man stood under the white canvas arch with hands on hips. His lower body was clad in fringed buckskin pants and moccasins. His chest was bare and hairless. Colorful tattoos of fierce snakes began above his wrists, coiled round and round his strong arms, and seemingly crawled over his broad shoulders. Their triangular heads were depicted over each breast with forked tongues, bared fangs, glassy black eyes, and flared pits. The vipers were drawn with effective skill, to entice fear and superstition.

Joe's alert gaze examined the disguise that covered the leader's face and half of his head, reaching to behind his ears and to the base of his neck. The painted metal mask that hid his identity was in the shape of a snake's head. The holes in it — eye, pit, and mouth — were small or shaped to prevent clues. The hair Joe glimpsed was black, dark, and silky. But shoulder length! Even if Orin's hair was sooted or dyed, Joe reasoned, he knew it wasn't long! He noticed the shade of the man's skin, which was much too dark for Orin's! In fact, Joe decided, the devil hinted at being . . . an Indian! He was baffled. He recalled Zeke's curious expression when he mentioned Orin's name earlier. Was it possible, Joe wondered, that

413

Orin wasn't the captain of these land pirates? Either way, he'd know the truth soon.

Zeke whispered a report, then fetched him. As they approached, Snake-Man spoke to the Indians. Despite new facts, Joe was surprised at not hearing a Scottish accent! He didn't recognize the deep voice, but listened carefully. He knew there had to be clues to glean.

"My friends, why do you doubt me? Have I not proven myself to you? I have given you guns, bullets, whiskey, and many gifts of friendship. Have I not sent word where the Lakotas hunt and camp so you can raid your enemies? Have I not shown you my big medicine? Have I not provoked the soldiers against your enemies? Have I not kept the bluecoats away from your camps? Did I not give Black Moon a magic present?" He tossed the musical watch that Wind Bird had delivered to him back to the Crow chief.

"You promise more rifles, but they no come," Black Moon replied. "Crow cannot fight enemies with whiskey and trinkets. You say, kill all Sioux. How we kill with no weapons?"

"More will come soon, my friend. You have captured the white man who destroyed your supply and who stopped more wagons."

The last part was a crafty lie. Joe caught how slowly and carefully the head of the gang spoke. He studied the man's physique, and culled his memory.

"I will speak with him. Then he will die. He will stop no more wagons from reaching Black Moon. Bring the captive to me, Hair Face. Rest, my friends, while we speak. I must learn if others work with him who will take his place to steal your supplies."

The Crow returned to the campfire in the center of the clearing, as the wagon was on its edge. Everyone except Zeke and his master joined the Indians there. The husky hireling yanked Joe closer to the lowered tailgate.

"You want me to stay?" he asked.

The man studied Joe a moment, then replied, "No, he will not run. Keep your gun ready. If he does, shoot him down. Strike only his legs."

Zeke checked Joe's bonds, then left him alone with

Snake-Man.

"You have much to tell me, Joseph Lawrence. Who sent you on this mission? What are your orders? Are you Army or Special Agent?"

Joe used a desperate ploy. "You can stop the ruse with me, Orin. That ochre dust on your skin and that fake accent don't fool me. Did you scalp an Indian for that hair or order Zeke to get it for you? Just tell me why you're instigating an Indian war before you have me killed."

Convinced he was safe by the length of time his men had been there and from fieldglass study, Snake-Man laughed and relaxed, basking in his power and success. "Sly tae tha end 'r' ye?" he jested near a whisper. "Good, nae need tae work sae hard tae talk like ye. Ne'er have I met ae man who's been such ae trouble tae me. Why, Joe?" he asked in a pleasant tone.

Joe was delighted the blackheart was incriminating himself before concealed witnesses. "I've already told Zeke and I'm sure he reported it all to you, so why repeat it? Let's get on with my dying and the why of it."

"Blarney, me lad, pure blarney. Ye're nae speaking with ae man who can be duped easy. Talk tha truth, and I'll make yer death easy and swift. Hold yer tongue, and I'll make ye beg for it all night."

"How about you tell me first why I have to die? I figured out what you're doing here, but your motive escapes me. I don't like holes in things, and I can't seem to fill the one to this situation, and that riles me as much as being defeated. Why would any man go to such lengths to take control of a vast wasteland? What's so valuable here?"

"If ye're stalling for help tae come, it won't. Me boys scouted tha area before we rode in; naebody for miles. If ye don't tell me what I want tae know, I'll send Zeke after yer woman. Ye'll be sure tae beg tae speak plenty when ye see what I can do with her. But it would be tae late then. Once I start me pleasures, it's nigh impossible tae stop until she's used up. Understand me, Joseph Lawrence?"

"Clear as a mountain stream," he responded between gritted teeth. He hesitated as he pretended to consider his predicament and decide his course. The kind of man this enemy assumed him to be would not yield easily or quickly. Orin waited patiently in confidence of victory. Joe shrugged and quipped, "Why not? No need to risk Little Flower's death or my torture for a job I've failed. I'm certain you'd carry out such vile threats. If there was any other thing to do, you can bet I wouldn't tell you a single word."

Joe perceived a begrudging respect for him in Orin similar to the one he had witnessed in Zeke. "To protect my wife, I'll do it your way," he said. "I'm a scout for a private company that plans to build a railroad from the Great Lakes to the Pacific, using Asa Whitney's route. They want this matter kept secret to prevent competition. President Fillmore has promised them federal land grants for surveys next spring. They hope to begin laying tracks in the East by late May. I was sent here to check out the terrain and climate, availability of supplies and protection, any Indian trouble, and possible opposition from landowners."

Joe took a breath and went on. "It didn't take me long to realize somebody was provoking the Indians and trying to prevent that treaty Agent Fitzpatrick promised my employers. They need that truce, Orin. They need the roads and forts it'll bring about; they need peace with the Indians to obtain water and timber and game to feed the workers. My run-in with Zeke helped get me started. That story about my wife is true, so is most of what I told Zeke. What you called 'blarney' is what happened before I took this job. It shouldn't surprise you that neither easterners nor southerners would accept my Indian wife. Taking this job served our needs. I nosed around until tracks led to you."

"Ye may be telling tha truth on most part, but ye're lying about ae trail tae me. I've been too careful tae conceal it."

Joe laughed. "Yep, until today." When Orin's head jerked around as if to search for trouble, he rushed on with, "Or rather until Zeke went to you after I destroyed those guns. Shipping those illegal crates through Pierre didn't fool me; a smart man would never be so careless. And you have to be one of the cleverest I've met to get this far with your bloody scheme. I realized Simon was an ignorant go-between. I figured Zeke would head there after he discovered my mischief.

416

He did, after he joined up with Farley. That kid isn't alert and skilled like Zeke; no problem dogging him. I trailed him to his meeting with Carnes at Tabor, then on to Pierre to meet Zeke. They steamed straight to your trading post—and you."

Joe rolled his shoulders to loosen their tautness. "I figured I had enough facts to get Captain Thomas interested in the case, so I left to convince him. Trouble was, Carnes had killed him, taken command, and declared me an outlaw. I knew by then he was in your pocket and trying to kill me, so explanations or threats were useless. The odds here were too uneven, so I decided to continue westward. It seemed best to report what I'd learned to my bosses and let them decide how to deal with you and your hirelings. But we rode straight into Black Moon's arms; the Crow should have been farther north that day," he muttered.

Joe exhaled in fake annoyance. "Anyway, I suspected you were the ringleader, but I didn't know for certain until today. You just fell for my last trick, for all the good it does me. Besides, I couldn't find another man clever enough to be pulling off your scheme. The railroad is important, Orin, so I'll be replaced. Better tell Zeke to be more careful with him. And next time, find a better man than Simon Adams to cast suspicions on."

Orin continued to make sure they weren't overheard. "Tae bad we work opposite sides, Joe. I could have used ae skilled man like ye."

"Pay me more than the East-West Railroad and I'll jump into your pocket. Survival is a big incentive to change jobs."

Orin chuckled in amusement. "I don't think sae. Ye strike me as ae man who's loyal tae who hires him first. I could ne'er trust ye."

Joe shrugged his shoulders. "Can't fault a man for trying to save his hide. But I'd still like to know why I'm losing it. You owe me the truth for the information I just supplied; it'll probably save your hide one day."

Orin's confidence was at a peak now. "Ye'll be dead before dark, sae I'll tell ye. I want tha Black Hills, and tha Sioux owns them."

"The Black Hills? Why are they so important to you?"

417

"They have e'erthing I need: timber, finest grazeland, plenty of game, abundant water, sheltered valleys for winter protection, strongholds against enemies, and gold."

Joe's astonishment was genuine. "Gold?"

"Plenty, maybe even more than California has. One of me men found some when he was raiding death scaffolds; he didn't tell tha others. He thought he'd become partners with me because I could help him get out more than he could do alone. He needed me backing and protection, but I didn't need him. He's dead, sae I'm tha only one who knows where it is."

Joe was relieved they were talking low and in a secluded location. Gold was one motive that no one must learn of! But if he allowed Orin to live, be arrested, and be questioned . . .

"Of course, timber is like gold in this territory. I know about tha push for ae railroad; it has tae come one day. With the Black Hills and her treasures in me possession, I can be their main and only supplier in these parts. I'll be rich and famous, ruler of this area."

"Except the Lakotas stand in the way of your plans."

"Ye're right. But not for long. I made ae deal with Black Moon tae supply him with guns and goods if he'd use them first tae kill off 'r run out tha Sioux. Then he'd control the rest of the territory."

"Until you provoked the Army to get rid of him for you."

Orin chuckled. "Yer wits impress me, Joe."

"Thanks," he scoffed.

"If ye hadn't of destroyed me last shipment tae Black Moon, with two more in ae few weeks, me war would have begun in a month. Now, it'll have tae be in October. When yer surveyors come next spring, I'll be the man they negotiate with o'er land, water, game, and timber rights."

Joe had one last thing to learn before he gave the attack signal. "Aren't you forgetting about the treaty council at Laramie in a few weeks?"

"Treaties 'r' made tae be broken. I'll be sure it fails before winter settles in. I'll give tha Sioux and Crow plenty of cause tae battle again."

Joe leaned against the wooden hull. "What if—"

Several incidents suddenly happened simultaneously: Joe

yelped and jerked aside as a bee stung his cheek; Orin, who had seen the insect land and poise to strike, leaned forward without thinking to brush it away; a startling war hoop sounded across the quiet clearing; and an arrow caught Orin in his left shoulder.

The Scotsman groaned and fell backward from the hit.

"What in blazes!" Joe yelled. If they hadn't moved at the same time, he would have been a lethal target! He jerked around to look for trouble.

Orin seized the shaft and yanked out the arrowhead. He held one hand over the bleeding wound as his gaze scanned the scene.

Another arrow thudded into wood too close to the bound Joe. His keen gaze retraced its flight path to Knife-Slayer. The warrior was trying to kill *him!* He needed cover fast in his vulnerable state. Joe saw the masked leader grab a nearby pistol and heard him murmur something about "ae war party attack." Joe knew he'd best get out of Orin's line of fire before the man realized his assumption was wrong. He ducked beside the wagon, hoping Clay Thorne could cover him with rifle fire and would come to untie him fast.

The trap prematurely exposed caused confusion on both sides, especially when Tom held off the signal long enough to give Joe time to roll under the wagon and no soldier showed himself. Melee ensued.

Orin's men backed toward their boss to defend him while firing at moving shadows in the woods. Crow dashed for cover, having been ordered to capture, not slay, the culprits. The sound and smell of gunfire filled the clearing, as did shouts back and forth between both sides.

As soldiers and warriors revealed themselves and called for the evildoers to surrender, Orin reached for his best weapons. He smashed the Oriental balls against the hard ground, creating an impenetrable veil. When the twinkling smoke vanished, Snake-Man was gone.

Clay rushed forward to free Joe. The two men joined their forces in a brief battle. When it was over, Zeke was wounded; two cohorts were dead; Farley and the last two were prisoners. On the other side, only four soldiers had minor injuries; three

Indians were wounded and two were slain: Hawk Eyes and Knife-Slayer.

It was revealed that the sullen Red Heart warrior had been the one to act before either signal was given. The shaman had caught one of Zeke's first bullets as he witnessed his son's treacherous behavior and apparently sacrificed his protection in an attempt to halt it. Knife-Slayer had been slain by Wind Bird while trying to kill Joe. No doubt the antagonistic warrior had intended to allege that Joe had given the attack signal and was aiming for Snake-Man to protect Sky Warrior.

Joe surmised the shaman had tried to perform the good deed to hide his and his son's past misdeeds, or to make up for them before his god. Surely Hawk Eyes had realized no one would believe the action was an accident, as Knife-Slayer was an expert shot. Justice, often strange and swift, had claimed both men.

Night Stalker was angered by his friend's deceit and his dishonorable conduct. During the past week, it had become clear to the chief's son that peace was the best trail to ride; working with whites, especially soldiers, had shown him most were not bad men and most wanted truce. He now knew that his father and others were right to seek peace, and he would obey the sacred vision. He pleased Sun Cloud with his change of heart and behavior.

Joe walked around the wagon and examined it. Near the front, he kicked the wooden hull and shouted, "Come on out, Orin, the game's over. We know about your hiding place." There was no response. "You want us to chop through your fake bottom or burn you out?" Joe threatened.

Everyone gathered around the white-topped wagon as Joe issued his warnings and kicks again. The clearing had been surrounded by their forces, so they knew Orin couldn't have escaped.

"Bring the hatchets, boys; we'll chop our way to him."

A shot rang out, and everyone jumped back as they assumed Orin was firing at them. Nothing happened for a while.

Then, Joe spotted blood dripping to the ground beneath the wagon. He climbed inside, and Clay followed. They searched for an entrance to the secret compartment and found it. They

420

were not surprised by the grim sight that greeted them.

Orin's body was hauled outside—dead from a self-inflicted wound to the head, preferring that to arrest and execution or prison. Joe removed his metal mask to show Black Moon and the others the truth. The flowing black hair was attached, so the mane left with the disguise. He watched Black Moon, his braves, and Red Heart warriors touch the tattooed snakes. He heard them laugh in relief to discover the man was human and the vipers unreal.

Joe recovered some of the "magic" balls and demonstrated how they worked. He passed out the remaining ones from Orin's supply. Despite the fact that the Indians knew the balls were tricks, they were amazed by them and continued to call them "big magic." Since Orin's target was the Oglalas, Sun Cloud was presented with the snake mask. To prevent jealousy, Black Moon was given the wagon, horses, and supplies. Both chiefs were pleased with their presents.

Tom and Stede were overjoyed by the removal of the final obstacle to peace in the territory. A burial detail tended to the chore of interring the remains of Orin McMichael, along with his two men, near the sacred location McMichael had craved. Joe related the motive behind the Scotsman's scheme, excluding one part: gold in the Black Hills. He would keep that fact a secret, except to warn Sun Cloud at a later date to make certain whites were kept out of the rich hills. Once gold was discovered, Joe was certain encroachment and a bitter war would take place.

When Black Moon comprehended how he had been duped, the Crow chief was silent in his shame. It helped matters when Sun Cloud told him they, too, had been falsely provoked against the Bird People by Orin's tricks. It made everyone happy to see the two leaders make truce. It was hoped that when news of their joint attack reached the ears of other Crow and Lakota tribes, it would entice them to lessen their hatreds.

Three camps were made as dusk appeared: Crow, Red Heart, and white. Yet men from each visited others and chatted with new friends and allies. The prisoners were held in the white camp by soldiers, to be taken to Fort Tabor the next day. It was decided to hold them there until after the treaty council to prevent any distractions from its importance. Men were assigned to take charge of Orin's trading post until a decision was made concerning it. They were ordered to search for the stolen payroll shipment from June eleventh, if the money wasn't already spent on illegal guns and whiskey.

Horses were fetched and tended. Wounded were treated. Meals were cooked and eaten. Chores were completed. Groups gathered to talk about this shared coup, the impending treaty, and future plans.

They were to split up in the morning. Sun Cloud and his band would ride home to prepare for their journey to Fort Laramie, to place the two warriors on death scaffolds, to send his people on the way to their winter camp, and to make Wind Bird their next shaman. Clay Thorne was to travel with them to speak with Buckskin Girl and Morning Star. He would journey to the meeting with his grandmother's tribe, with whom he would live. Then he would visit his family and people—the Cheyenne. Black Moon and his party would ride home to make their preparations to attend the joint council far away. Troops would ride to Fort Tabor with the prisoners, most to remain there until they were relieved in a month. The agent, Stede, Joe, and three soldiers would head for Laramie.

While Tom wrote out a report on this episode, Stede and Joe visited Sun Cloud's campsite. The three chatted genially for a time, with Sun Cloud praising the work of "Tanner" and his daughter. Neither white man revealed the truth of Joe's identity. That was something that needed to be handled in private and after the treaty was signed. Once the big council was over, Joe would go after Morning Star and expose the truth.

The treaty talk was scheduled to begin on September seventh, so each group had to hurry with their camp tasks and get to Laramie. Joe wanted to be present, and wished his love could be there. He wanted to witness the termination of their mission. He wanted to view the historic event so he could tell their children about it one day. It would enable Morning Star to leave home knowing peace ruled her land and protected her family and people.

Joe was eager to see her, hold her, kiss her. He dreaded the revelations they must make to Sun Cloud of their love and deceit. He had come to like and respect the chief more and more during his stay here. He prayed that time would soften the crushing blow. He grasped that what they must do would hurt the noble chief deeply. Joe hoped understanding and forgiveness would not be long in coming.

As the sun rose on a glorious day, Sun Cloud bid Stede and "Tanner" farewell until he saw them again at Horse Creek. He rode homeward with his band, a changed son, a new medicine chief, and two dead Oglalas. He carried his coup prize with him: Orin's mask. Elation surged through him as he imagined his parents — Gray Eagle and Alisha/Shalee — and his brother, Bright Arrow, witnessing this event from the Great Spirit's side. He knew how happy his beloved wife would be to see his safe return and to hear of their victory. There would be much celebrating in his camp when they reached home. He never suspected what grim news awaited him . . .

One of the main reasons Clay — Sky Warrior — Thorne accompanied the Red Hearts was to tell Morning Star not to expose anything about the couple's scandalous plan until Joe returned home with her father. Joe had asked him to warn her that if Sun Cloud learned they'd all tricked him, he might think he'd be tricked again at the peace council. "He mustn't have any doubts about the treaty or refuse to attend the meeting," Joe commanded. "Don't do or say anything to stop your father from coming." If Morning Star let their secret slip, he would be there to defend Joe's motives and character. Clay knew Morning Star might need his support and encouragement. He also wanted to ask Flaming Star for his daughter in joining, even though Buckskin Girl had already accepted him. By the time he returned from Laramie, the woman would have their tepee ready and their joining ceremony could take place. At last, his heart and mind were at peace. He felt he belonged here living as an Indian in the Dakota territory with a fine woman. He wished Joe and Morning Star the same happiness, but felt it would be long in coming.

Joe waved to Clay and Sun Cloud and watched them ride out of sight. He walked to the spot Zeke Randall was bound to force out of him the final piece of information he needed. Before he began, he had one of the soldiers take Farley to another area. "There's something I have to know, Zeke. Who—"

"You sorry bastard, I ain't telling you nothing!"

"I think you will. I know a few more things you've done here that I haven't mentioned in my reports yet. Be stubborn, and I'll gladly add them to the list of charges against you. That information should make certain you're hanged, or put a lot more years on your prison sentence. Tell me what I want to know, and I'll keep it to myself."

"What's so damn important to you?" Zeke sneered.

"I came here in early spring with a friend, Tanner Gaston, son of that man over there," Joe explained. "While we were in Pierre, somebody put a knife in him and murdered him. I want to know who's responsible. If you did it, I'll still honor my deal with you. I have to know who killed him before my mind can rest. His death is one of the main reasons I was so determined to defeat all of you. I'm offering you a good deal, Zeke, one you don't deserve. I advise you to accept it and not rile me again. I think you've witnessed how dangerous I can be when crossed."

"He a dark-haired man about your age, looked half-breed?"

"Yes," Joe answered. He was angered by Zeke's insulting tone and surprised the miscreant complied. "Tanner overheard something by accident, and one of you made certain he couldn't repeat it. Fact is, he lived long enough to give me a few clues that put me on your trail. It was probably about that wagon trip you took when we met. Talk. We don't have much time left."

"Ain't nothing you can do about it now; Clem gutted your friend. He's dead. It was his loose tongue that Gaston overheard, so the boys told him he had to clean up his mess. Me and Farley wasn't in Pierre that night, but they told me about killing a spy. Guess that was him. Too bad the boys didn't know about you that night and slit your miserable neck."

"Yep, it's a real shame they didn't commit two murders!" Joe growled. "If you've told the truth, our deal stands. If you lied, I'll let you hang for his death, guilty or not." Joe had Zeke gagged to make certain the big man didn't shout any warnings to his buddy. He went to the spot where Farley was captive, out of hearing range from his companion.

Joe intimidated Farley into talking. He was relieved in a strange way to hear the same account from him. Maybe it was because he knew he finally had the truth about Tanner's murder, and the killer was dead. Justice had been carried out without his participation. He had Farley returned to the others and Zeke's gag removed. While he waited for his party to move out, he completed his own report for Tom and the authorities. He left nothing out, and felt no remorse over duping Zeke. When Stede joined him, he related what he had learned about Tanner's death, and both grieved the heavy loss in silence for a time.

The detail mounted and departed with the prisoners, riding east to Fort Tabor. Joe was glad to have them out of his life forever. He was also glad the officer in charge was taking care of those false accusations against him and Morning Star. With Sergeant Bart Carnes in custody, the man would stand trial for the murder of Captain James Thomas and the deserter, George Hollis. Joe had liked Jim, and was sorry he had been slain while helping to solve this case.

Black Moon had left about the same time the Oglalas had, so the clearing was rather quiet, with only six men and horses present. Everything was packed and ready. The smallest group mounted and rode southwest. They entered the northwest section of the Black Hills to journey to the grasslands beyond it and on to Fort Laramie. The trek would require six or seven days.

As they traveled, Joe thought about Morning Star and his family. He wondered what she was doing as she spent her last few weeks with her family. He knew she must be experiencing an array of emotions. He was anxious to get finished here and head home. He wanted to see his parents, sister, and her family. He wanted to make certain everything and everyone there was all right. He wanted to roam the plantation, and enjoy life and peace to the fullest. He had experienced enough excitement and adventure to last him a long time. He was ready to get married, to settle down, to build his own home, and to have children. He knew the perfect spot on the Lawrence property for them to live. Soon, he kept telling himself, his dreams and goals would be realized.

The men made camp an hour before dusk. They were exhausted from yesterday's tense episode and their journey today. The weary horses, dusty and sweaty, were eager to rest and graze after being unsaddled. Joe and one of the soldiers cooked the evening meal. Tom and Stede conversed and relaxed. As they ate, another scout from Fort Laramie arrived, an extra horse in tow.

He dismounted, and one of the men tended his fatigued animals. He walked to the campfire and asked, "Which one of you is Stede Gaston?"

"I am," Stede replied, a curious sensation attacking his gut.

"Urgent message, sir." As he unfastened his pouch and withdrew the letter, he explained, "Colonel Mitchell ordered me to bring it to you at Fort Tabor. The boys there sent me to find you at Bear Butte. Before I reached it, I met the detail heading in with prisoners. They told me which route you were taking back to Fort Laramie. I rode across country to intercept you. This is it, sir," he finished his report and handed over the missive that was marked URGENT across the front in two places.

Stede tore open the envelope with shaky hands, fearing it was bad news about his older sister or her family. He had lost his only son here, and he prayed he wasn't about to learn he had lost another loved one during his long absence. He was shocked by the contents of the letter.

"What is it, sir?" Joe asked, concerned by his friend's reaction.

Stede's dark gaze, filled with sadness, met the younger man's. His voice was hoarsened by emotion as he revealed, "Bad news, Joe, about your father. It's from Annabelle. She thought I could locate you and get you home quickly. Joseph's very ill, Son, dying."

Joe paled, and a shudder raced over his body. He tossed his plate aside, intense apprehension flooding him. *Father, dying,* his mind echoed.

Stede had no choice but to continue with the terrible news. "The doctor says he can't linger more than six or seven weeks. Annabelle wants you to get home as soon as possible. She hired a man to deliver this to me, so it was written only a few weeks ago. If you hurry, there should still be time to reach home before . . ."

Joe was glad Stede didn't finish that awful sentence. His mind was dazed with many thoughts about getting home swiftly and about Morning Star. Retrieving his love and perhaps battling to win her from Sun Cloud would require precious time his father might not have. *Only weeks more to live* . . . and it took that many to reach home without any delays. *Any delays* . . .

Stede grasped how upset the man was, so he offered some suggestions. "If you leave in the morning for Tabor, you can catch a steamer there. At St. Louis, you can get a horse and cut across country to Richmond to the plantation. That's the quickest route. You can leave Star at Tabor. I'll see to him after the treaty. When Sun Cloud gets to Laramie, I'll explain everything to him. I'll visit his camp and tell Morning Star what happened. If you want, Son, I'll bring her to Virginia. You have to get home fast to spend any last days with him. You lost your best friend here, and I'll be losing a good one there. Life makes these demands on us."

Joe stood, paced, and protested, "I can't just leave for . . . I don't know how long without seeing her, sir. She'll be upset and afraid. She might not come with you, and I don't know when I can return. Sun Cloud may not let her leave home if I'm not there to persuade him I love her."

Stede understood his dilemma, but stressed that if he took the time to visit her or fight for her, he could reach home too late. "I haven't gotten over the fact I wasn't with Molly or Tanner when they died," he confided. "You need to speak with Joseph, Son; you didn't leave home with his blessing. And your mother needs you. Love is strong; it can wait a while."

"If you start trouble with Sun Cloud in your state of mind and rush him," Tom added, "you could stop him from attending the peace conference. We've all worked hard for this treaty to succeed, Joe. Don't ruin it now. I'm sure she'll either wait for your return or go with Stede. Will you be able to forgive yourself if you get there too late because of romantic notions? You have years ahead with her, but not with your father, from how it sounds."

Stede withdrew money from his pocket, handed it to Joe, and said, "You'll need this for passage and to buy a horse in St. Louis. Don't worry about anything here. I'll make sure the treaty is fair to Sun Cloud and his tribe. I'll tell you everything when I bring Morning Star to you in Virginia."

"You can use my other horse," the scout offered. "You can travel faster by changing mounts every few hours. Just leave him at Tabor, and the boys there will bring him to me when they return to Laramie. Both of them are fast and sure-footed."

Those kindnesses touched Joe deeply. "Thanks, you two. I'll leave right now," he decided, but Stede halted him with a grip on one wrist.

"No, Son. You and those horses are exhausted. You wouldn't get far before both of you collapse. Clear your head and don't be rash. It's a long and hard journey facing you. The trail is fraught with perils. Get a good night's sleep and ride out fresh and alert at dawn. We'll have your horses and supplies ready at first light. I'll see to Morning Star, I promise. Go straight home, Joe," he urged.

"I will, sir. Right now, I need to be alone for a while." Joe headed into a copse of hardwoods to get his emotions under control.

Chapter Nineteen

Sun Cloud and his party reached Buffalo Gap at midmorning. Red Hearts gathered around to hear the glorious tale of victory at Bear Butte and reports of Joe's perilous role in it. The ecstatic group was given food and water, and boys guided their horses away to be tended. Wives embraced husbands, mothers hugged sons, and children clasped the necks and legs of fathers. It was a time of celebration and happiness, a time of looking to the future, a moment of relief for safe returns.

The elated chief explained how they had worked with Crow, enemies for generations. He talked of the soldiers' friendliness and acceptance of him. He related the motive behind Snake-Man's greed and wickedness, and everyone comprehended why their Great Spirit had been eager to stop it. His party was praised and congratulated.

Sun Cloud held up his souvenir, then hung Orin's mask on a pole near the meeting lodge for all to see and study. He exposed the grim news about Hawk Eyes and Knife-Slayer, and the good news about Wind Bird becoming shaman. He called the man forward to demonstrate the "magic balls" Joe had given to him. The display drew sounds of amazement and approval of such "big medicine."

Morning Star was not happy about the two deaths, but she was relieved the bad influence of both men had been removed. She was glad when War Chief Lone Horn invited the grieving Waterlily into his tepee for protection and support until she recovered from her two losses and took another husband. She was relieved that her love was safe somewhere.

Sun Cloud spoke of his impending journey to Fort Laramie.

429

He planned to leave at sunrise with chosen warriors to sign a joint treaty with allies and past foes. He gave the command to break summer camp the next day to head for the Black Hills to set up their winter one. Men were assigned their duties during the seasonal trek.

As the people returned to their chores and families, Sun Cloud said to his wife and daughter, "It is a good day. The bloodline of my father has gathered many coups. My pride is large for you, Morning Star, and for Sky Warrior, grandson of my uncle. When Tanner returns with me after the treaty council, we will have a great feast to honor my daughter and blood brother. Truce, my loved ones, has been long and hard in coming. Until it is gone, we will enjoy peace and happiness. My heart is filled to bursting."

Singing Wind cast Morning Star a look of regret at having to spoil this glorious moment, but Sun Cloud was leaving tomorrow. She wanted to be the one to reveal the shocking truth to her husband, not risk his learning it from someone else while he was gone.

Morning Star's eyes pled for silence, but her mother did not catch the signal to postpone the revelation until another day. She wanted Joe here with her when their dark secret came to light; she had not thought of him riding on to Fort Laramie with Stede and the others. She prayed her actions would not delay the search for peace.

Sun Cloud noticed the curious behavior. "What fox walks in the heads of my loved ones?" he teased the two women.

"Come, my husband, and I will tell you."

While glancing at his nervous daughter, the intrigued chief let his wife guide him into their tepee. He watched her seal the flap, the signal for privacy. When she grasped his hand, pulled him to their sleeping mat, and drew him down to sit beside her, Sun Cloud misunderstood, and his desires flamed. He grinned and jested, "You grow brave, Singing Wind, to let others see your great hunger for me. It is good our hearts and bodies still burn for each other, and we have the strength to feed them at our ages."

"Love and hunger are not what burns in me this sun. I am sorry."

Morning Star stared at the closed flap of the tepee, then sought refuge away from camp. She sat beside a rushing stream and wished time would pass as swiftly. She wished Joe had returned with Sun Cloud. She needed him at her side when she faced her father soon. She had spoken with her mother many times in the last thirteen days. She had obeyed Singing Wind's urgent request to give the important decision more study, but nothing had changed her mind. She loved Joseph Lawrence, she wanted to marry him, she wanted to spend her life with him, and she wanted to bear his children. Whatever challenges confronted them, they would meet them together.

She looked up as Clay joined her to pass along her love's messages and warning. When he discovered the secret had been revealed to her mother who was presently telling Sun Cloud, he looked worried. As Buckskin Girl arrived, Clay offered her his help if there was trouble. Feeling there was nothing he could do, she smiled and told him to spend his short time with Buckskin Girl. The two walked away, hand in hand, to speak with Flaming Star about a joining ceremony.

Time passed too slowly for Morning Star in her state of dismay. Singing Wind had insisted on being the one to break the news to her husband. She had told Morning Star it was best for everyone involved if she related the decision and the reasons behind it. She had disagreed with her mother, but relented when it seemed so important to Singing Wind.

Her mother had spoken with her and had considered the matter at length. At last Singing Wind had said she understood and accepted that choice and realized how difficult and painful it had been for her daughter to make it. That and assurance of her mother's love eased her anxieties for a while, but they had returned with her father's arrival and the talk in progress.

Singing Wind was sad about her child's leaving. The older woman feared they would never see each other again. Her final words before Sun Cloud arrived were, "Go in peace, my daughter, and walk the path Grandfather makes for you. It will be long and hard, but do it bravely."

Morning Star dreaded the upcoming talk with her father, but

knew the matter must be settled. She could not stay here and lose Joe. She could not marry another and bear his children. Joe was her heart, her future. Her life here was over. With Joe, once the anguish of her decision passed and she eased into his world, she would be happy and free. Whatever the sacrifice to follow her true destiny, her true love, she would make it.

The nervous woman glanced toward camp and wondered what was being said between her parents. If only she did not have to shame and hurt them to make her dreams come true . . .

The exuberance of victory left Sun Cloud's heart and mind; now they were consumed by disbelief, anguish, turmoil, and anger. He listened to his beloved wife's stunning revelation about their daughter and Joseph Lawrence. He felt betrayed by them, their deceit, their weakness, their cowardice. He was hurt by their lack of trust in him, and their surrender to a forbidden union, as he knew they must have yielded to temptation while on the trail alone and in love. He wondered how his beautiful, gentle, sweet Morning Star could do this awful thing.

As promised before Singing Wind began this talk, he listened and held silent until she finished. Then Sun Cloud agonized aloud. "Does she not realize this cannot be? She and her family will be dishonored and attacked by pain. Has she forgotten our laws? It is wrong, shameful. I cannot break them or bend them for my child; that is unfair to all others. If I do not banish her, my people will see me as a weakling, unworthy to be their chief. If she is sent away, never can my eyes gaze upon the proof of her betrayal. She will no longer be my daughter. She will be cut from our lives, the story of our family, from our bloodline."

"Nothing can remove your blood from her, my love," Singing Wind refuted. "It can only be denied. She did not plan to trick us; Joe did not plan to trick us. Sometimes such actions must be taken. Remember what happened the night he came to us and understand why they did this. When Morning Star learned of the sacred vision and believed Joe was Sky Warrior, she acted swiftly to save his life. The Great Spirit silenced her tongue, my husband, not evil and defiance."

In his torment and shock, Sun Cloud disagreed, "There have been many times since that moon to reveal the truth; they have not. I trusted Sky Warrior; I made him blood brother and thought him a man of honor, a man of Running Wolf's bloodline. In secret, as the sly raccoon sneaks about in the night, he stole precious food from my tepee. Others know he is not Tanner — Stede, Broken-Hand, Clay, the soldiers — but none revealed his deceit. How do I know they will not keep other secrets from me? How do I know they will not make deceit for me and all Indians with the treaty?"

"Truce tricks are not in Payaba's vision, my love."

"My daughter's betrayal was not in Payaba's vision, but it is done."

"You are wrong, my husband. Their love is there, so, too, their leaving, but Wakantanka held Payaba's tongue silent until the right time to reveal them. That is now, my love."

Sun Cloud gaped at his wife. "Why have so many secrets been kept from me and Red Hearts? Why must she do this? It was selfish, defiant, and blind to jump on a wild horse she cannot ride."

Singing Wind caressed his cheek and reminded, "As we did long ago, my husband? Have you forgotten how we broke the laws of our peoples when we surrendered to love while I was promised to your brother? We risked banishment, dishonor, and death to have each other. I teased you that it would take more than an Eagle's fledgling to tame Singing Wind or to give her sweet pleasure, but you did both. Perhaps it will take more than an Indian warrior to do the same for our daughter. She is different from others, my love. She is strong, proud, brave, smart; but she is gentle and caring. She does not do this to be selfish. She does not wish to hurt us or to punish us. She is now as we were long ago — young, passionate, and in love."

"It is different, my wife; no one knew of our secret, our weakness."

"Does that make it any less true, or us any less guilty? We were not forced to choose between love and banishment, as she must do. We were not forced to choose between our loves and our families, as she must do. We were not forced to choose between joy and sadness, as she must do. We did not choose each other to love and join; Wakantanka put such feelings in our hearts and bodies, and He removed all obstacles from our union path. It is the same with Morning Star and Joe."

"How will the obstacle of our laws be removed, my wife? More whites and wars will come. If I change our laws, it will bring more palefaces into our tribe. If our bloods are weakened, we will know great defeats when the new battles come. When sides go to war, it will split the mixed families. My people listened to the words of Gray Eagle and obeyed them. They listen to mine and obey me. If I speak to change the law, it will bring trouble, sadness, and dissension. My people accepted whites in the lives of my father and brother. For my daughter to choose a white man sets a bad example. It will appear that the bloodline of Gray Eagle prefers white mates over ones of their own kind. I am chief and must think of my duty."

"Morning Star knows the truth about Alisha, my love," she revealed, then explained how the girl had learned the news. "How can we say it was good for Gray Eagle to love and join a white woman but it is bad for our daughter to do the same with a white man, one who has risked his life to save our people and to bring peace to our land? What of our child's coups and risks, my love? She faced as many dangers. She tried to obey our laws; she tried to remain strong. When fate seemed against us long ago, we battled our feelings, but could not stay strong and loyal to our ways. We knew what was right and wrong, but love swayed and ruled us."

"We are the same; they are not."

"Morning Star is half like him, my love, and she knows this."

"But he was raised white, and she was raised Indian. You take their side when you must fight it. You make excuses for them."

"As we did for ourselves long ago?" she asked in a gentle tone.

"It is not the same," he contended without raising his voice in anger.

"How is it different?"

"You think as a woman, with the heart."

"You think as a man and a chief, with the head. But Morning Star is a woman, and she has been a warrior. Her head battled fiercely with her heart. Only because she truly believes this is Grandfather's will did she have the courage to follow her heart.

Remember what you said to me when we were entrapped by our laws?' If evil has separated us, we must destroy it to be joined.' Hatred is evil, my love; war is evil, my love; they are destructive forces. They must be defeated. That was done at the sacred mountain."

"But only for a time, my wife," the chief reminded. "They will return, even stronger and deadlier the next time."

"Is that not a good reason to have our child far away, safe and happy? Do not let a man's pride be stronger than a father's love in this matter. Do not make us lose her heart along with her body. Do not make her suffer more than she must. Remember how Gray Eagle could not battle his love and destiny. Remember how we could not battle them. Accept it is the same for Morning Star and Joe," she urged.

Sun Cloud fused his troubled gaze with Singing Wind's imploring one. He had no more answers, only torment and sadness—and grief over the impending loss of his cherished daughter. He was glad Singing Wind had disclosed this news to him. If his daughter had done so, he might have said terrible things to her in his anger and dismay, and provoked a vicious quarrel. It was too late to change the situation, so he must deal with it in the only way left open to him. "I will speak with her."

Morning Star rose as her father approached. His gaze and expression revealed nothing of his turbulent feelings, a skill he used well when necessary. Her heart drummed in her tight chest, her mouth was dry, and her body trembled. She did not fear her father, but she feared the demands of this matter. "Mother told you?" she asked, her voice quavering, her eyes filled with anguish.

Sun Cloud did not speak for a time. His impenetrable gaze roamed her from head to toe, then settled on her face, which was lined with worry and tension. "Singing Wind told me of your secret. You have spoken with her many times and you know what sacrifices you must make. They are not yours alone, my daughter; we must share your dishonor and banishment. After the words are given to our people, I cannot speak your name or see your face again."

That news was expected, but still it was a crushing blow to hear him deliver it. "That is not my choice, Father. I love you. I do not want to hurt you or shame you before others. It cuts into my heart to lose you and Mother. I do not want to leave in banishment and dishonor, but that is our law."

"You know I cannot change it for you."

"Yes, Father, and I am sorry it must be so. I pray you to seek and find understanding and forgiveness as I take the true path of my Life-Circle. If it is wrong to love and join Joe, the Great Spirit would not allow it. I will learn the white ways, seek to understand their hatred and greed, and will send that knowledge to help my people."

"It will not stop what is to be, my child. When Joe's people come to destroy us, what then? Your heart will war with your mind once more. You must become white to live among them; you must deny your Indian heritage and blood to be accepted."

"War must end forever some day, Father."

"It will not until one side is destroyed or conquered. You rode Payaba's vision. Do not forget the rest of it—more war, a great and bloody war. Can you deny all and who you are, Morning Star? What of honor, duty, blood? What of love for your family, your people, your land? The line of Gray Eagle must continue; it must become strong and pure once more. Do not stain it with more white blood. Bright Arrow has only daughters, no son to carry on the chief's line. You must bear an Indian child, my daughter."

"The line will pass through Night Stalker and Bloody Arrow."

"What if they do not survive the next white man's attack? If you have no Indian son to take their place, the chief's line will pass from ours. When it has done so, we will be defeated, almost destroyed. That warning was in the sacred vision of Mind-Who-Roams when he was shaman to Gray Eagle."

"Bright Arrow has many grandsons from Little Feet and Tashina," Morning Star pointed out, "They are sons of chiefs. Little Feet has more sons with Thunder Spirit, child of White Arrow, best friend to Gray Eagle when they lived. If those sons are too old to ride as chief when the new war comes, there is the son of Soaring Hawk, child of Tashina. The Cheyenne shaman says he is marked for greatness; and he is of Gray Eagle's blood-

436

line. Have you forgotten how Red Cloud's father was a Brule, but he leads his mother's Oglala band? The Cheyenne are our allies and friends. Why could the grandson of Tashina not become Red Heart chief—if Night Stalker, Bloody Arrow, and all others are taken from his path?"

She caught his hand in hers. "What I do, Father, will not change the destinies of others. It will not halt or bring war. If I stay and join an Indian, that does not mean I will bear sons. Bright Arrow had no sons, and many others have no sons. All lives and fates are in the Great Spirit's hands. I must go to Virginia with Joe and become his wife. He helped rid our lands of evil ones. The Great White Chief has commanded peace, and all nations and tribes have agreed to sign the treaty. You must let nothing halt Sun Cloud from signing it. Joe needed my skills to win this great victory for our people. You, Father, are the one who gave them to me. You taught me the white man's tongue. You taught me warrior skills. You trained me to be clever and daring. You showed me how to be strong, how to do what must be done for the good of our tribe. Do you not see—Grandfather was leading you to prepare me for the sacred vision?"

"I do not deny such words and truths."

Before he could continue, she contended, "You said not to forget the rest of the sacred vision. I have not, but there is more Payaba must tell you about it. My love and leaving are parts of it, Father; they are His will, my destiny. Obeying is painful and hard, but I must and will do so. You are a great chief, a good father; you can expect nothing less of me. When Joe returns, you must not harm him. You must let me ride away with him."

Sun Cloud turned away to think and to master his warring emotions. His mind roamed to days long past, and to days beyond his birth that his parents had revealed to him.

Morning Star gazed at her father's back, still muscled and strong. She looked at the flowing ebony mane with its few streaks of white. Sun Cloud was still sleek and honed. He was still handsome and virile. He was loved, respected, and obeyed by the Red Hearts, and by most allies. Like his father, he was a legend awed and feared by their enemies.

She wanted to make his task easier for him, so she said in English, "I know how this pre-dic-ament must distress and torment you, Father. I know, as chief, you can not make ex-ceptions for me. I understand your duty and why you must stand taller and stronger than other Indians. Do what you must, Father, for I will love you and respect you forever, even more now because I know it is harder for you this time. I understand our laws, and we must both honor them."

At last, Sun Cloud made his heartrending decision and faced her. Despite his enormous strength of mind and will, his dark eyes glistened with deep and warring emotions. "I will say this but once, Morning Star, for the last time. I love you; I am proud of you; I will miss you. Go to live in peace, happiness, and safety. Have children where they will not be forced to live as half-breeds and where they will not endure wars and death. You have helped your people to survive many more years. I will sign the treaty, and I will honor it as long as I can. Your people love you and praise your brave coups, but they cannot disobey our laws for their chief's daughter. I must not coax them to change those laws, for they mean the survival of our bloodlines and race. I will tell them the truth this night. I will banish you before them. I will forbid the speaking of your name again. Only the legend of She-Who-Rode-With-The-Sky-Warrior will be upon our lips and on our tribal records. It pains my heart to deny you, but it must be this way for the good of our people. You must not return home, ever. It will do much harm for others to see you joined to a white man. He will not be safe in our land when the treaty is broken, and it *will* be broken." He drew her into his arms and embraced her. "Good-bye, my daughter. We will never touch or see each other again. What I must do this moon is hard, but it is for the good of our people."

"I know, Father. I love you. Come, end the pain of this matter."

Nearing four o'clock, Sun Cloud asked Wolf Eyes to summon the people to a clearing, and the ceremonial chief obeyed.

Morning Star stood beside her father with her head held high. She concealed her anxiety, and displayed courage and pride. She must not allow anyone to think she was ashamed of what the chief was revealing. Her gaze roamed the large group:

Sun Cloud, Singing Wind, Night Stalker, Buckskin Girl, Clay Thorne, Payaba, her kin, and her people. She saw Touched-A-Crow leave with a surly Bloody Arrow, and she prayed her brother could eventually change the boy's behavior. If the child continued to walk his rebellious path, he would become more like a son of Knife-Slayer than her brother. It was bad and alarming for Bloody Arrow to be in line for the chief's bonnet. Surely Grandfather would alter or remove him . . .

Morning Star saw girls whispering amongst themselves as they speculated on the reason of the tribal meeting and their friend's involvement in it. She knew from Buckskin Girl that unmarried braves wondered if the meeting was being called to announce her joining. She could not help but be relieved that Hawk Eyes and Knife-Slayer were not present to cause trouble. Her father lifted his hand for silence and attention. The moment arrived.

"Hear me, my people. Morning Star told me Sky Warrior is not Tanner Gaston; his name is Joseph Lawrence. Payaba said of his vision: 'The Great Mystery showed me two men. One's face was hidden from my eyes, but Grandfather said he carried Oglala blood . . . He will call the lost warrior back to the land of his people to share our destiny.' That man is Stede Gaston, son of Powchutu, Eagle's Arm. Payaba said of the second man: 'Trouble will be reborn, but its life will be cut short by the warrior Grandfather sends to us. A long peace will follow . . . He is a white-eye who will come to help us defeat our enemies . . . Peace lies within the grasp of the white-eye whose hair blazes as the sun and in whose eyes the blue of sky lives. His heart will side with us. Many foes, Indian and white, will try to defeat him.' This is all true of Joseph Lawrence and what has taken place. The vision did not say Sky Warrior carried Indian blood; Joe does not. It did not say Sky Warrior is the son of the man with Oglala blood; Joe is not."

Sun Cloud witnessed the shocked and baffled reactions to his words, but his people held silent, as was their custom. He saw how some looked at his daughter with suspicion and curiosity. "When Joe came to us to seek our help and friendship, many resisted him and some tried to have him slain. Joe came to our land with Stede and Tanner Gaston to work for peace. When

439

Tanner was killed by the evil ones and we scorned Joe, he claimed to be Tanner to win our acceptance. The Great Spirit works in mysterious ways. Grandfather allowed this trick to happen and to remain hidden until now, because Grandfather needed Joe to work for our peace and survival. When many resisted Joe's words, he believed the only way to win our trust, acceptance, and help was to claim he was Tanner Gaston of Running Wolf's bloodline. Joe did not want to trick us; he did not plan to trick us. It came to him as he was attacked and threatened with death. He did this to save his life to work on the sacred vision. His deceit was wrong, and our behavior that night was wrong. We are all living creatures and make such mistakes. It is true he wanted to save us and to get peace; he wished to do this for Tanner and Stede, who are as father and brother to him. When he came to know us, he came to like, respect, and accept us as worthy to save. One weakness in him does not take away his honor and many coups."

Many heads nodded in understanding. Sun Cloud awaited their reaction to his imminent disclosure. "When the treaty council ends, Morning Star will leave our land with Sky Warrior, to live in the white world and to become his mate." As people looked confused, Sun Cloud reminded, "They are not of the same bloodline, for Joe is not Tanner, not the grandson of Eagle's Arm, son of Running Wolf. Morning Star's destiny is not here with us. Payaba saw this in his vision, but Grandfather commanded him not to speak of it until peace ruled our land and the sacred mission was victorious. Payaba revealed it to me this sun; I believe and accept it as the will of the Great Spirit. Morning Star's destiny is in the land where her grandmother was raised. Perhaps our two Gods have made truce, as we make truce with our enemies. The white God sent Alisha/Shalee to my father, and the Great Spirit must send Morning Star to Joe. Gray Eagle claimed Shalee as wife. Now, Joe claims their granddaughter as wife. This is our great sacrifice for peace and survival; it is Morning Star's Sun Dance ritual to surrender herself to destiny and Wakantanka's will."

The hard part of Sun Cloud's task arrived. "But Payaba's vision also said: 'More white-eyes will journey here in great numbers. Their hungers will bring even darker and bloodier suns' than we have known for these past seasons. We must sign the treaty, though it will be broken one day, so we can enjoy many winters of peace, happiness, and survival. But, as Payaba warned: 'The white-eyes will come to fear and battle the Dakota Nation as they do with no other. The Tetons will lead all tribes of the Seven Council Fires and our allies in the last battle for survival.' It is our law not to join with our enemies, the whites. We must not change this law. We must keep our bloodlines pure and strong; they must stay Indian. If this law is broken, the guilty one is pushed from our camp and lives. This is what I must do with my daughter, for even a chief's family is not above tribal law."

As Sun Cloud took a few breaths, he saw people stare at Morning Star. Some reactions said his words were right; some said cruel; some said they felt empathy, but agreed with the law.

"No Red Heart, not even the chief and his family, must speak her name again. She must be banished. Our laws must not be changed. Morning Star understands and agrees. From this moon until our days cease, we must speak only of She-Who-Rode-With-The-Sky-Warrior, and she must never return to us. When my people break camp on the new sun to move into the Black Hills, she must remain here to wait for Joseph Lawrence."

Singing Wind, standing beside her daughter, started to protest the cruelty of leaving their child alone and in possible peril from renegades and wicked whites and from the forces of Mother Nature. But Morning Star grasped her hand and squeezed it to tell her to hold silent. It was one of the hardest things she had ever done, but she obeyed the message.

Morning Star locked her gaze with her brother's. Disbelief, anger, and disappointment filled Night Stalker's eyes. She smiled at him to let him know she was all right. As her father reminded everyone, her departure and mixed marriage were in the sacred vision and wills of the Great Spirit, Night Stalker returned the smile and nodded understanding.

To let those who resisted this decision know he wasn't being cruel and unfair or sacrificing an unwilling child, Sun Cloud added, "Morning Star loves this white man and chooses to go with him. From this time on to forever, Morning Star is dead to us, to her family and to her people; and we are dead to her. She must gather her possessions and make camp away from us until she leaves our land. She must be avoided; she must not be spoken to or looked at; she must not be helped with chores or visited. Morning Star is no more. Only the legend of She-Who-Rode-With-The-Sky-Warrior can be spoken, remembered, and honored."

Again, Morning Star squeezed her mother's quivering hand to halt the protest she perceived. Neither she nor her mother had thought of this part of banishment. Both had forgotten, once the words were spoken publicly, the deed was done and the punishment began. Her heart was breaking, and she wished Joe were here to give her courage. She prayed the peace council and his return would not be long in coming. Her father would tell him what had happened when he reached Fort Laramie and surely Joe would hurry to her side, here where she must camp alone and wait for him.

Sun Cloud commanded as chief, not her grieving father, "Turn your eyes and backs to her, my people. She is dead to us." To his lost child, he ordered, "Go, fetch your possessions and leave camp. Do not approach it again. This is our law. Live nearby until the white man comes for you."

Morning Star was consumed by anguish. She was cut off from her family and friends. They could not exchange goodbyes. To them, she must be as the wind — invisible, ignored. She must be as the flower — silent. She must be as the cactus spines — untouched. She was banished, forever. It was done.

The band, many with broken hearts, obeyed the chief and their law. They turned away from the beautiful creature with misty eyes. No one spoke, though many wished to do so, as it was their way and was necessary. Many said a mute farewell to the exquisite female, the brave vision woman.

Singing Wind did not care who witnessed her defiance. She embraced her child and whispered, "I love you, Morning Star. I will miss you and never forget you. You will always be my daughter. Be safe and happy."

She hugged the woman and whispered in her ear, "Be strong, Mother. I love you and will miss you. I will never forget all you have taught me. Help Father through this hard time. Soon I will be fine."

442

Night Stalker also embraced her and whispered, "Forever you are my sister and I will love you, no matter our law. I will be a good chief. Do not worry about our parents and people. I will take care of them."

Morning Star gazed into his dark eyes and smiled, as she knew he spoke the truth. Tears blurred her vision. She could not speak again, so she answered by caressing his cheek. She watched her mother and brother slowly turn away from her. She captured Sun Cloud's hand, squeezed it, and whispered, "I love you, Father. Never be sorry for obeying our law." It gave her strength when the man clasped her hand tightly for a moment.

Morning Star weaved her way through the silent crowd with lowered head. She went to her parents' tepee and packed her belongings, then walked to Hanmani, took his reins, and guided him out of camp. She did not look back, or halt until she was a mile from her people. She released the faithful animal's reins, dropped her possessions, and sat down to weep over her losses. Her decision was much harder than she had imagined, and it could never be changed or taken back. Tomorrow, her father and his band would leave for Fort Laramie; her people would depart for the sacred hills. She would be alone. "Come quickly to me, my love," she prayed.

Chapter Twenty

Joseph Lawrence reached his destination and dismounted. It was dark and quiet, and no one seemed disturbed by his late arrival. To make certain, he left Star at the edge of the camp and moved quietly to obtain the privacy he needed for what he must do. He realized his father did not have long to live. Yet, he was doing the best he could for everyone involved. He also realized that no matter how fast he traveled his father already might be dead, but he fervently hoped not.

Joe could not bring himself to leave without Morning Star. He would lose only half a day—a day at most if there was trouble—by veering off the route to fetch her. He knew Stede's urgings had come from a heart filled with remorse over missing last moments with his wife and son; the older man had not stopped to think how close to Sun Cloud's summer camp the route from their campsite to Fort Tabor would bring Joe. As best he could judge, the chief and his band should have reached home earlier today. That meant there had not been enough time to begin moving to the Black Hills.

Joe felt it was his responsibility as a man and a suitor to face Sun Cloud with the truth. He comprehended Tom's concern over damaging all their work with the confession, but he knew he must take that risk. He had to have faith in the chief's character and honor, in himself, and in God.

He approached Sun Cloud's tepee, knelt at the open flap, and called his blood brother's name. It was only moments before the chief responded and called him inside. Joe ducked and entered. His gaze widened and showed confusion when he did not see his love inside so late at night. He sensed a strange and alarming tension in the air. In the fire's small glow, he read expressions on the Indian couple's faces that worried him. Astute, Joe asked, "What's wrong, Sun Cloud? Where is Morning Star?"

"She is gone," Mahpiya Wi replied to the white man his child loved and had sacrificed all to have, the sacred vision warrior, the trickster, the power taking away his beloved daughter, his blood brother. Which—if any or all—of those things should rule his emotions and behavior tonight?

"Gone? Did she follow us to Bear Butte and get into danger?" *Please, God, don't let her be hurt. Don't let her be somewhere else. I don't have more time to spare. Help us get out of here quickly and painlessly.*

"No, she was banished this sun. She camps alone nearby. She is dead to us. We cannot speak her name or look upon her face again. It is our law."

Joe did not have to be told why the action was taken, but it shocked him. His gentle love was alone and in anguish. "My people will not banish me for choosing her. How could you do this to your own child?"

"It is our law. I could not break it for her." As the angry white man stared at him, Sun Cloud related all that had happened. "She is downstream waiting for your return. Why have you come tonight? Why did you halt your ride to the peace council?"

"A scout from Fort Laramie caught up with us that first night. He delivered an urgent letter from my mother. My father is dying. I must hurry home. Even now, I may be too late to see him. I have to ride fast and hard, Sun Cloud, but I had to come for Morning Star first. I wanted to be the one to explain everything to you. I wanted you to hear from me how sorry I am for having to deceive you about being Tanner. From what you told me, I can tell you think it was wrong, but that you understand my motives. I'm glad, because I don't want you of all men to think badly of me. Tanner was my best friend, like a brother to me. How I miss him. He wanted to help his father; they both wanted to help their Indian kin. At first, I took over his place to find his killer, but I became attached to Morning Star and her people. I really care what happens you and the Red Hearts; you must believe that. In all honesty, I took those risks more for your people than to keep the whites out of a war. This is Indian territory, and I wish it could remain that way forever. We both know it won't, and I'm sorry."

Joe related the talk that had taken place in his camp after the urgent message reached him and Stede's offer to escort his love to Virginia. "It wasn't right to let him be the one to face you about our secret. Stede and Tom, Broken-Hand, told me not to come here because they were afraid you'd be angry about my deceit and it would stop you from attending the treaty talk. I don't believe that, not of a man like the son of Gray Eagle. You might hate me and distrust me, but from what I've seen and learned about the Red Heart chief, you have too much honor to sacrifice peace for your people. You know this treaty is genuine, and signing it is vital to years of peace. What I've done wrong can't stop you from signing."

Joe was relieved when the chief allowed him to have his say before taking his turn. "I love Morning Star, Sun Cloud; I need her. She's a part of me now. I want to marry her. I want to share the rest of my life with her. I want her children. God knows we tried to prevent this from happening. We battled our attraction to each other as long and as hard as we could. It didn't work. We realized how difficult a mixed marriage would be. We knew what trouble and pain it would cause many people, especially her family. She's the most wonderful woman I've ever met. You raised her to be strong and skilled. She's my friend, my helper, all I want and need in a woman. I swear to you I'll make her happy. She'll be safe and free at my home. I won't let anyone mistreat her or harm her. You have my word."

Sun Cloud was pleased by Joe's confession, though he couldn't let it show. Yet his voice was not harsh when he informed the man, "I do not need your word, and you do not need my permission. She has chosen you; she has been banished. All you must do is go after her and leave. And you must never return to our land and camp."

"I know it's your law and I understand why you have to keep it, but I want you to understand our feelings. I want you to forgive us for tricking you. I want you to be happy about our love and marriage. I don't want to lose your respect and friendship. And I don't want the woman I love to suffer because of me. She doesn't deserve cruel treatment like this; she was the vision woman. She only obeyed it. Banish her if you must, but don't deny her; don't say she's dead to you and that her family is dead to her."

Sun Cloud studied the white man with blue eyes and blond hair. Joe's tone said he was sincere and honest. "It must be this way; laws are for every person. You must understand why we cannot change them. I believe your words, but they change nothing for her."

Joe took a deep breath, then released it. "You're right, but your decision hurts many people. I guess it was foolish, but I was hoping this wouldn't happen to Sky Warrior and the vision woman. Maybe I never believed it would, not even when Morning Star kept warning me of the grim consequences. What I don't understand is why you banished her before I spoke to you and made a claim on her. Until we exposed the truth, why was she sent off alone? What if I'd done as Stede urged and left for home? She could have been in great danger until Stede saw you at Laramie, then rode here for her."

Sun Cloud looked at the insect bite that had saved Joe's life from Knife-Slayer's treachery and the bruise from Zeke Randall's blow to his cheek. "She revealed the truth and forced me to act on it. By choosing you, she is your wife in our eyes. The Great Spirit brought you here tonight to rescue her and to take her home with you. She is a skilled warrior; I knew she would be safe until you came for her. I did not want you to come to our winter camp to claim her. I did not want my people to see my daughter—bloodline of Gray Eagle—ride away with a white man. I wanted them to remember you as Sky Warrior, not as the sly paleface who tricked us and took her from us. You have done much for me and my people. I thank you and honor you for this. But you have stolen my daughter from me; understanding and forgiveness will take time to fill my heart. But when they come, it will change nothing. You must understand this and not battle for what can never be again. You have been my friend and blood brother; never return as my enemy with my enemies. Keep her from harm and give her much joy, but never return," he stressed.

Joe perceived clues in the chief's speech: love and concern between the lines of it, the anguish Sun Cloud was experiencing, and the strength of this great leader to carry out his heartbreaking duty. "It will be as you say. We'll be gone at first light. But I'll contact you in the future to see if your feelings have changed. I won't tell Morning Star about my message until they do. If things are ever different, I'll bring her home to visit."

Sun Cloud used all his willpower not to reply in the way his heart begged him to do so. As chief he must not weaken. He did not.

Joe grasped the turmoil in his love's father. "I understand, and we'll obey," he murmured. "There's one last thing, Sun Cloud. I didn't reveal all of Orin's motives at Bear Butte." He related the last one, probably the most important to the greedy villain. He cautioned the chief to keep whites out of the sacred hills as long as possible. "I won't tell anybody about the gold, not even Stede. I don't want him to mention it by accident."

Sun Cloud clasped wrists with Joe. "You are a good and honorable man, Joseph Lawrence. I will long remember you and your coups. When you hear that the treaty is broken and war has come, do not return. It cannot be stopped next time; the sacred vision warned of this. Do not risk your life to challenge what is our tribal destiny; it cannot be defeated as you defeated Snake-Man. Do not bring her here to witness the sufferings and deaths of her family and people. If you love her, keep her there forever."

Joe noticed how Sun Cloud obeyed his law by not once

448

speaking his lost daughter's name. How he wished it didn't have to be this way for all of them. Maybe things would change in the future; he hoped so, for his wife's sake. "I love Morning Star, sir. We'll obey your words and laws. If you ever need to reach us, contact the President, our Great White Chief; he can tell you where we live." Joe glanced at the older woman who looked in great pain. "Good-bye, Singing Wind. I'm sorry we've hurt you. Don't worry about Morning Star. I promise to take good care of her." He turned to the chief and said, "Good-bye, Sun Cloud. I'll never forget you and my time here. And I won't forget all I've learned." Joe looked at his love's parents one last time, and left the tepee.

After a time, Sun Cloud joined his wife on their sleeping mat. He pulled Singing Wind into his arms. "He is right; do not worry. Payaba says she walks the path Grandfather planned for her. We must accept this."

"I will be strong, my husband, but it will be hard for a time."

"I love you, Singing Wind," he murmured against her lips.

"I love you," she replied, then kissed him to ease her torment.

Sun Cloud did not relate the rest of Payaba's vision for it would hurt and frighten his wife. What the past shaman had revealed in private about his daughter had given him the strength to banish her: "Let her go with Sky Warrior or she will die in the dark days ahead, as will many others."

The old man had spoken of a time when another great warrior—a legend larger than himself and Gray Eagle—would ride the Plains and war against the interloping whites. Payaba had spoken of another child in their tepee, a boy who would become a great warrior, whose prowess would blaze as a bright star in the darkened sky. But the old shaman did not know if the two men were the same. Payaba had warned of an arrow, dripping in blood and firing over the land, that must be watched closely over the years; and Sun Cloud suspected his identity—his unruly grandson.

"When dark shadows blanket our land once more, the

bloodline of Gray Eagle and Sun Cloud will become strong again," Payaba had said. "Do not resist what must be, or the vision will be defeated and all will perish."

Sun Cloud wondered if those parts of the prophecy—told only to him—meant they would have another son and the chief's line would not pass through Night Stalker and Bloody Arrow. They were no longer young, but the Great Spirit had the power to do anything. Until he was shown the meaning of those parts, he would keep them to himself.

The Red Heart chief accepted the Great Spirit's words and warnings. He closed his eyes and thought, *Good-bye, my beloved Morning Star . . .*

"Morning Star, it's me, Joe!" he called out to prevent startling her and getting shot in the process. "I've come to get you, love."

The overjoyed woman tossed down the bow and arrow. "Joe!" she squealed and raced into his arms.

He covered her face with kisses and held her tightly. His mouth covered hers, feasting in delight as she responded and clung to him.

When their lips parted and he nestled her head against his chest, he murmured, "I'm here now, love. Everything will be all right."

Morning Star leaned her head back, straining to see his handsome face in the light of a half-moon. "Why did you return early?"

In a hoarse tone, he related the grim news about his father and his decision to come for her before leaving the territory. "We have to get home fast, love. We ride at first light. I've seen your father; he told me what happened today. I'm sorry you had to face this alone. That won't ever happen again, I promise you."

"What did Father say? How was he?" she asked, worried.

Joe told her everything they had said to each other and his impressions of her parents' feelings. "What about Clay, love? Why didn't he help you? Why isn't he here to protect you?"

"I told him not to speak or act. There is nothing he can do about our laws, except cause trouble for himself and Buckskin Girl. No one must look at me, speak to me, or help me. If he disobeys, he must be banished. That is how the law makes all obey it. He did as I asked, what was best."

"Sometimes a person has to do what he feels is right, not obey unfair laws. I'm disappointed he would leave you in danger."

"Do not be angry with him, my love. He seeks a new life with a mate and with our people. This is our decision, our problem, not theirs. Soon, we will be far away forever; they will not."

"You're right, but I can't help feeling a little angry." He changed the subject. "We'll take a big boat, called a steamer, at Fort Tabor. We'll travel down the Missouri River to St. Louis. We'll buy horses and ride overland to my home. It'll take a few weeks."

"What will happen when we reach your home and family?"

"We'll take care of my father until . . . For as long as he's with us. I hope we make it in time. I want you two to meet each other. You'll like him, Morning Star, and he'll like you. We'll get married as soon as possible; I hope we can do it at Fort Tabor before we sail. We'll buy you some clothes there, so you won't feel different from other women we meet along the trail." The talk distracted and soothed them, so he continued with it for a while. "We'll live at the plantation. It's beautiful and quiet, and away from town. Mother and I will teach you all you need to know before we visit Alexandria; that's where our shipping business is. With Father ill, you might have to stay with Mother at the plantation while I check on things at the firm. You'll love her, Morning Star. She's a wonderful lady. She'll be so happy about our marriage. She'll enjoy her lessons with you; it'll take her mind off . . . Father's loss. Then, there's Sarah Beth, my sister, her husband, Andrew, who works with Father, and their little boy, Lucas. They'll all love you and accept you. With me gone so much, at least Father had Andrew to run the business for him. If we're lucky, we'll give Lucas some

451

friends to play with real soon."

Morning Star smiled, but knew from her woman's flow last week that she carried no child at this time. Perhaps children, grandchildren, would be the path back to her family. How could anyone not want to see the continuation of their bloodline? Joe's words about her laws changing one day gave her hope to pray for that occurrence.

As they snuggled on the buffalo mat and shared endearments, Joe murmured, "Do you want to be called Morning Star, or do you want to take a white name after we're married?"

"I will live in a white land with whites, so I will follow your customs."

Joe had pondered this several times and was ready with a suggestion. "What about Marie Lawrence? Marie was my grandmother's name."

Morning Star tested it upon her lips, "Ma-rie. Marie Lawrence. Marie Lawrence. Yes, it is a good name. I will take it."

Joe embraced her. "I love you, woman. Don't worry; everything will work out fine. Let's get some sleep. We have a long hard trip ahead."

They cuddled and closed their eyes, imagining what lay before them.

Light and the horses' movements awakened Joe and Morning Star. Both instantly noticed the man sitting at the meandering stream: Clay. Joe tossed aside their cover, and joined him.

"I didn't expect to find you here, Joe," Clay remarked. "I brought supplies and extra horses. I was planning to bring Morning Star to you at Fort Laramie. I figured by changing mounts back and forth, we could beat Sun Cloud's party there and let you know what's happened."

"Sun Cloud told me last night; I reached camp late." Joe explained why he had come, and he thanked Clay—Sky Warrior—Thorne for his help.

"I'm sorry about your father. I'll help you two get

to Tabor fast."

"You're a good friend, Clay; thanks," Joe said again. "But you'll be in big trouble. I understand what an awkward position you're in. If nobody knows you're here, get back before anyone finds out about your action."

"It doesn't matter now. I can't leave friends in trouble. I'm afraid I had to change my mind about joining the Red Heart Band. I don't agree with their law that banished Morning Star, not after all you two have done for them and for peace. Since I look more white than Indian, it could give me trouble down the trail. I don't want that to happen. I decided it was best to return to my family and people; the Cheyenne don't have that law. Buckskin Girl is helping her parents move to the winter campground. When I return, I'll take her home with me. She's agreed it's for the best."

Morning Star was relieved his change of heart didn't include giving up her best friend. She did not defend or speak against the law in question that demanded so much from her. Though it seemed cruel, it protected her people against diluting their Indian blood. That was important and good.

"Sun Cloud is riding in an hour. The others are breaking camp today. Don't worry about the treaty; it'll be signed. You two did a good job, and I'm glad I got to help out a little. Be proud of yourselves. Don't suffer over what it cost Morning Star. Get married, have a good life, and be happy."

"That's good advice, my friend. I hope you do the same. Let's eat and get moving. We've got a long ride ahead."

Five days later, the three entered Fort Tabor, having camped outside the previous night after a late arrival. Joe and Morning Star went to the sutler's store to purchase her several white woman's garments for their impending voyage and new life. Clay left them to check on the next steamer heading down the Missouri River. All three knew they must hurry, so tensions were high.

Fortunately the sutler's wife, a kind and plump woman, was present. Joe explained their needs. The gentle-spirited female walked around Morning Star and eyed her up and down to decide what sizes were best. She searched through stacks of ready-made dresses, undergarments, and shoes, then guided the Indian beauty into the back room to find her judgments were accurate. The two females exchanged smiles. Morning Star kept on the prettiest cotton dress and went to show it to Joe who was pacing nervously.

Joe's eyes brightened as he gazed at the lovely sight. He noticed that Morning Star had released her braids and brushed her ebony hair to shiny free-flowing tresses. Her dark eyes glowed with excitement. Joe thanked the sutler's beaming wife and paid the man. He lifted the three packages, wrapped in brown paper, and guided his love toward the door.

Before they could depart to look for Clay, their friend rushed to them and urged, "You two have to get moving pronto! The ship leaves in less than an hour. Here are your tickets. Your gear is already loaded."

"We have to see the chaplain first," Joe reminded. He hoped there was enough time to locate the man and persuade him to marry them.

"I just saw him leaving the jail. Guess he's been ministering to those prisoners we sent here. Lot of good it'll do them now!" Clay scoffed.

"I need a long bath and a shave before I see a preacher, but I'll have to do in this mess," Joe remarked with a wry grin as he rubbed the rough stubble on his face. "Let's find him."

They located the post chaplain in the small structure, the front of which was used for services, the rear, for his personal quarters. Joe explained his request and the rush for the ceremony.

The sympathetic man eyed both, then asked, "You two sure you know what you're doing? A mixed marriage has lots of problems. You love each other enough to confront whatever comes your way?"

"Yes, sir, we love each other, and we've given our future together a lot of serious thought. We know what we're doing. We'll be fine."

"What about you, young lady?" the chaplain inquired.

Morning Star glanced at Joe, then looked at the other

man. "Yes, sir," she responded in her best English, "I love him and will be a good wife. If trouble rides after us, we will flee it or defeat it."

The chaplain studied their pleading gazes, glanced at their clasped hands, and nodded. "I believe you. I just like to make sure couples don't rush into something as serious as marriage without lots of thinking. You two stand here," he instructed, placing them in front of him and opening his Bible. He found the place he wanted, then read two scriptural passages on love and marriage. He knew they didn't have much time, but a religious service had to be done proper even in a rush.

"Do you Joseph Lawrence, Junior, take this woman to be your lawful wife in the eyes of God and man?" the chaplain asked Joe.

Joe gazed into Morning Star's lovely eyes and replied, "I do."

"Do you Marie Morning Star take this man to be your lawful husband in the eyes of God and man?"

"I do," she responded, following Joe's lead.

"Do you both promise to love, help, protect, and keep only unto each other all the days of your lives?" he asked.

"I do," the couple answered at the same time.

"God being our witness in this holy place, I pronounce you man and wife. Let no man, other God, or trouble come between you or part you," he advised in a grave tone. "I'll fill out a paper to say you're legally wed. You'll both have to sign it, and your witness there, Mr. Thorne."

Everyone remained silent as the chaplain wrote out a makeshift license, but Joe's mind raced with thoughts. He wished his parents, sister and her family, Tanner, Stede, Sun Cloud, and Singing Wind could be present. He wished the ceremony hadn't needed to be performed so quickly and with such a lack of romance. He wished he had a ring to slip on his love's finger. He vowed again to himself to protect, love, and make this woman happy, as he had sworn to her parents a few days ago.

Morning Star's mind roamed, too. She was bidding one life farewell and greeting a new one. She wished some things could be different, but she had no regrets. She loved Joe and wanted to spend her life with him. It was as it should be.

The religious man turned the page toward Joe for his signature first, then to Morning Star, and finally to Clay Thorne. When all three had marked their names on the paper, the chaplain signed and dated it. He recorded the ceremony in his Bible, then passed the binding page to Joe.

It was obvious the couple loved each other. He smiled and said, "Good luck, Mr. and Mrs. Lawrence. God go with you and protect you."

"Thank you, sir." Joe shook the man's hand. He clutched the license in one of his hands and held his wife's hand with the other. "Let's go, Mrs. Lawrence."

Morning Star smiled, and her fingers tightened around his. She thanked the chaplain and left with her husband and Clay.

At the ship, they bade farewell to Clay Thorne. Both knew they would miss their half-Cheyenne friend. Clay shook hands with Joe and embraced Morning Star, knowing, too, how much he would miss them. She and Joe sent messages to her family and friends.

The horse Joe had borrowed from the scout had been left with an officer at Tabor, who promised to return it to its owner at Laramie.

Joe asked Clay to take his roan and her Appaloosa back to Sun Cloud as gifts to Morning Star's father, a small exchange for the treasure at his side. They waved good-bye and boarded the vessel. They watched Clay mount, gather the reins of their horses, the ones to the pack animal, then ride toward the Red Heart winter camp to claim Buckskin Girl as his wife.

A crew member showed the newly wed couple to their cabin, then left them alone. Their saddles and gear were stored beside the bed, as were their other possessions, including the new clothes Joe had purchased for her from the sutler at Tabor.

The cabin was small, so there was little room for settling

in comfortably. But the voyage wouldn't take long. Their eyes met as a whistle blasted the time for departure had arrived. When the ship moved into the swift current of the Missouri River their new life would be underway.

Joe left his bride to rest and adjust to the new experience before her while he went on deck to calm himself and to view the beginning of their voyage.

After many questions to passing crewmen and the revelation that he was an ex-sea captain, Joe was invited to join the *Lucy Mae*'s captain in the pilot house. He learned that the first steamship, the *Yellowstone,* had been brought up the river to this area in the early thirties by Pierre Chouteau.

The captain of the *Lucy Mae* chatted about how buying and trading had increased over the years until steamboats worked this area frequently when the climate allowed. He told Joe that most captains quickly learned how difficult the "Big Muddy" was to navigate with her shifting, changing, and twisting channels and with her perils of snags, logs, sandbars, and mercurial currents. Even in the best boat and with the most skilled captain, it was a hazardous journey.

Joe smiled, observed, and complimented the genial captain on his skills, courage, and wits.

An hour later, Joe headed for his cabin, to be with his new bride.

Most of the day, Joe remained in the cabin, cramped and barren though it was. He didn't want his love to become frightened by this sometimes scary voyage. The swirling water around the steamer was as dark as the coffee he had transported to his country from tropical ones far away. The winter thaw and summer rains were long gone, so the water level was lower than Joe or the pilot wanted for a safe and easy voyage. Joe knew there was plenty of time during the trip for Morning Star to witness the passing sites and learn about boats.

Joe could hardly wait to reach home where his mother would help Morning Star buy pretty clothes or have a skilled seamstress make them. He envisioned her begowned and bejeweled, and him the envy of every man present. The first thing he wanted to purchase was a wedding band to slide on her finger. He used such thoughts to keep his mind off what awaited him there: his dying father.

Joe was ecstatic about a few things. His dreams were coming true: they were married, man and wife, thanks to the chaplain at Tabor. They were sailing — steaming — toward their bright future.

They ate their evening meal in a small dining area, part of the ticket price. The other three passengers — trappers going downriver who were accustomed to seeing men with Indian wives — paid little attention them. Twice during the day, Joe had gone outside to catch a breath of fresh air when they halted to take on more wood for fuel. At last it was night, and they felt relaxed enough in the strange surroundings to share intimacy.

Joe bolted the cabin door and turned to gaze at his wife. He didn't know he felt a little shy about being alone and getting ready for bed. They had made love many times and had shared a sleeping mat even more times. They were married now, committed to each other for life.

Morning Star experienced the same curious feelings and thoughts. She could not understand why it seemed so different with him tonight. She was happy and excited, and she knew he was, too. Yet . . .

"Maybe it's because we know we aren't alone in this place," Joe suggested. "Out on the Plains or in the forest, we were away from other people. It was quiet and romantic. This room is small and ugly. We had fresh air and stars around us, we weren't closed in by brown walls. We'll be on this boat for a while, so I guess we'll get used to it."

"You read my mind as I read trail signs," she teased. "I miss the open places. But if we did not have this bed, the room would be like a tepee. I will get . . . used to walls and beds."

Joe sat on the bed and removed his boots. "At our plantation, the rooms are big. We have plenty of doors and windows to let in fresh air and sunshine. The walls are painted pretty colors, light colors. The floors have rugs with

458

flowers, as do the chairs and couches. Nice pictures are on the walls and the furniture is comfortable. It's nothing like this drab cabin, Morning Star."

"I am sure it is beautiful," she said, working with difficulty on the small buttons of her new dress.

"Let me help you," Joe offered. "These can be devils until you get used to them. I never understood why women have such little buttons on their garments. Men's are bigger and easier to manage."

As her husband did the task for her, Morning Star reminded, "You must call me Marie, my love. You must . . . get used to my new name."

"Marie Lawrence . . . Mrs. Joseph Lawrence, Junior. . . . Very nice."

"I have two new names?" she asked.

Joe explained the custom of a wife taking a husband's name and told her when she should use each of them.

"It is like the custom of marking spotted buffaloes, cattle," Morning Star teased. "You white men brand your women with your name."

"Yep," he replied, grinning as he slipped the dress off her shoulders. He placed a kiss on each one. "That's so other men will know they're private property. I wouldn't take kindly to any man trying to steal my woman. I want everybody to know you're mine: Joe's wife, Joe's love."

Both began to relax as their tensions melted and their surroundings were forgotten or ignored. They had been through a harrowing time, but now at last their future had begun.

"We're safe now, my love, and together forever," Joe said gently. "No more standing guard at night, at least not on this boat. No more dangers and hardships. I hope we reach my father in time, but if we don't, we did our best to get to him. He understands what I'm doing out here, and he must know I'm on my way home as fast as possible. I'm proud of what we've accomplished, and we should never be ashamed of falling in love. In a week, the peace council will begin. When Stede returns home, he'll tell us all about it. But until we reach St. Louis and take off on horseback, we can rest and enjoy ourselves. For a while, Marie Lawrence, we will think only of us."

"I like our words and plans, my husband. It has been a long and lonely time since we joined." Morning Star lifted her hand to caress his strong jawline, hairless after his shave. Her fingertips rubbed over his full lips and she could not resist the impulse to stroke his powerful torso and to feel his sleek flesh. She gazed into his eyes, a summer sky of inviting blue, and toyed with his sunny hair. She adored its texture and how it framed his face, how its color made his eyes look bluer and his skin darker. "I love you so much it causes me to feel strange inside," she said passionately. "I see and hear nothing except you. I want nothing but you."

"That's how I feel, too, Morning Star. It used to be scary to want you so much, to your effect on me. Not any more. I love you."

Morning Star unfastened the buttons on his shirt and peeled it off his muscled torso. She dropped it to the floor. His body was as sleek and toned as the best trained warrior's. He was a splendid man, and he was hers. With Joe nearby and touching her, nothing mattered except him and their love. There was no shame and no regrets. Their bond was pure and right. She was ready to face the challenges before her. As she unlaced the ribbons on her chemise, she remarked, "White garments are strange."

"But they're fun to remove," he teased, slipping it over her head. He pulled her back into his arms, their bare skin making blissful contact. Her nearness caused his heart to race with desire. He captured her hands and lifted them to his mouth to place kisses on her fingers, her knuckles, and her wrists. He turned one over and let his tongue play in its palm, which evoked soft laughter from her. Slowly, his lips journeyed up one arm to her shoulder, her throat, and then her face. His hands drifted up and down her back a few times, then sent his fingers into her cascading hair. He loved the way the ebony mane felt wound around them. His lips went to hers.

Their tongues played a seductive game of seek and find, then mated in a heady ritual. Their bodies trembled with passion, building to a frenzied level. Their flesh clung together, sharing warmth and pleasure. Their hands and lips teased and tempted. They were spellbound in a world of love and magic, and nothing could destroy it or break it.

Morning Star quivered and tingled. Her legs felt weak and her body heavy. It had been weeks since they had come together at Spearfish Canyon. Her heart was filled with longing. Her breath came in shallow, quick gasps; then it was stolen by his kiss. Her entire body experienced a rush of heat and tingling, a blend of wild sensations.

Joe's hands slipped around her sides and closed over her firm breasts. With gentleness, he kneaded them. His mouth roved her face and his nose inhaled her sweet fragrance. His manhood ached to be within her; it burned with a need only she could satisfy. Her tongue danced with his, and he savored the taste of her. He moaned in bittersweet need.

Joe paused to remove the rest of their constricting garments. He pushed the dress over her hips and followed it with her bloomers. He lifted Morning Star in his arms and placed her on the bed. Without delay, he was out of his clothes, naked, aroused, and lying beside his wife.

For a while, he made love to her with his eyes, caressing, tantalizing. To him, she was exquisite, perfect, beautiful, irresistible. He nibbled at her ears, and caused her to laugh once more. His mouth claimed hers again to explore and to heighten their desires. His hands were bold, determined, skilled.

Joe's hot breath on her made Morning Star's yearning for him flame brighter. She trailed her fingers over his honed frame, savored his manly scent. His body was hard, smooth, and golden. Her fingers wanted to trace every inch. She stroked the injuries he had received at Bear Butte and she felt the scar he had gotten from her rescue. Yet, nothing detracted from his beauty. She felt aglow with love, afire with passion, and fortunate to have him. No man could compare with Joe, in appearance or in character. He was more important to her than her life and honor, something she had proven with more than words. She was alive, elated, and fulfilled in his arms. For once she did not care if a man, but only this man, took control of her will and her body, of her entire being. She surrendered with eagerness. She responded and reacted to every touch, every kiss, every action, then she mutely begged for more. She had known great rapture in his arms, but tonight she found ecstasy.

Joe's hands trekked over her silky skin. She was so close, so intoxicating, so responsive. Her lithe body evoked him to stimulate it. As lightly as a butterfly, his lips brushed over her breasts. His tongue swirled round and round one bud to sample its nectar. His teeth teased at the taut nubs that revealed the intensity of her desire and his effect upon her. Their contact and her reactions played havoc with his mastery over his raging loins. He had never felt more alive or inflamed than he did now. He was almost mindless with hunger for her.

Morning Star trembled when his hand drifted down her flat stomach. Her entire being was enthralled by him. Reality had fled long ago. He and his actions were her only awareness. She wanted to relax and enjoy the sweet pleasures, but she was too ravenous with need. Each kiss and touch pleased her, but they whet her appetite for much more. She seemed swept away in a flood of bliss. Her hands grasped his shoulders and clutched them tightly. She wanted, she needed, she must have Joseph Lawrence or be dazed with starvation. Soon, there was no place upon her that did not cry out for his attention. As with him, muffled moans escaped her lips between feverish kisses.

Joe fingered the petal-soft flesh between her thighs until she urged him to end the sweet madness. He entered her body with a groan of delight. His breathing became labored and swift with his excitement and the strain of his self-control. He kissed her over and over as he murmured words of love and pleasure. "You're like a fierce desire burning within me. I need you and love you, woman." He felt her work with him, matching his rhythm.

Morning Star's legs wrapped around his and her arms clung to him. Her mouth meshed with his as her heart pounded and her blood raced hot and fast. She saw and felt the muscles of his arms and back as they rippled with his movements. "You are my air, my heart, my life. I want no one but you."

Joe tossed restraint aside and hurried after her. Higher and higher Sky Warrior soared with her on his wings. He grasped the star in his heaven and let it shine on him.

Morning Star held on to the all-consuming man and let her body yield completely to his touch, thrilling to the ecstasy they reached together.

Joe lay half atop Morning Star as he held her tightly in love's aftermath. His gaze roamed her flushed face. Her dark eyes glistened with joy. His heart's filled with love for her, pounded in his chest. He had never, even with her, experienced anything like this, a total joining of all they were. His fingers traced her lips, nose, and cheeks.

"Lordy, how I love you, woman. Every time I think my heart is so full it can't hold more, somehow it stretches and does. Every time I make love to you, it's better than the last time, better than all the other times put together. I don't know how it happens, but I surely do like it."

"I understand. It is the same with me. Perhaps it is the way of love, to grow larger and stronger each day, with each union. It is not the joining of bodies that does this alone; it is all the things that travel with it. I have made the right choice—you, my love, my husband."

Joe gazed into her serene eyes and smiled. They had faced thunder in the wind together, and they had found sweet ecstasy during that fierce battle. "We both made the right choice, my beautiful Morning Star, my sweet Marie, my wife, my woman, the true love of my heart and soul."

She laughed, a glow in her eyes. "I am many things to you, as you are many things to me. It is best of all things you are my love, my husband, my destiny."

Joe rolled to his back, and his wife curled against him. Her right leg slipped between his. Joe's left hand pillowed his head; the other one twirled ebony hair around playful fingers. Morning Star nestled her cheek to her husband's broad chest. The backs of her fingers stroked his damp flesh. For an hour, they remained quiet as each reflected on their lives before and since they met. They had experienced many dangers, tests, and adventures together. They had suffered and sacrificed for others. It was time for them, time for their own happiness. *Time for receiving life's rewards.*

Morning Star pondered the challenges behind her, and those still before her. She had Joe to make her strong and brave. Whatever tomorrow brought, she was ready and willing to face. She was Morning Star, daughter of Sun Cloud and Singing Wind; she was the granddaughter of Gray Eagle and Alisha/Shalee; she was Marie Lawrence, wife and love of Mahpiya Wicasta, the greatest white warrior to ever ride the open Plains. Each of them was controlled by fate, and she accepted that reality.

Thank you, Mother and Father, for your love and understanding, for all you taught me, she silently prayed. *Thank you, Payaba, for your vision long ago and for many years of friendship. Thank you, Great Spirit for giving me this man.*

Morning Star bid a final farewell to the past and welcomed the bright future before her. In the days ahead, she would draw courage, strength, and comfort from all she had been, from all she was, and from all she would become. Peace of mind filled the daughter of the Red Heart chief.

Joe also said his mental farewell to Tanner Gaston, and prayed that his best friend knew he hadn't lost his life in vain. He prayed for Stede's success at the treaty council and for the man's safe return home. He prayed for his father's survival until he reached him, and for strength to help his mother through the difficult days after her husband's death. He prayed for a future reconciliation between his love and her parents and people.

He realized how much he had learned about himself, about whites and Indians, and about life. He had changed and matured by coming here, by meeting Morning Star and the Red Hearts, and by giving so much of himself to others. Yet he had received far more in return. He had made friends, such as Sun Cloud and Clay Thorne. He had helped prevent a bloody conflict. He had helped establish a vital treaty.

Joe heard his wife sigh dreamily as she cuddled more snugly against him. He caressed her cheek and murmured,

464

"We have each other, my love, so we'll be all right. More than all right, absolutely wonderful."

Morning Star lifted her head to look deeply into her love's blue eyes. "Yes," the daughter of Sun Cloud replied, "I know we will."

Epilogue

Virginia, 1856

Marie Lawrence gazed at her sleeping children. She bent over to straighten the covers and to kiss their cheeks. They were beautiful girls, born two years ago. One had golden curls and sky-blue eyes like her father; the other had dark-brown hair and eyes like her. It seemed as if they proclaimed how the Indian and white cultures had fused into a lovely and precious reality.

Joe tiptoed into the nursery and joined his wife. He wrapped his arms around her from behind and looked over her shoulder at their twin daughters, who favored each other heavily but were not identical. He was proud of them, and of his wife and her numerous accomplishments.

After a moment, Joe released Marie, grasped her hand, and led her into their bedroom. He closed the door, then turned to smile at her. Her gown was stunning. The V neckline was trimmed in overlapping rows of narrow lace. The snug midriff exposed Marie's small waist before it, too, dipped into a V onto a full skirt with three tiers. Each layer was edged in delicate embroidery and wide lace. Marie's hair was dressed in a large bun near the back crown of her head, and several ringlets dangled near her ears. His love was a vision of genteel beauty. "You looked beautiful tonight. Every man present envied me," he said proudly.

"Thank you, my adoring husband. But you looked too handsome tonight and too many women tried to steal your eye from me."

He knew she was jesting, but he responded, "No woman could ever entice me away from you. They're only friends and wives of friends. I'm fortunate to have so many of them. They're yours, too."

"Yes, I have made many good friends here. I had a wonderful time at your sister's; Sarah Beth knows how to give a marvelous party." She removed his bowtie and placed it on the dresser. She helped him off with his frock coat with its contrasting revers and hung it in his wardrobe. She did the same with his vest.

As she worked, Joe grinned and said, "That's because everyone adores and enjoys my exquisite and intelligent wife."

Marie turned to him and he unfastened the diamond-and-emerald necklace and undid the buttons of her green satin gown. She slipped out of the rustling garment and hung it in her armoire as she responded to her husband's last remark. "That is because most whites are good people, my love. I wish—" Marie halted and took a deep breath. She removed her petticoat, chemise, and bloomers, all trimmed in ribbons and lace.

When his wife did not finish her statement, Joe ventured, "Your family and tribe could make that same discovery?"

Marie nodded, then listened to him as she continued her tasks. She took off her slippers and stockings, and put them away in their places.

"The problem is, too many whites who go west are evil and greedy, then soldiers have to play devils cleaning up their sorry messes. It sets bad examples and makes the Indians think all whites are that way. If your tribe and others could live around people such as the ones we know, they would learn the same truth you have. They will someday, my love; I'm sure of it. We made truce first with the British and other past enemies, then lasting peace and friendship resulted. It'll be the same between Indians and whites."

Marie recalled Payaba's vision about no lasting peace, but

467

she said, "I hope so, my husband. The treaty is still in effect, and we have heard of nothing terrible happening in that area. I pray it is not broken soon."

"Both sides worked too hard to establish peace and truce, my love, to let minor differences destroy the treaty," he comforted. "Both sides will be slow to instigate another war. Everybody realizes how destructive war is."

She prayed he was right. "I hope my family and friends are safe and happy. I only wish Father and Mother could see our girls."

"They will someday, Marie, even if we have to sneak them there and meet in secret to avoid trouble with your band. What grandparents could refuse to see their grandchildren when they're nearby? I've tried to keep an ear in their direction, but accurate news is hard to come by." Joe hoped that wasn't because the government wanted to keep bad news quiet. He was so settled and contented that he didn't want to receive alarming news, and he knew what his wife would want to do if it came. "When it seems the right time, I'll send someone to check on things for us. Stede's seventy now, so he can't make such a hard journey again. I'll find the right man."

"Thank you, my love." Marie mentally packed up her past once more and stored it in the back of her mind. She did not want to spoil this romantic evening. She put away her undergarments. White clothing no longer felt strange and uncomfortable to her. Over the past years, she had become accustomed to expensive jewels and splendid gowns. She had become accustomed to living in a house and had adapted to his culture with skill and enjoyment, thanks to her husband and Joe's mother and the tutors they had hired to assist her. "I miss Stede's visits," she remarked. "He took such trouble to bring us news of the peace council long ago, then checked on us several times. When the girls are a little older, we must go to see him in New Orleans. Perhaps next spring."

"I'm not sure that'll be possible; he's not in good health. You remember how quickly my father went—only a week after Mother wrote me to hurry home." To think of Stede's short time left on earth and of his deceased parents made Joe mournful for a moment. He placed the heel of his dress boot against a jack and wiggled it off his foot, then did the same with the other one. As he removed his shirt and evening trousers, he murmured, "At least Father left that special letter for me."

"Do not be sad, my love. Joseph loved you and was proud of you. He told you he understood why you left. He was no longer angry with you."

Joe finished undressing as he admitted, "That made it easier to get over not seeing him again. I just wish they weren't both gone. I wish Mother were here to help raise the girls."

"Father said long ago, 'It is good when mates leave the land at the same time or not long after the other. It is hard to live without your heart.' Annabelle was strong and brave. She hid her pain well, but it never went away. She was ready and eager to join her lost love. They were not young when you were born, and their Life-Circles were large and full. Be happy she was with us for several years. She taught me much. I shall never forget Annabelle and her kindness. Our pasts are gone; they must not trouble us."

Joe gazed at the nude beauty before him. Yes, his mother had helped him help Morning Star become a fine lady. Few would guess she hadn't been born and reared in her current social position. Her mind was quick and responsive. She never stopped learning and trying new things. She was a constant amazement, a rare treasure. In spite of all the forces against their marriage and their many cultural differences, their union had worked. Their love for each other was so strong that it had made it easy to brush aside problems and to compromise on important points. Love had conquered all.

Joe lifted her left hand and kissed the gold ring upon her third finger. "As soon as I finish my business here in town, we'll go to the plantation to relax. The girls enjoy the animals, open space, and fresh air. Especially Miranda. She's a bundle of energy." Joe removed the pins from Marie's hair, loosened the bun, and spread the ebony mane around her

469

bare shoulders. He gazed into her eyes, which sparkled with seductive mischief.

"Amanda is quiet and calm like you, my love, but Miranda's heart and body burn from the fires of nature as mine. She will be more of a challenge to raise."

"What you mean is, it looks as if she's inherited her mother's wild and willful streak," he teased, then nibbled at her chin.

"If you do not behave and be kind, my husband, I will send Captain Joseph Lawrence off on one of his ships until he learns how," she quipped.

Joe scooped up the laughing female in his arms, chuckled, and carried her to their bed. "You know I don't go to sea anymore, wife. I'm content to run the shipping business from shore, with Andrew's help." His voice lowered to a husky tone when he hinted, "What I'd like to do is spend time trying to get Lucas a boy cousin to play with; he loves those two girls, but he needs a Tanner like I had."

Marie rubbed her nude body against his naked frame. She caressed his cheek and trailed fingers over his lips. "If you do not remember how to make babies, my husband, I will refresh your memory tonight."

Joe laughed. He captured her wandering hands, brought them to his mouth, and kissed them. "From many nights shared with you, my beautiful wife, I know we've learned those delightful lessons well."

"Then, we must practice them," she murmured against his lips.

As Marie and Joseph Lawrence sailed away on an intimate sea of rapture, Morning Star and Sky Warrior soared the heavens in each other's arms and flew to the land of wild, sweet ecstasy—this time, forever . . .

Author's Notes

For those of you who want to know what happens to the characters in this book, their story continues in *Savage Conquest,* which is available from your local bookstore or Zebra Books. For those of you who missed any of the previous seven sagas in this series—*Savage Ecstasy, Defiant Ecstasy, Forbidden Ecstasy, Brazen Ecstasy, Tender Ecstasy, Stolen Ecstasy,* and *Bittersweet Ecstasy*—they will be available in the coming months from your local bookstore or from Zebra Books, with beautiful new covers.

Each book in the "Ecstasy Saga" features a story based on the lives and loves of Lakota warrior Gray Eagle, his white wife Alisha Williams, or their heirs. The series covers a time span from 1776 to 1873. Although *Savage Conquest* was not written originally as part of this series it fits in perfectly as Saga #9. It continues the story of Joseph and Marie Lawrence, their twin daughters, Sun Cloud, Bloody Arrow, and Blazing Star and it's one of the most suspenseful books of the series.

As *Savage Conquest* was published in February 1985 and was written before the intervening books, certain people and events do not appear in *Savage Conquest* or its genealogy chart; and that book controls part of the plot of this one. It is for this reason that the sacred vision, the adventures of Joe and Morning Star, the peace treaty, Stede and Tanner Gaston, Clay Thorne, and a few other events and characters are not mentioned in *Savage Conquest*. *Savage Conquest* reveals only that Morning Star was banished and Joe was called home because of his father's death, so I had to include those painful episodes here, and I tried to write them as sensitively as possible.

I hope you will enjoy the last book on these special characters. Having "lived" on pages with the Oglalas for thirteen years, I cannot bring myself to write another, as *Savage Conquest* takes my loved ones up to Custer's arrival and intrusion. I want to say good-bye to my people while they are free and happy, not carry them through agony and near annihilation. But if I do think of a spin-off story, you'll be sure to see it one day in the bookstores.

For those of you interested in what happened historically after this novel, the first of two Fort Laramie peace councils began with talks on September eighth of 1851 and ended on September seventeenth with the tribes signing to pledge eternal peace among themselves and with the whites. It was called the Treaty of Fort Laramie. At the invitation of the United States government, Thomas Fitzpatrick, and Colonel David Mitchell, more than ten thousand Plains Indians from many nations and tribes gathered at Horse Creek near Fort Laramie to parley. The terms and payments mentioned earlier in this novel are factual. The problem with the treaty was that many Indians did not grasp what they were signing away and initiating. Whites were granted permission to build roads and to travel through their territories and the Army was given the right to build forts to protect settlers and immigrants. These two provisions created a disastrously permanent and larger white presence in the territory.

Oglala Chief Red Cloud attended the powwow, signed the joint treaty, and tried to keep his word. Tragically, the whites did not keep theirs. Annuities were needed to replace the growing shortage of game and other supplies, but the American government reneged on the reparation terms of the treaty. What few supplies and cattle were delivered were of low quality or unusable. Added to the growing list of complaints or wrongdoings were corrupt Indian agents who carried out criminal and immoral deeds. As whites flooded the territory, buffalo, beaver, and other animals were hunted to near extinction or driven far from agreed upon intertribal boundaries. These problems led to conflicts between Indian nations and between greedy whites and near-starving Indians, who depended upon nature—particularly the buffalo—for survival. As hunters were compelled to forage other tribes' assigned grounds, the invasions provoked new outbreaks of intertribal wars.

In 1853, Thomas Fitzpatrick wrote that the Indians "are in abject want of food half the year. . . . Their women are pinched with want, and their children are constantly crying with hunger." His letters had no effect.

Hard feelings smoldered until a minor incident fanned the embers into a roaring blaze. In 1854, a Lakota brave was accused of stealing and slaughtering a pioneer's cow. A scornful, militant lieutenant named John Grattan rode into the Brule camp. Gratten became infuriated by what he considered hostile behavior, opened fire, and killed Chief Brave Bear. The outraged warriors attacked and slew the entire unit. General William Harney—"By God, I'm for battle, no peace"—was ordered to retaliate. Among other reprisals, he led the infamous Ash Hollow Massacre and earned the name "The Butcher" for his bloody tactics.

Oglala Chief Red Cloud could not bear the sufferings and abuses any longer. He later said, "The white men have crowded the Indians back year by year . . . and now our last hunting grounds . . . [are] to be taken from us. Our women and children will starve. . . . I prefer to die fighting than by starvation." At Horse Creek in 1851, "The Great Father made a treaty with us . . . We kept our word . . . but only once did [the promised goods] reach us, and soon the Great Father took away the only good man he had sent to us, Colonel [sic] Fitzpatrick. . . . When I reach [sic] Washington, the Great Father . . . showed me that the interpreters had deceived me. . . . All I want is right and justice. I represent the whole Sioux nation, and they will be bound by what I say. . . . We do not want riches, we want peace and love."

During years of conflicts and impending warfare, Tom Fitzpatrick urged the government to correct its mistakes of treatment and broken promises. His pleas and warnings were ignored and aggressive actions were taken against the Indians with whom they had signed a treaty.

It was the opening of the Bozeman Trail in '62 and the building of four forts between 1865 and 1867 to guard it that took their best hunting grounds, increased their miseries and fears, and provoked between 1866 and 1868 "Red Cloud's War." Until Crazy Horse, Red Cloud was the most feared and skilled Lakota chief. His daring and costly exploits eventually led to the Army abandoning the forts along the 967-mile trail and to new negotiations.

The second peace conference in 1868 concluded with the Laramie Treaty, which formed a "permanent" Dakota reservation. That parley ended the warpath of Red Cloud, who believed the United States government was being honest with him. He accepted that there would be no more encroachment of their lands that the whites would honor their new promises. It was the breaking of the second, better known, treaty that led to the series of events and clashes that finally allowed the invasion of the sacred Black Hills for gold, provoked the massacre of Custer and his men at the Little Big Horn, and caused the near destruction of the Dakotas and many of their allies.

In this novel, the Oglala rituals, societies, laws, and customs are factual to the best of the knowledge gleaned from thirteen years of research during the writing of the series. However, the Red Heart banishment law for interracial marriage is part fact and part fiction. I did not find authentication of such an actual law, but it *was* forbidden and scorned to intermarry, which was thought to weaken the Indian bloodline. The Oglala language—dialogue and sign— is genuine. Some words in past books, however, were translated incorrectly for the Lakota tongue due to dialect and spelling differences, but are correct for the Dakota. All forts, except Tabor, and all trading posts and fur companies, except for Orin McMichael's, are historically accurate. Throughout the series, all treaties used are authentic, except for the 1782 and 1820 ones used in previous sagas.

The mentions of Colonel Leavenworth, Francis Parkman, George Catlin, Asa Whitney, and the Topographical Bureau Survey are accurate. Events leading to the Indian/white conflicts portrayed in this book are true, as are the trails, states, and Indian chiefs mentioned. Sitting Bull, Crazy Horse, Gall, Red Cloud, Inkpaduta, Jumping Buffalo/Spotted Tail, Tashunkopipape (Man Afraid of His Horses), Little Thunder, Wacouta (The Shooter), Wamdesapa, and Tecumseh were real men.

The lives and fates of the most legendary chiefs were similar to one another. The great Sitting Bull, Tatanka Yotanka, battled at the Little Big Horn, was later arrested, confined to a reservation, resigned himself to his fate, but was slain there in 1890. Crazy Horse, Tashunka Witco, also battled Custer, warred many more years, surrendered in spring of 1877, lived on a reservation, but was slain there in autumn of the same year. Heirs of sculptor Korczak Ziolkowski continue working on a monument at Custer on Thunderhead Mountain to honor the legendary spirit of the Lakotas, whom he represents as an heroic leader who always rode before his bands.

Gall, Pizi, battled Custer, later surrendered and lived on a reservation, where he worked for peace, and died at home in 1896. Besides the mentions in the story and earlier in this section, ultimately Red Cloud, Mahpiya Luta, settled on a reservation, where he resigned himself to his fate. He had an agency named after him, and lived there until his death in 1909. The American government built a home for Spotted Tail, Sinte Geleska, his wives and children but he left it to return to life in a tepee. He was honored and respected by white leaders, had an agency named after him in 1873, but was murdered by a jealous rival in 1881. Today, there is a college named after him: Sinte Geleska in Rosebud. Tashunkopipape (incorrectly translated through history and should be "Man Of Whose Horses We Are Afraid") worked for peace until his death. Little Thunder, following the Ash Hollow massacre by General Harney, settled on a reservation, where he died in 1879. Inkpaduta fought at the Little Big Horn, then fled across the Canadian border; he never made peace with the whites or returned, and died there in 1882.

Some of the most enlightening and poignant speeches and letters in history were written by Lakota chiefs Sitting Bull and Red Cloud. Also, the Oglala chief and prophet Black Elk, cousin to Crazy Horse, is noted for his physical, mental, and literary prowess.

The Crow chiefs, warriors, and their roles in this story are fictional. My novel is about a Lakota maiden, her band, and their hereditary enemies, as told from an Oglala point of view. I read many non-fiction, including Indian, sources to understand the emotions and motivations of these two nations, who warred for many generations. I do not want to mislead or offend with the products of my imagination. It is my wish that the good traits in Two-Bulls counterbalance the evil ones in Black Moon. In all Indian nations there have been bands and warriors who resemble my characterizations. It was necessary to my fictional plot to use the Oglalas' strongest enemy and the Crow's weakest facet.

Historically, between these two nations existed "a rancorous hatred, transmitted from father to son, and inflamed by constant aggression and retaliation," wrote Francis Parkman in 1846. Sitting Bull's limp resulted from a Crow bullet. The Crow accepted and sided with whites during the Indian wars between 1850 and 1870. This was an action the Dakotas themselves could not do or understand any Indian perpetrating against his Red brothers, foe or not. In 1876, the Crow aided General Crook in tracking and battling the forces of Sitting Bull and Crazy Horse; the whites would have lost the Battle of the Rosebud if not for Crow prowess, courage, and tenacity. In 1877, Crow aided Colonel Sturgis in tracking and defeating the famous Chief Joseph and his Nez Perces at Canyon Creek. Custer used Crow scouts and allies.

It is implied that the Crow recognized and feared the power and intelligence of the white man, particularly the soldiers and their weapons, and that was why they allied themselves with whites against Indians. Crow served as scouts, guides, hunters, and couriers, some of the best skilled history has recorded. Crow saw the alliance as a path to retaliation, safe raids, and vengeance against their hereditary foes. Added to the traditional warfare and enmity between the two Red nations, the Lakotas and their allies disdained and hated Crow even more for such traitorous treachery.

I based Orin McMichael's and Black Moon's motivations on those of real men such as Absaroke chiefs Plenty Coops and Old Crow, and soldiers such as General Crook, Colonel Gibbon, Custer, and others. Many officers took advantage of the generational animosities as Gibbon did: "I have come down here to make war on the Sioux. The Sioux are your enemy and ours. For a long time they have been killing white men and killing Crow. I am going down to punish them. If the Crow want to make war upon the Sioux . . . [and] get revenge for Crows . . . now is their time." The Absaroke believed that "these are our lands, but the Sioux stole them from us. . . . the Sioux . . . heart is black. But the heart of the pale face . . . is red to the Crow. . . . Where the white warrior goes there shall we be also."

The historical quotations and facts featured in this story were found in too many sources to list for credit and are facts of public record. However, six nonfiction books helpful in clarifying people and events. I list for acknowledgment: *Forts Of The West,* by Robert Frazer, University of Oklahoma Press, 1965; *They Led A Nation,* by Virginia Driving Hawk Sneve, Brevet Press, 1975; *The Indian Wars,* by Robert Utley and Wilcomb Washburn, Bonanza Books, 1977; *Story of the Great American West,* edited by Edward Barnard, Reader's Digest Association, Inc., 1977; *Let Me Be A Free Man,* compiled and edited by Jane Katz, Lerner

Publications, 1975; and *South Dakota, Land of Shining Gold,* by Francie Berg, Flying Diamond Books, 1982, for information on the 1841 Pre-Emption Law. Thank you all—authors and publishers—for historical data and for written permission to use your research to enlighten and entertain readers. One last book I found useful is *Everyday Lakota,* collected and edited by Joseph Karol, in 1971 by the Rosebud Educational Society. It filled in translations missing due to the death of my Dakota friend and interpreter, Hiram Owen.

In South Dakota, there are two locations called Slim Buttes; I used the one near Reva, where the 1876 battle between General Crook and Lakotas took place. For reader recognition, I took the liberty of using the name Crazy Horse before this great legend received it in his vision-quest.

Many people in South Dakota were helpful with my extensive research and my attempts to be accurate, but the list in the beginning of the book acknowledges those who went to extra effort and cost to send me material and pictures. I want to thank each of you generous people again. Lawrence Blazek, aged seventy-five, *hand*-wrote me numerous pages of facts. He even entertained me with humorous tales of his boyhood days in Marcus.

To readers who enjoyed and supported this series over the years, thank you. Your letters, recommendations to friends, and kindnesses during tours and research trips have touched me deeply. In particular, I express my gratitude to: Eileen Wilson, who gifted me with ceramic busts she made of Gray Eagle and Alisha; Laverne Heiter, who made a beautiful and authentic white buckskin garment for me and had it beaded by One Sun with the symbols of Gray Eagle, Bright Arrow, and Sun Cloud. She also gifted me with a Lakota Medicine Wheel hair ornament (the female equivalent of the warrior's coup feather); Christy Johnson, who presented me with a Cheyenne Red-Tailed Hawk coup

CAPTURE THE GLOW
OF ZEBRA'S HEARTFIRES

AUTUMN ECSTASY   (3133, $4.25)
by Pamela K. Forrest

Philadelphia beauty Linsey McAdams had eluded her kidnappers but was now at the mercy of the ruggedly handsome frontiersman who owned the remote cabin where she had taken refuge. The two were snowbound until spring, and handsome Luc LeClerc soon fancied the green-eyed temptress would keep him warm through the long winter months. He said he would take her home at winter's end, but she knew that with one embrace, she might never want to leave!

BELOVED SAVAGE   (3134, $4.25)
by Sandra Bishop

Susannah Jacobs would do anything to survive—even submit to the bronze-skinned warrior who held her captive. But the beautiful maiden vowed not to let the handsome Tonnewa capture her heart as well. Soon, though, she found herself longing for the scorching kisses and tender caresses of her raven-haired BELOVED SAVAGE.

CANADIAN KISS   (3135, $4.25)
by Christine Carson

Golden-haired Sara Oliver was sent from London to Vancouver to marry a stranger three times her age—only to have her husband-to-be murdered on their wedding day. Sara vowed to track the murderer down, but he ambushed her and left her for dead. When she awoke, wounded and frightened, she was staring into the eyes of the handsome loner Tom Russel. As the rugged stranger nursed her to health, the flames of passion erupted, and their CANADIAN KISS threatened never to end!

Available wherever paperbacks are sold, or order direct from the Publisher. Send cover price plus 50¢ per copy for mailing and handling to Zebra Books, Dept. 3408, 475 Park Avenue South, New York, N.Y. 10016. Residents of New York, New Jersey and Pennsylvania must include sales tax. DO NOT SEND CASH.

feather on a beaded rosette; and Debbie Keffer, for the many pieces of Indian beadwork she has made and given to me over the years. I want to thank bookstore managers and their staffs for keeping the series available for their customers, and thank distributors and their employees for their support and hard work over the years by keeping the series in stock and by promoting it to stores. No author is more grateful and moved by reader and bookseller loyalties than I am.

Your satisfaction and appreciation make my work meaningful and worthwhile. I tried to the best of my abilities to give you a story, a series, and characters you will never forget and will love as much as I do. Of the twenty-three novels I've written, this series brought me special friends among Indians and whites and has been emotionally rewarding. To tell me you have learned about history and the two cultures involved thrills me. To tell me it inspires you to learn more about them warms my heart.

Until our next visit on the pages of my new book, keep reading, and learning, and loving!

For a Janelle Taylor Newsletter and bookmark, please send a self-addressed, stamped envelope (long size) to Janelle Taylor; P.O. Box 211646; Martinez, GA. Please print clearly.